For a chance to win an exciting getaway to Lake Tahoe and other fun prizes, please visit Joan Swan's website!

All the details are at joanswan.com/escapeandenjoy.htm.

FEVER

JOAN SWAN

BRAVA

KENSINGTON PUBLISHING CORP.
www.kensingtonbooks.com

BRAVA BOOKS are published by

Kensington Publishing Corp.
119 West 40th Street
New York, NY 10018

All Kensington titles, imprints, and distributed lines are available at special quantity discounts for bulk purchases for sales promotion, premiums, fund-raising, educational, or institutional use.

Special book excerpts or customized printings can also be created to fit specific needs. For details, write or phone the office of the Kensington Special Sales Manager. Attn.: Special Sales Department, Kensington Publishing Corp., 119 West 40th Street, New York, NY 10018. Phone: 1-800-221-2647.

ISBN-13: 978-0-7582-6638-5
ISBN-10: 0-7582-6638-3

First Kensington Trade Paperback Printing: March 2012

10 9 8 7 6 5 4 3 2 1

Printed in the United States of America

For Elisabeth—

I believe.

ACKNOWLEDGMENTS

The path to my debut novel has been a ten-year journey. There are so many people who have helped me along the way, and I am grateful to each and every one. Special thanks to Elisabeth Naughton, without whom this novel would not exist. My deepest appreciation to my wonderful parents for always supporting my endeavors; to my coworkers at UCSF Medical Center, whose enthusiasm has kept me motivated; my many special friends, whose interest in my writing has given me hope and inspiration. To my fabulous agent, Paige Wheeler, for loving *Fever* in its earliest form and believing in my abilities as a writer; my wonderful editor, Alicia Condon, whose appreciation and effort helped me take my writing to a new level and brought out the best in *Fever*.

Finally, my husband, Rick, who is endlessly supportive of my need for creative expression, and our two beautiful daughters who might not understand that need but put up with me anyway. I love you all. Deeply.

ONE

The *clank-clank-clank* of shackles echoed off the hospital's linoleum floors, rippling across Doctor Alyssa Foster's shoulders.

She headed toward the source, her muscles tense despite her fatigue. Normally, she didn't mind taking on additional duties when the department was short staffed like this. She didn't even mind carrying the everyday load for her attending physicians. And sure as hell didn't complain about it like her sorry-assed excuse of a rival, Greg Dyne, but this . . . This was the worst of the mundane chores. She'd rather perform the toughest procedure on the nastiest patient than be forced to interact with prisoners.

Before facing the hardened, violent psychopaths waiting at the end of the hall, Alyssa ducked into the restroom and took a minute to splash water on her face. Then she made the mistake of looking in the mirror.

Pale skin, bruise-colored shadows beneath her eyes, frown lines marring her forehead. She almost didn't recognize the person staring back. Her twelfth day in a row of twenty-fours didn't look so good in this light, and the unsavory chore awaiting didn't help.

"Fourteen more days," she murmured to her reflection. Her year-long fellowship would end in just two weeks. Had it really only been a year? She felt like she'd been at St. Jude's for a decade already. "And if you want to stay here, you'd better learn to live with jailbirds."

The hospital had contracts with five neighboring prisons and the forensic patients had prompted the budget increase, which in turn opened this new attending radiologist's position, one either she or Dyne would fill.

No. The one *she* would fill.

Alyssa yanked at the elastic band in her hair and smoothed the messy strands back into a ponytail with a damp hand. After stretching her back and popping her neck, she dragged herself through the closed double doors hiding the forensic wing from the general public.

She'd be the first to admit to a bit of a badboy fetish. Certainly had made her share of mistakes choosing men in the past. But her definition of badboys encompassed independent men who pushed the limits and lived by their own rules, not murderers, rapists and drug pushers.

The angle of sunlight spilling through the glass on the single exterior door at the end of the hall told her it was getting late. She still had patients in the intensive care units in need of procedures, the day's studies to read out and . . . oh, yeah, food. She hadn't stopped to eat anything all day.

Her teeth met and her jaw muscle flexed. She didn't have time to be doing other people's work, but if she didn't, Dyne would. And she damn well wasn't going to lose this position to that cocky, substandard excuse for a rival.

Alyssa paused at the doorway to the already darkened exam room and nodded to the officer in the hallway. The one with a weapon. The one who kept a safe distance from the inmate so the prisoner wouldn't have an opportunity to steal a gun. One sweep of his twenty-something, clean-shaven, sweet Midwestern face, and Alyssa knew this was the perfect place for him—well out of the felon's reach.

"Ma'am." Farmboy shifted to allow her past the partially curtained opening. "Sorry we're so late. The transportation sergeant screwed up."

She couldn't quite muster the words, *that's okay*, because it was really messing with her day and her mood, but it also wasn't his fault. She nodded acknowledgment. "What facility are you from?"

"San Quentin, ma'am."

Alyssa resisted the urge to close her eyes and slump her shoulders. Quentin: death row capital of the California state prison system. Home to the most notorious serial killers and mass murderers of the decade. Definitely an apropos ending to this hellacious shift.

With a slow breath directed deep into her chest, Alyssa prepared her emotional shields then passed the guard and scanned the prisoner's paperwork: *Teague Creek, thirty-four, right upper quadrant pain. Abdomen ultrasound.* Piece of cake. It would take her ten minutes, tops.

She surveyed the prisoner from shoulders to toes. He was tall, but little else stood out. His periwinkle-blue prison uniform was too similar to hospital scrubs for Alyssa's taste. Probably because it made her wonder if she was a prisoner of sorts as well. Especially on days like this.

The second officer—this one inside the room and without the weapon—was older, maybe fifty, also Caucasian.

"Officer," she greeted, "I'll need his shirt off and his hands uncuffed from the waist chain."

"Yes, ma'am."

Alyssa pulled the curtain halfway closed and set the papers on a foldout desk. Her gaze paused on the box labeled RELEASE DATE where the word *life* had been scribbled. Her lips pursed with an involuntary shake of her head. *So young. What a waste.*

She slipped on a glove, picked up a bottle of warm gel and turned to find the prisoner leaning on the edge of the gurney. Something dark caught her eye and her gaze passed over his face without seeing it, honing in on the coal black tattoos covering a wide muscled chest.

A swastika the size of a basketball stamped the left side of his torso. The right side of his abdomen flaunted an eagle holding a shield with the letters "A B" and two swords crossed in the background. Barbed wire spiraled his biceps. All classic insignia of the Aryan Brotherhood .

Apprehension clenched her belly in a tight, hot fist. Her eyes darted to his face, looking for something—disgust, venom, condescension—some reaction to her ethnicity. Anyone with two eyes could tell she wasn't a hundred percent lily white. But he'd tilted his chin down, his gaze now cast on the floor, and Alyssa found herself looking at the top of his head, shaved nearly to the skin, and—surprise, surprise—another swastika centered on the dome of his cranium.

In a last ditch effort to quell her anxiety, she took a quick look at his hands. They'd been released from the waist chain and secured with another set of regular cuffs, standard procedure for high-risk prisoners. Suspicion confirmed. This guy had trouble written all over him. Capital T. And Alyssa already had all the trouble she could handle. She already felt brittle enough to shatter. This would be the fastest scan she'd ever performed. The typical ten minute exam just dropped to three.

She gestured to the gurney, keeping her focus on the crisp white sheet. She didn't want to meet his eyes, didn't want to see whatever was there—or not there. "Lie on your back, please."

He obeyed, without even attempting a side glance her way. Seemed he wanted to avoid eye contact as much as she did. Something was finally going right with her day.

Alyssa tapped information into the ultrasound machine with tense fingers and grabbed a chair. "Can you raise your arms over your head, please?"

As he moved, so did the bulk beneath his tan skin and black tattoos. Alyssa could have used him as an anatomy model to delineate each muscle. Inmates were often physically fit—after all they had all the time in the world to work out—but this man was extreme. As a physician, the sheer beauty of his body intrigued her to distraction. As a woman half his size, it scared the hell out of her.

The officer in the room edged toward the partially open curtain, meeting up with the other guard. "Did you buy that golf pass yet?"

"No," Farmboy replied. "I have to wait until my next paycheck."

"You're gonna miss the deadline, man. Can't beat those prices. Thirty bucks for eighteen holes on a course like that? Includes a cart, too."

Alyssa angled the transducer between Creek's ribs to get a good shot of his liver, half listening to the idle conversation. She darted a look at his face. His gaze was locked on the ceiling, his jaw ticking. The darkened room shadowed his features, but his looks still caused a double take. Just as striking as his body, his face was all handsome angles and perfect proportions. Too bad the good looks had gone to waste on a racist, criminal pig.

"Do you have AIDS?" she asked as she clicked pictures of his right kidney.

His eyes flicked toward her, held. Light eyes. Sharp eyes. "No, ma'am."

The low, smooth timbre of his voice gave her belly an uncomfortable twist.

"Hepatitis? A, B, C?"

"No, ma'am."

Her arm brushed his ribs and heat stung her skin. Alyssa startled, attention refocused. She tipped the transducer so she could lay the back of her hand against his belly. "You're burning up. How long have you had this fever?"

He shifted away from her touch and turned his eyes to the ceiling again. "No fever, ma'am. I'm fine."

"I can feel it through my glove."

"Normal for me."

Alyssa squinted at him in disbelief. That level of heat wasn't normal for anyone. He had to be near a hundred and five degrees.

As she continued to scan, she searched for a source of infection to explain the fever, but ultimately found none.

In an effort to get him talking in hopes of gaining more information, she said, "I haven't found anything that would cause the pain you're having."

Creek said nothing. His jaw resumed ticking.

With a mental shrug, Alyssa used a washcloth to clean the gel off his skin, his body heat burning through the cloth. *Weird* kept repeating in her head. But if he wanted to let his blood boil, so be it.

"Turn toward me," she said. "You're almost done."

The officers ignored her conversation with Creek as they debated club grip and swing arc.

When he rolled onto his side, he was only six inches away. His intense body heat closed around her like an embrace, creating an intimacy that left her squirming in her chair.

Alyssa's eyes lifted to his face again, expecting to find him staring at her, but again, he was looking down and away, his gaze fixed on the officers' boots, all that was visible of the men now situated just outside the curtain.

With one last image of yet another perfect kidney, Alyssa dropped the transducer into its holder and laid a towel on the table beside him. This man's cut physique would linger in her mind for a long time.

Which meant this place must have finally pushed her over the edge, because fantasizing about prisoners was not what lingered on a normal woman's mind.

"Done. You can clean up." She turned away and pushed to her feet. "You need to mention that fever to your—"

The hair on her neck barely had time to lift before heat washed her back. Creek's hard body closed around her. A cool chain cut across her throat. *No.* She sucked air. *No.* Her fingers clawed at the metal. *No!*

"Don't make a sound." He spoke softly, slowly, his chin on her shoulder as he bent over her and pressed his cheek against hers from behind.

Her brain finally came back online. Air wisped into her lungs and fed the new baseline of fear. When Creek straightened, he rose ten inches above her. And she now registered not only his size, but the sheer strength in all that corded muscle she'd been admiring. His movements were controlled, purposeful, almost Zen-like in confidence.

"You idiot . . ." She barely breathed the words, the metal and pressure restricting her vocal cords. "Let go—"

The chain jerked once, cutting into her trachea. "Shut. Up."

Pain cut off all thoughts of arguing. She wedged her skull against his collarbone to allow a fraction of relief on her airway. Oxygen wisped through the stricture. In. Out. In. Out. Her gray matter slugged back to work, edged with hot, sharp panic that threatened to invade every crevice and drive her insane.

The officers' boots were still visible beneath the curtain where they stood in the hall, but she couldn't draw enough air to speak, let alone scream. And the links of metal weren't cool anymore. They burned, as if Creek's body heat streamed through the chain.

The older guard chuckled. "You have to stay away from those sand traps, man."

"Water holes are my problem," Farmboy replied. "I could pay for the damn pass with the cost of the balls I lose in those lagoons."

Creek leaned sideways, reaching for something on the desk. With his chest pressed against the width of her shoulders, his hips fitted to the low curve of her spine, he dragged her along. Alyssa strained her peripheral vision toward his reach. Toward the coffee cup holding pens and pencils and . . . He plucked up a pair of scissors.

Jesus. "Put . . . those down." A spurt of terror gushed up her chest. Her fingers searched for a millimeter of leverage between the chain and her skin. "You're . . . burning . . . me."

Creek's head tilted down, his whisker-roughened chin scraping her cheek. "Fuck."

The pressure eased and Alyssa ran her cool fingers over raw skin, choking in blessed air. Her relief was short-lived as the rasp of metal on metal sounded in her ear. A hard blade pressed against her neck, and she squeezed her eyes shut.

"Not another sound," Creek whispered, "or I'll cut your throat."

"All right." The older guard sounded relaxed and jovial as he swooshed the curtain aside. "Are we all done in—?"

The room went completely still. The extended, shocked moment expanded, taking on weight and mass and volume like one of the cancers Alyssa fought so hard to find and fight in her patients.

"Creek, what the fuck are you doing?" The older guard's voice cracked the silence. "You're not thinkin', man. This stunt will get you thrown in the hole for a month."

"Not if I don't go back." His forearms locked over Alyssa's shoulders, keeping her tight against him. "Give me the gun."

Oh, no. God, no. Alyssa's eyes popped open. In front of her, the older man had both hands held palms out. His face had lost two shades of color.

This *really* couldn't be happening. She could almost convince herself if Creek's body heat weren't wearing on her as if she'd been hiking in the sun.

"Listen, Creek," the guard said, "I heard about your appeal, but you're not out of options, man. You know how this works. Just have to keep bucking the system. You'll get another chance. This kind of shit will only get you—"

"Out of that living hell," Creek finished. "Now, give me the damn gun before I cut her open."

Something pinched Alyssa's neck. She gasped. Or at least

she tried. Only a thread of air got through. Warm liquid trickled down her neck. "Do . . . something."

"You heard her, boys." His voice dipped to a dangerously desperate tone. "Do what I say or she'll be dead before she hits the floor. And you know where I'll be? No worse off than I was when I woke up this morning. Give me the gun, *right fucking now*."

To Alyssa's utter disbelief, the older guard pursed his lips, dug his hands into his hips and nodded at the younger officer. "Do it."

"*What?*" Alyssa squeaked. If that gun reached Creek's hand, every chance she had evaporated. "No!"

The younger guard stepped forward, the weapon held out, butt first. After one more glance at the older officer, he slapped the gun into Creek's palm. Alyssa's vision blackened at the edges.

"Give me your gear," Creek ordered. "Both of you. Now."

They obeyed, setting their radios, sticks and whistles on the foldout desk. Creek pressed the gun to the base of Alyssa's skull. The scissors rasped closed and disappeared. She took one luscious, deep, shaky breath. Air had never tasted so good.

"Keys," Creek said. "Uncuff me."

The older guard unhooked his keys from a belt loop and dropped them on the desk, his expression angry but resolute. "Make your new girlfriend do it for you."

"You bastard." If she could have reached that guard, she'd have decked him. "How dare you—"

"Dump your keys, kid," Teague said to the younger man.

Once Farmboy's keys joined the others, Creek lifted his chin toward the half bath tucked into the corner of the room for patient's use redirecting the weapon toward them. "Both of you, in."

He pushed Alyssa forward as the men crowded into the tiny space. Within sixty seconds she'd be alone with Creek. No one came down this hallway but prisoners and guards, and look how well that had worked out.

Creek's grip shifted and the chain loosened, offering instant relief, but her skin still simmered as if it had been fried in oil. "Oh, my God. What's on that chain? You *burned* me."

His arm came up and across her throat. "One twist, and I'll break your neck. Then you'll forget all about the burn. You're no safer now than you were a second ago, so don't get cocky."

Fear and betrayal mingled with confusion and exhaustion, resulting in white-hot anger. "I'm not cocky, I'm *pissed off*. If you want to screw up your own life, go right ahead, but I can screw up my own just fine."

His chin scraped her temple when he looked down at her.

"You won't make it past the others," Farmboy said.

"Others?" Creek's voice lightened with sarcasm and victory, yet still sounded starkly powerful and authoritative in comparison to the guard's. "I happen to know there's only *one* other. And I'd tell you to watch me, but the first one who sticks his head out that door will get a bullet to the brain.

"Close the door," he ordered in Alyssa's ear, "and put that chair under the knob."

She did as she was told, trying to do the lousiest job possible. Not hard considering she had a two-hundred-pound—*burning*—proverbial monkey on her back.

"Do it right," Creek said. "Or you'll be responsible for getting their heads blown off."

Just what she needed—a guilt trip. She wedged the chair's metal bar beneath the knob. With the cabinets securing the chair's feet, those guards wouldn't be going anywhere anytime soon.

"Good girl. Stay that way and you'll be fine." Creek walked her backwards, pausing at the desk. "Pick them up."

Gladly. Alyssa wedged the individual keys between her fingers like claws.

"And put them in your pocket," he said.

Dammit. "I don't have pockets."

Creek tightened his arm on her throat. "You *have* pockets."

She couldn't swallow. Could barely breathe. And, damn, her neck *hurt*. Alyssa shoved the keys into the breast pocket of her scrubs.

"Good girl." Creek loosened his hold and dragged her toward the door. "I don't want to hurt you, but I will if I have to. Got me?"

"You've already hurt me." Alyssa took deep, quick breaths, savoring the oxygen. "It would be smarter to let me go and get the hell out of here as fast as you can. I'll only slow you down."

He didn't respond. He was busy perusing the length of the hallway, empty now at nearly six o'clock. The side doors, where all prisoners entered and exited the hospital, were just twenty feet away. Twenty feet. Surely, he'd release her when he hit the exit. She couldn't consider any other outcome.

And just to push her own desired outcome forward, she kept talking. What man in his right mind would want a pissy, ranting female along for the ride? "Look, I really don't have time for this. I've got critical patients in the ICU who could die if I don't get PICC lines in them A.S.A.P."

It was true they could die, just not from the lack of a PICC line. But he didn't know that.

"Not my problem. And stop talking in acronyms. It's annoying as hell."

"I'd be a lot less annoying if you let me go."

"I can see you're going to have to learn to keep your mouth shut. That's not what I expected from you."

"From *me*? What does that mean?"

He didn't answer as they approached the exit, where late fall sunlight filtered through the glass. Screw whatever he might have meant. Freedom inched closer with every step. That's what she had to focus on: reaching that door.

But Creek stopped too soon.

At a doorway leading into a holding area, he tapped the fake paneling with the muzzle of the guard's gun in some cryptic Morse code-type pattern. The door burst open with such force, Creek jerked Alyssa back and twisted, putting his body between her and whoever or whatever was in that room. In that moment, his massive body engulfed hers giving her a flickering sense of complete protection.

"Hey, man." A rough voice, filled with almost boyish glee, sounded on the other side of Creek. "You gotta see this."

He straightened and turned them both back around. Another prisoner stood at the door, no cuffs, no leg irons. He had a gun stuffed in the waistband of his navy prison sweatpants, and the grin on his unshaven face matched the mischief in his tone. But his eyes . . . There was definitely something wrong in the brain behind those eyes. Alyssa had worked with too many mentally deficient patients to miss it.

Reflexively, she pressed back against Creek as Psycho Prisoner eyed her up and down, too thoroughly, too slowly. She caught a whimper in her throat before it escaped.

His lips lifted in more of a sneer than a smile. "Would have preferred a purebred, but she'll do." He squinted at her throat. "What'd you do to her? That's wicked cool, man."

Creek took a step and nudged her forward. Alyssa pushed back. He shoved again, harder. A frantic edge cut at her belly. Bile lunged up her chest, burning the back of her throat.

"Look at them." Psycho tossed a hand toward the back of the holding area, filled with empty gurneys and chairs. Another officer sat in the corner, his hands, feet and mouth bound with compression tape. "Stupid sonofabitch. He was so easy it wasn't even fun." He pulled a pair of handcuffs from his sweats. "Got some toys, too."

"Great." Creek's gaze darted toward the hall, the exit, then back. "Let's get out of here."

Yes! Alyssa almost yelled the word. Relief and hope broke through the fear. She was almost free. This time, when Creek pushed her, she moved. Five more steps . . . four . . . three . . .

They stopped just inside the doorway. This was it. As soon as these jerks were gone, she'd hit the bathroom, clean herself up, grab some burn gel from the E.R. and call one of the radiologists from their partner clinic across the street to cover for the night. Then, she'd head to the nearest bar and drink this whole nightmare away.

"Get these off of me." Creek's voice interrupted Alyssa's fantasy. He extended his hands in front of her face. "Keys are in her pocket."

Psycho scanned Alyssa's shirt, a lewd grin on his face. "My pleasure."

He pushed his hand into her pocket and grabbed her breast. Disgust twisted Alyssa's throat closed. She knocked his arm up and away. The knit of keys flew out of his hand and across the room.

The pupils of Psycho's eyes expanded, turning his muddy hazel irises nearly black with rage. Alyssa identified with the emotion. She'd been attacked by someone she'd been trying to help, abandoned by someone who should have helped her, and now, she'd been molested by scum living off her tax dollars. Rage? Yeah. She definitely identified.

"Don't *touch* me, you—"

Creek turned, pulling Alyssa with him. "Stop fucking around, Taz."

Psycho whipped another key from his own front chest pocket, but his cold, cutting eyes stayed on Alyssa. He slipped the key into the cuffs, and with a *click,* Creek was free.

An instant later, Creek had his big hand around her wrist. The cuffs were so warm she didn't feel them close. By the time her reflexes kicked in, she was captive. She stared at the contrast of her fine fingers and slender wrists against the thick metal cuffs. Hands her mother forever insisted were made for dishes and diapers. Hands Alyssa eternally argued were destined for helping and healing.

Surreal. Absurd. Fallacious.

This isn't happening.

Creek put one hand in the middle of her back, pushed her into the hall and turned her toward the exit door.

This is *happening.*

Her stomach lifted, then dropped, then went queasy, like it did when she rode a roller coaster.

Alyssa planted her feet and leaned back. "I'm not going out there."

He fisted the back of her scrub top and used the bulk of his body to force her through the doorway.

Alyssa twisted, grabbed the metal frame with both hands. "I'm *not* going."

"Oh, yes, you are."

"No!" Alyssa held on with every last muscle fiber in her fingers. "You got what you wanted. Leave me here."

Psycho elbowed his way out the door. "There's the car. I told you it'd be here. Let's go."

"Don't make this harder than it has to be." Creek's tense voice ground in her ear. "Let go of the door before I break your arm."

"No." Her feet skidded forward as he pushed harder. Her wrists ached from the bite of the cuffs. Her fingers burned from grasping the metal. "No! I'm not go—"

Psycho's hand blurred in front of her eyes a split second before her head snapped sideways. Fire erupted in her cheek, spread through her face. Blood seeped onto her tongue, the metallic bitterness adding another level of realism to this nightmare.

Taz gripped her face in one meaty hand and jerked her toward him. "Shut the fuck up, you goddamned *gook.*" He smacked a piece of tape over her mouth. "You fuck this up for us and I'll gut you."

Creek yanked her out of Psycho's reach, and closed that big body around hers again. "Chill, Taz. The only person who's going to fuck this up for us is you. Get the car."

Alyssa let her eyes close. Pain buzzed across her face. Shock numbed her brain. At some point, she'd started to shake, and couldn't control it. She'd never been hit before. Not by any man she'd ever dated, even in the most heated argument. Not by any one of her four older brothers, even during a tussle. Not even so much as a spanking as a child, even though she'd given her parents plenty of cause. She'd spent the entire twenty-eight years of her life abuse free. Until now.

She'd also never been taunted with racial slurs, probably because she looked more Caucasian than Asian. The combination of violence and racism shook her solid foundation.

"Don't fuck with him." Creek's hold loosened. "The quieter you are, the less trouble you cause, the better this will go."

She opened her eyes and looked at him. His gaze darted to her cheek, then away, scanning the parking lot, as if her suffering meant absolutely nothing to him.

Primal anger sank deep and overlaid the fear. She'd be quiet all right. And in the silence, she'd watch. And wait. And plan.

Two

With a solid grasp on the girl's upper arm, Teague dragged her into the shadows of an overhang outside the hospital. The chilled air bathed his burning skin. Inwardly, he took a moment to appreciate the sensation, grateful for the city's distinctive evening mist.

He pressed his back against the cool brick building and pulled her in front of him for cover, focusing his mind to control the body heat that had winged out of his control. Not a great start. His heart knocked so hard and high in his chest, he thought it would choke him. If he didn't slow his breathing, he'd hyperventilate.

Luckily, hardly anyone ventured to this side of the hospital but prison guards and inmates, and he and Taz were the last trip of the day. Teague had pulled every last favor he'd accumulated in prison to get right here, right now.

It amazed him how a city the size of San Francisco could have so many dead spaces where few people ever tread. But when he'd started looking for them months ago during other outings, he'd been surprised to find them everywhere—walkways, alcoves, or alleys between soaring buildings, like the one they were in now.

In a side parking lot, the GTO's engine rumbled to life. Tires squealed.

"Idiot," Teague mumbled. "Let's just fucking advertise."

The adrenaline raging through his body made him nauseous. Or maybe it was the welt on the girl's face that made him sick to his stomach. Or the burns on her neck. Or the blood trail.

He couldn't even remember her damn name. Emma? Anna? Something sweet and passive, just the kind of woman Luke always seduced. Only this woman was neither sweet nor passive, although she was a beauty. A goddamned, exotic Barbie-doll, wet-dream beauty. At least that part of Luke's criteria hadn't changed while Teague had been rotting in prison the last three years.

The bright red, chain-shaped scars on her smooth, sun-kissed skin looked like a twisted S&M necklace. He couldn't stand the sight.

You're burning me. The memory of the pain in her voice nagged. None of this was her fault, other than her lousy taste in boyfriends.

Teague flexed the fingers of his free hand, took a slow, deep breath and focused. He settled his fingertips over the burns at one side of her neck and slid them slowly across her fried skin. She stiffened at his touch and strained against his hold.

A sizzling current of mellow heat ebbed from his fingertips and melted into her flesh. He knew the instant the relief registered by the way her spine softened and her eyelids drifted closed. Her spidery black lashes curved against cheeks flushed bright and hot. Teague had the deepest urge to press his mouth to the corner of one eye and let her skin sizzle across his lips.

He repressed the random thought just as he had all such longings that surfaced during his years in prison. The progression of his fingers transitioned the burnt tissues from chafed, angry red to plump, irritated pink.

So soft. Even damaged, her skin was so incredibly soft. How long had it been since he'd felt a woman's skin against his? Three years? Four? He'd lost count. Something about touching her made his mind haze in a very dangerous way under the circumstances. With her, under any circumstances.

Sensations seemed to boomerang back at him. Enticing currents drifted down his arm, through his chest and straight to his groin, pumping blood to a part of his body that had no business being aroused.

He steered his mind toward curling his fingers into his palm, stepping back, and looking away. But before he did, her head tilted, as if she could barely hold it up, and her cheek eased to his shoulder. Her body swayed, hips curving forward and crushing their joined hands between her soft pelvis and his aching dick. A geyser of lust blasted up his chest and out his limbs. He shuddered. The muscles in his legs went lax. Pleasure blurred the edges of his mind.

Oh, no. Hell, no.

Some part of his sesame-seed-sized brain evidently still worked. Teague nudged her backwards and steadied himself on the building with his free hand. He had no idea if he looked disinterested on the outside because he was a mega fireworks display gone awry on the inside.

"Stand up, for God's sake." He pushed her back another step. "Don't pull any fainting bullshit. We still have a long way to go."

God help him.

Her lids fluttered fully open. She stared at him with those eyes, some curious color between sand and hazel. They were a little dazed, a little confused and plenty suspicious, but they were most definitely not afraid. And, yeah, he may have been out of the game for years now, but he couldn't mistake that edge of lusty heat, even if it was now fading. Quickly.

Taz steered the hot rod to a stop alongside them. Grateful for the diversion, Teague swung the back door open and tugged on the girl's cuffs. The motion seemed to knock her back into reality, back into that little spitfire she'd been inside the hospital. She pulled, yanked, kicked, twisted like a frigging pretzel.

"Dammit." He fought to get a solid grip on the squirming target without hurting her. "What did I just tell you?"

With one good yank, she popped her arm from his grip. And ran.

"Fuck." Teague took off after her. And shit, she was fast. She headed toward the front of the hospital, toward Divisidero, the busiest street in the goddamned city. If she made it to the sidewalk, he'd lose her. If he lost her, he might as well just cuff himself and walk right back into prison.

She reached a grass patch near the southeast corner of the building. Before she broke into public view, Teague lunged. He clipped her around the waist with one arm and broke their fall with the other.

The GTO rumbled up next to them, door still open, Taz yelling, "Kill her or leave her."

Teague sure as hell wasn't leaving her. He fisted her scrub top and yanked. Smoke plumed from beneath his fingers. When he made a move to hoist her by the waist, she thrust her head back. Her skull connected with his cheekbone. Pain exploded behind his eye, traveled up his temple and gripped his brain. But he didn't let go. He kept his fingers wrapped in that fabric, because it wasn't *as if* his life depended on keeping her—it *absolutely* depended on keeping her.

"You little witch." The thin scrub fabric disintegrated in his hand and he lost his grip. He bent at the knees, tossed her over his shoulder and shoved her into the car, then slid in beside her. The vehicle skidded out of the parking lot before Teague got the door closed.

"We don't need her anymore," Taz yelled. "And I don't want a piece of ass bad enough to keep that cunt-eyed bitch around."

"Shut up and drive." Teague wiped at the warmth sliding down his face and pulled his hand back covered in a mixture of sweat and blood.

He leaned across the seat and slammed the lock on the girl's door with his fist. Even after years of effort, he still couldn't harness the heat that came with anger. His healing powers needed work, too, but at least those he could control.

Her hair had come loose from the ponytail and fell everywhere. It was long and straight and nearly solid black but for a bittersweet chocolate undercurrent in the natural light. Her face looked so much softer, so much more innocent with the soft strands framing the high cheekbones and little nose. And those eyes seemed even more piercing with the new contrast.

Teague retreated to his own side of the car. He needed to clear his head and think. All things considered, this had gone pretty well—aside from getting beat up by a goddamned girl, of course. *Hannah*. That was her name. And nothing about her had worked out quite right. He had to admit, the tape over her mouth had been a brilliant move on Taz's part. No doubt she'd be smacking up a whirlwind if she weren't gagged.

"Where to, boss?" Taz grinned over his shoulder as he turned onto the freeway. "We can dump her somewhere off Highway Five. That'll give you time to get your fill. Don't worry, I won't look." He laughed. "Much, anyway."

Teague rubbed a hand over his face. For the love of God, that was the very last thing he needed to be thinking about. Even an impromptu sprint and a cracked cheekbone hadn't cooled him down.

He cast a look at Hannah to gauge her reaction to the threat. She tossed her head to get the messy strands out of her eyes and watched him with a look that clearly said, "try it and I'll kick your teeth in." How could such a small woman, handcuffed and gagged, look so . . . formidable? Why couldn't she have turned out to be Luke's typical fragile-flower type?

Maybe, after two years of living without Keira, Luke had finally realized his mistake. Maybe he'd pulled his head out of his ass—at least in one area of his life—and was reverting back to the type of woman he belonged with.

Stupid thought. Luke wasn't that evolved.

The girl's hands lifted toward her face, distracting Teague

from his thoughts. He pointed at her with one rigid finger. "Don't touch that tape."

Without taking her eyes off him, she ran her fingers over the newly healed skin of her neck. The I'll-kick-your-teeth-in expression transitioned into what the fuck? Teague knew what came next: You're a freak. He'd seen it before, and he didn't want to see it again.

He turned away and watched the streets flash by his window. Dusk came early to the city with the sun falling behind skyscrapers. Funny, he didn't feel any different. He didn't feel free. Probably because he was still a long way from what any sane man would consider *free*.

"Just stick with the original plan for now," Teague said. "Turn on the radio to the local news and head for the Bay Bridge. Is the money in the glove box?"

"Yep." Taz held up a wad of folded bills two inches thick.

"And the clothes?" Teague scooted forward to look in the front seat.

Taz lifted the brown grocery bag with a C scribbled on the outside, and tossed it to Teague. "That's yours."

Teague nearly drooled as he rummaged through the contents. Brand new Levi's, crisp T-shirts with cool logos like NASCAR, Harley Davidson, Hurley and Volcom. Packages of boxer briefs, snow-white socks and lightweight suede work boots. "I never thought I'd get so excited over clothes."

At the bottom, Teague felt plastic and pulled out a Ziploc baggie filled with toiletries: soap, shampoo, toothbrush, toothpaste, razors and . . . condoms. Lots of condoms.

He cast a sidelong look at Hannah. She was inspecting the cuffs on her wrists. Probably trying to figure a way out of them. Teague had spent his three years in prison honing his abilities in an effort to bend metal with hopes of getting out of those irons. The closest he'd gotten was transference, the kind that had burned Hannah. Useless and pathetic.

But he was glad she was preoccupied now, because it gave

him a moment to shove the bag back beneath the clothes and try to clear his head. 'Cause what filled his brain when he looked at those condoms was clear all right. Crystal clear.

A pristine fantasy of him lying naked in the middle of a big, comfortable bed with her equally as naked, straddling his lap with a sexy smile on that beautiful face instead of that perpetual scowl. Her hair fell forward over her shoulders as she split the foil condom wrapper with her teeth. Popped the latex securely between those full lips. Rolled it over his extended length with her mouth. Seated it in place with a suction that made his hands clench the sheets and his body arc off the mattress. Molded it to every rib of his dick with mercilessly confident strokes of those long, lean fingers before taking him deep inside her body and riding them both into ripping ecstasy.

Blistering lust hit him square in the solar plexus and spread to his groin, where his blood ran hot. His eyes fell closed. He dropped his chin to his chest. The universe was against him. That had to be it.

Sweat slid down his cheek, slipped off his jaw and hit the back of his hand. The irritation dragged him back to the second-to-last place he ever wanted to be. This was a fucking nightmare. He had a hard-on for a woman who was sleeping with a man who'd once been Teague's best friend. A man who'd once been someone Teague would have died to protect. A man who'd ultimately betrayed Teague in the worst possible way.

Thoughts of the past and all that had gone wrong eased the sexual ache. He dragged jeans, underwear, socks and a T-shirt from the bag. "What about the girl's stuff?"

With a disgusted scowl, Taz chucked another, smaller bag into the back. It hit Hannah in the face and dropped in her lap. "Should just strip her naked and leave her that way."

Shit. That was not an image Teague needed in his mind. Not after having their bodies plastered together for the last half hour. He already swore he knew every damn curve she had. Every damn perfect curve.

Don't go there.

"Change your clothes." He snapped the order without looking at her, leaning down to unlace his prison-issue work boots. He needed to keep his eyes off that side of the car. Avert his mind from the fact that she was getting naked only a foot away.

He rattled the thoughts from his head with a hard shake, tugged off the boots and socks, then checked her progress from his peripheral vision. She hadn't moved.

Teague shot her a look. "You can do it my way or his way, but you're gonna do it. So choose and get busy."

He didn't wait to see if she did what she was told. He could bet she wouldn't. And he didn't relish the idea of undressing and then redressing her. Not at all.

They cleared downtown and merged onto Highway Eighty headed east. Traffic was still light, which was good. The faster they got out of the city, the better.

Teague leaned back in the seat and untied the waist of his CDC pants. Hannah had turned her attention out the window toward Treasure Island, her fingers stroking the skin of her neck again. He whipped off his flimsy boxers and pulled on the new boxer briefs, allowing himself a moment to enjoy the feel of solid support and soft fabric.

God, the little things he'd missed. Ordinary, everyday things people took for granted. He'd never do it again.

He shook out the Levi's and pulled them on. "Perfect fit, man. Your woman does good work."

Taz's laugh was low and filled with double meaning. "You know it."

"Come on," Teague said to Hannah as he yanked a soft cotton tee over his head. "Get moving."

Her eyes narrowed in a scowl. She held out her hands and muttered beneath the tape, something Teague interpreted as, "Hel-lo."

"I know what you can do with those cuffs on, girl. Don't try to pull that shit on me. Just do it."

They'd traversed the Bay Bridge when a siren trilled behind them. A gush of adrenaline burned beneath Teague's sternum and spread over his ribs. He twisted to look out the back window.

"You see 'em?" Taz asked, voice tight.

"No. Did I miss something on the radio?"

"I didn't hear nothing."

Teague reached into the front seat with one hand and pulled on a Giants baseball cap with the other. "Give me the map."

"Traffic's choking down, man." Taz slowed and slapped the map into Teague's hand. "What should I do?"

"Whose car is this?" Teague searched for alternative routes to their destination, but didn't want to veer too far off course. This plan had been hashed out too hastily as it was. Adding twists to the path would only lead them into an even bigger mess.

"Cousin of a friend of a friend of a cousin," Taz rattled. "But it's registered to his stepfather. Different last names, different addresses. And he changed the plates with his brother's stepsister's Dodge Durango."

Well, hell. Those convoluted strings would never get untangled. The only snag would be anyone who had seen them leaving the hospital and reported it to police. But that was the great thing about San Francisco. There were so many people everywhere, nobody paid any attention to anyone else.

The siren grew closer. Louder.

"Probably an accident up ahead," Teague said. "Change lanes. Move to the right. It'll look like you're trying to let the emergency vehicles through."

As soon as they'd settled in behind a purple spray-painted VW bus, Teague saw the cruiser's lights flashing a half mile back. They were in the emergency lane, road dust swirling in their wake. He reached across the seat and wrapped a hand around the back of Hannah's neck, pulling her down until she was out of view through the window.

Taz's shoulders curled forward. The slower the traffic crawled, the more drastically he hunched over the steering wheel.

"Play it cool, Taz." Teague tried for a reassuring tone, but had to work for it. He held his breath as the siren grew so loud it filled his head and scrambled his brain. The cop was directly behind them, then beside them, then in front of them. And kept going.

Teague let all his air out in one heavy *swoosh*. His eyes closed as he dropped his chin to his chest. That's when he felt it—the soft, warm skin beneath his hand. He opened his eyes and found Hannah's head on his thigh, where he'd, evidently, been holding it.

His hand splayed over the side of her face, his fingers caressing the shadowed bruises on her cheek from Taz's backhand. The blood beneath her skin changed color as his fingers eased her body through the healing process—burgundy to purple to green to gold. And with every stroke, a zing of attraction traveled back toward him, squeezing his chest, drifting south and tightening his jeans.

Her eyes were closed, her head heavy on his leg. For an instant, he considered letting her stay there, using the opportunity to complete the mending process for the damage he'd caused. She was so pretty. So soothing to look at. Her dark lashes were a beautiful contrast to her skin. Her nose small and straight. Her lips full and pink. And for the first time, her scent registered—something soft, a mix of floral and spice.

As soon as the buzz of lust pulsed in his groin, Teague forced his hand back. Forced himself to shift away. No way could he do this—to himself or to her.

Hannah sat up with sluggish movements, eyes bleary. She sent him a confused look before turning her attention out the window again.

Teague reached over the front seat and clicked off the radio. Tense silence swamped the car, joining the white noise of the tires on asphalt. With his arms curved over the top of the bench seat, his gaze followed the cop's lights. Just before the toll booth, where the freeway split to take traffic either north or south, a dozen police vehicles clustered. Uniforms stood out on the road, directing traffic.

"Sonofabitch." Teague smacked the vinyl seat. "It's a goddamned fucking roadblock."

"What now, man? I got a full tank of gas. I say I put the pedal to the metal and blow by these cops, take a few out in the process. They won't know what hit 'em."

Teague's stomach clenched as tight as his fists and rolled with nausea. He wasn't about to mow down a bunch of cops. Then again, he wasn't about to go back to prison, either. He'd die first.

"Stay to the right. It doesn't look like they've got it completely blocked yet." Teague knew from his years of responding to traffic accidents how slow the cops moved. "We'll take the Eight-Eighty exit, back into Five-Eighty by way of Nine-Eighty."

"I don't do numbers, jackass. Just tell me where to go."

Teague's hand still tingled from where he'd been touching Hannah's face. That was a switch for him—being on the receiving end of the heat. And the attraction, that was new, too. He'd never felt anything when healing in the past, granted that had been long ago, before prison.

He rubbed the warmth against the roughness of the new jeans. "Like I said, stay right. Way right. Squeak through before it's blocked."

Taz nosed the GTO mercilessly toward the right. Sirens closed in from every direction. Police units burrowed in along the shoulder, between lanes. Cops swarmed on foot over the quickly stagnating freeway.

"Almost there," Teague reassured, struggling to keep his anxiety under control and his body heat level. "Just another few hundred feet and we'll be clear."

"Cop coming up on the left, Creek."

Teague darted a look in that direction. An officer walked toward their lane, carrying a yellow-striped sawhorse adorned with red lights like Rudolph.

"Keep going," Teague crooned. "Sit back in your seat, relax your shoulders."

As they inched forward, movement beside him caught his eye. He turned. Found Hannah's taped mouth pressed against the window. Her cuffed hands lifted. She thrust them toward the glass.

Teague caught one wrist on the downward swing inches from a solid *thwack* on the window just as they rolled past the cop. Teague locked an arm around her shoulders and pulled her into a hug. She squealed, squirmed. The cop hunched and peered into the car. Teague buried his face in the soft mass of her hair, put one hand against the back of her head and held her face to his shoulder.

And, he couldn't help himself. He took one long deep inhalation of her gently floral, vaguely spicy, helluva sexy, one-hundred-and-fifty-percent female scent.

They said every agent had one case in their career that haunted them. One they dreamt of in the night. One they reflected on during the day. One they took to their grave. This was that case for Jason Vasser.

Jason leaned his elbows on the metal balcony railing outside DARPA Deputy Director Dargan's office and squinted over the lights of downtown Arlington, Virginia. He took a deep drag on his Marlboro, pulling every last molecule of tobacco smoke into his lungs and holding it there. If he had to take this to the grave, that grave would damn well come sooner than later.

He'd secretly hoped Jocelyn had called him here for personal reasons. It had been months since they'd been together. But, inside her office, the hard smack of plastic signaling the end of her phone call also indicated alternate motives for this meeting. And considering the recent news of Creek's escape, Jason didn't have to guess it also signaled the beginning of his hellish last days as a federal employee.

She appeared beside him soundlessly, mirrored his stance and looked out over the darkened city. "Can I have one of those?"

Jason pulled the pack from his pocket and shook one forward. He lit it for her with the flick of his lighter. And waited.

"Schaffer is ballistic." The quaver in her voice matched the tense vibration in her small body. Jason slid his barrier into place. Her stress was as contagious as H1N1, and far more lethal.

"Senator Schaffer wouldn't have this problem if he'd taken care of the situation five years ago." Jason shrugged and stared at the red-rimmed glow of his cigarette. "All seven of those firefighters should have been eliminated at that warehouse explosion. Compassion always bites you in the ass."

"It wasn't compassion."

"Oh, right." Jason chuckled, knowing very well Schaffer didn't have a compassionate cell in his flabby body. "Election year. Those are big ass-chompers, too."

She wrapped one arm around her waist and stared into the night. "Where would Creek go?"

"Why ask me?"

She turned those sharp, light eyes on him. "Because you interviewed him initially after the fire. You followed him after he was released from the hospital. You were the first to notice his . . . abilities."

"Long time ago, Jocelyn." Jason winced at the slip of weariness in his voice. Definitely time to retire.

"He's your responsibility, Jason." She turned toward him, anger, frustration, fear shooting off her in laser beams. "You've just had it easy for the last three years while he was in prison."

He blew out a long stream of smoke, looked down at the street fourteen stories below and watched the remainder of his cigarette plummet into the darkness. Wondered what would happen to his own body if he jumped. Wondered if it would be an easier way to go than what he suspected lay ahead.

"I'm tired, Joce. I've got a one-way ticket to Costa Rica in three weeks. A bungalow on the ocean. Fishing all morning. Siesta at two. Margaritas at five. Dancing at eight. I'm not the guy to send after Creek."

She stiffened, tilted her head and stubbed out her barely smoked cigarette on the railing, then flicked it over the side. Both hands on slim hips, she shook her shoulder-length blond hair back. "In fact, you are. He wants Creek stopped. Schaffer's 'compassion' has faded over the last five years."

Jason's dream bubble burst. "Schaffer's the same fucking cocksucker now as he was then. Creek may have been the biggest problem child of the group five years ago, but he's an escapee now. He's looking toward the border, not the media. Give me a break."

"I agree with you, Jason. Schaffer *should* have killed them all years ago. And I'm sure Creek *is* headed for the border. But you're going to make sure he doesn't reach it."

Jason's stomach hardened. Sometimes always being right was such shit. He turned his squint on Jocelyn. She was a handsome woman. Might even be beautiful if she let go of this bloodsucking career. Needed some meat on her bones, some sun on her face, but that could happen in Costa Rica. If he could get her to buy into his pipe dream of going there with him to retire.

"Effective now," she broke into his thoughts, stuffing a sock in that hopeful pipe, "Creek has a priority kill order in place. Make sure you're discreet, Jason, or you may never see that shack in Central America."

Three

Alyssa rested her head against the car window, her mind wrangling thoughts for answers. Maybe she'd had some kind of chemical reaction to the metal in Creek's cuffs. An allergy she hadn't known about. Only they weren't burning her wrists now. The thought brought her back to the pain in her face.

Even with the cool glass pressed against her cheek, her skin still felt like it was going to split. The pain had ratcheted down after Creek had touched her, which was another oddity logic couldn't explain. Along with the way her libido skyrocketed in reverse proportion to her pain.

This whole situation was beyond bizarre. She was caught somewhere between scared-out-of-her-mind and ready-to-jump-him every time he touched her.

Snapped. She'd finally snapped. Just like her mother and brothers said she would if she didn't slow down. Didn't ease up. Didn't stop working and start living. What they'd never understood was that her work *was* her life. But, maybe that's where she'd gone wrong, because look where it had gotten her.

By the dashboard clock, they'd been driving an hour and a half. With every minute closer to nightfall, Alyssa's anxiety amped. Her fatigue also dragged at her, not to mention the grind of her stomach reminding her she hadn't eaten in nearly twenty hours. And the way her mind pinged around beneath her skull didn't help with the developing stress headache.

Where were they going? Why did they keep her? What were they going to do to her? She found herself wondering about death, what it would be like to get to that final moment. Those questions led to thoughts of her patients, ones she'd lost, ones she'd saved, which then led back to her work and her future. And the cycle started all over again.

Taz had mellowed with time and blaring classic rock. He sang along with an endless lung capacity, his choruses almost more painful than her throbbing face, aching wrists or morbid thoughts.

" 'Take me down to the Paradise City where the grass is green and the girls are pretty,' " Taz belted, completely off-key. " 'Oh, won't you please take me hooowooome. . . .' "

Creek hadn't looked at her for over an hour. At least not directly at her. He sat as far on the other side of the bench seat as he could get without climbing out of the car. Every time she moved so much as her little finger, he cast a surreptitious side glance at her. Since the incident with the roadblock, he'd dropped the whole idea of her changing clothes, which was good. She was not getting naked, or even close to it, in this car with these guys. For any reason. Ever. Period.

Despite the sheer noise level and her mounting anxiety, Alyssa had to force her eyes to stay open, her mind to catalogue landmarks. She needed a plan. Several plans. One for every situation that held the possibility of escape. But right now her brain felt as numb as her butt, and if she didn't get blood flowing, she'd definitely pass out—Guns and Roses at a hundred and thirty decibels, or not.

Alyssa straightened away from the window. That one movement gained her Creek's complete attention. He stiffened and twisted toward her, fingers curled into fists resting on his thighs. And she had to admit, he looked more human in street clothes. A lot more like one of those intriguing bad boys. But she'd already seen the tattoos. She knew where he'd come from. He was not the typical good-looking, rough-around-the-edges man she liked. He had hurt her. Would hurt her again if he deemed it necessary. Had told her so himself. Yet . . . something about him suggested that wasn't entirely true. Maybe his attempts to ease her pain. Maybe his efforts to shield her from Taz. Of course, maybe it was just her own warped psyche bending reality.

She lifted her cuffed hands and gingerly peeled the tape off her lips, grimacing as it pulled at the tender skin. Creek made no move to stop her, only watched with a guarded expression.

She looked directly at him, meeting those very light, intense blue eyes. "I'm car sick, I'm hungry and I have to pee."

One brow lifted. His mouth quirked. "You're sick *and* hungry?"

With that one look, Creek turned into a regular guy off the street. But more. He was a guy who would stop traffic. A guy who would warrant double takes. A guy she would have tripped over herself to meet under normal circumstances. She had to glance down at her cuffed hands to get her head on straight. In less than a second her anger and fear swung back around full force.

"I always get sick in the backseat of a car," she lied, "I haven't eaten since midnight, and my bladder is going to burst if we don't stop for a bathroom."

Creek heaved a sigh and rubbed his eyes. "Stop somewhere, Taz. A quiet gas station with a bathroom in the back would be good."

"Screw that," Taz said. "Why should we give a shit about what she needs?"

"Because it was your decision to kidnap me, and it was your decision to keep me." She'd had enough. The tension, the bizarre emotions, the uncertainty had turned her into someone she didn't recognize. "Now you have to deal with the consequences. As opposed to you, I'm human. I have human bodily needs. If you don't address them, we'll *all* be very uncomfortable, very soon."

"Put the tape back on that big mouth of hers, Creek, or I'll stuff it with something that's sure to shut her up."

Alyssa's back went up. Her mouth opened to spew something fierce and foolish, but someone touched her first. She jumped and turned toward Creek. His big, warm hand closed over her forearm with just enough force to send a message. The same message he delivered with that potent stare: Don't antagonize him.

He didn't look away from Alyssa as he talked to Taz. "You find me a private bathroom, and I'll make sure I tire her out good."

Alyssa jerked her arm back. Why she'd thought for a flicker of an instant they were on the same side she didn't know, but his nasty retort put everything in perspective. When would she learn men were all the same? Crude. Selfish. Controlling. Competitive. Self-serving.

And these men were the worst of the worst.

"What's wrong with what you got, Creek? If I'd known you were gonna waste all this time, I'd have made you drive. I know just how to fill a couple hours with a dink like that."

Alyssa's throat convulsed. The thought of rape pushed at the edges of her mind, but she shoved it right back out. Someone would die first. And it wouldn't be her. She'd already catalogued every possible way she could use her own body to end another's life, because her body was her only weapon.

"Just take the first exit with a gas station once you hit Highway Five," Creek said. "Pick the lousiest dive you can find."

"This is a shit hole, man, everything is a dive. Nothing but niggers and spics live here."

"Just find something and stop."

They slowed and traveled down the ramp. Taz hummed, low and troubled. "I don't like it."

Alyssa shifted in her seat to relieve the pressure on her bladder. She did have to pee—bad—but, more, she needed to develop a plan for the stop. "How long?"

"Couple minutes." Creek surveyed her, mouth turned down in disapproval. "Take off your shirt."

She scrunched one side of her face in contempt. "No."

"That blue thing has the hospital logo on it." He gestured at her with one careless hand. "Everyone's going to be looking for you in those . . ."

"Scrubs," she finished for him. "And, let me rephrase so you understand—*hell,* no."

He met her eyes with determination and a set jaw. "Take it off, or I'll take it off for you."

"Aw, yeah," Taz piped up. "Now we're gettin' some action."

Alyssa had to press her mouth tight to keep from telling the idiot to shut up. When she made no move toward taking her shirt off, Creek slid over the vinyl bench and snagged the hem that had come untucked hours ago.

Alyssa leaned away, her cuffed hands pushing at his. A sweep of panic heated her chest. "No. Don't. Leave me alone."

Taz laughed and chanted, "Go-go-go."

Creek grabbed the back of her shirt and pulled it up and over her head. He yanked the fabric down her arms into a bundle at the cuffs. The cool air prickled her skin beneath the white tank top remaining. She curled in on herself to minimize exposure. That's when she noticed the hole in her scrubs, irregular brown marks along the edge. She *wasn't* imagining things. He *had* burned her.

Taz watched in the rearview mirror and hit a curb as he pulled alongside a closed gas station-slash-mini mart. He shoved the car into park, twisted and laid one arm over the seat.

"Look what the skinny bitch was hiding under those baggy clothes." Taz's excited, bright eyes raked over Alyssa and fastened on her breasts as if he could see through her clothes. "Thought I felt a melon in there. Keep going, Creek. I wanna see that rack."

Stomach in her throat, Alyssa scanned the area, searching for an escape route. For someone who could help her. But the gas station wasn't closed as she'd first thought—it was abandoned. Tendrils of panic coiled around her lungs.

Creek fisted the chain between her hands, shoved the door open and dragged her across the seat. Would he beat her? Burn her? Kill her? She forced her mind back to the vulnerable areas of the body she could target: a fist to the temple, flat of the hand to the nose, knuckles to the philtrum, side chop to the adam's apple—

"Keep watch," Creek said to Taz as he pulled Alyssa to her feet and grabbed the smaller bag of clothes from the floorboard. "Don't do anything. No stroll, no smoke. Nothing, got it?"

Taz jerked his chin. "Am I gonna get a piece of her when you're through?"

"We'll see." Creek slammed the door and towed Alyssa toward two doors, where painted blue circles identified men's and women's bathrooms.

No. She couldn't go in there with him. She'd be trapped. But running wasn't much of an option either. The landscape around the deserted gas station was a barren sea of flat dirt and scraggly shrubs. Nobody within screaming distance. No haven within running distance. But the approaching darkness might actually be her friend.

Without any solid plan, Alyssa gathered all her strength, drove down with both hands, then jerked upward. To her utter shock, her hands wrenched free of his grip. A second seemed to float, suspended in time, before she could make her feet move.

As the surprise cleared from Creek's face, he made a grab for her hands. Alyssa spun and pushed into a kick start. Gravel slipped beneath her feet. Creek's big hand grabbed the back of her tank. Fabric ripped. Bra snapped. Creek whipped an arm around her waist. Twisted her body. Slung her over his shoulder. Just that quick, as if he'd done it countless times before.

"Fucking A," he growled. "You are the biggest pain in the ass."

"Let me go." Alyssa beat on his back with the cuff edge, kicked her feet, and twisted. Nothing loosened his grip. Nothing broke his stride. And his body heat had ramped up again.

Creek was still muttering as he kicked in the bathroom door. The *bang* made Alyssa flinch. Taz's full-bellied laugh followed them until Creek slammed the door shut.

Alyssa's feet hit the cement floor so hard her teeth knocked together. Pain ricocheted through her jaw. Creek let her go with a partial shove. She stumbled backwards and hit a wall. The scent of stale urine swamped her lungs. She pressed her hands against the tile to gain her balance, and waited a beat to catch her breath. When she was steady, Alyssa used both hands to comb the hair out of her face and look around.

The fading evening light dribbled in from a single window over the door. The chipped tile floor was stained brown around the toilet. Graffiti painted the walls.

With his handsome face focused into a piercing glare, Creek tossed the brown bag at her. "Use the bathroom and change your clothes. And if you even *think* about arguing with me, *think again*."

"You leave, and I'll change."

"No. You'll change right here, right now."

He pulled something from the pocket of his jeans and took two giant steps toward her. Alyssa scuttled backwards until her back was pressed up against the tile again. Creek flexed and curled his fingers, then rubbed both palms down his thighs, as if preparing himself for some drastic feat. Before she could find more words, Creek grabbed the chain binding her hands, pushed back the wadded scrubs and shoved a key into the cuff lock.

"And don't worry," he said without lifting his eyes from his work, "I'm not the least bit interested in looking at you, or . . . anything else, either. Just take care of your business so we can get back on the road."

So the fleeting attraction she felt when he touched her didn't go both ways. Even a criminal who'd been incarcerated didn't want to look at her. She was strangely offended, which only confirmed her earlier conclusion that she was also seriously screwed up.

When he retreated, Alyssa looked down at the one cuff still clasped around her arm, the other closed and dangling. "Can't you take them off?"

"No."

"Can't you even give me some privacy to pee?"

"No."

She jerked her scrub top over her hands and balled it up. All she wanted to do was put the flimsy fabric back on and cover herself. Instead, she not only had to change in his company, she had to pee in his company, too. After so many years in medicine, after all she'd seen and done, she shouldn't care. But she did. And if her bladder weren't ready to burst, she'd hold it.

She untied her scrubs and slid them over her hips, as little as possible to get the job done. She covered her face with her hands, resting her head as much as hiding her embarrassment. Fresh red welts encircled her wrists. Allergy. Had to be.

"Where are we going?" Her question came out muffled.

"Don't ask questions. Just do what I tell you."

When she'd finished, Alyssa pulled the clothes out of the bag—a pair of dark, low-riding, boot-cut jeans and a white spandex top with a deep, lace-trimmed vee neckline. In the very bottom of the bag, she found a pair of strappy, black, three-inch, ice pick heels.

Nothing would fit her. The pants were too long and a size too big. The shirt's cleavage would reach her navel and the sleeves would hang to her knees. She could fit two of her feet into one of the heels. A strange sense of wrongness edged in. For the first time she realized they'd planned to take someone. To take a woman. To keep her for some time if they'd thought to get her a change of clothes.

Panic resurfaced. Alyssa's gaze fastened on Creek where he paced the length of the bathroom like a caged animal. He had been serious about not wanting to look at her, because he hadn't so much as flicked his eyes her way.

"Look . . ." She paused, trying to get her words together. "I have a brother. He's the best criminal attorney in San Francisco. If you let me go, I know I can convince him to look into your case. I'll make sure he gets your appeal through the system, and—"

"A lousy goddamned lawyer is the reason I'm here." His voice emerged slow and tight as if he were growing close to the end of his patience. "No one can help me. Change your clothes. Now."

"Or," she tried again, "I could make a phone call and have money wired from my credit card to a Western Union. That way you wouldn't have to depend on that other guy for money. You could break off and go your own way."

"Sonofabitch." Creek stopped pacing, his back toward her. He crossed his arms, pulling the black fabric of the tee across muscular shoulders, and dropped his chin to his chest. He pulled off his cap and rubbed his head with both hands. "How does Luke fucking live with you?"

Alyssa's stomach jittered with unease. She was starting to think they existed in parallel universes. "Who?"

He slid the hat back onto his head and swung around, eyes hot with irritation. "I swear, woman, if you don't start moving, I'll strip you myself. Don't make me do that."

His tone made it clear undressing her would be a disgusting chore. *Jerk*. She pushed the stupid thought aside and focused on her goal.

"Get me a phone," she said, "and I'll make the call right now, while you're standing here. You can confirm the money is waiting for you before you leave. Then tell that idiot"—she gestured toward the door—"that you killed me and that you two need to get out of here before the police come. I'm nothing but another problem for you to deal with."

Creek crossed his arms. His strong jaw jumped beneath tan skin and golden stubble. "Last warning. Don't make me tell you again."

Alyssa had never begged for anything in her life. Demanded, maybe. Asked, okay. Pled, no. This sick feeling of helplessness made her angry and desperate.

"You're out now," she said, imploring. "You don't need me."

One side of his mouth turned up, but the expression was more cunning than humorous, his blue eyes reflecting anger. Maybe resentment. "Girl, you are the *only* thing I really need."

Bang! Bang! Bang!

Alyssa jumped at the rap on the door. Creek swung that direction.

"You done with her yet?" Taz yelled. "I've got a boner the size of a Louisville Slugger and nowhere to put it."

A rush of bile stung Alyssa's throat. She clutched the clothes to her chest.

"Jack off in the car," Creek yelled back. "I'm keeping her." He met Alyssa's eyes directly. "It's him or me, Hannah, and *he* doesn't need you. I suggest you do things my way."

Hannah? The circuits of her brain sparked, shorted out. "Hann—? Who . . . ? What . . . ?"

Holy shit. Hannah. He thought she was Hannah Svelt, the sonographer Alyssa had filled in for. Which meant he'd never met the girl, because she and Alyssa were polar opposites. Hannah was five-foot-ten inches of pure Scandinavian beauty. Tan skin, white-blond hair that reached the middle of her back, model looks. She also had a curvy figure, which explained the clothes, but left Alyssa with a whole host of new questions.

She opened her mouth to clarify her identity; then another thought dribbled into her brain. If she wasn't Hannah, then Creek didn't need her. If she wasn't Hannah, then Creek had no incentive to keep her safe or alive.

In that moment Alyssa decided she could damn well be Hannah, at least until she could find a way to escape.

"I'm changing." Alyssa slid her pants off without a hint of embarrassment. Dragged on the poorly fitting clothes without a murmur of complaint. She tied her broken bra strap into a knot and kept her tank on beneath the spandex. Then she slid back into her comfy clogs instead of the heels and used a section of her hair to tie a knot around the rest, pulling the unruly strands off her face. And she did all of it while Creek paced the bathroom, his eyes averted.

With her little emergency wallet holding her identification still in the pocket of her scrubs, she balled up the thin garments and stuffed them into the corner behind the toilet.

"Good try." Creek's voice made her jump. "Pick them up. We're taking them with us."

Like a hungry crow, he'd snapped up her bread crumb. As she bundled the clothes into the bag, he waved her over, the cuff key in his hand. She hesitated only a moment before stepping forward, hands outstretched.

"Doesn't look like Taz's woman did as good a job picking clothes for you." Creek frowned as he settled the metal on her wrists, looser than the first time. His warm fingers lingered on her skin, rubbing the red welts there. A gentle, relaxing heat flowed through her wrists just before the lines started to fade. Right in front of her eyes the red swells turned pink, then melted into her own flesh color. Alyssa squeezed her eyes shut in disbelief, but when she opened them again, the marks were still gone. "How'd you do that?"

"Do what?"

She darted a look at his face to gauge his expression. He was calm and serious. "That. Take away those red marks?"

"You don't have any marks." He released her hands with a

disgusted grunt. "Women. Always milking the situation. Give it a rest."

Had she imagined those rings on her wrists? Had she imagined his intense body heat? Maybe St. Jude's had finally driven her over the edge. Or maybe this whole thing was one big nightmare she'd wake from, shuddering like a child.

A muffled shout sounded outside the door. Teague straightened and turned. More voices drifted in. Men's voices. Not just Taz's. Hope sparked. Alyssa had to fight back the urge to call out for help.

"Creek," Taz yelled, clear and sharp. "Get your ass out here."

A wall of heat blasted off Creek and hit Alyssa with the force of a desert wind.

"Creek!" Taz's voice rose with urgency.

"Shit." Teague grabbed the chain between Alyssa's cuffs and yanked her close.

The heat was definitely back. She might not be able to explain the science behind it, but there was no mistaking the hot current traveling through that metal.

"You stay behind me," he said. "Understand?"

She nodded, her thoughts already sprinting toward the anticipation of bolting into the arms of police or F.B.I. or C.I.A. or whatever the hell agency handled kidnappings.

Creek tugged her close at his back and opened the door.

FOUR

During their time in the bathroom, dusk had turned to night. The area streetlights now cast an eerie yellow hue over the gas station. Everything beyond hid in the deepening shadows.

Alyssa peered around Creek's arm, hope welling so fast her throat ached. She swore she could taste the sweetness of freedom on the back of her tongue. But what she saw filled her mouth with bitter fear.

Four black men stood in an arc around Taz, blocking his path to the car. Instead of the uniforms she'd hoped for, they wore low-slung pants, unzipped oversized sweat jackets with the hoods up, two with no shirts underneath. Black bandanas covered their foreheads and hung over their eyes.

"It's about fucking time." Taz's eyes cut between Creek and the other men with a wild edge, one Alyssa read as part excitement, part fear. "These fucking porch monkeys say we're in their territory."

The twenty-somethings shuffled closer, shoulders back, chins up. The tallest gave Teague a one-sided superior grin. "These 'porch monkeys' gonna pound your cracka faces into the pavement."

Creek pulled on the chain between Alyssa's hands, forcing her fully behind him. She gladly curled into his bulk, hoping to disappear.

The guy with dreadlocks craned his neck to see around Creek. "Ooooowee. Whatcha got there, wigger?"

Alyssa cringed. She scooted closer to Creek and wrapped her fingers around the wrist of the hand holding her cuffs. Just like that, they were on the same team again.

She peeked around his arm and found three of the four making noises of interest as they inspected her. One remained between Taz and the car, where Alyssa assumed Taz had left the gun he'd stolen from the prison guard. Judging by the bloodthirsty look on Taz's face, if he'd had the weapon on him, she had no doubt all four of these men would be dead.

"Ni-i-ice." Dreadlocks laughed as if he'd found some hidden treasure. "Whatch you doin' with these honkies, pretty? Come on over here with us. We'll take good care of you."

"These white boys ain't got half of what we got." The stocky one cupped his crotch. "You know what they say . . ."

"Once you've had black," the tall one finished, "you never go back."

All four hooted with laughter. Dreadlocks tipped his head and waved her forward. "What do you say, baby? Wanna taste of black meat? It's an all-you-can-eat buffet."

Alyssa's stomach flipped and twisted. Her airway constricted. She pressed her face into the furrow between Creek's shoulder blades, curled her free hand into the back of his shirt and tightened the fingers wrapped around his wrist. This time, the intense heat radiating from his body reassured her. Gave her hope he might just be able to get her out of this.

"We don't want trouble," Creek said. "Just stopped to use the bathroom. We're leaving."

"There's a charge for use of the facility," one of them said. Alyssa didn't know which. Her forehead was still buried against Creek. "Leave her and we'll let you go."

Oh, Jesus, no. She shook her head against Creek's back in a silent plea. She'd never imagined choosing to stay with convicted criminals, but she had no doubt in her mind that if he abandoned her here, she'd be gang-raped and left for dead.

"Dump the whore," Taz said. "Let's get the hell out of this dive."

"She's not up for negotiation." Creek's voice dropped in warning. "We'll just leave and it will be like we were never—"

Shhhhh-click.

Everyone went silent.

Creek stiffened. A shot of heat traveled through the cuffs and snapped at Alyssa's skin like a firecracker. The pulse at his wrist picked up another twenty beats per minute.

Alyssa looked around Creek's thick bicep. The stocky gang member stood ten feet away, twisting the handle of a knife, the blade glinting in the light from a distant street lamp.

"No one's going anywhere until we say so, white boy."

"Look"—Creek pushed her back and to the right, angling her away from the guy with the weapon. "We don't want any troub—"

The attacker lunged. The knife sliced the air. Teague dodged, dragging Alyssa with him. She stumbled and lost her balance.

"Come on, man," the attacker's groupies jeered. "Stick 'em."

The look in the attacker's eyes as he twirled the knife and maneuvered for position was something Alyssa had never seen—not even in the angriest or most insane patient. Something that made her stomach chill. Something malicious, vicious. Animalistic.

She struggled to get into sync with Creek as he dodged, but her mind was muddled with fear.

The man stabbed again. Creek leaned. Twisted. But Alyssa was too slow. The *rip* of fabric met her ears before the stab of pain enveloped her right side. She wasn't sure whether or not she screamed. If she did, she didn't hear it. In fact, she heard nothing. All sound ceased. Her mind shut down. Her legs lost strength. She broke from Creek's grip and hit the pavement on her butt, jarring her tailbone and knocking the air from her lungs. Fire engulfed her ribs.

The smack of flesh on flesh drew Alyssa's gaze up as Creek nailed his fist into the attacker's jaw. The blow rocketed the gangbanger back five feet. With restricted use of her hands, Alyssa pressed her elbow to the injury and struggled to a sitting position. Sticky warmth pumped from the wound, but she didn't have time to assess the damage. Taz still circled with the tallest gang member, while the remaining two pulled knives similar to the one that had cut her. They angled toward Creek from both sides.

Alyssa searched the ground for something, anything to use as a weapon. But any substantial pipe or board was secured to the building or the ground. Three feet away, the concrete gave way to a pea gravel border. She pushed to her knees and crawled to the rocks. With her teeth gritted against the pain, Alyssa scooped up a double handful of gravel and heaved it toward the men going for Creek. Pain ripped up her side. A cry burst from her throat.

The men shielded themselves as they swore and looked at each other in pissed-off confusion. Alyssa sucked in a breath and scooped again. Just as the men turned their menace fully on her, she hurled another double fistful of rocks as hard as she could. Like BB's, the little rocks peppered the men. Falling back a step, they shielded themselves once again, cursing.

"You goddamned bitch!" One of the men started for her. "I'm gonna tear you apart."

If she thought she'd seen the worst expression on a man's face a moment before, she'd been wrong. The eyes aimed at her now were ruthless, ferocious. The saying "tearing her limb from limb" didn't seem at all clichéd in the moment.

Alyssa scuttled backwards, but didn't have the coordination or the strength to run. Her body was as incapable of responding to commands as her mind was of making them. She backed into something, or someone. A bite of fear ripped at her belly. She looked up. Found Creek pointing a gun at the men.

"You're not going to touch her."

She darted a glance at the car. The back door stood open. Relief pushed the air from her lungs. Pain rushed in, all her senses coming back online as the adrenaline seeped away.

"You heard him, monkey meat," Taz said. "Get the fuck out of here before he shoots your ugly black faces clean off."

A siren sounded somewhere close. All four gang members looked around, and made a collective decision to bolt. As soon as their backs were turned, Creek swooped in and picked Alyssa up, one arm behind her back, one under her knees.

"Back here," Taz yelled from beside a Dumpster.

Creek jogged that direction, each step stabbing pain through Alyssa's torso. She gripped the front of his shirt with both hands and jammed her head against his chest for stability.

He dropped to one knee behind the Dumpster and looked down at her with those clear, sharp eyes. But something new floated there—obvious, serious concern. Maybe even an edge of guilt. "How bad is it?"

"I need a hospital."

"No fucking way," Taz barked.

Sirens drew closer. Louder. Creek tightened his arms around her and drew her into the support of his chest. Despite the situation, Alyssa found the gesture unnervingly tender and . . . compassionate. She rested her forehead on his shoulder, wincing at the heat radiating through his shirt, wishing she had the strength to hold her head up, praying those sirens would stop, boots would hit the pavement and the words *Freeze, police!* would jump out of a dozen different mouths. But her luck stayed true to the day. The cops kept going and going and going, until the sirens faded entirely—along with Alyssa's hope.

Her muscles went lax and she softened against Creek's bulk. Tears leaked from beneath her closed lashes. The warmth on her cheeks felt foreign and awkward. She rubbed her face on his shirt.

"I'm bleeding a lot," she tried again. "I really need a hospital."

Taz scoured the area and hoisted himself to his feet. "How 'bout if I just kill you and put you out of your misery? If I have to listen to one more word, I'll put a Glock in your mouth." He turned to Creek. "I'll wait for you in the car."

Alyssa's skin rippled and the fine hairs on her arms rose. She realized this was one of the first times Taz had spoken directly to her, and she discovered she preferred him speaking *about* her as if she wasn't there.

Creek pulled away and yanked at Alyssa's clothes. "Let me see how bad it is."

"Don't." She shoved at his hands, but might as well have been pushing him with a feather.

"Stop moving, would you?"

He nudged the warm, bloody fabric out of the way. Cool October air licked at her skin and sent goose flesh over her torso. She glanced down at the gash—six inches long, four to five millimeters deep and still oozing fresh blood. And, damn, it hurt, a combination of throbbing ache, fiery burn and deep, stabbing pain.

"I need to stop the bleeding." Creek coiled and flexed his fingers. Every time she'd seen him do that, he'd subsequently touched her.

"Wait . . . What . . . ? Don't . . ."

He pressed the full length of his hand to her side.

She sucked in a breath at the immediate burn along her skin. The first thing that zipped through her mind was *infection*. "Don't . . . don't . . ."

The heat penetrated her skin, sinking into muscle. The throb eased to an intense ache. The ache melted into a dull twinge. Her mind softened around the edges. *Don't what?* She couldn't remember. Couldn't think about anything other than the instant pain relief his touch offered. But how? *How?* Her brain grasped for answers. Counterpressure. Had to be the counterpressure.

Only counterpressure had nothing to do with the way another type of heat kicked up in her body when the pain receded. Or the way that heat traveled to other parts and created other sensations. The way her chest filled with an entirely different ache that made her breasts tingle and her nipples tighten. The way her pelvis felt warm and heavy and made her want to rub her thighs together to ease some vague need.

Her forehead grazed his chin as she let her head loll forward. Let her face press against his neck, her mouth against his throat. He was rough and soft at the same time. And so warm.

"You need stitches." His voice sounded low and unsteady, vibrating against her lips. She was just about to open her mouth against his skin. Just one little taste of the forbidden. He abruptly put space between them, yanking her out of this luscious lull he'd tempted her into.

She gave her head a swift shake, and didn't even attempt to quell the automatic *duh* in her tone when she said, "That's why I mentioned the hospital."

He avoided her eyes. "You know I can't do that."

"You can do anything you want."

"This isn't just about me."

"What? You mean that perverted asshole? His needs are more important than mine? I've never committed a crime in my life. I've dedicated my life to helping people."

Screw this. She struggled out of his grip and set her feet on the ground. As soon as she broke contact, she looked down at her wound and the dark blood crusted along the incision. The bleeding had stopped.

Counterpressure, one piece of her mind reassured while another nagged, *I've never seen counterpressure work that fast*. The pain crept back, and she found herself craving his touch again. The proximity between them had become too comfortable. She needed to remember who she was with and why.

"Forget it," she said. "Like you give a damn."

"Hannah—"

"I said, forget it. Can we just get to where we're going? Get this whole stupid game you're playing over with? I have a really screwed-up life to get back to."

Still crouched behind the Dumpster, Creek dropped his head, rubbed his face with both hands, then repositioned his ball cap. He paused to rest his elbows on knees, as if he was thinking about something deep and all-important. She would have walked away, but she didn't want to be alone with Taz. She sure as hell didn't want to run into those four lowlifes again, either.

When Creek stood, took her arm gently and led her to the car, she didn't protest.

Taz looked up from his spot crouched near the rear passenger side tire. He pushed to his feet and started straight for her. "You fucking bitch. This is all your fault."

"Back off." Teague smacked a hand against Taz's chest and stepped between him and Hannah. "We've got more important things to think about."

Taz's edgy eyes cut into Teague. "Yeah, like how the fuck we're getting out of the hell hole that bitch got us into now that those niggers jacked our ride."

Teague's gaze fell to the rear tire. Flat. Then it jumped to the front. Flat. Taz pushed against Teague's hand as he reached for Hannah again. "I'm going to fuck the living shit out of this slant-eyed cunt."

Teague had heard enough racial slurs for a lifetime. He shoved Taz so hard the other man stumbled back and hit the trunk of the car.

Taz's dark eyes narrowed on Teague. "What's wrong with you, man? Why is this bitch so important?"

"Not your business."

"It is if she gets our asses thrown back in the hole."

"That won't happen."

Taz leaned forward and pointed a rigid finger in Teague's face. "If it does, you're *mine*."

A dark film inked Teague's stomach. The threat reminded him of exactly why he would die before he went back to prison. It was the fear he'd lived with day in and day out at Quentin—the fear of being gutted, strangled, stabbed, beaten, raped or worse. He was convinced the twisted severity of his crime had kept the other animals at bay so far. That and the fact he benched more than three of them put together. Teague didn't work out obsessively to kill time. He did it to stay safe. To stay alive.

"Where the fuck we getting another car?" Taz's arms flew as they typically did when he was on the edge of "throwing a nutty." Bad things always happened when Taz wigged, things like death and dismemberment. "Look around you, Creek. We're in the middle of fucking mud country."

Teague scanned the surrounding industrial area, devoid of pedestrians and traffic. He doubted there was civilization within two miles. Besides, Hannah couldn't walk that far. He might have stopped the bleeding for now, but too much movement, too much pressure could break open the wound.

"There." He tightened his grip on Hannah's cuffs and started for a parking lot two blocks away where three U-Haul vans sat alongside a building. "Come on."

Hannah resisted when he pulled her forward. He swung toward her without any effort to hide his annoyance, but she didn't cower.

"Take these off me." She lifted her hands and the cuffs shone in the low light. "I need to put pressure on my side."

"Fucking A." If it wasn't one thing, it was another. He unlocked the cuff on her right hand and, much to his own distaste, secured it to his left wrist. "Sooner we get to the truck, the sooner you can sit."

Taz fumed under his breath, muttering a rash of racist, cursing comments with each step toward the yard. When Teague had made the deal in prison to take Taz on as an escape partner, he'd rationalized the desperate move by telling himself he'd be rid of the jackass within hours. Unfortunately, Teague's plans hadn't panned out as expected, and now he was ready to ram Taz's head into the chipped stucco wall on his right. The only reason he didn't was because he didn't want to burn Hannah's wrist again.

When they reached the lot, Teague realized the trucks weren't out in the open, but behind a twelve-foot, chain-link fence with razor wire spiraling upward another two feet at the top.

Teague ran his hand over the stubble of hair on his head. "Aw, fuck me."

Taz picked up the padlock secured by a thick chain and slammed it back into place. "How is this going to help us?"

Teague dragged Hannah fifty feet from the entrance and pointed at the pavement. "Sit."

He released the cuff on his wrist and fastened it to the chain link, then surveyed the barrier. A familiar sense of impotence nagged at him. If he could just harness the powers he knew he had inside, he could use his finger as a freakin' welding torch. But no. He hadn't found the secret yet.

"Nothing about this could be easy," he muttered. "Let's go."

"You go," Taz said. "I'll wait here with the *princess*."

"No, you won't." Teague stretched his arms overhead, gripped the fence and pressed a boot against the chain. "If you can't help me get this truck, you can't ride in it."

Grumbling, Taz climbed the fence with Teague. Swore when he nicked himself on the wire. Ranted when he dropped to the ground and twisted his ankle. By that time, Teague was already at the truck, peering in the window. As long as Taz was on the opposite side of the fence from Hannah, Teague didn't give a shit what the ass did.

"How you gonna get in?" Taz asked. "How you gonna start it?"

Teague looked around the lot for something to break the

window. "Don't tell me you don't know how to hot-wire a car."

"I never have to. Just stick my gun in the driver's face and say *get out*."

The gun. Teague pulled the weapon from his waistband. "Great idea."

He looked past the fence in all directions. Dead quiet except for the distant swoosh of freeway traffic. He stepped back several feet and pointed the weapon at the window, angling the muzzle down at the floorboard. His finger hesitated on the trigger, apprehension tightening his gut. He'd never fired a gun and didn't want to start now. But with no other adequate choice, Teague closed his eyes, turned his head and fired.

FIVE

The gun kicked Teague's arm back. The blast rang in his ears. Glass shattered and sprayed the truck's interior. He peered around the neighborhood again while his heart hammered, half expecting a rush of cops, or at least a few shocked spectators. But no life stirred beyond the fence, and the only thing Teague heard was Taz laughing.

"Yee-haw. Creek, you are one resourceful prick."

Teague put a hand against the muzzle to test its temperature. When he decided it wouldn't scald him, he tucked it back into his jeans. With a pop of the lock, he opened the door and dove beneath the dash. He yanked wires, checked colors, used his fingernail to strip the plastic covering away. A twist of the reds, and he was ready for the big moment. Teague positioned the third red and a single brown wire in either hand. *Please start*. He touched the wires together. A mechanical grind sounded near his head.

"Yes," he hissed. "Come on, baby."

Another grind. Another.

"We don't have all night, Creek."

"If you think you can do better, get your ass down here."

Sweat dripped across Teague's forehead and he wiped it away with the back of his hand. This wasn't working. He needed more amperage. More spark.

He closed his eyes, focusing. He visualized a fiery, electrically charged ball of power deep in his gut. As he channeled the energy, the globe spun and fizzed and popped and grew. Golf ball to tennis ball. Tennis ball to football.

He settled the two wires together, squeezed his eyes shut and gave a mental push.

The engine rumbled and turned over, then quit. Teague gritted his teeth, tightened his fingers and pushed again.

Grind. Grind. Whoosh. The engine roared to life and kept going.

"Woo-hoo." Taz slapped Teague's back. "You're the man. Now what about the fence?"

Teague uncoiled from the cab, sweating, nauseous. He pressed one hand to the side of the truck to steady himself. "Run it."

"You drivin'?"

"No, you are." No way was Taz sitting next to Hannah.

Teague checked her spot on the sidewalk. She was huddled on the ground, still and quiet, her arm hanging limp from the fence. The sickening guilt that had leaked through his barriers the instant he'd wrapped that chain around her neck was back, dousing the residual heat from his powers and leaving him cold.

He gripped the front of Taz's shirt and shook the jerk to attention. The last thing Teague needed was Hannah's arm ripped from the socket. "You make sure you wait until I unhook her from the fence."

"Whatever." Taz jumped into the cab and revved the engine.

Teague climbed the fence, picked through the razor wire and dropped to the ground next to Hannah. He unlocked the cuff, inspecting her face for signs of shock. She was pale, her eyes glazed, but fire still sparked beneath.

"We'll stop and get you fixed up before we move on." He hooked the free cuff to his own wrist.

"Why did you involve that idiot in the first place?" she

asked, her gaze fastened on the truck behind Teague. "He's an anchor. You're the one with the muscle and the brains." Her eyes skipped to Teague's face and sharpened. "Or do you need him, too?"

Brains? She thought he had brains? Laughter swelled in his chest and he almost let it out. Only nothing about this was funny. Not one goddamned thing.

"I need him, too." Teague helped her up, put an arm around her waist. "He's the one with people on the outside. He's the reason we had a car, money and clothes."

"You don't have people?"

Teague's mind drifted to the team of firefighters who'd once been his family. Before his perfect life had been blown to hell. Before that damned warehouse fire. Five long years before. Luke had already turned on him, and the other five had suffered enough. Everyone had suffered enough.

"No, I don't have people. I don't have anyone." He pulled her against his chest. "Cover your head."

She pressed her face to his shoulder. Her free hand clutched his shirt in a way that made him feel needed. Something he hadn't experienced in so very long. Yet she needed him in all the wrong ways, for all the wrong reasons, taking all the sweetness out of the emotion and twisting it into another source of guilt.

Taz revved the truck. Tires screeched. A second later, the explosive shriek of metal on metal filled the air. But all Teague could focus on was the way Hannah squeezed closer until her body was flush with his. She was warm and strong. She was intelligent and gorgeous. She was way too good for Luke.

Hannah lifted her head and looked toward the street. A tremor rocked her delicate frame, drawing out Teague's protective instincts. He was so tempted to trash this asinine plan, ditch Taz, find a safe place for Hannah and call the whole thing done.

One fleeting thought of Kat wiped that option right out of his mind.

"I don't know how much more of this I can take," she said, her voice feathery soft.

"We'll be rid of him by morning, then things will smooth out." He put up a mental shield. Focused on his goal, on what really mattered. "All goes as planned, you should be home by tomorrow afternoon."

That thought should have thrilled Teague. And the prospect of seeing Katrina's perfect cherub face smiling at him, of hearing her little voice calling to him, did make his heart ache with anticipation. But he had mixed feelings about letting Hannah go. And those mixed feelings became even murkier when he thought about letting her go back to Luke.

Hannah searched his face with a clear look of cynicism, and he couldn't blame her. He climbed into the cab, positioning himself in the center of the bench seat, and leaned over to pull her into the cab beside him. She grimaced with the movement, but didn't complain. Once she was settled, Teague uncuffed his wrist and secured her hand to the passenger's door. He didn't need to be in those cuffs a minute longer than necessary.

They drove to the handicapped GTO a few blocks away and threw their things in the back of the U-Haul.

"Directions," Taz said as he pulled onto the main street.

"Stay on Thirty-Three. Head for Los Banos. There's a Walmart there."

Taz looked at Teague as if he'd turned black. "Why Walmart?"

"We need supplies."

Taz didn't respond. All his excitement from the confrontation with the gang and the carjacking had drained, leaving him in a hole, burrowing deeper by the minute. Teague let it go, hoping Taz came out of it on his own. Hannah laid her head against the seat and closed her eyes. After a few minutes, her head slid sideways and rested on Teague's shoulder.

"I think we got a problem, you and me." Taz finally spoke

after fifteen minutes of cool, dark silence. "I think that chink is more important to you than I am."

Teague didn't look at Taz, didn't show any emotion. "She's a bargaining chip, nothing more."

"What you want bad enough to put up with her?"

"Not your business."

"I ain't goin' to no Walmart."

"You don't have to go in. It would probably be better if you didn't."

"I'll drop you off and go find myself a whore," Taz said. "I know where they hang out in town."

Hell, no. Taz was not disappearing with this truck. "She's in no condition to sit around and wait for you to get back. I'll drop you and pick you up when we're done."

"You're a bossy sonofabitch, Creek. I'm gettin' tired of it."

"We agreed on the inside. My rules, your contacts. If you don't like it, I'll drop you back off at the GTO and make a phone call to the cops to let them know where you are."

"I could do the same for you."

Teague thought back to Hannah's comments at the fence. "But you won't because you know you can't do this without me. After tomorrow, you can make every goddamned call on every goddamned day for the rest of your life. For now, you have to live with me."

They rode in silence for the next fifteen minutes. As they came up on the outskirts of Los Banos, Taz made a few turns and slowed where three women stood clustered around the stairwell of an apartment building—two black women, one white.

"You girls workin' tonight?" Taz called toward them.

"You know it, baby," one of the black girls answered. "Come on over."

Taz set the brake and pushed open the door.

"Hey." Teague caught his arm. "Leave me some money."

Taz peeled off a dozen bills and pounded the remaining

wad into Teague's hand. Teague caught his partner's grip and infused heat into the connection until Taz looked him in the eye. "I'll be back in an hour and a half. If you're not here, I'll assume you're going the rest of the way on your own."

Taz yanked out of Teague's grip, and shook the burn from his hand, casting Teague that anxious you-freak look. Sometimes others' suspicions about his abilities worked to Teague's advantage. "I'll be here."

Teague scooted to the driver's side, dislodging Hannah's head from his shoulder. She woke and straightened in the seat, her eyes sleepy, making her look sweet and sexy all at the same time. "Where are we?"

"Go back to sleep." As Teague pulled away from the curb, he glanced back at Taz. The animal had one arm around each black girl, and the threesome walked toward the stairwell. Teague hit the brake. "Shit. That's no good."

Hannah groaned as she shifted in her seat.

"Goddammit," Teague muttered as he watched Taz and the two black girls disappear into the building. The single white girl strolled off around a corner.

"Oh, God," Hannah whined. "I think I'm going to be sick."

Her tortured voice brought Teague's attention around. The color in her face had paled several shades in the last hour. His gaze drifted to the bloodstains on her shirt, which made him realize there was no real decision to be made. He pounded the gas and headed toward Walmart.

"You need something in your stomach," he said.

"Yeah, like stitches."

Teague's mouth quirked. With Taz gone, a certain relief settled in. One less wild card to worry about. "I was speaking of food and water, but stitches would be good, too."

"If I eat, I'll throw up."

Teague sighed and rubbed at the stubble on his head. He hadn't shaved his skull in a week, and the new hair growth made his scalp itchy. "Do you argue with everyone or am I just lucky?"

"You're about as lucky as I am."

"That's not a good sign."

"Tell me about it. Where did that jerk go? You said he'd be gone tomorrow morning."

Teague was too tired to make up a lie. "He went to get laid."

His statement was met with extended silence.

"He has a girlfriend here?" she finally asked.

"No."

Another silence. Then, "Why didn't you go get laid, too?"

He darted a look at her, surprised by her candidness. And irritated with the zing of heat in his groin. "Because I have more important things to take care of."

Her eyebrows shot up. "There's a man on the planet who believes there is something more important than sex?"

Teague bit the inside of his cheek to fend off the growing lust the subject brought on and pulled into the parking lot of Walmart, stopping the truck a respectable distance from the store.

"You really *did* want to go to Walmart? I thought that was a code name for something." She turned confused eyes on Teague. "This is the last place on earth I'd expect you to stop."

"Where *would* you expect me to stop?"

"I don't know, a liquor store, local drug dealer's house, a McDonald's drive-through . . ."

"I didn't eat McDonald's even before I went to prison."

Her lips turned, just barely. The lids of those sultry eyes lowered, almost imperceptibly. The effect was a little dreamy. Extremely sexy. "Then you've missed out on the best French fries on the planet. Mmm."

His throat squeezed. Mouth went dry. That hum nearly popped the button on his damn jeans. Fuck, he so didn't need this. "You don't look like you've ever eaten a fry in your life."

"I just don't eat them all day, every day. Why are we here again?"

Hell, if he knew. All his blood was somewhere below his belt.

"We need supplies." He pressed his fingers to his eyes and forced his mind clear. "I think I can get them all here."

"How long have you been in prison?"

He dropped his hand, opened his eyes and stared out the windshield, half sure he'd imagined the question. But when he looked at her, she peered back with such keen interest, Teague was convinced she was waiting for an answer. In a sick way, he was glad she'd asked, because every degree of heat she'd fueled immediately chilled.

"Too long."

"For what?"

"I don't want to talk about it." Or think about it. Or remember all the unbearable details.

Teague pushed the driver's door open, dropped to the ground and rounded the truck. He opened Hannah's door and settled a serious look on her. "Here's the deal. You stay close to me. And I mean close. If you try to get away or make any stupid move, like scream, complain, fake an injury, whatever, I'll make sure Taz knows not only where you live, but where every member of your family lives as well."

He paused, waiting for that information to sink in, then put the punch behind the statement. "He murdered his baby sister for sleeping with a Mexican. He tied them both up, took them into a lettuce field, threw them into the dirt and ran them over with a discer while they were still alive. Do you know what a discer is?"

Her big eyes glazed with shock. "I . . . I don't think I want to—"

"It's a tractor with a couple dozen rotary blades on the back. Each blade is the size of a semi's tire. They're used to till fields."

Hannah's face scrunched as if she was in pain again. And he knew just how she felt. The stories Taz boasted about had caused Teague nightmares for months. But in this case, he needed to make a point, and she needed to get it.

"They were picking up pieces of them both for weeks," he continued. "The coroner came out to the farm with a bulk supply of evidence flags and stuck one where they found every body part—"

"Okay." She closed her eyes and held up her hand. "Okay. I get it. Jesus, you're lucky I haven't puked on you yet."

"With my luck, that'll change soon, won't it?"

Alyssa didn't know if Creek's luck would change anytime soon, but she was about to give her own lousy luck a kick in the butt. This was the first public location she'd been to since Creek had kidnapped her, and he could tell her every gruesome story he could dream up, but she wasn't going to let this opportunity pass.

Creek pulled a shirt from his bag of clothes and tossed it on the seat, then released the cuff attached to the door. "Let's get you into something clean. It may be October, but somehow I doubt all this blood will come across as a Halloween prank."

Alyssa wanted the blood to show. She wanted her bruises and burns exposed. They were bound to garner attention. She didn't have to fake the exhaustion slumping her against the seat. It was bone-deep real. "I can't change clothes. I hurt too much."

Creek thought a second, then brought both hands to the collar of her tank. "I'm going to tear it. Don't scream."

Before Alyssa had time to process the information, he yanked. She tensed, anticipating a rip of pain in her side, but amazingly, her body hardly moved. The tank however, halved like tissue paper, exposing her chest to hips. The cold air hit her skin and made her shiver.

Creek inspected the gash in her side. "The bleeding's stopped."

She knew that. Knew that whatever he'd done with his hand behind that Dumpster had clotted the main flow of blood. Something beyond counterpressure. She let herself acknowledge that much, but her mind continued to search for another possible, if not logical, explanation.

She'd come up with cauterization. The heat he seemed to harbor in his body must have performed some type of cauterization of the bleeding tissues. While that eased her mind, it didn't alleviate the fatigue from the blood she'd already lost. Or the radiating pain in her torso. Or the knowledge she'd have an ugly, welted scar that would need plastic surgery if she ever planned on wearing a bikini again.

"You know I need a hospital," she said.

Creek ignored her. He drew the soggy fabric off her body and eased her into a white, collared T-shirt with a colorful NASCAR logo across the chest. He slid her left arm in first, then stretched the fabric and eased her right arm in.

He was amazingly deft and gentle, yet efficient. He was also all business, without any hint of interest in her body, which irritated her, considering how she seemed to react to his every touch.

He reached across the seat, and with one tug, covered the swastika on his fuzzy head with the baseball cap. Then, to her surprise, he unlocked the remaining cuff and pulled the metal off her wrist.

A giddy wave rolled through her stomach. Her first step toward freedom. But, now what? She scanned the parking lot, searching for . . . something. But only found a smattering of cars dotting the darkened asphalt.

"What time is it?" she asked.

"About nine last time I looked." He adjusted the collar of her shirt up around her neck and over the injuries. "Why?"

"Just wondering." Wondering where everyone was. Wondering if this sparse crowd would be any help to her at all. Wondering if this night would ever end.

"Remember." Creek lifted the bottom of his tee to reveal the handle of the gun. "I still have this."

Alyssa's eyes skipped past the weapon to the delineated abdominal muscles beneath. This guy had blown right by a six-pack. He had an eight-pack going, and then some.

"You're going to be a good girl," he said. "Right?"

Alyssa's mind took a wrong turn somewhere. It veered from the clean city streets and headed straight to a seedy alley, picking up a dozen different innuendos on the trip.

Looks mean nothing. He is a criminal. A lifer.

Those facts gave her mind the kick it needed to get back on track. "Don't talk to me like I'm five years old."

Creek slung one strong arm around her shoulders and walked her toward the store. Alyssa searched the area for a police car or security vehicle. None. She studied the patrons traversing the parking lot for someone formidable enough to take Creek on. No one.

He accepted the grocery cart offered by a smiling, elderly woman at the door and placed Alyssa's hands on the cart's handle, then covered one of hers with his own. His palm was warm, his fingers strong. He came in close behind her, one arm securing her at the waist, making her feel protected and imprisoned at the same time.

He headed from one department to the next with focus and purpose, dropping selected items in the cart and moving on. But the objects he chose seemed haphazard, almost like he was on a scavenger hunt. Disposable cell phones from electronics, fishing line from outdoors, Gatorade from beverages, bandages from pharmaceuticals, power bars from grocery, upholstery needles from crafts, a blanket from housewares.

Creek zigzagged his way around the store so that every aisle he chose was empty, which wasn't hard to do because the store was quiet. Way too quiet for Alyssa's preference.

The cart filled with merchandise, signaling her dwindling opportunity for escape. Jittery panic grew in the pit of

Alyssa's stomach. "I should go to the bathroom while we're here," she said, her mind clawing for options. "I need some water, too."

"You can wait."

"I've been waiting for hours." She made a concerted effort to raise her voice, yet the massive store swallowed her words. "I've lost a lot of blood. I'm dehydrated."

"Keep it down," he growled in her ear and steered them toward women's clothing, where the store opened, and she could see beyond one aisle at a time. "And pick some clothes for yourself."

Her eyes skimmed over round racks and past shelves. A middle-aged couple browsed belts and socks across the aisle in the men's department. She watched them, willing them to look up, hoping they could read the panicked message she prayed her eyes conveyed. But they wandered to the baseball hats and drifted around a corner, out of sight.

A young boy scampered down the center aisle and grabbed his mother's hand as she looked at sleepwear, then tugged her toward the toy section.

"Never mind." Creek huffed in apparent exasperation at her lack of interest in the clothes and walked toward the men's section, where he eyed a shelving unit of sweatpants. "What size are you?"

"I have no idea. I don't shop for men's clothes."

He pulled a pair of small size sweatpants and a sweat jacket off the shelf. Turned and plucked a small T-shirt from a round rack.

"Are you going to make me wear men's underwear, too?" She couldn't hold back the smart remark, nor did she want to. This situation became more absurd by the moment.

A woman wandered into the area and stopped at the same rack of T-shirts. Alyssa's stomach inflated like a bubble and floated toward her throat. With Creek positioned behind her, she reached for a hanger and pretended to look through the shirts, her head turned so her bruised cheek was angled toward the woman.

In her mid-sixties, with short, straight, gray-brown hair and dark brown eyes, the other woman flicked a quick smile of acknowledgment toward Alyssa, then did a double take. When her eyes scrutinized Alyssa's face, Alyssa lifted her hand to scratch her ear, but let her fingers drop to the neckline of her shirt instead and dragged the collar down.

The woman's eyes fastened on Alyssa's neck, and her expression shifted from uncertainty to pained concern. "I'm sorry, I don't mean to stare. Looks like you're a little banged up."

Alyssa felt Creek stiffen behind her. Maybe it was just her imagination, but she could swear the air temperature rose. Her skin grew damp. Her heart picked up speed.

She hadn't expected the woman to *say* anything so direct. And not in front of Creek. Which was stupid. How was anyone else supposed to know this was all a big secret?

"Are you all right?" the woman asked, her eyes flitting toward Creek, then back.

She opened her mouth to respond, but found herself at a loss. "Um, I um . . ." *I . . . um . . . should have thought this through better.*

"We were in a car accident earlier tonight," Creek said from behind her, his voice smooth and congenial. "The doctor said she didn't break anything, but she'll be sore for a few weeks."

Damn. Alyssa's bubble of hope deflated. He was so much better at this game.

The woman's dark eyes lifted to Creek again. This time, she studied him. Assessed. Then she took Alyssa's hand in a compassionate gesture and pressed something into her palm—a business card she guessed from the size and shape. "That's good news. Get some rest, sweetheart."

Alyssa watched her lifeline walk away, her throat swelling

with the need to call out to her. Creek's hand covered Alyssa's. She startled and tried to evade his grasp, but he was faster and stronger and hotter. His fingers burned hers as he pried her hand open and pulled the card out.

" 'Geraldine Hummel, L.M.F.T.,' " Teague read. " 'Director of Therapy House, a safe haven for the . . .' " His face twisted into a sour expression. " 'Domestically abused.' "

He fisted the card and dropped his hand to his side. The faint scent of smoke met her nose a second before a miniature plume drifted toward the ceiling. She looked down just as he opened his fingers. Ashes fluttered from his palm. She stared at them, eyes wide, mouth hanging open.

"How . . . ?" Her thoughts wouldn't solidify. She grabbed his hand and turned it over. No burns on his skin. No soot on his fingers. She looked down at the ashes on the linoleum.

As if those gray flakes kicked her mind into gear, Alyssa dropped Creek's hand and stepped back. "How can you do that?"

Something glinted in his eyes—a mixture of anger and hurt—before the blue irises turned slate gray. He closed his hands around hers on the handle of the cart until her fingers were mashed painfully against the metal bar, and headed back toward the center of the store and all those lonely, deserted aisles.

"I'm starting to think you're a fucking nutcase," he said. "Which would explain your involvement with Luke."

"Nutcase?" Fear ignited her anger and, in turn, her mouth. "You think *I'm* a nutcase when your body temp is twice the normal person's and paper burns in your *hand*? If anyone in this situation is screwed up, it's you. You're the one who dragged me into this. The only thing I hate more than the victim mentality is being a victim myself. You've cut my professional throat, exposed me to life-threatening situations—"

"Shit happens." His voice was dangerously low and flat. He passed by two rows with people browsing in them and turned down an aisle of office supplies void of customers.

"You can't always control what life throws at you. Sometimes you just have to make the best of it. And right now, the best thing to do is get the hell out of here."

"This isn't a 'shit happens' situation." Alyssa continued to fume as they headed toward the front of the store, mostly to keep herself from freaking out over the fact that this man had just burned paper with nothing but his bare hand. " 'Shit happens' is a flat tire on the freeway in the middle of the night or someone stealing your wallet. Comparing this to 'shit happens' is like comparing a traffic ticket to first-degree murder."

He stopped abruptly in the middle of an aisle and twisted toward her. *"Lower your voice,"* he ground out, his own voice strained. "In fact, just shut the hell up, Hannah. You're like a goddamned two-year-old who doesn't know when to stop."

He started forward again with a jerk of the cart. The sudden tug sent a stab of pain through her stomach, a harsh reminder of her weakness and his strength.

"This . . . this . . . this is . . ." Her mind couldn't grasp the enormity of the situation, of the aftermath this would leave on her career, on her reputation, on everything she'd struggled so long and hard to build. "This is unbeliev—"

Creek came to a hard stop at the end of the aisle. As he did, the handle of the cart knocked Alyssa's wound. Pain burst in her torso. She doubled over and cried out, but the air stuck in her lungs. Creek released the basket and turned into her, yanking her against him. With a hand behind her head, he gripped her hair and smashed her face to his chest, where the pained moans that eventually leaked out were absorbed by his bulk.

She breathed through the torture and tried to push away, but he had her trapped in those big arms that felt like crushing steel.

"What did you say to that woman?" It was an accusation, not a question.

"You were right there, moron." Her words came out muffled against his chest. "You know I didn't say a darn word to her. Let me go. I can't breathe."

"There are all kinds of ways to say something without words." He unwrapped her, but closed his long fingers around her wrist and edged toward the end of the aisle to peer around the corner toward the far bank of registers.

Alyssa tried to twist out of his grip, his fingers like hot rings on her skin. "You're burning me again."

He ignored her, his attention riveted to the front. Alyssa craned her neck to see what he was looking at. The woman who'd approached her minutes ago stood at the customer service desk talking to two men in uniform. A surge of hope made Alyssa gasp.

Then she looked closer, scanning the men for weapons. None. They weren't real cops. They were unarmed security guards. And, unbeknownst to them, they faced a desperate escaped convict with a gun and a hostage in a store still occupied with at least a few customers. They didn't know it yet, but they were way out of their league. As was Alyssa.

Her mind fast-forwarded through her options, then over the repercussions of each. Nothing panned out favorably.

If he didn't have that damned gun . . .

The *gun*. Her gaze dropped to his waist, to the outline of the weapon beneath his tee. Just the thought of taking that risk pushed her heart into her throat. But if she could get it, if *she* had control over the gun, all her options turned a hundred and eighty degrees.

Her gaze skipped to his face. His attention was still focused on the front.

She had to do it. It was the only answer.

Adrenaline rushed up her chest.

Alyssa sucked in a breath. Held it. And made the grab.

SIX

Alyssa didn't remember the second between reaching for the weapon and finding it in her hand. She put as much distance between herself and Creek as his grasp on her opposite wrist allowed and pointed the gun at his chest.

"What the fuck?" Creek turned on her with shock and anger darkening his eyes to navy. "Give it back, Hannah."

A sickening combination of terror and hope rolled beneath her breastbone. "Now who sounds like a two-year-old?"

"This isn't funny," he rasped in a furious undertone. "Give me the gun before someone sees it."

"Let me g-go." The pathetic stutter would have embarrassed her if simply holding the gun didn't scare her enough to pee on herself. The thing was so heavy, so awkward. She didn't know the first thing about how to hold it or fire it. "That's all I want. Let go of my hand, turn around and walk away. I won't stop you. Just let me g-go."

"Or what?" His gaze dropped to the gun, then lifted to her face again with something new floating there, something sly. "You'll shoot me?"

No. "Y-yes."

"Honey, you can't shoot me with the safety on."

Safety . . . ? Her gaze dropped to the gun. But by the time her eyes landed, it was gone. Whipped out of her hand by Creek.

He slid the gun into the opposite side of his waistband, out of her reach. A fresh anger floated in his eyes, one that sent a chill over the back of Alyssa's neck, despite the heat still searing her wrist.

"Try to remember this for next time," he scraped out from between clenched teeth. "Glocks don't have safeties."

He took hold of both her hands in a hard, hot grip and lowered his face to within an inch of hers. His eyes were so clear, so crystal blue. So cold. "We're going to check out. Don't make a fucking sound, Hannah. Don't try another goddamned thing. A man can only hold his patience for so long and you've been testing mine from the moment I set eyes on you."

He reached around the back of her head, his fingers digging into the knot she'd secured in her hair.

"Ow!" The binding gave and her hair fell everywhere.

"No more showing off your bruises. Got it?" He grabbed one arm, yanked her forward and pushed the cart up to the closest unoccupied cashier.

Alyssa checked the length of the store from beneath her downcast lashes. There was no sign of the woman or the security guards. "The bathroom's right there—"

"No," he whispered in her ear. "And unless you want a set of knuckles in your side, stop bringing it up."

With one arm around her waist, Creek used the other to unload the cart. His body heat continued to simmer, as if in silent warning. Alyssa kept her gaze on the tired, middle-aged woman at the checkout, but she never even looked up. They could have been aliens and the cashier wouldn't have known the difference.

"Ma'am," Alyssa said, "is there a water fountain—?"

Creek settled his hand on her side, just below her cut, enough of a warning to stop Alyssa in mid sentence.

"Right over there, by the bathrooms." The woman never made eye contact.

Creek kept darting looks toward the aisles, but ultimately

managed to pay and exit before the Good Samaritan and security guards returned. He continued to watch the parking lot like a skittish fox.

At the truck, he lifted the rear door. "Get in."

"I'm not riding back there," she said. "I don't care how mad you are, I'm not—"

One shove was all it took to tip her into the cargo space. She stumbled, but managed to stay on her feet. He tossed in the bags alongside her, then climbed in as well, closing the roll-up door halfway.

She eased to the farthest wall of the enclosure as Creek rummaged through the bags with jerky, angry movements, muttering to himself. He pulled out a small lantern and a strip of batteries, plunked the light on the floor, and with a hard, quick push to his feet, swung around and kicked the side of the truck. The bang exploded in the small space, echoing off the metal walls.

Alyssa started and squeezed into the corner.

"Stupid," he muttered, then kicked the wall again. "Stupid." And again. *"Stupid."*

Alyssa jerked with every bang. Her shoulders crawled up around her ears. Now she was captive in the back of a truck with an armed escaped convict who had cuffed her, burned her and jerked her around for the last few hours. On top of that, he was royally pissed off.

A strategist she was not.

With a new level of calm, Creek opened the packaging, stuffed the lantern with the batteries and turned the lever until bright light filled the truck. Then he unfolded the blanket and set out supplies in what Alyssa slowly started to recognize as a procedure area.

She knew it was a bad idea to ask him anything right now, but she couldn't help herself. "What are you doing?"

"We've got to get that gash closed." He knelt alongside the blanket and leaned over to lower the rear door all but a couple inches. "Lie down, let me get a good look."

"Wh-what? A few minutes ago you were ready to skin me alive. *Why* in the *world* would I let you treat me now?"

He pressed both hands to his thighs and leaned back on his heels. "Because I was a paramedic for twelve years in my past life." His blue eyes stayed steady on hers. "I'm not happy with you right now, but I've never hit a woman in all my thirty-four years, and I'm not going to start with you."

"A-a *paramedic*?" She didn't like this new stutter. It was annoying as hell and undermined her already failing self-confidence.

"Yes, a paramedic and a firefighter. Let me look."

As if she'd donned a pair of those funky red-and-blue glasses for three-D movies, Creek rounded out into a full-fledged human being. A man with a past, a present, a future. A man who'd once contributed to society, who'd healed the injured, who'd saved lives. A man who had a mother, father, siblings, possibly a wife and children . . . *I don't have anyone* . . . or not.

"How did you go from paramedic to prisoner? For *life*?" she asked, incredulous.

"I'm not giving you my life story. Just lie down and let me look at this cut. It needs to be cleaned and bandaged, minimum. Or would you rather get an infection that could kill you a hell of a lot faster than I ever would?"

While she debated, Alyssa examined the supplies he'd laid out, wondering when he'd put most of them in the cart. The combination of blood loss, sleep deprivation and stress was turning her mind into mush.

"Looks like you're planning surgery," she said.

"Just a few stitches."

How did she know he wasn't a pathological liar? She had no proof he'd ever seen a stitch before let alone placed one. He obviously had some altered body chemistry he wasn't talking about, and—

An alternative idea clicked.

"What about . . . ?" Alyssa shifted on her feet and gestured in his general direction. "What about that . . . that . . . heat thing you do?"

"I don't—"

"Don't you dare tell me I'm imagining things." She held out her wrist. "Those are your fingerprints burned into my skin."

His gaze lingered on her arm. "What about it?"

"Can't you . . . fix me with that?"

"No." He looked away, as if embarrassed. "I'm not . . . it's not . . . I can't."

She hadn't thought so. But she'd had to ask. "If I let you . . . do *this*, will you tell me how you do *that*?"

His mouth compressed. "Fine."

Dammit. He'd agreed too easily. Now she had to decide. "How many times have you done this?"

"Stitches? Couple dozen. I'm competent."

"What method will you use?"

"Won't know until I get a good look at the cut. Either a horizontal mattress or a Smead-Jones. Depends on length and depth of the cut." He paused, and while no grin turned his mouth, Alyssa sensed a smile simmering inside him. "Do I pass?"

"I suppose." With a sick sense of anticipation, Alyssa lay down on her back. She lifted the T-shirt over her belly, exposing her injured ribs. They both inspected the wound. Creek's touch was deft and gentle, checking the depth of tissue damage. Heat sparked beneath each point of contact. "I can't believe I'm considering this."

"Considering?" He sat back and met her eyes. "If you don't let me do this, you'll have one hell of a scar."

"No matter what, I'll have one hell of a scar."

"Not if I can help it."

Alyssa remained fearful over the grave mistake she was probably making, but didn't protest as he poured instant hand sanitizer in his palms and scrubbed thoroughly before uncapping the hydrogen peroxide and cleaning the surface of the wound.

Her gaze focused in on the shamrocks on his knuckles, a well-known Aryan Brotherhood symbol, and her mind jumped to Taz. "Is there enough time?"

"There has to be. I won't be responsible for a red, welted scar on this perfect body." He tossed the bloody gauze into an empty Walmart bag.

"Was that a compliment?" Alyssa asked. "If I weren't already lying down, I might faint."

When his mouth tilted up, a fluttery sensation winged around her stomach. One she hadn't felt in a long time. One she shouldn't ever feel with this man. She forced it away. Forced herself to refocus as he poured saline into a Ziploc.

"What are you doing?" she asked.

With the nearly bursting plastic bag in one hand, he turned it bottom-side-up and ripped a hole in the corner with his teeth. "Cleaning the wound." He spit out the plastic bit and poised the bag to turn it over. "Brace yourself. This isn't going to feel very good."

The cool saline hit her skin and stung as it flushed the gash. Then Creek squeezed the bag and drove the sterile solution out under pressure. The water knifed into her side. Sweating, panting, Alyssa fisted her hands in the blanket beneath her. She clenched her teeth around a scream and seethed air. Just when she thought it would never stop, the stream ended and the torture along with it.

"Sorry," Creek said, his voice low and sincere. "That will be the worst of it."

Dizzy with pain, Alyssa opened her eyes and stared at the scraped metal roof, illuminated by the lantern's glow. "Liar," she breathed. "I know the stitches are going to kill me."

"I've got something to take the edge off."

He flipped open a bottle of topical anesthetic and poured

the solution on gauze four-by-fours, then dabbed it along the length of the wound. Sure enough, her skin started to tingle, then numbed.

Creek performed another round of hand sanitizing, threaded the smallest of the curved upholstery hooks with the nylon fishing line and set a pair of scissors nearby. The stress of the cleansing had left Alyssa weak and exhausted. She relaxed against the hard surface beneath her and watched Creek.

A kind of peace and purpose shimmered around him like an aura, giving Alyssa an unfounded confidence in his abilities. For the moment, she felt secure in his hands.

He tested the needle on the far edge of the wound. "Feel that?"

"Barely."

"How about that?"

"A little. It's fine. Let's get it over with."

She continued to amaze him. Teague made the first pierce of her skin at the distal edge of the wound. A wound, he'd discovered after inspection, that was far more extensive than he'd expected based on the way she had continued to function. He'd seen many a grown man—child molesters, rapists, murderers—howl like whipped dogs with injuries far less severe.

His limited attempts to heal her had done nothing but temporarily quell the bleeding, but then he hadn't had the time or opportunity to make additional passes over the wound. Not that it would have mattered. His powers were too weak to heal this deeply.

"You promised." Her voice brought his gaze up from her firm abs. Her eyes were closed, her fingers curled into the hem of the shirt bunched up beneath her breasts.

"Promised what?"

"To tell me about all that heat."

He'd love to tell her about all this heat. Better yet, show

her about all this heat. Tell her *while* showing her just how hot it could get.

Sweet Jesus, the images that filled his head would get him arrested all over again. He wiped at the sweat forming on his temple with his forearm. Too damn bad the heat she was talking about and the heat he was talking about were not one and the same.

"Right." He pulled the nylon through and secured the anchoring stitch. "I don't know."

Her eyes opened and her head came up, tightening her stomach muscles and shifting his supplies. "What do you mean you don't know?"

"Put your head down. You're messing up my work space." When she complied, Teague continued stitching. "I mean, I don't know what it is. An anxiety disorder or something. When I get angry or stressed, my body temperature rises. It happens to everybody."

She released her shirt and shoved her hand into his line of sight. "This level of heat does not happen to everybody."

"If you don't want a scar, stay out of the way." He nudged her hand to the side and continued stitching. "I can't tell you what I don't know."

As he made another stitch of her inner tissues, she tensed and turned her head away. Her fingers curled and released in the fabric of her shirt.

With her attention averted, Teague followed each stitch with long, steady pressure from the fingers of his free hand. He'd purposely chosen hand sanitizer instead of gloves because he'd never tried to heal through a barrier, and he wasn't about to start now. And though he might not be able to wipe out her injury instantly, he could speed the healing and hinder scar formation while helping with pain relief. Of course, the whole sexual attraction thing that seemed to flow in its wake—that he hadn't counted on.

As he steadied her skin and muscle for each double stitch, his subconscious kept whispering reminders of how soft and warm she was. Kept influencing him to peek at her supple belly and the swell of her breasts. He succumbed briefly to a vision of himself hovering over her, kissing his way up that belly toward those breasts, and the simmer in his body boiled to life. He imagined sinking down, pressing his body to hers, feeling all that satin skin against his own. He felt the supple play of her nipple against the roof of his mouth as he suckled, the roll of muscle and pressure of flesh as she arched against him in pleasure.

In the next instant, his traitorous mind replaced his own image with Luke's. His fantasy shattered, as violent as boiling water on frozen glass.

"What's wrong?" Hannah's voice brought Teague back to where his hand hovered over her ribs. "Why'd you stop?"

He shook his head, clenched his teeth and resumed. "Just making sure I'm catching all the edges. It's not going to look like a pretty package when I'm done. I'm exverting the edges so the skin won't pucker and sink in, leaving a big divot. But it'll invert on its own and heal flush."

Hannah put one arm behind her head and watched Teague work.

"How long have you and Luke been together?" He hated the fact that he couldn't keep these nagging questions inside. That he cared about the answers.

She didn't immediately respond. Her brows furrowed, gaze steady on the ceiling. "I don't know." Her response came clipped and irritated. "I don't keep track of that kind of thing."

"Well, like weeks, months? What?"

"I supposedly hold some sort of leverage for you. Why don't you already know this?"

"Why are you so evasive? Just answer the question."

"I don't know, a few, several . . . a couple months . . . maybe."

He frowned at the bizarre answer. "Has he introduced you to Kat?"

"I work a lot. I don't have much time to socialize."

Halfway up the gash, Teague paused and took a closer look at Hannah's face, trying to read her. "Some vague answers from someone who's supposedly hot and heavy with the guy."

Her light eyes flicked toward his. "Who told you that?"

"Friends."

"I thought you didn't have any friends."

He looked away, irritated with her sharpness. Or maybe more irritated with the truth of the statement. Time for a change of subject.

Teague channeled all his focus, sent the heat down his arms, through his palms and into his fingertips as he slid his skin over hers, each pass healing another several hundred thousand cells at a time. "Am I hurting you?"

"Not much. Whatever you used for anesthetic is working."

It's called touch. That topical junk had only been a prop. A scapegoat on which to lay the pain relief. Teague had learned how to hide his abilities years ago. His thoughts of the past brought his mind back around to Luke, to Kat, to all that had happened, to all that had gone wrong in his life.

Hannah closed her eyes on a half-sigh and laid her head back again. Supple muscle moved beneath velvet skin. Teague would have to be dead not to notice.

"What do you see in Luke, anyway?" The words were out before he had a chance at a second thought.

Her lashes lifted halfway. "By your tone I think the question you *wanted* to ask was what does *Luke* see in *me*."

"Maybe. Since he broke up with . . ."

Teague shook the thought of Keira from his mind. He would have liked nothing more than to call on his long-time friend for help in this situation. She would have been there in an instant. But Keira had left the fire service for the F.B.I. months before, which only increased her risk of personal and professional catastrophe if she was ever connected to him.

And unlike Luke, Teague would never put her in a situation where she would be forced to choose.

"In recent years," Teague continued, "he seems to prefer the meek, bombshell, save-me type."

"And since you see me as obnoxious, plain and independent, you don't think he could find anything about me attractive."

Hardly. "You might be obnoxiously independent, but you are not the least bit plain." A fact which pissed him off when he thought about it too much and led him to his next taunt. "You know he's a player, don't you? Doesn't stay with any woman long and often goes back and forth between two or more?"

The emotion that passed through her eyes appeared more relieved than surprised or angry. "So? What makes you think I'm not a player, too?"

He shrugged, but something deep in his gut tingled the way it did when a situation wasn't quite right. "Guess you just don't strike me that way. How did you meet him if you work so much?"

"Why the twenty questions?" she snapped. "What is it about Luke that you're so obsessed with? What do you think you're going to gain by keeping me?"

That tingle in his gut grew into a burn. He paused mid-stitch and looked at her again. She answered too many questions with questions. She was too defensive, too evasive. Something she'd said earlier, something that had seemed off-beat at the time, popped to mind again. "What did you mean when you said I'd cut your professional throat?"

"When?"

"Inside, after that woman came up to us."

She heaved a breath and closed her eyes. "I'm competing for my job against someone else. This other guy is a total manipulator. By the time I get back, he'll have wormed his way into making everyone believe they can't live without him."

"You already have the job." He knew at least that much

from his hasty research, from the stories his teammates had told him on their occasional visits to the prison. "You've had it for two years. How can you be competing for it?"

"They're cutting back. Only keeping one of us, and he's got seniority. They're letting one of us go in two weeks."

"Where's the competition? Seniority usually wins out. Why don't they just let you go?"

Alyssa shot him another angry look. "Because I'm *better*. Way the hell better. I work my butt off while he schmoozes." The anger seemed to drain her energy. She closed her eyes and turned her head away. "He's a frigging con man. No one like that is going to beat me."

He admired her fight. Saw his own reflection in her struggle. And felt guilty for interfering in this important piece of her life, not to mention all the trauma and injury she'd sustained in the last few hours.

"Don't worry." He tied off the last stitch and cut the nylon. "I'll have you back to your boyfriend and your job before you know it."

"Then what? Where are you going? What are you going to do?"

Teague brought up an image of Kat's face, those big, dark, sparkling eyes. He savored the idea of feeling her in his arms. The security of knowing where she was every moment of the day. The peace of having control over her safety, her growth, her well-being. The pure, unadulterated joy of hearing her laughter, experiencing her unconditional love.

A smile started in his soul and ended up on his face. "Then I disappear, and you'll never have to see me again. I'll be like a bad dream."

She rolled onto her side and pushed herself to a sitting position. Her hands darted out and grabbed his. "Let me see your hands."

He tugged back in automatic reaction, but she held firm. His smile vanished. "Why? Let go."

"Let me see them, and I'll let go."

Exasperated, he turned his hands over and indulged her inspection. To humor her, not to feel her skin against his. Not to experience the gentle heat of her strong fingers. The pad of her index finger skimmed his palm, sending an erotic signal directly to his groin.

"Okay, enough." Teague pulled out of her grasp. "See, no magic bullet. Just normal human parts. Now lie down so I can finish."

"But—"

"No more buts, Hannah. Lie down."

She stared at him with lingering questions in her eyes, but he was done. She was getting too curious and way too comfortable and, dammit, so was he. He needed to put a stop to all this small talk. And then get the hell away from her before he did something really stupid. Like told her the truth. Or found something else completely inappropriate to do with his mouth, like taste every inch of that glorious body.

She obviously sensed he was serious, because she obeyed.

Teague cleaned the wound with another dose of hydrogen peroxide, plastered it with Neosporin and bandaged her up tighter than he probably needed to. "There. It's about time to pick up Taz."

Hannah sat up and pulled her shirt over that tight belly. But this time she didn't look at him. She didn't touch him. And she sure as hell didn't speak to him.

And that, he knew, was the way it should be. The only way it could be.

Just as he reached down and offered Hannah a hand getting to her feet, headlights swept over the truck's rear entrance, darting beneath the partially open door like knives.

Teague shoved the supply bags to one side of the truck and turned to watch. Waited for them to either go off or retreat. But they remained on and focused on the truck.

Apprehension crept under Teague's skin. He shifted toward Hannah, put his arm around her shoulders and drew her close. Outside, a car door closed. Footsteps neared the lift gate.

His heart kicked into high gear. He pressed his mouth to Hannah's silky-soft, floral-scented hair and murmured, "Do the smart thing here."

SEVEN

Acid swirled in Teague's stomach. This was it. Faced with the very confrontation he'd planned to avoid at all costs. And the question remained, did he have what it took to use the Glock if push came to shove?

"Follow my lead." He took a breath and forced out the remaining words. "Or I'll shoot him."

Several raps on the metal door made Hannah jump. Teague tightened his arm around her.

"Hello?" a voice called. "Police. Anybody in there?"

"Yes, sir." Teague lifted the rear door, then shaded his eyes against the headlights. The cop was young, early twenties with a face so clean-cut fresh he'd have been on the dessert menu in prison. No partner sat in the passenger's seat of the unit, no additional unit hovered as backup. "Evening, officer."

The cop's hand hovered over the butt of his weapon. "Can I see your hands, please?"

Teague removed his arm from Hannah and held his hands out, palms up. Hannah lifted hers as well.

"Okay," he said, hand easing away from his gun. "Just leave them where I can see them, please."

"Yes, sir." Teague relaxed his arms, but turned his hands so the clovers on his knuckles wouldn't show.

"What are you two doing here tonight?"

"We're moving this weekend." Teague softened his voice into an eager-to-please tone. "Just stocking up on some supplies. Am I parked in a bad spot or something?"

"No." The cop's serious eyes assessed Hannah, who had her head turned to avoid the light, which, luckily, also hid the healing bruises on her other cheek. "We had a report of a possible abuse situation. I'm just checking the area. Are you all right, ma'am?"

Hannah lifted her hand to shield her eyes from the light and hesitated long enough to push bile up Teague's throat. Finally, she said, "I'd be better if those lights were out of my face."

Someday, he'd look back on this moment and laugh. Although this wasn't the best time for her to show it, he had to admit, he liked this girl's spunk.

"I'm sorry, officer." He offered a contrite smile. "She's a little . . . stressed . . . with the move."

The young man shared Teague's grin. "My wife and I almost divorced when we moved here so I could take this job. Where are you headed?"

"Keizer, Oregon." Teague said the first thing that came to mind—his cellmate's hometown. "Just south of Portland."

"Pretty country." The officer took another look at Hannah, then stepped to the side, allowing them to exit. "You two have a good night. Good luck with your move. I'll wait until you're safely on your way."

Teague climbed from the truck and turned to help Hannah down, pulling her close to keep pressure off her injury.

"You can go to sleep now, honey," he crooned as he walked her to the passenger's door. "I know you're tired." He helped her into the cab and whispered, "Good job, Hannah. Don't make any mistakes now, and he'll go home to his wife."

"Shut up." The angry words scraped out of her throat. "I hate your manipulation. I hate what you stand for. I hate *you*."

Her opinion shouldn't sting, but it did. "You hate what you see. You don't know anything about me."

She laid her head on the seat and turned away, a clear gesture of disgust. Teague shut the door and waved to the officer before rounding the hood and climbing into the driver's seat. When he reached over Hannah and cuffed her hand to the door, she turned her head the opposite way and pushed back into the seat as if she couldn't get far enough away from him.

Better, he decided.

Teague kept his eyes on the cop in the side-view mirror as he dug beneath the dash and restarted the truck, connecting the wires by feel alone.

Hannah didn't say a word as Teague slowed in the lousy neighborhood where he'd dropped Taz and slid up next to the curb where the man paced the gutter. No girls stood beside him. In fact there was no one on the street at all. Teague set the parking brake and slid into the center seat, leaving the driver's spot open for Taz.

Taz hefted himself into the front, revved the engine and took off down the street. He smelled of sweat, sex, booze and something else, something dark and disgusting Teague couldn't place.

"What the hell took you so long?" Taz asked. "I banged them both twice and still had time to spare. I was about to make that phone call."

Right. "With what?"

Taz pulled a cell from his back pocket and tossed it in the air. Teague automatically caught it. Small and light, the thing barely registered as a weight in his hand. What did register was the dark, sticky liquid that smeared onto Teague's hands.

"What the fuck . . . ?"

"Sorry." Taz laughed, low and superior. "She really wanted to hold on to it. Had to beat her unconscious before she let go."

Teague vaguely registered Hannah's dismay. He dropped

the phone on the floorboard and wiped the blood on his jeans.

"Sonofabitch," Teague muttered, stomach roiling. "Stop somewhere, man. I need to wash my hands."

"How about a motel? My homies are going to meet me in Chowchilla tomorrow morning. Then you and I part ways." Taz let out an extravagant yawn. "I'm tired. Those jigaboos can fuck, man. Those fat lips are the best for blow. They can fucking suck white off rice—"

"Enough," Teague barked, thoroughly disgusted—with Taz for being who he was, with himself for not making the phone call he should have made to the cops. "We'll find a motel for the night."

"Wouldn't be in such a bad mood if you got yourself some real pussy. That rice-picker ain't got no meat on her bones and all she uses her big mouth for is spewing shit."

"There." Teague pointed to a building not much bigger than a shack, with a neon motel sign. At this point he'd sleep in a hole in the ground just to get away from the bastard. "Stop there."

Taz pulled in and parked the truck in the back of the lot along a border of trees with an empty field beyond. Teague got out the driver's side after Taz and rounded the truck to help Hannah down. Just as he released the cuff from the door handle, Taz jerked her arm from Teague's grasp.

"Get two rooms," Taz said. "I'm gonna teach her some respect. We'll need privacy."

"You're a disgusting excuse for a human being," Hannah spat, jerking against Taz's grip. "I'll kill you before you touch me."

Taz's face twisted in fury. His hand rose, fingers curled into a fist. Before he made contact, Teague knocked Taz's hand down and shoved the animal away from Hannah. "You know the rules. She's mine. Period."

Taz pulled something from his pocket. A familiar *shhhhh-click* sounded loud in the darkness. An icy mix of dread and fear perked beneath Teague's breastbone as he stared at the long, serrated blade reflecting in the single light illuminating the parking lot.

Fucking A. Would this night ever end? "And where the hell did you get that?"

"Amazing what whores carry around nowadays. As for the rules—*fuck* your rules. She's been nothing but a mouthy cunt and it's time for some payback."

"You're drunk. Don't do something you'll regret tomorrow. Go get two rooms, Taz, but she'll be staying in mine."

"New rules." Taz stood his ground, twisting the knife in his hand. "Play by them or get your ass out of the sandbox."

"You'll have to go through me to get to her." Teague's chest rocked with quickening shallow breaths. His skin burned. Sweat trickled down the indentation of his spine. "Without me, you're SOL."

"Guess I'll be taking my chances, because that bitch is going to pay."

Taz lunged at Hannah and jabbed. Teague dodged, caught Taz's wrist and twisted. A sense of déjà vu lightened his head. Only this time, he'd make sure Hannah didn't get hurt for her unsuspecting role in Teague's plan.

He poured all his energy into the heat sparking through his body like electricity. Taz screamed just as the scent of burnt flesh wafted past Teague's nose.

"Aaaaahhh! Let go, you fucking freak." Taz went straight for the dirty fight and dug his teeth into the fleshy palm of Teague's hand.

"Fucker." Teague pounded Taz's temple with his free palm, ending the bite.

All Teague's pent-up hostility exploded, and he directed every flash of frustration right back into Taz. They kicked and twisted. Their heads knocked together. If it weren't for the damn knife, Teague would have had the asshole pinned in seconds.

Taz elbowed Teague's ribs. Teague tightened his grip on

Taz's wrist and jerked on his arm, dislodging Taz's elbow and pounding the other man in the chest. Taz grunted, the sound an eerie guttural wheeze.

"Come on, asshole." Teague panted through the words. *"Give."*

Taz's body went rigid a second before he lost all strength. The brunt of his weight fell on Teague, and he staggered.

A sick sensation slithered into Teague's gut. He pulled back and found Taz's eyes glassy. Blood streamed from one side of his mouth. In a flash of panic, Teague let go. The other man slumped to the ground and rolled onto his back. Teague's eyes landed on the knife sticking out of Taz's chest, the blade buried. Taz coughed. His body jerked. Blood bubbled in his throat and erupted out his mouth.

Teague's own stomach heaved in response. Fiery terror burned through his chest.

"Oh, fuck. Oh, Chriiiiiiiiiiist, no!" He dropped to his knees, slid a hand behind Taz's neck. "Taz, you dumbass. Taz. Shit. *Taz!*"

Taz's eyes rolled back in his head. Air wheezed in and out of his lungs in wet, bubbling, labored breaths. He went still. Then limp.

"Fuck, fuck, *fuck*!" Teague shook Taz's shoulders. "Taz!"

Teague pushed his fingers against Taz's throat, hoping for a pulse. If he was still alive, Teague could call for help, then run. But no blood beat beneath Teague's fingers. He repositioned, searching for the faintest beat. But, again, nothing.

He dropped Taz's head, curling and flexing his fingers as a mental argument flitted around beneath his skull.

You can't save him now, you idiot.

But I have to try.

You can't even heal a freaking cut.

But I have to try.

With a quick jerk, Teague pulled the knife from Taz's chest and tossed it aside. The residual gurgle made Teague's stomach flip and fold. With his hands layered on top of each other, he rose up on his knees and used a CPR position to compress the wound. He ignored the warmth of the blood, the softness of Taz's belly, and leaned into the pressure.

Teague's entire body staged an uncharacteristic revolt. His stomach rose to his throat. He gagged, and heaved, but managed to keep himself from puking. How many times had he been in this position in his career? How much blood and dismemberment had he seen in his life? Never once had he gone queasy. Yet never once had he been the cause of the injury.

With closed eyes, Teague focused and forced a rush of energy straight from his chest down his arms. He envisioned Taz's heart kicking to life. Willed him to live.

He had no sense of time, no idea how long he tried to infuse life back into the limp body. Exhaustion was the decider. By the time Teague fell back on his heels in defeat, he was drenched in sweat, his arms shaking, his breathing labored, his stomach swirling like a wild river eddy.

His legs brought him upright, and he staggered backwards until his ass hit the hood of the truck. He'd killed Taz. He'd *killed* a man. Horrifying reality ambushed him. He looked around, scouring the parking lot for witnesses. The area was empty.

His mind turned to Hannah. Shit. Hannah. Good God. *Hannah*.

Breathing hard, he wiped the thick, quickly-cooling blood off his hands and onto his jeans. Teague peered toward the passenger's side of the truck. Empty. His stomach bottomed out. He pushed himself into a sprint toward the other side of the truck. He pivoted around the open door. Empty.

"Hannah." It was absurd to call to her, but her name burst from his throat anyway. He jogged to the back. Threw open the door. Empty.

Gone. Hannah was *gone*.

He turned in an arc, his eyes darting through the night,

searching the darkness. The office, the parking lot, the tree line on the opposite side of the property. Movement. A shadow. Someone darting into the eucalyptus grove.

Relief, fury and fear mixed with adrenaline, pushing a bellow deep from his gut.

"Hannah!"

With one arm pressed to her injured side, Alyssa sprinted across the parking lot and into the opposite bank of trees. Creek might have called her name, but she couldn't hear much over the beat of blood in her ears, the raspy pant of her own breath.

She'd only been running for a few minutes, but her lungs burned and her side ripped. She stopped and rested against a smooth tree trunk, peering into the distance but finding nothing but shadows.

What now? Her brain wasn't working. Couldn't ever remember being so panicked. So damned scared.

Get yourself together, Alyssa.

Alyssa took one long, steady inhalation to quell her nerves. The pungent scent of eucalyptus cleared her head and invigorated her system. She couldn't say she'd been through worse, but she could get through this. She didn't have a choice, did she?

Careful to keep her hands out in front of her, she dodged trees as she made her way . . . somewhere.

Just keep going. Just keep going.

An arm wrapped around her waist from behind.

"No!" She pried at his fingers, elbowed at his arm. Her wound tore and burned and stabbed. "Let me go. *Let me go!*"

Her mind flashed with violent images. Knives, fists, teeth, blood. She twisted out of his grip and ran. Harder. Faster.

Creek came after her again. Caught her again. This time his momentum took them airborne. When they hit the ground, the blunt force ripped through her from shoulders to knees.

Pain swallowed her whole. She rolled onto her side and curled into a ball, unable to draw air. When her lungs kicked in, the expansion of her chest stabbed pain through her torso.

"Goddammit, Hannah." Creek knelt over her, his hands pulling at her shirt. "Why do you have to make this so impossible? Lie flat. Hold still. Let me check your stitches."

She blocked his hands, panting through the pain. "Don't you dare . . . touch me with . . . all that blood . . . on your hands."

He stopped probing and sat back on his heels, chest heaving with hard, fast breaths. "You're right." He swiped at his face with his forearm. "You're right."

Fresh fear had her hands digging into the earth beneath her. She pushed herself into a sitting position and scuttled away from Creek. "You . . . you . . . Did you kill him? Is he d-dead?"

Creek's eyes darted around the darkness. "We have to get out of here before someone finds him."

"Oh, my God. Oh, my *God*. You did. You *killed* him."

Creek's hand snaked out and grabbed her ankle. "We don't have time for you to freak out."

She kicked her foot from his grasp and tried to crawl away. He yanked her back, dragging her along the rough ground until she lay at his feet. With one click he'd connected the dangling cuff to her free hand, imprisoning her once again.

"If you'd just do what I tell you to do, if you'd just keep your damn mouth shut, this never would have happened."

Creek lifted her into his arms, quickly and easily, but not gently. The movement sent another slice of pain through her belly. She slapped a hand at his face, but didn't have any strength behind the hit, and Creek simply shook her off with a growl. He was on fire, his body as hot as she'd ever felt it, burning through clothes and along her own skin.

When they reached the truck, he dropped her feet to the ground and fisted the back of her shirt. He lifted the rear door of the truck with one hand and shoved her in with the other. Her knees hit the metal floor. Her hands followed. The door clamored down, then slammed shut.

Alyssa collapsed onto the cold surface beneath her, torn between relief and fear. The space was completely black. No light eked in from beneath the door. She slithered to the side of the truck and put her cheek against the cool wall, catching her breath.

Taz's face drifted into her mind. Then Teague's words. Maybe she should have known better than to antagonize Taz as she had, but that wasn't why the scum was dead. He was dead because Teague had a deep, compulsive urge to protect.

He doesn't need you like I do.

More than ever she wanted to know what it was about this Kat woman that drove Creek to such lengths and what possible leverage Hannah could have over this Luke guy. Why didn't Creek just run? Cross the border and disappear, for Christ's sake? And why would Creek want Kat if he knew she'd been with Luke? Why would he want to be with a woman who would want a man who, by Teague's own admission, jumped from woman to woman?

Alyssa just didn't get it.

The truck's engine ground, coughed and kicked over, and all Alyssa's wondering faded. All that mattered was getting away. Getting out of this alive.

The metal rumbled beneath her as the truck moved backwards. She worked herself into a corner, bracing her back on the walls, her feet on the floor and found some stability.

With her elbows settled on her knees, Alyssa rested her head in her hands as morbid thoughts traipsed through her mind. Maybe he was taking her to some remote location to kill her and dump her. Maybe he would abandon the truck somewhere and leave her inside to suffocate or starve to death.

She tortured herself for at least another twenty minutes with similar ideas before the truck slowed and turned. Alyssa lifted her head, and listened. The engine cut out and the driver's side door slammed. Her heart pounded harder in her chest. Her muscles tightened.

A loud click sounded at the back door, then the metal rolled up with an ear-ripping screech. Creek stood silhouetted at the opening.

"Get out." His voice was a low, flat void, as dark as the landscape at his back.

Los Banos had been a metropolis compared to this place. She couldn't even call it a town. A handful of lights shone in the distance, broken by miles and miles of dark as far as she could see, the night air thick with the pungent odor of fertile farmland.

Cautiously, Alyssa scooted toward the door on her butt and paused at the end of the truck bed with her legs hanging over the edge. They'd stopped in some kind of parking lot. Dim lights dotted the small space and across the asphalt, a flashing neon light signaled: VACANCY.

Another motel.

"Where are we?"

"Doesn't matter." Creek reached for her hands, stuck the key in the lock and popped the metal open. This time she didn't feel any sense of hope, only fear for what would come next.

Without looking her in the eye, he wiped blood off her arm with the bottom of his T-shirt. And his hands were shaking.

His fingers slid around her upper arm and bit into muscle as he walked her toward a small room at the front of the motel labeled OFFICE. At least his body temperature had returned to something closer to human. "You're going to get a room. One room, Hannah. Do you understand me?"

No, she didn't understand him. She didn't want to understand him. She also didn't want to get a room. "Why are we here?"

"Because I can't stand this blood on me another fucking minute." He pulled her alongside the office door, where warm light poured through the glass, and shoved cash into her hand. With his eyes directly on hers he said, "I'll be watching. If that desk clerk picks up a phone or looks the least bit confused or shocked by something you say to him, I'll walk in and shoot him in the face, right in front of your eyes. Got it?"

She considered arguing with him, but there was something in his eyes, something determined and desperate and dangerous. Alyssa turned and put her hand on the doorknob.

"Hannah," he said from the shadows. "Don't fuck this up."

She took a deep breath, pulled open the door and stepped inside. A bell tinkled over her head. The front desk stood empty, but a television played somewhere in an adjacent room.

"Yeah, yeah. Just a minute." The grouchy voice emerged from the same direction as the television monologue.

A woman came through the doorway of what appeared to be a break room. She looked about as well cared for as this shack of a motel. And about as old, too. Alyssa had to fight the urge to look over her shoulder to see if Creek was really watching. The thought of taking a chance terrified her, yet her instincts screamed to ask for a phone.

She was trying to think of a way to do that when a young boy wandered out of the other room. Straight, dark hair, big, dark eyes, round little face. About eight years old.

I'll walk in and shoot him in the face, right in front of your eyes.

Thoughts of crossing Creek evaporated, along with the remaining sliver of Alyssa's hope.

"Can I get a room for the night?" Alyssa's voice didn't sound like her own. Deep and rusty and flat. "Two beds please."

"Grandma." The little boy tugged on the woman's arm. "I'm hungry."

"Two beds? Who the hell ever wants two beds?" The

woman reached for a key on a hook by the register. "All the rooms got one bed. Take it or leave it."

She'd like to leave it, but one more look at the little boy and she realized that wasn't an option. The idea of taking two rooms separately was completely out of the question. Creek would never let her out of his sight.

"Do you have roll-a-ways?" Alyssa asked.

"What does this look like? A Motel Six? Make up your mind, lady. I got a hungry kid here."

"Fine. How much?"

"Sixty-two including tax. Pay now."

Alyssa paid and took the key. As soon as she stepped out of the office door, Creek skulked out of the shadows and grabbed her arm. One cuff clicked on, then the other. He took the key from her hands and led her toward a row of rooms.

"Wait," she said, "let me get the Gatorade from the truck. I'm dying of thirst."

"I'll get it. You're not in any condition to carry anything."

A black number three stared at Alyssa as Creek unlocked the door. He pushed it open and shoved her inside, then dragged her toward the bed and yanked on her arm.

"Sit," he instructed.

"You treat me like a dog."

"A five-year-old or a dog? Which is it?"

"Both." Alyssa perched herself on the edge of the bed and peered around the sparse, dingy room. Creek uncuffed one of her hands and closed the free metal around a lamp base secured to the nightstand. "Don't make a sound. Anyone who comes in here to help you will end up just like Taz. I'll be back in sixty seconds."

Creek's footsteps crunched on the asphalt, then slowly faded. Obviously screaming was out of the question. She couldn't risk him following through on his threat. But whatever she did, she had to do fast. Fifteen of her sixty seconds were gone.

Alyssa's gaze honed in on a phone sitting atop a dresser ten feet away. She held her breath against the pain and stretched the distance allowed by the cuffs, reaching for it, but came up four feet short. Neither the nightstand nor the lamp budged. She braced her feet on the floor for leverage, brought her other arm around, curled her fingers through the cuff and pulled.

Pain stretched through her side. The metal lamp base bent. Just a fraction of an inch. The effort made fresh sweat slick Alyssa's face. She gritted her teeth, refastened her fingers on the cuffs and pulled again. The metal groaned as it bent a little more.

Alyssa tried for the phone again. Managed to catch the spiraled cord between her fingers. Yanked the receiver off the base. It hit the floor with a *kerplunk* just as the door to the room swung open again.

"Goddammit." Creek dropped two armfuls of supplies on the floor and kicked the door closed. "Can't you hold still or shut up for one minute?"

Alyssa recoiled as Creek picked up the receiver and slammed it back onto the base, then raked his fingers across his head and paced. She watched every step, her emotions toggling between fear, anger, guilt, frustration and empathy.

Without warning, Creek swung around and approached her. In automatic defense, Alyssa's hand came up. But he didn't strike. He released the cuff around the lamp and pulled her into the bathroom. Her heart rate spiked again as his angry gaze scoured the small space. With a hand on her shoulder, he pushed her to sit on the closed toilet lid and dragged the free cuff below the sink. The ratchet of metal signaled its closure around an exposed drainpipe.

"What are you doing?" She twisted her wrist against the metal, trying to position her body to alleviate the strain on her side.

Creek stripped off his shirt, balled it up and chucked it into the corner, then pushed the curtain aside on the shower /

tub combination and bent to flip on the faucet. The muscles beneath his skin flexed and rolled. That's when a fresh form of anxiety wedged in. She couldn't sit here and watch him get naked and shower. She really couldn't.

"I can't sit like this," she complained, hoping to play on the sympathies she'd seen. "It hurts my side."

Without acknowledging her, he moved his hands to his waist, unbuttoned and unzipped his jeans and shucked them so fast Alyssa didn't have time to look away. And, okay, yeah, maybe she could sit here and watch after all.

He wore burgundy boxer briefs that clung to his muscular ass. He was tan everywhere but for a pale line mid thigh where he'd obviously worn shorts. She could swear every muscle was outlined in perfect relief. Her gaze traveled over the lines and dips and swells and curves. God, he was beautiful.

A beautiful, racist, murdering, escaped convict.

Alyssa grimaced. Before he took off his underwear and Alyssa lost her last shred of human decency and ogled the beautiful, racist, murdering, escaped convict, she laid her elbow on the edge of the sink and pressed her eyes to her forearm. "Why couldn't you just leave me in the other room?"

Her only answer came in the *swoosh* of the plastic slides on the shower curtain rod as he closed the drape.

Alyssa stayed there, resting her head on her arm, for what seemed like endless minutes. Without any immediate threat, her adrenaline flagged. When her butt went numb and her arms tingled from lack of blood supply, she finally raised her head. Steam filled the room, creating ethereal clouds she could barely see through.

Searching for Creek behind the frosted shower curtain, she discovered him sitting on the tub floor, knees drawn up to his chest, arms wrapped around his legs, head bent.

She'd seen many a broken man in her line of work—the distraught father, the grieving husband, the heartsick son—

and the man behind that curtain had all the signs of a broken man.

Alyssa stared, unable to assimilate this man with the one who had wrapped a chain around her throat. Or the one who'd killed Taz right in front of her. That one was a force to be reckoned with. This man looked overwhelmed. Vulnerable. Defeated. Her compassionate streak—the one that most of her coworkers swore she didn't have—flared to life, urging her to give him the benefit of the doubt against all common sense and good judgment.

"Cr—" Her voice caught. At some point she needed to tell him she wasn't the woman he thought she was. Or she needed to do something to make sure he never found out the truth. She cleared her throat and tried again. "Creek? I need to . . . um . . . talk to you about something."

His head came up, eyes peering at her over the edge of his arm. "It's Teague. My name is Teague." His voice was soft and flat, without animosity. He lowered his head again. "And not now."

"O-okay, but when you're done. It's . . . important."

No response. No movement. With no other options, Alyssa put her head back down and closed her eyes.

She woke to the rake of the plastic curtain rings. Her head jerked up to find Creek staring at her from the tub, a white towel wrapped low around his hips. She rubbed her eyes, trying to clear them. And when she did, the sight that met her nearly made her drool.

This was the first time she'd seen his chest bare in any substantial light, and she wasn't disappointed. His shoulders were wide, his chest strong, his belly flat. A thin cluster of golden hair formed a vertical line down the center of his abdomen, starting just above his belly button. *Oh, yum,* was the first, involuntary thought to flit through her mind. *Amazing*, the second.

Peeking out from beneath the towel, spreading over his right hip and pelvis where his leg met his torso, a deep red streak of skin, much like a healed burn but with more style, more design, tempted her eyes. Curiosity spiked at the extent of the mark, its shape, its origin. Then about his body as a whole. How hard, how often, did a man have to work out to obtain that level of fitness?

She forced her gaze to his face, pleased when she only lingered on his chest and the dusting of dark gold hair over his pecs for . . . okay, more than a moment. That's when it registered. He looked . . . different, but she couldn't figure out exactly how. He looked . . . cleaner, more human. More attractive—if that was possible. But there was something else, too. Something in his eyes, a dullness, a veil. Something flat. Distant. Pained.

He stepped out with a key in his hand and reached for the cuff holding her hand to the sink. The scent of soap drifted to her nose. He no longer smelled of sweat and blood, and as he leaned in to reach the cuff, the warmth of his body floated close. Her eyes lingered on his head. On the swastika covering his scalp, which was noticeably lighter. Confused, she brought her free hand up and ran her fingers over it. His short, soft hair prickled her skin.

Creek jerked away. "What the hell?"

Frowning, she inspected his body again, this time with attention to the other tattoos. The ones on his chest, his arms, his belly, they'd all faded. Instead of that intense black, the images had turned a strange shade of brownish-gray.

When reality dawned, she looked up at him and found his eyes averted. "They aren't real?"

He reached down to take the other cuff off her wrist, and neither met her eyes nor answered.

"Why would you do that?" She rubbed at her wrists, which had grown raw from the chafe of metal, but her mind was still unraveling this new knot in Creek's personality.

"Why would you pretend to be something you're not? What's the point, anyway, if they wash off so easily?"

"It wasn't easy. I had to scrub my skin raw. Come in here." He straightened and walked ahead of her into the other room. "I'm going to make a phone call."

Her mind dropped the confusion over his tattoos and refocused on the immediate problem. "Who are you calling?"

He didn't answer. When he reached the bed, he dropped his towel without warning and reached for a pair of underwear from the bag on the floor. And the seconds between seeing him naked and seeing him step into those boxer briefs seemed to stand still.

He had the most gorgeous ass she'd ever seen. Muscle definition, shape, size, the way his body was so flawlessly proportioned, he made her mouth go dry. And that scar or birthmark or whatever it was and the way it curved around his hip, the tip of a pointed section touching high on one perfect glut, was way too intriguing.

With heat kicking up in her body, she forced herself to turn away and pressed her fingers to her eyes. "Can't you warn me before you do that?"

"It's nothing you haven't seen before."

She dropped her hand and rolled her eyes toward the ceiling. He was dead wrong. He was like nothing she'd ever seen before. "Are you done? I want to talk to you."

"In case you haven't noticed," he said, his voice muffled behind what Alyssa guessed was a T-shirt coming over his head, "I'm a man. I do 'talk' about as well as you follow directions."

Oh, she'd noticed—the man part, at least. She took a chance and looked at him from her peripheral vision. He was dressed again in fresh jeans and a black tee. She breathed a sigh of relief, then stiffened as he picked up one of the cell phones he'd bought at Walmart.

"Wait." She held out a hand, anxiety heating her neck and face.

"Be quite, Hannah. This call is as important to you as it is to me." He gave her a serious look. "If you want to sleep in your own bed tomorrow night, or Luke's bed, or . . . whatever"—he waved the idea away with an irritated fling of his hand—"then keep your mouth shut."

EIGHT

Teague tried to block Hannah out of his mind as he dialed. He needed total focus. But the woman seemed to inspect every inch of his body with a mix of appreciation and interest, leaving his skin tingling as if she'd touched him. Sure, she was sexy as hell. Sure, he was hornier than sin. Still that didn't account for this level of extreme and immediate attraction. Especially after all he'd put her through. Sonofabitch, if this didn't qualify as a clusterfuck, he didn't know what would.

As he paced the small room, Teague chalked up the heat between them to his warped imagination, and his attraction toward her to the fact that she belonged to Luke. There had to be some subconscious temptation to take something of Luke's the same way Luke had taken something of Teague's.

He pushed the weak idea to the back of his mind and focused on what he had to do next. The words had all been worked out. Studied. Rehearsed. Yet now they skittered around his brain like frightened birds, banging into cage walls.

Just get it over with.

Teague dialed Luke's cell. Hannah eased onto the desk chair, back straight, attention riveted on the phone, hands clasped between her knees.

On the third ring, his ex-best friend, ex-brother-in-law, ex-partner picked up. "Ransom."

Teague hadn't heard Luke's voice in three years, yet recognized it immediately. A rush of emotion pumped through his chest: hurt, anger, betrayal, loss. He opened his mouth to respond, but nothing came out.

"Ransom," Luke repeated with a familiar irritation edging his bark.

"Luke," Teague managed.

"You goddamned idiot!" Luke bellowed. "Did your brain turn to jerky in prison? When they catch you, you'll be in the hole so long, you won't see Kat until she's eighteen."

"If you had your way"—Teague's voice emerged rusty and torn—"I'd never see her again. Period."

A beat of silence passed. "Ever heard of a fucking phone? A goddamned letter? Ever think of discussing something before you go and cut your own throat?"

"Don't insult me. We both know nothing I could have said would have gotten you to bring her to see me."

"Prison is no place for a little girl."

"Living without me is no way for her to live."

Another tense moment of silence passed before Luke said, "Then why'd you call? You can't think I'm going to let you talk to her."

"No." Teague's resolve solidified with Luke's rigid defiance. "You're not going to let me talk to Kat. You're not going to let me see Kat. You're going to let me *have* Kat."

"You're out of your fucking mind."

"I'm not asking for a gift, Luke. I know understanding and compassion are completely beyond you. I'm offering a trade."

"You don't have anything to trade. And what the hell makes you think I'd trade anything for—?"

"I have Hannah."

The silence that followed filled Teague's chest until he thought it would crack.

Luke finally breathed. "Holy shit."

"You give me Kat; I give you Hannah. Simple. Easy."

"Not simple or easy." Something filtered through Luke's voice. Something that sent sickness to the bottom of Teague's gut. "You don't have Hannah. At least you don't have my Hannah, actually my *ex-Hannah* as of a week ago."

Teague's eyes darted to Hannah. Her attention was still focused on him. Eager. Anxious. Frightened.

"Don't fuck with me, Luke. You have no idea how much I've been through these last few years. You could never know."

"Just like I'll never know what you did to neglect my sister so badly she killed herself. Just like I'll never know what your girlfriend went through those last minutes of her life, the ones when you bashed her head in with the fireplace poker, or the ones when you poured lighter fluid on her, or the ones when her flesh burned off her body while she screamed, or—"

"Stop!" Teague blocked the images assaulting his mind and turned the conversation back to the only thing they had left in common. "Kat belongs with me and you know it. Stop being an arrogant, stubborn asshole and do the right thing for once in your sorry life."

"I am. I'm raising my dead sister's daughter. And I'll continue to raise her. In case you haven't heard from Seth in the last couple days, the judge made his final decision on custody. She's mine. One hundred percent, full-time, *mine*."

Pain slashed through Teague, so swift and sharp it stole his breath.

"And, just so we're clear," Luke continued in Teague's silence, "I talked to Hannah about half an hour ago. She called all freaked out because some convict abducted one of her doctors at the hospital while she was at a dentist appointment."

Teague's heart dropped like a rock and landed in the very pit of his stomach.

"In perfect Creek-fashion," Luke said, "you've fucked up again."

Teague forced the phone away from his ear and slammed it on the hook. His hands came up, fingers scraping his scalp, over and over.

"Fuck me."

For the first time since this whole nightmare started, Teague felt hopeless. Hollow. Gutted.

"Fuck me."

He'd lost his leverage. He had nothing. No, worse than nothing. He now had multiple life-sentence charges hanging over his head. And, as opposed to the ones that had sent him to prison originally, these he'd actually committed.

"Fuck me!"

He swung toward . . . the woman. Whatever the hell her name was. Advanced two steps before he stopped himself. "Who . . . the fuck . . . *are you*?"

"I . . . I tried . . . I wanted to tell you. . . ."

He took another step.

She cringed. "Alyssa. My name is Alyssa. Foster."

"What were you doing in Hannah Svelt's ultrasound room?"

"She left early for an appointment. I was trying to . . . My boss told me to . . ." She looked up with the light of defiance still shining in her eyes. "It's part of my damn job. There was no one else to do it."

"And, what, exactly, is your damned job?"

"I'm a . . . doctor. A radiologist." She lifted her chin, and infused her voice with that know-it-all edge. "And if you'd stopped for a minute to match the name with the person, you'd have known I couldn't possibly have been Hannah *Svelt*."

"You're obviously some mixed heritage." He slashed a hand at her. "I just figured . . . It doesn't matter what I figured anymore."

He dropped his hand and rubbed his face. Now what? His plans had been gutted like a target in a prison yard brawl. But instead of anger raging inside him, the fury receded to make way for despair. His head filled with memories of Kat: her brand-new baby smell, her first smile, her first steps.

Those led to thoughts of the last time he'd seen her, six months before in the visitation room. Seth had brought her, because Luke never would. She'd winged herself into Teague's arms and chattered nonstop. Showed him her new haircut, her new doll, her new glittery shoes. How she'd learned to write her name, how she could spell *daddy*. Then she cried when time was up and she had to leave. His last vision of her was one with fat tears wetting her red face, her arms outstretched toward him as Seth carried her away.

Teague picked up the towel on the floor and threw it at Hann—Alyssa. "Go take a shower. I need to think."

He turned his back to hide the tears welling in his own eyes. That would make for one scary convict, crying like a baby because things didn't go his way. Alyssa hadn't shed one tear in the hours they'd been together. At least not one he'd seen. Surely he could be tougher than a friggin' girl.

"I can't get my stitches wet," she said.

Teague picked up a roll of duct tape from a Walmart bag. He ripped a strip off and turned to her. "Lift up your shirt."

When she complied, he plastered her bandages with the silver tape, far less gentle than he should have been. "That should get you through the shower. I'll put fresh bandages on when you get out. I have to check the stitches anyway."

She eyed him as if questioning his sanity, then wandered into the bathroom.

"And keep the door open," he called after her.

She shot him a look over her shoulder, gauging his seriousness, then left the door halfway open and disappeared. The shower turned on. In the opening, Teague watched her toss her clothes over the sink. His body may have perked up at the sight, but his mind and heart both still ached, the need to hear Kat's voice overwhelming.

He picked up the phone and punched out Seth's number, praying Kat answered. On the fourth ring, Teague's hope dimmed. On the fifth, Seth picked up, irritable and distracted. "Yeah, hello?"

"Seth, it's Teague."

"Teague, Jesus. Where are you?"

"Not important. Where's Kat?"

"She's asleep. It's been the day from hell. We heard from the judge—"

"I know. I already talked to Luke."

"Bastard." Seth's normally easygoing voice held a bite Teague had never heard. "What did he say?"

"Just that the judge ruled in his favor."

"Did he tell you we weren't granted any visitation?" Despair joined Seth's anger. "That seeing her is at Luke's whim? Fucking asshole. Partial custody wasn't enough. He had to have Kat all to himself. Do you realize what this is doing to Tara? I had to give her Valium to keep her from having a nervous breakdown."

Guilt welled from every angle. "I'm sorry, Seth. I never imagined Luke would turn on me, on us, like this."

"Where the hell are you? Why did you break out?"

"I think that's self-explanatory, don't you? When does Kat go to Luke?"

"Judge gave us—" His voice broke. "Judge gave us three days to turn her over."

So many emotions tore at Teague's heart, chewing at his conscience. He had to put those aside for now. Use his brain. Guilt and pain wouldn't repair Alyssa's life. Wouldn't take away Teague's status of murderer. Sure as hell wouldn't get Kat back.

And now he knew where she was, but he only had three days to grab her. He'd never get her away from Luke. But, Seth . . . Tara . . .

Focus on Kat.

"I don't know what Luke has told you," Teague said, "but—"

"He hasn't told me anything. I'm not talking to the asshole."

Teague blew out a breath. That saved him from having to explain the threat he'd made to Luke. "I need to see her, Seth."

"What . . . ? You've *escaped prison*, Teague."

"We both know that once she's with Luke, I'll never see her again."

"Tara won't go for it. This is already tearing her apart—"

"Don't tell Tara. Just take Kat for ice cream and meet me somewhere."

"Christ, Teague, I don't know."

"I know what I'm asking. But this may be the last time I see her. She's the only reason I'm still alive and we both know it."

Another length of silence fell over the line. Finally, Seth exhaled. "I'll have to set the house on fire to distract Tara long enough to get Kat away from her for ten minutes over the next few days. No promises."

Alyssa turned off the water, pulled the towel from the rod and pressed it to her face. Every one of her cuts and scratches had bitten her again when the warm water touched them, and now her body throbbed.

Creek's voice drifted in from the other room. She tilted her head toward the partially open door. Only one voice. A one-sided conversation she couldn't clearly pick up. He had to be on the phone again, which seemed odd given his claim of being in this alone.

She wanted to believe he'd let her go now that he knew he'd taken the wrong woman, but he wouldn't. She knew too much. She'd seen too much. She was a huge liability.

She took her time drying off because she dreaded putting

those dirty, bloody, lousy-fitting clothes back on. But it was that or face Creek in a towel. Resigned, Alyssa reached for her clothes. Her hand landed on soft flannel. She picked up a pair of men's pajama bottoms so new they still had fold creases. Beside them sat a crisp navy T-shirt. Her ratty clothes were gone.

Her insides softened. Dammit. She shouldn't feel anything for him. Anything but anger, contempt, disgust. But she did. *Dammit all to hell.* She did. She felt sorry for him, embarrassed for him, lost for him, scared for him. The other things, the sexual things . . . those were just too twisted to contemplate.

In the other room, his voice ceased and the television clicked on, filling the space with the direct voice of a male news anchor.

After Alyssa dressed and pulled her fingers through her hair, detangling the damp mass, she peered through the partially open door. Creek stood at the window looking out, hands pressed to the sill, shoulders hunched. The blanket from the van had been spread over the bed, and the supplies he'd purchased at Walmart were unpacked on the small table.

Without turning around, he said, "Lie down." He had this eerie sixth sense of knowing where she was at all times. "I'll change your bandage."

She complied, too tired to continue the useless fight. He sat on the edge of the bed and peeled up the edges of the tape, which had already loosened from the shower. His fingers were warm and sure and gentle. Alyssa couldn't help thinking about how inappropriately comfortable they were with each other.

"What a hack job," he muttered.

"It worked. Stitches stayed dry."

He unpacked the bloody gauze and inspected the stitches from every angle. With one finger he probed a couple spots, heat tapping everywhere he touched. Soon her attention had honed in on every sensation and how the heat drifted to other parts of her body.

"Looks like your luck's changed. They're all intact. Thought for sure you'd pulled at least half a dozen."

"Show me." Her voice came out softer and more tentative than she'd planned. His eyes lifted to hers, suspicious. And hot. She knew how it sounded, but that didn't keep her from saying it anyway. "Show me how you do it."

He looked away, started fiddling with the gauze. "Do what?" His voice went all smart-ass. "Bandage a wound? It's called gauze and—"

"You know what I mean."

He shook his head. "I told you—"

She pushed up on her elbows, challenging him to look her in the eye. "Don't treat me like an idiot."

"A five-year-old, a dog, an idiot . . . Make up your mind. But do it lying down so I can finish."

"You tell me how you do it, and I'll lie down."

He seethed an exasperated sigh and pushed her shoulder until the burn in her side made her give up and fall back. "I told you before, it's just the way I am. I don't know why or how. It just *is*."

"Were you born with it?"

"No."

"When did you know you had it?"

His hands dropped to his lap as he sat back. "You make it sound like a fucking gift. Look at your neck, your wrists. It's nothing but a nuisance. One that hurts people. One I can't control."

"But you can also heal. The bruises on my face should be purple. The burns on my wrists and neck should be blistering and raw." She pointed to her stitches. "Look at the way my skin has already started to fuse at the edges. That shouldn't happen for another week. I know the stages of healing. More than that, I know my own ability to heal, and it's not this damned good."

In the new, tense silence, the TV weatherman's perky voice spoke of continued cold nights and crisp, sunny days through the rest of the month.

"Let's change the subject," he said, eyes steady on his work. "Are you married?"

"Avoidance. That's beautiful."

"Boyfriend?"

"What do you care?"

"I'd like to know who the hell I kidnapped and who might be worried about you. I've already got the cops after me. Would be good to get a heads-up if I've got a psycho significant other ready to hang me by the balls, too."

Alyssa's frown deepened. No. No significant other. In fact, she had very few people who would worry about her. Her competitor, Dyne, would be thrilled she was out of the picture. Her attending radiologists would be irritated she wasn't around to do all their work. Her coworkers would be curious, possibly mortified. But there were only a few people who would be truly concerned.

"My family will be worried."

Well, *some* members of her family would be worried.

Creek placed fresh gauze over the wound and taped it securely. He picked up four ibuprophen tablets and a bottle of water and handed her both.

"Your hand works better," she said, taking the medication. "But I suppose you won't acknowledge that either."

His eyes met hers with a spark of something she might have considered lust if he hadn't shown such complete lack of interest in her so far.

"*New information has surfaced on the day's top story.*" On the television, a female news anchor took over where the weatherman left off. "*Earlier today, two prisoners from San Quentin Penitentiary escaped custody while receiving care at St. Jude's Medical Center in San Francisco.*"

Creek's head turned sharply toward the television.

"*Sources say Francis Sanders and Teague Creek, both in-*

mates serving life sentences at the prison, were transported to St. Jude's for routine medical tests." Mug shots of Taz and Creek flashed on the screen.

"Francis?" Alyssa said, incredulous. "His name is . . . was . . . *Francis*?"

"Shhh." Creek silenced her with a wave of his hand.

"*The San Quentin inmates subdued guards and reportedly escaped the facility with a woman whose identity remains undisclosed. It is unclear at this time whether that woman was a hostage or an accomplice.*"

"*Accomplice?*" Alyssa sat straight up and swung her legs over the side of the bed. "You've *got* to be kidding me. Why would they . . . ? How could they . . . ?" Her mind shot back to Creek's one-sided telephone conversation, and she set her eyes on him. "You."

"What?" One brow dropped in a look that said, "You're crazy. I've been with you this whole time."

"Not while I was in the shower, and when I got out you were on the phone."

"You think *I* was on the phone with a *news reporter*?"

Okay, when he said it out loud, it did sound ridiculous. Still . . . "Look at everything else you've done tonight. Seems you're capable of just about anything."

His brows evened out as a menacing shadow crossed his face. "Watch it. Think about what you're saying. It's not smart and it doesn't even make sense."

"And this does?" She threw her arms out, indicating their hideout. "*Nothing* makes sense anymore. Seems to me you didn't plan this very well. If you're making decisions as important as these on the fly, you're bound to make mistakes."

His eyes went flat. Up until that moment she hadn't realized how much of his guard he'd dropped. Now that he'd thrown up the wall again, she wanted to tear it down. "I guess we can't all be as perfect as you, *Doctor* Foster."

Pounding on the door made Alyssa jump. Creek spun toward the door and pulled the gun from his jeans at the same time. He held the weapon tight to his thigh and put his index finger over his lips in a silent order to stay quiet.

"Yeah?" Creek said through the closed door.

"Manager." The deep rasping voice of the woman from the office came through loud and clear. "I'm getting complaints, which is hard to do when there's only two other people staying here. Keep it down or find another place to sleep. And no refunds."

Creek's shoulders relaxed. "Yes, ma'am."

He continued to stare at Alyssa as the manager's footsteps faded down the walk. He pushed the gun back into his jeans and nodded to the bed. "Go to sleep. I have a feeling that's the only way you're going to stop arguing."

"Takes two to argue."

He slid the cuffs from his pocket and rounded the bed. Alyssa pushed to her feet, crossed her arms, tucked her hands into the crooks of her elbows and stepped back. "You're not putting those back on me."

"You're right about one thing," he said as his hand snaked out and pried one wrist away from her body. "It does take two to argue, and God knows I can't compete with an expert like you."

"Stop!" She pulled and twisted, but nothing fazed Creek. With a quick snap, the cuff encircled her wrist. "You can't expect me to sleep in these."

"I'm not that cruel." He pulled her toward the bed, leaned down and closed the other cuff around the metal lamp base secured to the wall by the headboard. "I only expect you to sleep in one."

Reflexively, she yanked against the restraint. The grating of metal on metal clanked through the room. She gnashed her teeth. "You . . ."

He lifted his brows. "Yes?"

She caught herself before the word *prick* came out of her mouth.

As she sank to a seat on the edge of the bed, she couldn't help thinking how everything could change in an instant. How one person could make one decision and send multiple lives into a tailspin. And wonder how in the hell she was going to put it all back together.

Or if it were even possible.

Nine

Something hit Alyssa's leg. She startled to consciousness with a surge of fear, the type that burned her chest when she woke from the midst of a nightmare.

"We have to go." The male voice, familiar yet unknown, pushed another spurt of adrenaline into her chest.

She lay frozen on her side, eyes open, staring at a blank, white wall, the room mostly dark but for a light drifting in from somewhere nearby. Where was she? Hospital? No. Apartment? No. Parents' house? No.

She rolled to her side and pain erupted from every part of her body—her ribs, her stomach, her shoulder, her left knee, her right hip—everything hurt. She winced. A groan ebbed from her throat.

"You're going to be sore for a few days."

The voice clicked in her memory and with it, a rush of emotion: anger, anxiety and fear. So much fear—for the present, for the future. And now that the incident had been on the news, her family jumped onto the list—specifically, her father.

She eased onto her back, grimacing against the pain. Creek set a covered paper cup on the nightstand by her head. She didn't have to look to know it was coffee. The rich scent filled her nose with each breath.

"It's not Starbucks," he said, "but it'll wake you up."

He pushed the key into the cuff at her wrist and clicked it open, then took her hand and rubbed warm, gentle fingers over the red lines digging into her skin. Instant relief trickled through her wrist, but there were other places that needed his touch more. She hurt so badly she could barely breathe.

Alyssa unfastened his fingers from her wrist, pulled his hand to her side and pressed it flat over her wound. Heat gushed with an initial, almost painful burn, then immediately receded to a deep, soothing, pulsating wash of relief.

"Oh, God, that feels good." At her words, he pulled back. Alyssa tightened her hold and held him there. "Just another minute. Please."

His light eyes were intense as he stared down at her. His cheeks and jaw were covered with fresh stubble, outlining his full lips and highlighting the hollows beneath his cheekbones.

She didn't want to notice his looks, had been fighting the temptation since she'd first seen him in the exam room, but there was just no way to miss them. He was a handsome man, one with a very *GQ* look that could go rugged high-class or gangster sexy-chic. And with his humanity starting to show, she couldn't discount his attractiveness as she had before.

And it was even harder when the pain receded and the heat turned deeper, more sensual. It spread in various directions. Lit her up in a whole different way. And as a deep yearning bloomed low in her gut, she shifted her gaze from his mouth, back to his eyes, wondering . . .

Oh, yeah. He felt it, too. His lids had gone heavy, his eyes a little glassy. And with that edge of tension gone from his face, Alyssa glimpsed a window inside, that same sliver of vulnerability she'd seen when he'd been in the shower, looking broken and defeated.

"Enough." He twisted out of her grasp and made tracks to the opposite side of the room.

Pain returned in the absence of his touch and she forced herself to sit up. "Where did you get coffee?"

"The motel office." He stuffed supplies back into the Walmart bags with jerky, irritated movements. "Get going. You've got five minutes to change. If you're not ready, you go in what you're wearing."

"Go where?"

"Just get dressed."

"Leave me here. I'll get home on my own."

"You're not going home just yet."

"But you promised—" Alyssa cut off the ridiculous statement. "I'm not Hannah. Luke doesn't want me. You don't need me now."

"I need you just as much as I did before, only in a different way. And that promise was made to Hannah Svelt not Alyssa Foster."

"You don't understand. I have to get back to the hospital. What I told you about competing for a job wasn't a lie. I've already lost a lot of ground. They're making their decision in just a couple weeks. I've been working toward this for years." She waved a hand at the television, now dark and quiet. "And now I'm going to have to refute that rumor about being an accomplice in this whole stupid scheme."

He lifted a newspaper from the table and tossed it onto the bed beside her. "You're going to have to do more than that."

She looked at the blaring front-page headline: SAN QUENTIN ESCAPE CONSPIRACY.

She picked up the paper and read.

Yesterday's escape of two convicted killers from St. Jude's Hospital in San Francisco was reportedly aided by an insider.

Twenty-nine-year-old Dr. Alyssa Foster, a radiology fellow at St. Jude's, was performing a routine study on Teague Creek, one of the prisoners, when guards say she gave him access to a pair of scissors, which he then used to hold Foster as a false hostage.

"Oh, my God." Her fingers curled into the edges of the paper.

> *Creek subsequently subdued the officers, locked them in a room and escaped the facility with Dr. Foster and fellow inmate, Francis Sanders.*

"Come on." He walked over and pulled her to her feet. Alyssa stood, but didn't take her eyes off the paper.

> *Creek and Sanders were both sentenced to life in prison without the possibility of parole for particularly heinous murders. Creek was convicted of beating his girlfriend, a prosecutor for the Nevada County D.A.'s Office, Desiree Tapia, unconscious, then setting her on fire while she was still alive. For several months prior to the murder, Tapia had been investigating a serial arsonist. Investigators believe Creek, a former firefighter and paramedic with Nevada County Fire Protection, was that arsonist and that Tapia had uncovered his identity, leading to the attack.*

Alyssa's stomach lurched. Her gaze blurred over the words. Her mind tried to absorb the information, rejected it, tried again. She skimmed the rest of the article, which confirmed the information Creek had told her about Taz's crime and then read:

> *Creek and Foster should be considered armed and dangerous. If you see either of these individuals—*

"They know we stole the U-Haul," Creek said. "They found our fingerprints on the metal fence posts. We need to find another car, and we need to leave. Now." He searched in one of the bags, and pulled out the sweatpants and T-shirt he'd picked up from Walmart the night before and tossed them at her. "Get dressed."

She stood and faced him. "I'm not going with you."

"We are *not* going through this again."

Alyssa looked back at the paper, ignoring his frustration. "This has to be some stupid reporter taking liberties to sensationalize the story."

Teague shot her a look from beneath heavy brows. "Did you miss the part that reads 'guards say'?"

"They wouldn't—"

"Don't be so naïve. Honey, the only difference between guards and inmates is that guards carry a badge and a gun."

Alyssa dropped the paper and rolled her eyes. "Don't even—"

"Who the hell else told the media? You and I were the only other two people there." Creek picked up the towel he'd dropped on the floor the night before and started wiping down every hard surface in the room. "A screwup like the one they made by leaving you alone with me will cost them their jobs. The young guy was a newbie. He'd have been instantly canned. Titus is a couple years away from retirement. He'd lose his pension. That guy is a bad seed."

"You're saying *Titus* is a bad seed?" Alyssa lifted the paper. "You're a . . . You . . ." She waved the paper, her stomach rolling with disgust. "Is that true? Did you really . . . *do* that?"

Creek paused in his cleaning streak to settle flat, emotionless eyes on her. "You tell me, Alyssa. Did I?"

She couldn't fathom it, yet it was all in black and white in the paper, and he changed moods and personas like a psychopath.

When she didn't answer, he huffed a bitter laugh. "Another believer."

"What are you doing?"

"Eliminating fingerprints."

He tossed the towel aside and stalked toward her. Before she could move away, he lifted the bottom edge of her shirt and pulled up.

Alyssa caught it just before he cleared her breasts. "Stop! *Now* what are you doing?"

"If you're not going to change yourself, I'm going to do it. We have to *move*."

She stepped back. "You move. I'm going back to fight this bull."

His expression changed with the twist of his mouth. "You know, somehow I knew that even after I explained how screwed you were, you'd insist on defying reality. So, I took the liberty of adding a little . . . leverage . . . to the picture." He rested his hands at the waistband of his jeans. "I've transferred five grand from my credit card into your checking account. You can consider it restitution for the damage my rash stupidity has caused in your life, but I'm sure the authorities will see it a little differently."

Alyssa's mouth dropped open. Her mind struggled to comprehend. "That just doesn't make any sense. Why would you even go to the trouble—"

"Because I can't let you go yet. And I can't spend all my time fighting you either."

She shook her head, not ready or willing to accept reality. "There's no way you could have—"

He picked up a thin billfold from the table—the same one she kept in the back pocket of her scrub pants. With a flourish, he pulled out the single blank check Alyssa kept there for emergencies and let it float to the bed. "I could, and I did."

Her brain remained a solid block of denial. "No. That's not possible."

"You've obviously never had to take a cash advance off a credit card and deposit it into a checking account. All it takes is a phone call. They wire the money immediately, from my account to yours. We're linked now, baby. Officially. Like it or not."

He was bluffing. He *had* to be bluffing. Because if he wasn't, he'd just implicated her in this whole mess with hard evidence—the escape, the auto theft, the murder. "You *can't* get access to my checking account."

"Not to withdraw money or transfer money out, no. But just about anyone can make deposits. Banks don't inhibit the influx of money, only the outflow."

Her chest heaved with shallow, quick breaths. Sweat broke out on her neck and back. For the first time in her life, her mind stopped working. Completely.

"I . . . I need to call my dad." If she could just talk to her dad, hear his voice, his reassurance, her world would right. "He's bound to know about this by now, and he's going to be worried sick. You can monitor the call. I just want to tell him I'm okay."

"Not going to happen."

"*Please*. He has a heart condition that's aggravated by stress. I don't want this to kill him, for God's sake. Do you want another murder on your conscience?"

"I like it much better when you don't talk." He pointed toward the bathroom. "Get. Changed. Now."

For once, the girl did what she was told, and even kept her mouth shut while she did it. Teague watched Alyssa turn on her heel, long black hair whipping over her shoulder, and stalk into the bathroom. Then she did exactly what he expected—she slammed the door, cutting off his view of that cute little ass.

He could qualify her butt as a cute little ass now that she wasn't Luke's girlfriend. He could fully appreciate her beauty. Remember the feel of her amazing body. Imagine how they'd fit together.

His rational mind knew it would never happen. His repressed male mind wrestled with its nemesis to complete a simple fantasy.

He waited in front of the bathroom door until it swung

open sixty seconds later. Alyssa stood there like a raging bull ready to charge, head dipped, brow furrowed, mouth tight. All she needed was a little steam pumping from her nostrils and a pawing foot to complete the picture. The thought almost made him grin. But it was the way she looked in those oversized sweats that finally turned his mouth up at the corners.

"I'm glad you're getting some pleasure out of this." She chucked the bunched nightclothes at him.

He caught the clothing and tossed it onto the bed. "It's not all that bad." He reached out and grabbed her left hand, now balled into a fist, and closed one cuff around her wrist. "Besides, you'd look good in a brown paper sack."

"I don't get it. Why'd you bother transferring the money if you're going to keep using these?"

"You've got a thick skull and an impulsive nature. Not a great combo. I'm just giving the ramifications of the information time to get through."

"You've got the most annoying way of flipping between being complimentary and condescending." She looked down at her hand, twisted her arm in the cuff, testing the fit. "I'm not the woman you want. I can't help you. It's obvious you're not going to hurt me, so why keep me?"

Hell, yeah, he wanted her, but in a whole different way than she meant. He clipped the other cuff to his own wrist, frowning. "What makes you think I won't hurt you?"

"We both know you would have already. Besides, I don't know if you even could."

His gaze lifted to her face, searching for evidence of cunning, lies, ulterior motive. No one truly understood or accepted his abilities, including himself. The fact that she was intrigued instead of appalled touched a cold, rejected part of himself he'd closed off a long time ago. It had been years since anyone had believed in his humanity. Unfortunately, this wasn't the time for her to see him as harmless.

"Didn't you read that article? Weren't you there when I

gutted Taz?" His stomach turned at the memory of sickening sensations—the knife piercing Taz's skin, sinking into flesh, driving through muscle. "Maybe you're not as smart as I thought you were."

He scooped up the Walmart bags and opened the door a couple inches to peer out. Streetlights glowed over the main road, clear of traffic. The shadowed parking lot beyond was quiet and empty but for a few cars and the U-Haul. He glanced up and down the walkway outside the room and found it clear.

He turned and met Alyssa's eyes, trying to ignore their soft almond shape and the long fringe of lashes. "Let me make one thing very clear: I am not going back to prison. Ever. I'll die first. You may not believe I'm dangerous, but I'm also not backed into a corner at the moment. And you have a lot more to lose now. I can either explain that five grand away after this is over and clear your name or throw your life to the sharks. You choose."

She held his gaze without responding. She'd heard him, and that was all he needed to know. He pulled her alongside him as he stepped out.

The motel was made up of two buildings, configured like an L. Their room was on the short end of the bottom leg. The office, closer to where the truck was parked, lay at the end of the longer section.

Despite the gray light of dawn, Teague kept to the shadows of the building, dragging Alyssa behind him. As he traversed the corner where the two sections met, a door closed near the motel office. Teague pushed Alyssa into an opening between the buildings, home to an icemaker and vending machine, and peered around the siding. A woman shuffled to the edge of the parking lot, a bathrobe wrapped around her chubby figure, a cigarette between her fingers. It was the office manager he'd deliberately avoided when he'd picked up the coffee and newspaper earlier.

"Great," he muttered. "Right between us and the truck."

Alyssa leaned into him to see around the corner. "What is it?"

Her warm breath bathed his ear, sliding down his neck. He nudged her back to put more distance between them and shushed her. Something wasn't right. He could feel it in the way his scalp tingled and his shoulders tightened. In the way an uncomfortable pinch took up residence in his stomach. That was a sixth sense he'd developed in prison, unlike his lame, struggling pyrokinetics that had been chemically burned into him one terror-filled night.

He couldn't chance walking right by the woman, so he waited. It seemed like forever as the manager continued to stare out at the parking lot, shifting her weight from one foot to the other, the cigarette taking quick trips to her lips. In the distance, tires hummed on the asphalt, growing louder. The hair on Teague's neck prickled.

He scanned the length of the motel for another exit. If they went around the back and approached the truck from the opposite direction . . .

The drone of a car engine brought his gaze back to the parking lot. A police cruiser pulled in and coasted toward the manager, who waved it down.

Dread settled in Teague's gut. He gripped Alyssa's hand and pulled her with him as he crossed the breezeway between buildings and peered out the other side. The neighborhood beyond was barren, the only inhabited building within sight another shacklike hotel half a mile down the road.

Before he'd strategized a plan, another police car passed the hotel—this one with lights flashing, but no sirens.

"Fuck." Teague jumped back into the shadows and collided with Alyssa. A cry of surprise and pain rumbled from her mouth. Teague pressed her face into his shirt with a hand on the back of her head.

The click of another door drew Teague's attention. A man wandered out of his motel room with an ice bucket in one hand, the other rubbing at his eyes as if he'd just woken. The man stopped and looked toward the parking lot, squinting at the red-and-blue flashing lights.

While he was distracted, Teague walked Alyssa back into the shadows alongside the vending machine. Her face was still pressed into his chest. Her breath, hot and fast against his T-shirt, filtered through the cotton and slid along his skin, making his mind blur around the edges.

"Oh . . . my God . . ." she said between breaths, her voice raspy with pain. "My side . . . hit that stupid . . . gun."

The other motel guest grumbled something unintelligible as his attention shifted from the cops back to the ice machine. The sound of his feet dragging on the cement brought Alyssa's focus around, her eyes wide with surprise. And in the fraction of a second that followed, Teague realized that if he didn't act fast, Alyssa would act faster.

Before she could speak, Teague put one hand under her chin, turned her face and covered her mouth with his. She stiffened and squeaked, pushing at his chest. The hand cuffed to Teague's pulled hard. He tightened his grip on her face and pulled back just enough to murmur, "Kiss me back, Alyssa. Please. Don't push me into a corner."

He couldn't read her expression in the shadows, but her mouth softened under his, her hand stopped tugging, her muscles lost some of their tension.

"Oh, hey, man," the other man stammered. "Sorry. Don't mean to . . . uh, er . . . I'm just gettin' some ice."

Teague broke contact only long enough to mutter, "You ain't botherin' us. Is he, baby?"

Before she had a chance to answer, Teague kissed her again, and not solely for the purpose of keeping her quiet. He kissed her because he had to. After feeling those lips against his, he had to feel them again. And again. Her mouth was warm and soft. And with each press of his mouth, hers relaxed. Within seconds, she'd leaned into him, abandoning resistance.

Teague tightened the arm at her waist and pulled her

closer until they were chest to chest, hips to hips. He shifted, allowing her body to rub against his, allowing him to get a better feel of all her soft swells and lean muscle.

And that was the moment she responded. Her hips met his pressure. Her mouth moved under his. The hand at his chest gripped the fabric of his shirt, as if to keep him close.

The clatter of ice hitting a plastic bucket echoed in the small space. "Did you see the cops out there, man?" the guy asked. "Do you know what happened?"

Teague didn't answer. There was nothing that could make him pull away from Alyssa short of a cop holding a gun to his head, which he fully understood could happen at any moment.

The man's voice seemed to nudge Alyssa from a trance. She broke their kiss and looked up at Teague. Her eyes glimmered in the dim light, heavy-lidded, filled with surprise and confusion and heat.

"Can't you see I'm busy here?" Teague didn't have to fake the irritation in his voice.

The other man harrumphed and continued to fill the bucket. Teague ran his thumb over Alyssa's bottom lip, slid his palm to her jaw, and his fingers into her hair. He let his other hand drop to the low curve of her spine and pulled her hips against his again. Fully erect, he indented the soft swell at the center of her pelvis. She sucked in a breath, met his pressure, closed her eyes.

Teague's mind hazed over. Almost slid right out from under him. His groin pulsed with heat. His hands ached to roam. He couldn't stop himself when his mouth fell back to hers. And she didn't resist. Her hand pressed against his face in the most endearing way as she tipped her head and opened to him.

The leash on his restraint snapped. He kissed her back with a hunger that reflected all those dark, desperate years alone. Years he thought he'd never feel a woman's lips again.

Her hand slid over the back of his neck as she tilted her

head a little more. Up and over his scalp as she teased her tongue into his mouth. After an instant of shock, he accepted her invitation with a groan that felt as if it rumbled all the way from his feet. Lost himself in the texture of her, the heat of her. The sexy play she elicited with her lips, teeth, tongue was like unlocking a private playroom door, giving him a glimpse into the secrets she kept for a classified few.

And he liked the private disclosure of those secrets. Really liked it.

Teague's veins were filled with high octane, his body ready for a long, hot, steady burn followed by an intense, shattering explosion by the time the racket from the ice machine ceased and the man started back down the walkway.

"Might want to head back to your room," he muttered. "Cops'll find any excuse to bust you."

Alyssa pulled away in one sharp movement, leaving Teague dizzy with lust. His heart beat double time, his chest rocked with quick breaths, his muscles strained for action.

And his brain was definitely focused on one thing, and one thing only.

Whoa. He shook off the haze and peered around the side of the building toward the parking lot. Only minutes had passed, but it felt as if he'd been floating in an alternate universe.

Lights swept over the parking lot as another vehicle pulled in. But not a cop. Teague forced his mind to clear. He sharpened his attention on the man who emerged from the idling SUV and made his way to where the two cops stood talking to the woman. An eerie trickle of familiarity cut at Teague's belly. Something about the way the man carried himself, the slant of his shoulders, the arrogant tilt of his head, but most of all, the stagger of his gait. Not quite a limp, but definitely not right.

Teague had only met one man who'd walked that way and that man had no business showing up here. Now. Ever in Teague's life, for that matter. Not again. Even the possibility threw Teague's screwed-up world way the hell off kilter. If it was Vasser—Teague would never forget that bastard's name—then nothing was as it seemed, and Teague was screwed beyond imagination.

One cop held a hand out to the hotel manager, gesturing her to stay put as all three men pulled weapons and trotted toward the U-Haul. And all Teague could focus on was that man's damned limp.

Fuck.

With his heart still pounding, his damn dick still hard, he scanned the parking lot for a vehicle to jack, but the few cars present were all out in the open. He moved back to the opposite side of the passage and peered down the length of the building. An older model Honda Pilot sat in the manager's space.

He looked down at Alyssa. "You're going to have to move fast."

Her tongue drifted over her bottom lip. Her eyes remained downcast, her head turned away. Her body language screamed embarrassment. She'd probably shocked herself as much as she'd shocked him with that kiss. The possibility that she regretted it nagged at his ego, but there was no time to dwell.

He dug in his pocket and found the cuff key. With a quick click, he released the metal from his own wrist. It was simply too awkward to keep her tethered to him.

He wrapped his arm around her back, using the good side of her ribs for support. "Put your arm around me and hold on."

They scuttled along the building, obscured by the motel's shrubbery. Two more cop cars came blaring onto the scene just as he and Alyssa reached the Honda. The cops would search the rooms first, but that wouldn't take long. And as soon as they found Ice Man, they'd know which direction to look. Teague had five minutes, tops. And if that other guy was really Vasser, the cops were the least of Teague's problems.

If he had thought his spiraling plan had hit rock bottom when he'd killed Taz, he'd been wrong, just like he'd been wrong about everything else.

He dropped the Walmart bags at his feet and secured Alyssa to the driver's side door handle.

"Come on." She jerked against the metal. "This is so unnecessary."

"Where you're concerned I never know what to think."

He dragged the lantern from one of the plastic bags and worked at its metal handle, but couldn't pry it loose. Anxiety pumped through his body. Teague closed his eyes, cleared his mind and channeled the energy into his hands. The metal softened and twisted and finally snapped off one side. Before the heat slipped away, he worked the thin metal rod in his palm to straighten the curve then create a hook at the end.

"That's just . . ." Alyssa's soft voice brought Teague's gaze up. She was peering around his shoulder, her eyes wide with awe.

"Weird," he said. "I know."

"Amazing, not weird," she countered. "You have to change your thinking patterns."

"Whatever." He slid his new tool between the glass and the window frame on the driver's side. The metal hooked around the interior door handle on the first try, and he popped the door open. He uncuffed Alyssa from the door and pushed her forward.

"Get in." He glanced over his shoulder. Still clear. "Climb across."

She moved too slow for his amped state. Teague slid halfway onto the driver's seat, grabbed her thighs and shoved her over. He didn't have time to be gentle.

He clicked her free cuff to the passenger's door handle, then leaned under the dash on the driver's side. One ripping jerk and the dash's plastic cover popped off. With a handful of wires, Teague yanked, searched, plucked the colors he needed. His hands were shaking too hard to manage the fine work of stripping the plastic coatings, so he stuck the wires between his teeth instead, bit into the rubbery outside and pulled them off.

Red to red. Twist. Red to brown. Focus. Channel. Spark. Channel. Spark. Grind. Churn. The engine turned over.

"Yessss." He swung an arm over the back of the seat and whipped out of the parking spot, turned the wheel, and with one last look for witnesses, jammed the vehicle into drive.

The cops were still on the other side of the building, probably doing a room check as Teague reached the street by mowing down the border shrubs and driving right over a weedy grass patch. He hit the road, turned left and had to squeeze the steering wheel until his fingers turned white so he wouldn't gun the damn car to a hundred. With a steady speed, he kept his attention divided between the road and his rearview mirror.

"Where did you learn to do that?" Alyssa's voice dragged Teague's attention across the car to those big, light eyes looking at him through a haze of suspicion, frustration and pain.

"Do what?"

"Break into a car. Not exactly the kind of thing you learn in Boy Scouts."

"No." The veiled accusation burned. Especially after that kiss. "The kind of thing you learn as a fireman, to help people who either lost their keys or locked them in the car."

Her eyes narrowed. "What about the hot-wiring part?"

His fingers wrung the steering wheel. "The hot-wiring part works great when someone has lost their keys in the snow or the sand or the water and would either be stranded or waiting hours for a locksmith when they've got another set at home."

"Hmmm."

"Maybe you should change your own thought patterns." Irritation replaced the immediate fear of being caught. No one was following them as Teague took the ramp onto the freeway. "Why do you think everything has to have a nefarious purpose?"

"Nefarious. Nice word choice. You're a convicted mur—" She cut herself short, her eyes going dark and troubled. "Felon. What do you expect me to think?"

A familiar stab of disappointment dug deep, cooling the heat she'd stoked so readily just moments before. "Looks like I should go back to expecting you to think just like everyone else."

TEN

Alyssa watched Creek drive, fighting the guilt trying to creep into her mind. She'd judged and accused him. The disappointment in his eyes was far too familiar for her to miss, and considering how much pain that emotion had caused her over the years, she felt sick that she'd inflicted it on someone else. On *him*.

She remained quiet as he drove, unsure what to say. Unsure how to feel. Her body was still buzzing, her lips still burning from those kisses. In just twelve hours her life had been turned inside out, her future thrown to the wind, all her hard work trampled. She was now bound to a stranger who had evidently committed the hideous murder of someone he'd supposedly cared about, but part of her simply couldn't reconcile the man with the act.

As they hit the edge of town, she studied his profile, trying to gauge his state of mind. When she couldn't evaluate his expression, she found her gaze drawn to his mouth. He was a forceful, hungry kisser. An amazing kisser. Passionate, the way he encompassed her in his arms as if he wanted to own her. Erotic, the way he'd responded to the advance she hadn't been able to keep herself from making, the way he'd rubbed his hips against hers. And that erection. Criminy. She wiped a hand across her damp forehead. Just the memory caused a burst of white-hot fire between her legs. He was a freaking rock-hard ball of fire. And he was big. Like . . . wow.

Not that it mattered. She was sure he'd be an awesome lover, regardless. Passionate, intense, demanding and erotic. He'd be like no other man she'd ever known, no doubt in her mind. He'd already blown every one of her past boyfriends out of the kissing department.

"Didn't your mother teach you staring is rude?"

Alyssa's gaze jumped back to Creek's eyes, where he split his attention between her and the road, looking both concerned and irritated.

"You shouldn't have kissed me." The words hung between them. "There's a line, you know? We have to draw a line in the sand and stay behind it."

He hesitated, looking at her as if he didn't quite understand what she'd said. Then a little grin tipped his mouth. "Who are you trying to convince? Me or you?"

"Shut up."

The little grin grew into a smile that held more irony than humor. "I may have started it, but, damn girl, you finished it."

Heat rushed her cheeks. Her chest. "Shut. Up."

He snorted a laugh, propped his elbow on the door and ran his fingers over his mouth, reminding Alyssa how he'd rubbed his thumb over her bottom lip before he'd kissed her again. The gesture so sweet just before he'd taken her mouth like a man possessed. She could still feel the sizzle of it to her toes.

Her mind traveled to all the wrong destinations. Her body pulsed with heat in all the wrong places. She looked straight ahead out the window as the sunrise cast a coral glow on the horizon. "Can I call my dad now?"

A heavy sigh rocked Creek's wide shoulders. "Will you sleep for twelve hours if I let you?"

"Probably not twelve, but I promise to stop talking for a while."

"Define 'a while.' "

"At least two hours."

He chewed on the inside of his cheek as he rolled the thought over in his mind. She could tell by his expression that he was going to cave, which gave her the opportunity to enjoy the sexy twist of his mouth as he pretended to consider.

"Two hours isn't much for that kind of risk."

"Give it up. You're transparent. And I won't relent until I talk to him."

"Transparent," he repeated, and his brow lifted as he thought about the comment. Then out of nowhere he asked, "Is your mother dead?"

"No. Why?"

He shrugged. "I expected you to ask for her, that's all."

No, Alyssa didn't want to talk to her mother. Especially not now. "Stop stalling and give me the phone."

He dug the cell out of his back pocket and held it out to her. "Conditions."

"I know." Alyssa rolled her eyes. "No hints, no codes. Blah, blah, blah."

"And the conversation is on speaker."

Discomfort trickled into her belly. "Why?"

"I think that's obvious." He lifted his brows at her. "Problem?"

She couldn't—no matter how she tried to force her eyes to stay locked on his—keep her gaze from falling to his mouth. Dammit.

She swept the phone from his hand. "Fine."

Now that she was holding it, her mind veered toward her family. Would talking to her father make his anxiety worse? What would she say? And, her mother . . . She cringed.

"Change your mind?" Creek asked.

"No, I'm trying to figure out how to tell them a lunatic kidnapped me and that I don't know where we're going or when I'll be home, or even *if* I'll be home, in a way that won't freak them out and make things worse."

"Maybe you shouldn't call."

"No." She'd learned better during her years in medicine. "Knowing, no matter how bad, is always better than not knowing."

Dialing, Alyssa prayed her father would answer. He was usually the only one up at this hour of the morning, and definitely the only person she wanted to talk to.

"Speaker," Creek said. "And make it quick."

Alyssa pressed the speaker button and the ring at her parents' home filled the car.

On the second ring, a rough, breathless, expectant, "Hello," came over the line.

She hesitated, confused to hear her twin brother's voice. "Mitch?"

"Oh, my God, Lys! Are you okay? Where are you?"

She darted a look at Creek and found him watching her with only occasional glances at the road. She pointed to her own eyes with two fingers, then at the road and mouthed *watch where you're going*. His lids dropped low in warning before he turned away.

"Alyssa?" Her brother's worried voice redirected her.

"Yes, I'm here. I called to tell Dad that I'm okay. Can I talk to him?"

"Not until you talk to me. Where are you?"

"I, um, can't say."

"Is he right there? Are you still with him?"

"Yes. How's Dad taking it?"

"How do you think he's taking it? He's a mess."

Alyssa's brain tightened as her thoughts sharply refocused. "Have you taken his blood pressure? Are the nitroglycerin patches handy?"

"Hold on. You're the one who's God only knows where with some fucking murderer—"

"Mitch, don't swear." She cast a look at Creek, whose hands were wringing the steering wheel, mouth pressed into a hard frown. "I've heard enough to last me the rest of my life."

"You're the one I'm worried about," he continued, talking over her as he often did. "Give me something to go on, Lys, anything."

Creek lifted a hand and gestured in a circle, a get-going sign.

"I can't talk long. Put Dad on the phone."

"You tell that motherfucking sonofabitch that I'm going to make sure he is prosecuted to within an inch of his life."

"He's already got a life sentence, Mitch—"

"Then I'm going to nail his ass to the electric chair. He picked the wrong people to fuck with. I've got my best two investigators on your trail, Lys. We'll find you soon. Here's Dad."

A moment of silence passed before her father came on the line. "Lyssie, baby? You there?"

"Yeah, Dad—" A thick shot of emotion clogged her throat. She swallowed past it, but her voice still came out rough. "I'm here."

"Are you okay? Are you hurt?"

"I'm fine," she lied.

"What can we do, baby?" His voice was smooth and calm, but Alyssa heard the hidden fear. "How can we help?"

Tears burned her eyes. "You can take care of yourself, Dad. I called to let you know that I'm all right so you won't stress. I want you to take your medicine and do what Mitch tells you to do."

Creek lifted a hand beside her and snapped his fingers to get her attention, then made a cutting gesture over his throat.

"For God's sake, Lys," her father continued. "Don't worry about me." Her mother's voice droned in the background, running over her father's, which was probably where Mitch had picked up the habit. "Hang tough, sweetheart. I love you. Here's your mother."

"What? No, Dad wait—"

"Alyssa Naoko." Alyssa flinched at her mother's harsh voice. "Didn't I tell you not to take that job? Those ridiculous hours, that low-life population and crime-ridden city . . ."

In her peripheral vision, Alyssa saw Creek's head whip toward her. She swore she could feel the heat of his stare on her face.

"Mom, please—"

"But do you ever listen? No. You always have to be the best. You always have to go after the biggest challenge. One day, young lady, one day, that hard head of yours will get you—"

Creek jabbed at the receiver, hitting the disconnect button. Startled, Alyssa looked up at him. His brow was a tight vee of wrinkles, and the dark spark in his eye reminded her of when they'd first met.

"You just hung up on *my mother*," Alyssa said, caught between shock and anger.

"She deserved it." He stuffed the phone between the driver's seat and the center console. "How is it that I can't say 'boo' to you without raising your hackles, yet she can ream you without even a tap on the wrist?"

"Why do you care?"

"You've been kidnapped by a convicted murderer and she yells at you like it's your fault?" Anger seethed through his words. "That's no way for a parent to act. It's no wonder you're a daddy's girl."

A different kind of emotion tightened Alyssa's chest. Only Mitch and her father had ever pushed her mother back during one of her famous tirades. But Teague hadn't only pushed her back, he'd knocked her out.

Teague. Alyssa realized it was the first time she'd thought of him by his first name.

The car went over a dip in the road, jolting Alyssa. Her ribs compressed and released, punching a burst of pain through her abdomen. The cuffs on her wrist jangled against the door, and reality rushed back in a hard smack.

She sat in a stolen car, handcuffed to the door with a convicted murderer-slash-arsonist, headed for God only knew where for no coherent reason—

Arsonist.

Alyssa's head turned sharply toward Teague.

"What now?" he asked.

"Your . . . whatever it is . . . ability-thing. You said you can't control it. It gets out of hand when you're angry. Is that what happened? With your girlfriend?"

He looked at her in pissed-off confusion. Then her meaning clicked. His face smoothed into a mask of indifference.

"Naoko?" he changed the subject again. "You lied about your last name, too? Are you even a doctor?"

"Naoko is my middle name, genius." Alyssa's teeth gnashed. "Talk about evasion. You're a master."

"Japanese?"

"And Philippino and Irish and Italian, yes. You have a problem with that?"

"No, I don't have a problem with that," he snapped right back, "but I would have guessed Hawaiian or Hispanic or, yeah, maybe Italian. You don't look Asian."

"I did to Taz. And what's with those tattoos of yours? The ones that fade? Did you use black henna? Do you realize that stuff seeps through your skin and poisons your bloodstream? You're not going to have to worry about an electric chair. You've probably shortened your life span fifty years with that stuff."

"It's not black henna, *genius*. It's ink from a plant that grows in the rainforest. Completely harmless."

"How in the hell did you get ink like that in prison? And why waste your time if they're going to wash off?"

"You can get anything you want in prison, if you know how to go about getting it. And, inside, fitting in is more important than anything else. Being who they expect you to be means life or death." He changed gears again. "Does Naoko mean something?"

Alyssa snorted. "Obedient."

"That conversation makes a whole lot more sense now."

"Well, I'm glad someone got something out of it." Other than heartache. Alyssa always got plenty of that from her mother.

"What about your brother? You said he's a defense attorney, but he was mouthing off about prosecution."

"He used to work for the D.A. Still has friends and contacts there."

"Let me get this straight. I not only have the cops after me for escaping, but the F.B.I. for kidnapping, and now private investigators have jumped on the bandwagon."

"Sounds like." She let her head rest against the seat, suddenly exhausted despite the fact that she'd slept deeply and dreamlessly the night before.

"And on top of that," he continued, "I've committed a dozen felonies in the last twenty-four hours, all of which you've witnessed."

"I'll say anything you want me to say. I could have suffered stress-induced amnesia after everything I've been through. I just want to get back to my life."

A combination of nausea and fatigue washed over her like a wave. Had to be the stress, the anxiety, the frustration. She needed to sleep it off. Yes. Sleep. The perfect solution. She could escape Teague, his questions, his comments, his stupid scheming, her own worry, maybe even this damned gnawing pain that seemed to spread through her body.

"This is just beautiful. Your brother was sure right about one thing. I certainly did choose the wrong person—or people—to fuck with."

"I don't know why I bother talking. No one listens to me outside hospital walls." She wiped at the dampness on her forehead with her free hand and closed her eyes. "I meant what I said to my brother—enough with the swearing already."

* * *

Alyssa didn't know how long she'd been asleep. In some ways it felt like days; in others it felt like she hadn't slept at all. She couldn't get comfortable. Couldn't figure out if she wanted to scream or sleep. Couldn't decide whether she was hot or cold. Couldn't keep her mind firmly in consciousness. Couldn't let herself slip into the deep abyss she so desperately wanted.

She scooted her shoulders sideways against the poorly padded surface behind her, shifted her butt against the seat and whimpered at the rip of pain along her side. With her knees pulled up toward her chest, hands clasped between her thighs, she laid her cheek against the cool surface and relaxed again.

A shiver rocked her from shoulders to hips. Her muscles tightened against the spasm and pain rocketed through her body. She grimaced and moaned.

"We're here." A cool hand swept across her cheek, brushing her hair back, smoothing away the film of sweat she hadn't realized was there until it was gone. "Wake up, beauty."

Oh, that voice. Smooth and deep and filled with compassion. The one that had been crooning to her as they drove. Although she couldn't remember what he'd said, she knew it made her melt into the surface beneath her. And that voice was connected to the hand whose thumb now stroked her temple, whose fingers combed the heavy strands off her neck allowing cool air to bathe her hot skin.

Movement ceased, and Alyssa came slowly to full consciousness as the comforting touch abandoned her. Her eyes opened to a dull, muted canvas of gray. Gray asphalt, gray storefronts, gray sky. Dark gray mountains in the distance covered in a lighter gray snow. She was looking out a car window at the only splash of color in the whole dang landscape, a red neon sign screaming PET EMPORIUM.

Her stomach dropped. She was in the same car she'd been in that morning, with the same man who'd destroyed her life the day before. She glanced over her shoulder as he pulled into a parking space, killed the engine and pulled on the baseball hat. Confusion mottled her brain. "What are we doing?"

He ignored her, got out and rounded the car. Alyssa shifted in her seat and whimpered at the discomfort erupting from every cell in her body. He opened her door and unlocked the cuff on her wrist.

Frigid air snuck in, floated over the sweat filming her body and made her shiver hard. "My God, it's cold out there. Where are we?"

"That much closer to where we're going."

"And where would that be?"

He pressed the back of his hand to her throat, his eyes sharp in concentration. "It's getting worse."

His comment brought everything into focus—her pains, her sweats, her chills. "I have a fever."

"I'm pretty sure it's worse than that. Sit up. Let me look at the stitches again." He didn't wait for permission, simply pulled her shirt up and eased the bandage back.

Alyssa peered down at the red welts forming a pattern around the nylon he'd used to stitch her. "Damn, they're infected." She winced and dropped her head against the seat. "I can't believe this. I need a hospital and you bring me to a pet store."

"Sonofa—"

"*Stop* swearing. It's the least you can do if you're not going to let me go."

"Now do you see how pathetic my so-called *abilities* are?"

"Refreshing to see you embracing your uniqueness, Creek." She pushed his hand away and tugged down her shirt. Now she felt guilty for making him feel bad. This was so ridiculous. "May just be a reaction to the nylon."

"Nylon, my ass. You don't get a raging fever from a reaction to nylon. You think I'm an idiot?"

"That's a rhetorical question, right?"

"Come on." He gripped her arm, encouraging her to move. "Let's go."

As she lifted her head off the seat, a roll of nausea rumbled through her belly. "Go in without me. I feel sick."

He reached across and unclicked her seatbelt. The heat of his body drifted over her. The lingering scent of soap and maleness filled her nose. Surprisingly, both soothed the queasiness.

"No way," he said. "Even as sick as a dog, you'd run given the chance." His eyes flicked toward her with a spark of humor. "No pun intended."

"Ha-ha. In case you hadn't noticed, I'm getting impatient with this whole escape-plan-gone-wrong thing. What could you possibly need in a pet store?"

He propped both hands on the Honda's roof and looked down at her. "Just so we're really clear, this will *not* be a repeat of your Walmart escapade. You will *not*—"

"Don't lecture me." She pulled at the edges of her sweat jacket and crossed them over her chest, searching for warmth.

"I'm *reminding* you."

"Like I need reminding?" A burst of anger gave her the strength to sit up and glare at him. "I'm reminded every damn second I'm awake. I'm reminded every damn time I try to move."

"Which is why we're here. I'm going to get something to help you." He tugged on her hand. She tugged back. "The more you resist, the longer it will take to get where we're going, which in turn means the longer it will take for this to end."

An end to this nightmare—now there was something she could focus on.

"Touch me, first." She grabbed his hand and pressed it against her abdomen. It was big and warm and strong. Heat traveled through his palm and fingers and into Alyssa's side, spreading much-needed relief through her torso. With one hand pressed over his, she slid the other up his forearm searching for more warmth. She found it, in supple muscle and soft skin. "You need to bottle this. It's amazing."

"I'll get right on that." He drew her from the seat, supporting her with his arm at her waist.

"How long 'til we stop for more than ten minutes?"

"About an hour."

"And when will this all be over?" she asked as they approached the entrance. "When will you let me go?"

He didn't answer.

A young woman with her dark hair in a ponytail greeted them. "Can I help you find something?"

"Fish," Creek said.

"Along the back wall," she said, gesturing. "Fresh water on the right and salt water on the left."

"Thanks."

Teague led Alyssa past the cash register where a young man sat talking on the phone, a newspaper spread out on the counter in front of him. He glanced up as they passed and returned his gaze to the paper, hardly more than an uninterested blink. Just as Alyssa looked away, the man's eyes jumped up again. She continued to watch him from the corner of her eye as the conversation on his end of the phone ceased, and he slowly pushed to his feet.

They turned down an aisle and Alyssa lost sight of him, but by the way his eyes grew wide as they'd disappeared, she was sure he'd recognized them. Instead of excitement, the sighting brought apprehension.

Creek turned and looked down at her, his steps slowing. "What?"

"Wh-what do you mean, what?"

"You squeezed my hand."

"I didn't . . . I mean, I didn't mean to. . . ." She was torn between pulling him from the store and stalling to keep them there as long as possible. This was exactly what she'd been silently begging for at Walmart and here it had been handed to her without even trying. "Never mind. Nothing."

She turned her attention to the shelves where he'd stopped and stared at the contents in disbelief. "You brought me in here to buy *fish food*?"

"Little trivia for you, doc." He crouched and picked up a bottle. "Fish ailments are treated with human medications. Antibiotics."

Her mouth dropped open and her mind temporarily veered from her turmoil. "You expect me to take off-the-shelf medication for *fish*? Okay, this nails it, Cr—" She stopped herself and forced his first name out of her mouth. "Teague. You are officially certifiable."

A grin tilted his mouth as he looked up at her and something strange and uncomfortable twisted in her chest. His teeth were straight and white, his eyes a sparkling blue beneath the hat's dark brim. A glimpse of someone else shone out at her. Maybe the man he was beneath the fear and desperation. Maybe the man he'd been before he'd gone to prison. She didn't know, but whoever it was touched her in a way she hadn't been touched in a long, long time. Maybe ever.

"Here's the thing," he said. "The emergency room would have asked too many questions and then called the cops to report a knife wound. Internet sources would take too long, and I'm not in the mood to knock off a vet's office. So." He pointed at two more bottles on the shelf. "You have your choice of Amoxicillin, Erythromycin or a sulfa-combo. What'll it be?"

Curiosity won out and Alyssa took one of the bottles from him. Sure enough, as far as she could tell, it was the same stuff she'd given out prescriptions for in the past. "How is this legal?"

"Let's not worry about that right now. Just tell me which one you can take and we'll get back on the road."

That comment had her looking up and toward the front of the store. The two young clerks loitered there talking, their heads together, body language hunched and tight.

"Well?" Teague prodded.

He'd truly made this stop to help her. He'd risked being seen just to find antibiotics for her infection. So many thoughts zoomed through her head at the same time, she couldn't prioritize or sift. She looked back at him. "Do you have that gun on you or is it in the car?"

His face tensed, eyes sharpened. He glanced in the direction she'd been looking and watched the clerks. "I have it on me. Why?"

Let me make one thing very clear: I am not going back to prison. Ever. I'll die first.

"I think we should go." Alyssa pulled him toward the opposite end of the aisle.

He resisted. "Why the rush?"

"Come on."

He pulled on her hand until she was forced to turn back around and face him. "Talk to me first."

She lowered her voice to a whisper. "I think they recognized us."

Teague's mouth went stone hard as his bright eyes scoured the store. Pocketing several bottles, he urged Alyssa toward the rear corner of the building.

"Where are you going? The front doors are that way."

"Which is exactly where the cops will come in if they've been called."

They reached a single rear door with a banner reading, NO EXIT. FIRE ALARM WILL SOUND. Teague tinkered with a lever on the big red bell over the door, then pressed the metal bar. Alyssa cringed, expecting an ear-piercing alarm, but it never came. Teague poked his head out the door, took a quick look around, then pulled her out behind him.

"Keep your head down." He draped an arm around her shoulders and pulled her to his side. "Walk straight to the car without looking around."

Tires crunched on the asphalt nearby. Teague's hand lifted

from her shoulder and gently pressed the back of her head. He leaned in nuzzling her temple. Despite the urgency of the situation, a delicious shiver trickled down her neck.

"Don't look up," he murmured, his voice intensifying the tingle. "Keep walking."

The police car darted through the parking lot and angled in at the front double doors of Pet Emporium. Another car appeared within seconds.

Teague opened the passenger's door of the Honda and eased Alyssa into the seat. Sirens whined in the distance. Without cuffing her, he shut her door and rounded the car. He slid into the driver's seat, reached below the dash and fiddled with wires. A flash of light burst from the darkness of the floorboard, and Alyssa jumped.

"Just a spark," he said. "There'll be a couple more."

And there were. They lit up Teague's face in quick, bright flashes. The engine finally cranked over, and as he drove leisurely from the parking lot, Alyssa watched the growing spectacle in front of the pet store. Vehicles screeched to a stop at all angles surrounding the store. Doors flew open and officers crouched for cover as they drew their weapons. Off to the side, men in F.B.I. Windbreakers stood questioning the store clerks.

A complex blend of fear and relief whipped inside Alyssa like a firestorm. All those police, gunning for Teague. For her, too. And as if they were invisible, she and Teague slipped right out onto the main road, where a sign directed them immediately onto the freeway.

Her mind was already miles ahead, on the road to that safe haven Teague had promised, when the car jerked to a stop. Alyssa flew forward. She threw a hand out to catch herself on the dashboard. The impact jarred her chest. Before she could gather enough air to let out a scream, Teague's arms came around her. One hand pressed her face to his shoulder, the other slipped beneath Alyssa's jacket and rested across her ribs. Heat penetrated deep into her body, relieving the pain enough to turn the scream into a gurgle.

"I'm sorry," he murmured. "Shh, shh, I'm sorry."

Within twenty seconds, the pain had vanished. Before she started to feel the desire that always seemed to follow, she pushed back, still breathing hard and fast, and wiped at the tears on her cheeks, unable to remember them falling. "What happened? Why'd you stop?"

He wasn't looking at her, but over her shoulder, out the window toward the multitude of flashing lights and milling people. "Thought I saw someone . . . Nothing. Stupid."

But it wasn't nothing. It wasn't stupid. Alyssa could see fear in Teague's eyes.

The car started forward again, Teague now focused out the front window. "Fasten your seatbelt. Please," he added.

As he took the on ramp to the freeway, Alyssa looked back over the crowd. All she could see was a bunch of cops and a few guys in dress shirts and ties. They all stood near the storefront, conferring, interviewing, taking notes. But there was one man, dressed in civilian clothes—khaki cargo pants, long-sleeved shirt over a tee underneath, brown work boots—standing off to the side. He had his arms crossed over his chest and his butt planted against the grill of an F.B.I. vehicle. His gaze scanned the parking lot from beneath a tan ball cap. And as he turned his head, one of the lights flooding the lot shone across the side of his face, illuminating the dark red scar spiking over his jaw and the absence of at least part of his right ear.

"Who is that?" she asked.

"No one."

"What happened to his face?"

Teague's head snapped sideways, his eyes sharp on Alyssa's. "What about it?"

"What do you mean, what about it? He's missing an ear."

Teague turned green. He rubbed his hand over his mouth and closed his eyes for an extra-long second.

"What?" she said. "You didn't notice? Little hard not to notice. That *is* who you were looking at."

"I was hoping . . ."

"You were hoping it wasn't who you thought it was."

His hand slid to his scalp and rubbed. "Fuck me."

"Stop saying that. And why does one man upset you more than a hundred cops?"

Teague didn't answer. He remained silent as he drove, his hands busy in a familiar wringing of the steering wheel, his brow heavy in thought.

As Alyssa's mind turned back to the fiasco they'd just fled, nausea rolled in her belly. She'd just walked away from her chance to escape, and she wasn't sure if the queasiness stemmed from *missing* the opportunity or from nearly *getting* the opportunity.

At the first exit, Teague veered off the freeway and drove half a block to a gas station-slash-mini mart. Her muscles tensed, jutting another round of pain through her torso.

"Can we stop somewhere else?" Alyssa asked. "Anywhere else? I think I'm suffering PTSD."

He parked around the corner from the front door, jammed the car in park and got out without a word. The slam of the door made Alyssa flinch. Instead of coming to her side of the car, he walked directly into the store without looking back.

A fresh sense of uncertainty tightened her chest. He'd left her in the car unattended and uncuffed. She looked out the window at a vacant office building with a FOR RENT sign out front, then to a darkened church next door, the parking lot empty. There was no immediate shelter within running distance, but she should still run. She *should*. So what kept her there?

He wasn't gone long enough for Alyssa's heart to slow to a regular rhythm, let alone for her to form an answer to the question. He approached her side of the car carrying a bottle of water and a newspaper. Popping the door open, he pulled the antibiotics from his pocket and twisted the top off, then held both out to her. When she took them, he closed the door without saying a word and walked around to the driver's side.

He slid into his seat and sat there staring straight ahead without putting the car in drive. His fingers fiddled with the edge of the newspaper in his lap.

Alyssa downed a healthy dose of the fish meds, hoping they didn't kill her, then looked at him again. "You're kind of freaking me out."

"What the hell is PTSD?"

"Post-traumatic stress disorder."

He rolled his eyes, then turned to look at her with a quick snap of his head. "Why'd you do that? At the pet store?"

"I just . . . I don't know. You made it clear you'd die before you went back to prison. I . . . I . . ." *Didn't want to watch you die.* "I didn't want to see anyone get hurt."

The paper crinkled in the quiet car as he dropped it on Alyssa's lap. "Too late for that."

Her gaze fell on the front-page photos of herself and Teague. They'd used her smiling medical graduation photo alongside Teague's mug shot, his mouth tight, his eyes defiant. The stark contrast between their images couldn't have been more blatantly designed to elicit sensationalism.

The headline read, ESCAPED CONVICT FOUND STABBED. The subtitle said, ANOTHER STILL ON THE RUN WITH CONFIRMED ACCOMPLICE.

"I can't *believe* this. *How* does this *happen*?"

"I told you how it happens." He backed out of the parking space and navigated onto the freeway. "It's Titus—the older guard. You can't do anything about it now, but when the time comes, I'll give you enough evidence on the bullshit he pulled inside prison to use as leverage to get him to retract his accusations about the escape, make a public apology or something. Extortion, drug running, more crap than you'd ever believe. And if that brother of yours is half the attorney you say he is, he'll be able to put Titus away until he's a very old man."

"That's like putting a Band-Aid on a severed limb." Alyssa recognized his effort to make amends, but it was way too little, way too late, especially when he'd only added fuel to the fire. "And then there is your money transfer."

He tipped his head in concession. "Yeah, there is that."

She rolled the paper into a tube and chucked it into the backseat. As the sun set against a dark blue sky, sinking behind majestic pines, Alyssa knew her life had changed forever.

"Are you going to tell me who that guy at the pet store was? I think after everything I've been through, I deserve to know what I've really been dragged into here, and I'm getting the impression it's even uglier than it looks on the surface. Which is pretty damn ugly."

Teague's mouth twisted in consideration. "Let's focus on one thing at a time." He shook his head slowly. "I can promise you, *that*, Dr. Foster, is one bridge you'd prefer not to cross."

Eleven

Teague took the Fallen Leaf Road exit off Highway Eighty-nine and slowed until he was crawling alongside the lake. He checked the rearview mirror for other vehicles, but the road remained empty. The sun slumped behind the Sierra Nevadas, casting deep shadows over the valley. As a boy, exploring the surrounding terrain with his best buddy, Quaid Legend, he'd dreaded the loss of sunlight. As a man, with a hostage and a shattered escape plan, he welcomed the darkness.

The car's headlights lit the strip of asphalt, but Teague couldn't see much more than the glow from an occasional porch lamp along the roadside. A recent snowfall had left a few inches of ice over the mountains, and a plow had scraped the white layer off the road and piled it along the borders.

Teague passed the familiar sign: WELCOME TO FALLEN LEAF LAKE, POPULATION 423. The little place had grown since he'd last visited, five years before. Fortunately, 421 of those 423 residents were fair-weather part-timers. They'd all be gone by now. The other two inhabitants were the mom and pop who ran the general store and lived in a dinky cabin on the opposite side of the lake.

The Legend family cabin came into view while Teague was still several hundred yards away. Relief crept in, but he choked it off. That sighting at the pet store made him realize there would be no relief until he was deep in Mexico with Kat.

Vasser. Lieutenant Colonel Jason Vasser. The man who'd interrogated Teague while he'd been in the hospital after the explosion. The man who'd sat in the back of the courtroom during Teague's trial.

The fact that the guy was still hovering five years later brought all the strange circumstances surrounding Desiree's death and the trial swarming back to Teague's already overwhelmed brain.

"Fuck," he muttered under his breath.

His instincts were leading him down a very ugly path. He'd spent years trying to figure out who had set him up and why. The thought it could possibly have been someone connected to the Department of Defense—or so Vasser had claimed at the time—was just too enormous to contemplate.

As he scoured the area for signs of life, something dark and heavy and sinister hovered over Teague's shoulders like a sooty blanket. He didn't expect the cops to look for him here. At least, not initially. And by the time they dug deep enough to consider this place a possible hideout, Teague would be across the border, sipping iced tea, while Kat splashed in the warm waves.

Vasser, however, was another story entirely.

He turned off the headlights and eased off the gas until the car was barely moving and turned into the drive. Stopping halfway up the snowy gravel path, he reached for the gun he'd stashed between the seat and the door panel. With his other hand, Teague flipped the lights on and hit the brights.

The little house appeared in a wash of halogen. No movement. No shadows. No sound. No footsteps or tire tracks in the snow. The porch sat barren. The forest-green shutters were closed and locked over every visible window. A little of Teague's tension eased as he studied the familiar cabin. By the looks of the place, Quaid's family didn't have any plans to return until the first thaw, sometime around May. And

Teague didn't feel the least bit guilty about using the cabin. Quaid would have supported this crazy-ass scheme one hundred and ten percent.

The thought of his long-time friend and fellow firefighter still pinched his heart even five years after Quaid's death. That warehouse fire had damaged the lives of every team member, and the injustice still burned. But he pushed aside the pain and anger, just as he did every day, because there was nothing he could do to change the past.

He left the engine running, the heater on, and climbed out of the Honda. The icy air stung his skin and scraped his throat. With the headlights illuminating the area, Teague held the gun down by his thigh and walked the perimeter of the building, flipped the breakers and found the spare key.

Inside, he pulled space heaters into the two bedrooms and the open living area, turning them on full blast before returning to the car. Alyssa was still asleep. He opened the door and nudged her shoulder.

"Wake up, sleeping beauty, I've got a real bed for you."

She shifted, grimaced, moaned. Sympathy pains twined through Teague's body. The first few days after an injury were always the worst, and he expected the infection to wipe her out before the antibiotics kicked in.

"I know," he said as he tugged on her arms to turn her toward him. "You'll feel better tomorrow."

Her eyes cracked open, hazed and dull, then immediately fell closed. "Where are we now? Siberia?"

"Funny. Somewhere safe. With heat and water and beds and food."

She struggled to her feet, then swayed. Her hand fell against the car to steady herself and a shiver rocked her body. Teague leaned down, tucked one arm behind her shoulders, the other behind her knees and lifted. She relaxed against his body without complaint and laid her head on his shoulder.

Teague climbed the stairs, kicked the front door closed and carried Alyssa into the first bedroom. He dropped her feet to the floor and supported her weight with one hand as he drew back the covers with the other.

She fisted her hands in his shirt and kept her face snuggled against his chest. "Sleep with me."

His breath froze in his lungs. Dick rose to attention. Muscles contracted. Heat raced beneath his skin. That hadn't been the sweetest whisper he'd ever heard. The kind from his dreams. That had been his sick psyche, torturing him again.

"Please?" The test of his inner strength, his character, his moral fiber continued. "I hurt, I'm freezing, I . . . just . . ."

She sighed, the heat of her breath sliding along his skin. He curled his fingers in the covers to keep from curling them into her hair. Kept his body still to keep from rocking and rubbing against her.

"Make me stop hurting." She turned her head, pressed her cheek to his chest and tipped her chin so the tip of her nose grazed his jaw. "Make me forget."

Her hands roamed down his chest, fingers feeling along the muscles of his belly before finding their way beneath his shirt. His stomach muscles jerked. His struggling mind knotted. Warm palms, strong fingers. Rubbing, touching, enticing.

"I know you can," she whispered against his throat.

Hell, yeah. His dick throbbed. Demanding.

Her lips pressed. Kissed. Lifted. Moved. Pressed again.

His mind filled with those secrets he'd shown her earlier. The slide and dash of tongue. Nip and scrape of teeth. Brush and suckle of lips.

Her hands slid around his ribs, nails scratching skin all the way to his back as she aligned her body with his.

Yes. Please. Yes.

No. Don't. Stupid. Don't.

His dick jerked hard. Possessed. Angry.

"Teague?"

A fist grabbed his heart and squeezed. For the love of God, why did she choose this moment to call him by name?

He dropped the covers, and pulled her fully into his arms. Her hands slid up his back along his spine and a long, satisfied sigh exited her lungs. He closed his eyes, swallowed the regret thick in his throat and savored the feel of her slim, strong body against him. Beneath one hand was the narrow waist, curve of spine, swell of hips. Beneath the other, slim shoulders, graceful neck, silk fall of hair.

"You need sleep," he said. "Not me."

He had no idea where that had come from. Some small, sane sliver of himself. Surely not from the animal standing here ready to devour her.

"I know what I need."

Damn, but she was stubborn. He leaned away, pushed her back by the shoulders. As he expected, her gorgeous eyes were dark and angry and confused. Even hurt.

He cupped her face, ran his thumbs over her cheeks, regret thick in his throat. "But you don't know who you're asking to fill those needs."

"Maybe I do. Maybe that's what you're afraid of."

An arrow pierced Teague's gut: bull's-eye.

He pointed at the bed. "Sleep."

She turned away, dropped to the bed and curled onto her side, arms tucked to her torso, knees tight to her belly. Teague slid off her shoes and covered her with the comforter, then pulled two more blankets from the closet and added them to the pile. When he was done, she was nearly invisible beneath the mound.

He left her there with mixed relief and regret. She was too damned perceptive. Too damned insightful. Too damned intelligent. Add to that gorgeous, sexy and freaking willing . . . and he had definitely taken the wrong woman.

Teague swapped the Honda for the four-wheel-drive Jeep Cherokee Quaid's family kept in the detached garage behind the house.

Inside, he got to work filling the hearth, trying like hell to get Alyssa and all she'd offered out of his mind. He forced his thoughts toward the reason he was here, toward the attic access panel over the kitchen entry door. That's all it took to replace the attraction with apprehension.

He'd stored all his precious memories of his past life in that space. More importantly, he'd hidden everything he needed for his new life up there before his trial had started, just in case.

As the fire caught and the sizzle of wood replaced the silence, Teague stood, dusted off his hands and headed toward the kitchen.

The big question that started his heart hammering against his ribs—were his documents still there?

Alyssa was on fire. Flames raced up her leg and across her belly. Panic clawed at her chest. She dropped to the ground, rolled, kicked, and slapped at the fire searing her knee, her thigh, her belly. A figure appeared, a shadow moving toward her. Just as she called out for help, his face came into view.

Teague.

He stood at a distance, firelight reflecting off his skin, lighting his eyes with an eerie glow as he watched her struggle. He reached out to her, but instead of helping, a fireball illuminated the palm of his hand. The flames shot from his fingers and hit Alyssa in the chest. Heat exploded.

Alyssa's eyes popped open. Air rasped in and out of her lungs, fast and painful. Disoriented, she pushed up on her elbows and immediately suffered a stab to her side.

Light drifted through the bedroom door, softly illuminating Alyssa's sparse surroundings. *Somewhere safe.* Teague's words came back to her, and the air left her lungs in one long whoosh as she fell back onto the bed. She closed her eyes. Forced her breath to slow, her mind to clear. A nightmare. Just a nightmare.

The reassurance did nothing to control the quiver along her limbs. She was alone in a remote cabin with a man convicted of murder.

No. It didn't fit.

Or did it?

Her mind returned to his comment when he'd rejected her advance—another nightmare.

I know what I need.

But you don't know who you're asking to fill those needs.

How humiliating. She could blame her behavior on the circumstances, but it didn't ring entirely true. She was attracted to him. Had known what she was asking and what part of her still wanted despite all the unanswered questions. Despite all she didn't know about him.

Alyssa thought of his previous girlfriend, of the horrible way she'd died, and familiar questions surfaced. Had she become a threat to him, as Alyssa was now? She couldn't see any sound reason for Teague to keep her, and he wasn't offering any justification. It didn't matter what she *thought* she saw in the man. What mattered was the risk Alyssa presented to his freedom—the freedom he'd vowed to retain at all costs. Hence the money transfer, the handcuffs, the continued captivity.

She pushed back the covers. As soon as she tried to stand, she realized where the pain in her dream had come from. Stabs and aches and burns erupted with every movement.

The heat she'd imagined had come from the fever still lurking in her body, dampening her skin and clothes with sweat. Clenching her teeth against the pain, she picked up her shoes and made her way down the hall toward a dim light. At the opening to the living room, she peered around the corner. A fire smoldered in the hearth. A single lamp shed light on a sectional sofa, rocking chair, low coffee table and a few file boxes settled by the arm of the couch. All the windows were blocked by exterior shutters.

Teague lay on his back, stretched out on one arm of the L-shaped sofa, arms and ankles crossed. Eyes closed. Breathing even, deep and slow. And he was stripped down to a pair of gray gym shorts. She supposed if she harbored that much body heat on a consistent basis, she'd wear minimal clothing, too. Only she wouldn't look half as good. Man, he was gorgeous with the firelight bouncing over those muscles, creating dramatic shadows in their valleys.

While physical beauty had never been one of the most important elements of attraction for Alyssa, Teague was downright distracting. Evidently, he didn't find her quite as irresistible. Probably for the best.

She scanned the kitchen counter for car keys, then the tables, the floor, the hook by the door. No keys. Looked like she was going it on foot.

Only when her feet were supposed to move toward the door, they stayed planted there in the hallway. She could swear she had an angel sitting on one shoulder and a devil sitting on the other, each urging her in opposite directions.

There was a lot of good in this man, more good than she'd seen in most men. How a woman had died at his hands, in a reportedly brutal fashion, she'd never understand, but her deeply rooted common sense simply wouldn't allow her to stay in a dangerous, potentially life-threatening situation when she had the opportunity to escape, even if another part of her, the rusty emotional part, urged her to stay, to get involved, to help.

Misgivings twisted her guts as Alyssa side-stepped her way to the kitchen door without taking her eyes off Teague. When he hadn't moved so much as an eyelash, she set her shoes on the floor and stepped into them. The fire crackled. Fear spiked in her stomach, then receded to a slow burn as she lifted a heavy jacket off a peg nearby. Still, Teague didn't move. She eased the deadbolt lever to the right, wincing in anticipation of the *click*, but the lock rolled with nothing more than a *shhhhh*.

Alyssa twisted the metal in her hand, and the door cracked open. Purposely avoiding another glance at Teague, she held her breath and slipped out the door, closing it quickly and quietly behind her.

The cold hit her with a clean, icy stab to the throat, then it closed around her in one frigid sheet, eking out a violent, full-body shiver. She hustled into the jacket and pulled it tight, fumbling with the zipper as she tip-toed down the steps. She scanned the area and found nothing but darkness. No streetlights, no other homes or structures, no cars. Nothing but black pine trees silhouetted against a navy sky, the sliver of moon her only light.

She had no idea where she was, but instinct led her down the drive while another part of her mind nagged, *You impulsive idiot, get your ass back in the house with the man who hasn't once intentionally hurt you.*

Eventually, she had to reach a road. Unless she froze to death first, which was a very real possibility she hadn't considered. As she moved, her traitorous mind kept at her, reminding her of all Teague had done for her—every instance he'd gone above and beyond, every offer of comfort, every sweet touch or kind word.

To escape the haunting voice, she eased into a light jog. Her stiff body protested, but she ignored it. For all of sixty seconds. Then she was out of breath from the altitude, her throat raw from the frozen air. Her teeth chattered as she dropped back into a quick walk, pulling her hands into the sleeves of the jacket to protect her now-aching fingers.

I've never hit a woman in all my thirty-four years and I'm not going to start with you.

Alyssa stopped in her snowy tracks. The voice in her head came out of nowhere. Teague's voice. She'd believed him in that moment. The statement had been made with spontaneity and sincerity. But if he'd never hit a woman, then he couldn't have beaten his former girlfriend, Desiree. Couldn't have murdered her.

Is that true? Did you really . . . do *that?*

You tell me, Alyssa. Did I?

The voices rattled around in her brain as she turned in a slow circle.

Looks like I should go back to expecting you to think just like everyone else.

Her breath created billows of icy clouds in the clear, frozen air. She glanced at the cabin, so quiet and serene in the distance. Something deep inside pulled at her to go back. And it pulled hard. She looked over her shoulder toward the wilderness. The only thing urging her in that direction was obligation. What she thought she *should* do. Going back to Teague was what she *wanted*.

She groaned as she dragged her feet in the direction of the house. "I'm s-so s-s-screwed."

Something rustled in the trees. Alyssa whipped toward the sound, lost her balance and stumbled. Her butt ended up in a mound of snow, her hands submerged in an attempt to break her fall. Her ribs jammed her injury, spearing pain through her side and sucking the wind from her chest. Another rustle sounded, closer. A low growl floated out of the darkness. Panic cinched her chest.

She scrambled to get back on her feet, but kept slipping on icy snow pack. By the time she succeeded, her jeans were soaked, her hands scraped, her shoes filled with ice.

Another growl sounded in the midst of more rustling. Closer. Maybe. She couldn't tell. She could see the cabin steps now. Just a little farther.

The scuffle of paws on ice rippled through the night, followed by a howl so high, loud and long, the echo shimmied down her neck and rocked her body.

At the base of the stairs, Alyssa swiveled toward the sound and steadied herself with a hand on the banister.

A wolf trotted out of the forest and crept along the edge of the moonlight shimmering through the treetops. The animal was silvery gray with a white undercoat and shiny yellow eyes.

A high-pitched sound eked from Alyssa's throat.

The animal's shoulders hunched, head dropped, muzzle peeled back, baring a mouthful of pointed white teeth. It let out a throaty growl and approached.

Her fingers tightened on the banister. Panic sliced her thoughts into fragments. She wouldn't make it to the door before those teeth sank into her leg.

Another shadowed animal appeared at the tree line, tilted its head back and belted an ear-piercing howl.

The outside light flipped on, blinding Alyssa. She threw her arm over her eyes. The bay cut off midstream.

"Get out of here, you stupid sonsofbitches." Teague's voice bellowed over her head, ricocheting off the trees and fading into the forest. "She's no meal, for God's sake. Look at her."

Heavy footfalls pounded down the stairs, joining the wolves' retreating barks and whimpers.

Frozen in place, Alyssa watched the carnivores disappear.

"You goddamned idiot." Teague's angry voice bit at her ear. "What in the hell is wrong with you? Get in the house. You're going to freeze to death out here."

"T-too l-l-late." She tilted her head back and zeroed in on his eyes, filled with irritated indignation, as if she was nothing but a nuisance. Why had she turned around again? "Y-y-you're what's w-wrong with m-me, you j-j-jackass."

He rolled his eyes. "Come on. It's seven fricking degrees out here." As he seemed to have done a dozen times in the last two days, he lifted her into his arms without effort. "Yell at me in the house."

Alyssa couldn't find the motor skills to speak. She'd never known how physically painful the cold could be until she ached with it. Or the way true terror ripped from the inside out until she'd been so completely vulnerable to those wolves. Her jaw felt frozen into place, so many parts of her on the throbbing edge of numbness. Her mind wasn't working well enough to drum up treatment strategies, but she knew getting her body back to regular temperature would involve hot water and a lot of pain.

Teague bumped her ribs as he started up the stairs. A pathetic moan bubbled out of her throat, drowned by the thud of the front door hitting the wall as it opened, then slammed at her back. The warmth of the house immediately wrapped around her, and Alyssa groaned at the beauty of it. What had ever possessed her to leave?

Teague set her down on the sofa in front of the fire. "Don't move."

He disappeared down the hall and Alyssa sat watching the fire in the hearth, wishing she could jump into the flames. As her body temperature rose, she shivered uncontrollably.

Teague returned with a space heater in one hand and a stack of towels in the other. After plugging in the heater and pointing it directly at Alyssa, he dropped to his knees in front of her. He pulled off her shoes and socks, then tugged the jacket off her shoulders and threw it aside. He curled his fingers into the sleeves of her shirt at her wrist and pulled one arm out, then the other.

Alyssa gurgled a protest. Her arms were as stiff as tree limbs, her teeth clenched as if the hinges of her jaw were rusted shut. With one pull, her shirt came off over her head and joined the jacket on the floor.

He picked up a towel, threw it over her head and started scrubbing. Icy droplets from her hair needled her back like little knives. "S-s-s-so c-cold."

She barely got the murmur from her mouth. Nothing was working right—not her body, her voice, and most definitely not her mind.

"I know. Give me a minute." Teague slid the towel off her head, made one swipe of her back and tossed it away. "Lie down."

She cast a sidelong look at the sofa, wanting more than anything to obey. "I c-c-can't move."

Teague lifted her legs and eased her back. Alyssa rolled onto her side and closed her eyes, soaking in the feel of the lush, warm corduroy fabric. Then his hands were on her again, pulling at her sweats. Before she could push his hands away, her pants were gone.

"Everything has to go," he said. "You're soaked."

With a simple flick of his fingers, the knot she'd tied in her pathetic excuse of a bra opened. Alyssa pulled in a surprised breath as he yanked it off. Then his hands were at her hips. A second later, her panties had disappeared. She found herself caught between shock and embarrassment before something soft layered over her, cocooning her in warmth. A breath of relief slipped through clenched teeth. Teague stood in front of her, bare-chested, his hands unbuttoning his jeans.

Excitement spiked in her chest, and melted into her pelvis. "W-what are you d-d-d-doing?"

"Getting you warm as fast as possible." He toed out of his boots and dropped his jeans.

Alyssa was too exhausted, and honestly, too interested, to look away. He was so beautiful, like a work of art she could study for endless hours. The tattoos were shadows of her imagination now, his body perfectly pristine and tan as if he spent a lot of time outdoors.

"W-w-warm w-w-water," she said. Preferably with him in it, too.

"The water heater is ancient." In an abrupt move, he lifted the blanket and lay on the sofa alongside her. "No warm water until tomorrow morning at the earliest."

He pressed his body full length against hers, worked his arms around her back, laid his top leg over hers and ratcheted his body close. Alyssa sucked in a breath at the feel of him, so supremely warm, all hard muscle and soft skin.

Oh, man. Okay. This worked, too. Maybe even better.

"Jesus Christ," he growled. "You're a fucking ice cube."

"S-s-stop—"

"Swearing," he finished for her. "I know, I know."

His hands were everywhere, sliding, rubbing. And every place of her that he touched warmed instantly, the feeling so primitive, so perfect. Alyssa pried her arms away from her chest and slid them around his back, pulling him until the flat plane of his chest pressed to hers. His warmth instantly seeped into her skin. This was just what she'd wanted a few hours ago. Now she was too damned frozen to take advantage.

"Oh, my, G-god," she murmured against his chest. "You feel so g-good."

She shifted closer, a leech searching for heat, and she found it when his hips aligned with hers. His erection pressed along her thigh, pumping heat through his cotton briefs and directly into Alyssa's skin. A mixture of excitement and nervousness tangled in her throat. His arms tightened around her on an irritated groan, and he tried to shift his hips away. But with the edge of the sofa at his back, he didn't get far.

"Stop wiggling, for God's sake. You're going to push me off the couch." With a kick of the blankets, he tightened the fabric around their feet, then rubbed the arch of his foot over her instep and toes. And somehow managed to put space between her hips and his. "Your hands and feet are the parts I'm most worried about."

Those should be the least of his worries. He should be concerned with the craving deep in her belly, the one that made her mouth want to taste and her hands want to touch. Between the moment he'd dragged her into the house and now, one vital fact she'd suspected had been confirmed: He had no plans to hurt her. She'd given him the perfect opportunity to get rid of her quickly, quietly, permanently, and without any involvement. All he'd had to do was leave her out there. Yet he'd saved her, not only from the wolves and the elements but, ultimately, from herself.

She pried one hand from his grasp, slid it up his chest and around the back of his neck. With her face pressed between his thick pectoral muscles, Alyssa rubbed her cheek against his warmth and strength. Dragged in the smell of hotel soap lingering from his shower that morning and his purely male and unique scent.

She hummed in pleasure. "How can you c-create so much h-heat?"

"We've been over this, remember?" His voice sounded thick and rough. "You know, my father, Hades, god of the fires of hell and all that?"

She would have at least snickered, only her face would crack. She wedged her other arm underneath him, trying to align every inch of her skin with his. He might not have had much room, but he managed to scoot away again.

Frustrated with both the lingering chill and his resistance, she pulled on his shoulder to roll him into her. "Hold m-me."

"I am," he snapped.

"Closer. I'm s-so cold."

"Honey." His voice dropped to a raspy growl. He slid a thigh between hers, wrapped his arm around her back and pressed their bodies together. "We can't get a whole lot closer."

She'd like to prove him wrong. Dammit. Only he was still resisting. And she just didn't get it. She might not be a Swedish goddess like Hannah, but she wasn't the Hunchback of Notre Dame, either.

She tightened her arms around him, soaking in his heat, revelling in the feel of him while the fire inside kicked up a notch. He smelled good, he felt good, he looked good. He was the only good thing in the moment. She couldn't look ahead, couldn't look back, or everything fell apart. All she could do was live right now.

He wanted her, too. There had been hunger and passion in their kiss earlier in the day. There had been ownership and control in the way he touched and maneuvered her body in his arms. There had been demand and need in that thick, heavy shaft pressed against her pelvis.

Her thoughts raised her body temperature, and closing that last bit of distance between them gained appeal by the moment.

There was no time left for second-guessing herself. She knew what she wanted and she was going to reach for it. Now.

TWELVE

Alyssa let her hand drift down Teague's ribs, her fingers playing along each indentation as she kissed his chest.

He groaned, a pained, frustrated sound. His hips rocked and pressed into hers. His erection was thick and hard and so damn hot. Now this was more like it. Alyssa absorbed the deep zing of pleasure pulsing through her core.

His fingers curved around her upper arm and pushed her back. His eyes skimmed her face and paused on her mouth.

Yes. Kiss me.

"What happened to that line in the sand?" he asked.

Damn you.

"What line?" She added pressure to the back of his head to bring him closer, craving the feel of his mouth.

His hand fisted in her hair. *Yes. Yes. Yes.* Her mouth parted in anticipation of the pressure of his lips, the swirl of his tongue.

But he pulled back instead of diving in. "You just went out in ten-degree weather to get away from me, remember?"

Why was he being such a pain in the ass? That throbbing shaft pressed against her leg made it clear he wanted her. He'd been in prison for years. But maybe he didn't want to want her. Or maybe it wasn't *her* he wanted at all. A familiar determination prompted her to slide the inside of her thigh along his. "I changed my mind, didn't I?"

His brows dipped. "What?"

"I came back. That's what I was doing when you found me. Coming back, not running."

He continued to stare at her, his expression shifting from confusion to disbelief to fear and finally to anger.

"Fucking A." He released her hair and rolled his shoulder back so their bodies were still touching, but not in the most sensitive areas. With gentle pressure, he pushed her head to pillow it on his shoulder. "For a smart woman, that has to be the stupidest thing you've done so far."

Her chest pinched. Anger rushed up to soothe the hurt of yet another rejection. "What? Running or coming back?"

"Both. Didn't take you long to figure out you'd freeze or be eaten, huh?"

She wasn't quite ready to declare her faith in his innocence. Not because she didn't believe, but because she doubted he'd believe her. "Maybe I decided since you're the one who created this mess for me, you should be the one to get me out of it."

"I don't know how the hell you expect me—"

"You'll find a way. I'll make sure of it."

"I'm sure you'll do your damnedest."

"Have I told you lately what a jerk you are?"

"Not in the last hour, but I think it's been implied from day one."

A hard shiver came out of nowhere and racked her body. Teague tightened his arm around her shoulders and made a sweep down her arm with one big, warm hand.

She cuddled closer, his warmth finally settling in and easing her muscles. "I didn't come back to fight with you."

He didn't respond, but the silence remained tense, as if all the unspoken issues between them sat like parrots on swings swaying above their heads.

Teague continued to stroke her back and arms, and she tried to think about something other than the way she felt pressed against the hard muscle of his chest, his ribs, his thigh. But every other topic that came to mind brought trauma. Her work, her future, her family.

Alyssa's thoughts turned to the same topics for Teague, which brought a flood of questions, the first and foremost centering around this Kat—evidently the whole reason Alyssa was here in the first place. And the sudden realization that she might have very well been throwing herself at a married or otherwise committed man made her feel queasy.

Alyssa decided to drag the biggest parrot off its perch and start plucking feathers.

"You must really love her, this Kat." She murmured the thought, wondering, maybe hoping, that was the reason he'd rejected her. "I mean, it takes a big man to, you know, overlook the fact that the woman he loves has been with another man or might love another man."

Teague's hand stilled. His body tightened. "It's not like that." His voice was oddly soft. Filled with an emotion that reached out and tugged at Alyssa's heart. "And I do love her. More than I could ever explain."

Not like what? was the real question she wanted to ask, but she already sensed he was shutting down. "Does she know how much you're risking to get back to her?"

"That doesn't matter." His tone took on a determined edge. "All that matters is that we spend the rest of our lives together."

Alyssa's eyes floated closed. She would have to get stuck with the best-looking man around who still had morals after being imprisoned for three years. She thought of his conversation with Luke. Teague had threatened to kill himself if his freedom was placed at risk. What would he do if Kat rejected him?

"Will she be there when you get wherever it is you're going?" she asked.

His fingers increased the pressure over her shoulder blade, then released. "She'll be there."

The surety, the finality, the forceful determination in his

voice made Alyssa pull back and look up at him. The firelight cast shadows over the planes of his face, making him look fierce in the sexiest way.

"Teague." She waited until he tilted his chin and looked at her. "You have to be prepared for the possibility that she doesn't want the same things you want. It's been a long time."

His eyes glazed over as if he was remembering, then hardened with resolve. "She wants to be with me. I have no doubts about that. We love each other—unconditionally."

Unconditionally. Envy niggled deep in Alyssa's psyche. The only person who'd ever loved her to that degree, had been her father. But somehow her mother had always interfered with that love.

Alyssa closed her eyes, shutting out the ever-present source of disillusionment. She shifted closer to Teague, feeling warmer by the moment.

"She must be something," she murmured. "Two men who love her enough to fight for her."

Teague's hand lifted to Alyssa's head and stroked down her hair, then paused at the ends to twirl a lock around his fingers. The gesture was so sweet, it sent uncomfortable mixed messages considering the conversation.

"Are you going to marry her?" She dreaded the answer, but had to know. "I mean, after going to these lengths to get back to her, you must be planning on marrying her, right?"

Teague had known this would happen. It hadn't taken long to realize Alyssa's curiosity would bring them to this subject.

He breathed a frustrated sigh and pulled away from her. He couldn't take it anymore. Her body was the most beautiful thing he'd ever seen and every time he closed his eyes, he saw it again as he'd undressed her. With all that luscious skin and those perfect curves pressed against him, he was about to go insane.

Not to mention her advance. The warmth of her lips on his chest, the slide of her leg over his, it was enough to make him come in his shorts. Now she was pushing about Kat, and the two thoughts combined brought up too much frustration to bear. Then there was the fear she'd unearthed—one he'd kept buried somewhere deep and dark—that Kat wouldn't want him when he came for her. . . . He planted his feet on the floor and stood.

"Wait," she complained from the sofa. "Don't go."

He glanced back to find her reaching for him. And Jesus-God-Almighty she was so beautiful. And so naked. And warm. And soft. And . . . *fuck*. It took everything he had to turn away and crouch in front of the hearth to fiddle with the fire.

Part of him wished she'd just kept going, escaped tonight and gone back to where she belonged. But another part of him ached at the thought of her absence. And, logistically, it was too soon. He needed her to stay quiet a while longer so he could follow through with his plans. But, hell . . . keeping her close under these circumstances . . . Yeah, complete hell.

"I'm sorry," she said. "I don't mean to upset you. I just want you to realize that things may not go your way."

"That's an interesting comment coming from you."

"Don't get all pissy. I'm worried about what you're going to face when you see her again. I'd rather not have to witness you getting your heart broken or have to deal with the fall-out."

"When did you turn into Miss Compassion?"

"You know I'm right. You've considered the possibility or you wouldn't be so defensive."

He looked over his shoulder. She was still turned on her side, huddling beneath the blanket, her tousled black hair spilling everywhere, those light eyes sparking with what had become a familiar look of determination.

Teague didn't want to think about the repercussions of failure when it came to getting Kat back, because if it didn't happen, there was only one option, and the thought of putting a bullet in his brain wasn't particularly appealing.

"Kat's my flesh and blood. She's my daughter. She belongs with me. Period. I *will* get her back." He turned back to the fire and tossed on three more logs.

"D-daughter?" she squeaked. "She's your *daughter*?" The shock in her voice made a grin turn the edges of his mouth. "You have a daughter? How old is she? Why does whoever this Luke is have her? And where the hell is your *wife*?"

His grin dimmed to a bitter smirk. Those inevitable questions were exactly why he'd avoided the subject. He heaved a breath, pushed to his feet and turned back toward the sofa. Each time she looked at him, her gaze traveled over his body with such hunger. Hunger that in turn brought the lust he'd been harboring to the surface.

When her eyes reached his face again, she veiled them. "*Are* you married?"

He thought of Suzanna. She'd been gone so long now, he sometimes believed she was a figment of his imagination.

"No, I'm not married, but I *am* tired. And I don't want to be peppered with questions."

She pushed herself up on her elbow. The blanket slipped off her shoulder and dipped at her chest. Teague told himself to look away, but didn't. Couldn't.

"You can't just dump that bombshell and expect me to accept it," she said. "You've put me through a hell of a lot the last couple of days. The least you can do is tell me *why*."

"Playing the guilt card," he said. "That's good."

She lowered her chin and glared at him, then sat up, swinging her feet to the floor, holding the blanket up around her chest. Her dark hair fell over her forehead, skimmed her cheeks, drifted down her shoulders.

Teague's fingers curled into his palms. He wanted her so badly, she eclipsed all rational thought. He'd bet she'd be a fireball in bed. A woman who gave as much as she took. He pictured sweeping passion and erotic satisfaction. And she was five feet away, completely naked and willing. Even inviting.

And that would be a really stupid move. If he started something with this woman, he was well aware there would be consequences—mind, body and soul. Yet . . .

The ring of the phone startled him back from the edge of fantasy. A streak of panic shot through his chest as he turned toward the kitchen, where an old rotary hung on the wall.

The phone rang again. Not the kitchen phone. Teague swiveled toward the sound, but the ring traveled with him. His jeans. The pocket of his jeans. The cell?

"Aren't you going to answer it?" Alyssa asked.

He dug into his pocket, pulled the phone out and looked at the display, which read "private caller" with no number. He picked up the gun and went to the front door, tilted his head and listened. No voices, no crunching footsteps, no car engines. With the phone still ringing in his hand, he cracked the front door and peered through the inch-wide space. Nothing but blackness beyond the porch.

He exhaled, long and slow, closed and relocked the door. Then he punched the answer button on the cell and put it to his ear, but didn't speak.

"Teague?" Seth's voice drained all the remaining tension from Teague's shoulders. "You there?"

"How did you get this number?"

"It's called caller I.D. It was in effect long before you went to prison."

Yeah, but Teague had thought the number on a throwaway cell was blocked. "Who else knows I called you? Who else has this number?"

"No one, shithead. You think I ran around the neighborhood telling everyone that I'm taking Kat to see her escaped convict father?"

Teague closed his eyes on the rush of excitement, his anxiety from moments before forgotten. He could almost feel

Kat's warm little body against his chest, her arms wrapped so tightly around his neck she choked off his air, just like the last time he'd seen her in the prison visitation room. "When and where? I'll be there."

"Tomorrow," Seth grumbled. "I convinced Tara I needed a little time alone with Kat before . . . before . . . *fuck*."

Teague could relate to the pain in Seth's voice. He'd lived it every day for the last three years. A certain amount of guilt nagged in the back of his mind. But either Luke would take Kat away from Seth or Teague would.

"Okay," Teague said. "That's doable. Give me the details."

"I'll have to call you tomorrow. The atmosphere around here is volatile. Tara's been under so much pressure. She's anxious and . . . Anyway, I have to play it by ear to gauge everyone's mood."

Teague ground his teeth. "Call me by eight to let me know what's going on. I'm going crazy here."

"Fine." Seth sounded distracted. "What are you going to do now? After you see Kat, I mean?"

Teague had more than a little doubt about that moment himself, the moment he'd have to take Kat from Seth and walk away. He only hoped Seth would see the rightness of Teague's plan.

"I'm still working that out. Just focus on Tara. She's the one who needs you now." He closed his eyes and scratched at the new hair growth on his scalp. "I'm sorry it all turned out like this. Sorry it's been so hard on you two."

"Not your fault," Seth mumbled. "Talk to you tomorrow."

Teague disconnected and stared at the phone a moment. He dropped his head back, closed his eyes and hissed, "Yessssssssssss."

"What was that about?"

Teague startled back to the present at the sound of Alyssa's voice. For a moment, he'd forgotten she was even there. But it only took one look at her huddled in that blanket, the firelight playing over her beautiful face and all that dark hair to remember where his mind had been before the phone call.

"That was about something finally going right."

Alyssa floated out of sleep gradually, like a diver breaking the surface of the water. She didn't open her eyes, but snuggled into the warmth surrounding her. She knew exactly where she was and whose lap her head rested on. And this time she didn't wake fearing him.

He'd stayed in the living room with her all night, made sure she was warm, continually monitored her for fever, checked her stitches twice and plied her with ibuprophen and antibiotics. In between, he'd spent long moments with healing fingers stroking her injury, his palm laid over the stitches. Not once had he attempted to take advantage of the situation. Much to her disappointment.

In fact, he'd refused to climb back under the same blanket with her after his phone call and had taken up residence on the other side of the sectional sofa. At some point during the night, he'd fallen into the corner seat and laid his head back. Alyssa had seen the opportunity and scuttled close until her cheek lay against the supple warmth of his thigh.

Now, as she lay curled as close to him as she could get, the most comfortable she'd been in days, Teague's fingers toyed with her hair. He picked up a strand, ran it through his fingers, then curled the tip round and round before doing it all over again. Continuously.

She didn't know what it was exactly about the gesture that made her want to purr like a kitten. The touch was sweet and endearing, intimate and loving. It was something no man had ever done before. In fact, none of the other men in her life had ever acknowledged her softer side. No one except her father. Maybe that's why Teague could see it, because he was the father of a daughter himself. One risking the very freedom he swore he'd never jeopardize to get back to his baby. A fact that twisted her image of the man a hundred and eighty degrees.

Alyssa repositioned her head on Teague's thigh, rubbing her cheek against the muscle, tipping her nose to his skin and breathing him in. Warm. Masculine. She opened her eyes, and took a moment to let them drift over the small room. Since there was no source of natural light, it looked exactly as it had the night before. "What time is it?"

Teague lifted the cell he held in his hand and looked at the display. "Seven-fifty-seven."

The tightness of his voice exposed the impatience he was stifling as he waited for his call.

Alyssa looked up at him. His eyes were as sharp as an eagle's, clear and bright, the color she imagined the sky would be today. His jaw ticked beneath the stubble of overnight beard. The hair on his head was already half an inch long, and it was coming in lighter than she'd expected, more golden than brown.

"Did you sleep at all?" she asked.

"Some."

"You're in another talkative mood."

His eyes flicked down to meet hers, then rolled away. "Don't tell me you're a morning person."

The gesture made her wonder more about his daughter. "Does Kat look like you or her mother?"

He hesitated. "Her mother. Dark hair, brown eyes, fair skin."

Wow, he'd actually answered her. She felt a sense of accomplishment. Wanted to push forward with questions about Kat's mother, but knew she'd instantly stop the flow of information.

"Straight or wavy?" she asked.

"What?"

"Her hair. Straight or wavy?"

"Wavy. Curly, actually." His voice softened. "Hard to get a brush through it some days."

"Hmm. Turned-up nose? Freckles?"

"No. She's got delicate little features and perfect skin with these cheeks that are constantly pink." He sighed. "She's beautiful."

The love in his voice tugged at her. "I bet she is. Is she shy or friendly?"

"A social butterfly. She makes friends with everyone she meets. Totally open. No fear. Starts up conversations in the supermarket line."

"How old?"

"Almost six."

Which meant she'd been only two when he'd gone to prison. Probably just a baby when the crime occurred. "She's in kindergarten then?"

"Next fall. Her birthday missed the cut-off." His voice turned distracted. He lifted the phone and looked at the display, mumbling, "Come on, Seth."

Alyssa waited, letting the comfort of their conversation sink in. She snuggled against his leg again, but her mind couldn't stop wondering how he had possibly been accused of killing his girlfriend.

"Who is Seth to you?" she asked.

"A friend." The clipped tone was back, warning her off the subject.

"And Luke?"

He hesitated. "My former brother-in-law."

So he *had* been married. "Your wife's brother. Kat's uncle, then."

"Yeah."

There was bitterness in the word. A world of conflict and hurt between them. It killed Alyssa not to be able to uncover the cause.

"Why is Kat with Luke and Seth and not her mother?" She half expected her question to kill the conversation altogether.

"Because she's dead." Teague slid his leg out from beneath her head and shifted to the edge of the sofa. "And before you ask, no, I didn't kill her. She committed suicide when Kat was a baby."

Alyssa sat up, but before she could find any words in her shocked brain, Teague's cell rang. He stiffened, the muscles across his shoulders and back tensing.

He jabbed at the phone and put it to his ear. "Seth?"

The other man's voice filtered to Alyssa from the earpiece, garbled and inaudible.

"What do you mean, you don't know where she is?" Teague pressed his free hand to his forehead. "Where in town? How long will she be?"

Seth said something Alyssa couldn't make out, then she caught: ". . . will have to call you . . ."

"You're not fucking with me, are you, Seth?"

Alyssa laid her hand on his back. He jumped and twisted toward her, frowning.

"Don't piss him off," Alyssa whispered. "He won't work with you."

He closed his eyes, tipped his head back and clenched his teeth. "I'm sorry, man. I didn't mean it that way. I'm just . . . I miss her so much. I need to see her."

". . . couple hours . . ." Seth said. ". . . promise to call . . ."

Teague hit the disconnect button with excessive force and swore under his breath. He stood and pulled on his jeans without looking at her.

"Go take a shower," he muttered. "I'll make breakfast."

"With what? There can't be any fresh food here."

"I'll manage."

She pushed up on her elbow, hugging the blanket to her chest. His physical absence left her chilled despite the fire or the blanket or the fact that the old baseboard heaters combined with the space heaters were finally warming up the cabin. The "hot" part of a shower didn't sound bad, except she knew the "shower" part would hurt like hell.

"Will the water be hot yet?" she asked.

"Enough for a quick shower, at least." He wandered into the small kitchen and pulled the refrigerator open, peering inside. "Don't expect to spend all day in there."

She pushed to her feet and wrapped the blanket tightly around her body. Teague stood in the kitchen wearing only jeans hanging low on his hips. He reached for an upper cabinet and rummaged through the contents. Alyssa watched the play of muscle beneath his skin, appreciating the taper of his shoulders to his waist, the length of his legs.

"What did he say?" She knew the answer but wanted to see what Teague told her.

"Tara took Kat into town to run errands. He doesn't know when they'll be back, so he can't pick a time or place for us to meet."

He sounded disgruntled and impatient. But he wasn't the only one. She looked at the sweatpants laid out on the table in front of the fire where Teague had put them the night before.

"Are my clothes dry?" she asked.

"Not yet. You can look in the closets to see if there's anything you can wear, but I doubt it. None of the men who came here were small."

Well, that explained the clearly male décor. "Why didn't anyone bring his wife or girlfriend here?"

Teague pulled a can from the cupboard, set it on the counter and started searching the next. "It's a hunting and fishing cabin."

"No girls allowed."

"Something like that."

"Is it yours?" she asked.

"No."

"Your family's?"

"No." He looked at her over his shoulder. "Go take your shower."

Frustration consolidated into anger. "I know you have a lot at stake here, but so do I. I've already put up with a hell of a lot. I really don't need your attitude. So stuff it."

Alyssa turned and headed for the hallway, muttering, "Jerk."

In the bathroom, she slammed the door. In a completely idiotic move, she pushed in the flimsy lock on the handle, which gave her an irrational sense of satisfaction.

Teague obviously didn't need her. He, evidently, didn't want her either. And in a matter of hours, if he'd been honest with her yesterday, she'd be returned to her old life and he'd be nothing but a memory.

So, okay. She didn't need to be banged over the head to take the hint. What she needed to do was stop thinking about him, why he'd done what he'd done or what he was going to do about his daughter and start focusing on her own problems. On the things she could fix. Namely, what the hell she was going to do regarding the mess he'd made of her career.

Alyssa flipped the shower on and shed her blanket. This wouldn't feel good, but what about the last few days had felt good? For that matter, what about the last few months had felt good?

Her life was screwed.

But that was about to change.

She wouldn't lose all she'd worked for without one hell of a fight.

Thirteen

Teague opened the freezer door and surveyed the contents. His stomach jittered like it had the day Kat was born. He felt all the same crazy emotions at the prospect of seeing her again now, and dreaded the drastic measures he'd have to take to actually get Seth to let her go. The thought of his lifelong friend explaining the loss of Kat to his wife made Teague sick to his stomach.

He tossed bacon in the microwave, telling himself he had to do what he had to do. Kat was his daughter. His *life*. He'd been there for her first diaper rash, her first smile, her first ear infection, her first tooth, her first steps, her first words, her first tantrum. All while trying to keep his career intact and managing Suzanna's medications and ultimate hospitalizations.

Teague's mind drifted back to the night before, to the man who'd been at the motel, the same one who'd caught his eye at the pet store, rekindling ugly memories. Lingering questions resurfaced. Suzanna had been struggling with depression for a long time, but she'd gotten progressively worse after that warehouse fire. If he hadn't been called out that night, would his wife still be alive? He'd never know.

He moved through breakfast preparations in a fog. His mind bounced from Luke to Seth to Tara to Kat and lingered on Alyssa. She was such an intricate, fascinating, frustrating, maddeningly beautiful woman. Yes, he'd been imprisoned for three years. Yes, he'd probably react to any woman. But what had developed between them over the last two days was far more complex than simple physical chemistry.

"Okay, look." Alyssa's voice brought his attention around. She stood near the counter, waving a hairbrush in one hand. "I'm not going to keep doing this in the dark. I want answers and I won't let up until I get them."

She was wearing jeans that rode low on her hips with her pink-painted toes peeking out beneath the hems. A long-sleeved, deep green, v-neck sweater clung to the breasts that had been pressed against his chest last night and a tight abdomen he'd seen and felt firsthand. Hot damn, she looked good in clothes that fit her cute little body.

"Where'd you get those?" He shifted on his feet to relieve the sudden tension in his groin and turned back to the griddle.

"Bedroom closet. I hate to tell you this, but one of the boys has been sneaking girls into the fort."

"Seems times have changed." Teague waved the spatula at the table. "Sit down, food's ready."

"Did you hear me?"

"How could I not hear all ninety-eight pounds of you threatening all two-hundred pounds of me?"

"A hundred-and-twenty pounds, thank you."

"Not even after you ate every scrap of food on that table."

He set the pancakes down in the only vacant spot on the table. Alyssa stared at the feast in amazed confusion.

"How could you possibly . . . ? Where did you get all this . . . ?" Her stomach rumbled so loud the sound drowned out the still-sizzling griddle. She put a hand over her belly, her cheeks blushing to a beautiful hue. "Oh, my God. I didn't realize how hungry I was until I saw this food."

Teague didn't wait for her. He sat and forked steaming pancakes onto his plate. Alyssa set her brush on the counter and pulled out a chair. She heaped two ladlefuls of scrambled eggs onto her plate, plucked up four strips of thick-sliced bacon, then started in on the pancakes.

"Eggs," she mumbled around her food. "Where did you get eggs?"

"They're powdered. That fish food must have worked because you've got to be damn good and hungry if you're eating those without noticing. Your eyes are about twelve times the size of your stomach."

She pointed at the dark circles embedded in the hotcakes. "What are these?"

"Blueberries."

She smirked at him. "These can't be from a powder."

"No, those are from the freezer. You don't get out much, do you, doctor?"

"Ha-ha." Alyssa clopped off a chunk of butter and slathered it over the cakes, gushed on syrup and butchered them as she tried to cut them into bite-sized pieces. Then she heavily salted her eggs. Once the preparations were done, she started eating. Or rather devouring.

With a strip of bacon in one hand, her fork in the other, she started a two-handed method of eating Teague had never seen outside a firehouse. A lopsided grin pulled at his lips as he watched.

She flicked an absent glance his way. "What?"

He chuckled, reached across the table and wiped a smudge of syrup from the corner of her mouth with his knuckle. "You look like a chipmunk hoarding for winter."

She scowled. "Mind your own food and leave me alone."

Once she'd demolished the quadruple stack of cakes, she reached for more. And more butter. And more syrup.

"For a doctor, you aren't very heart healthy."

She looked up at him through her lashes with a don't-start expression. "At the moment, the longevity of my life based on my diet isn't among my top concerns."

Her quip brought their reality into focus and punched a

hole in Teague's distraction. He set down his fork and started clearing the table.

"Hey." Alyssa grabbed the edge of the bowl holding the scrambled eggs. "I'm not done with those."

He set it back down, shaking his head. "You eat as much as two of my biggest firefighters. You're going to make yourself sick."

She swallowed a mouthful of food. "What I'm sick of is being kept in the dark. I want to know what you're planning."

Teague ignored her demand as he washed the frying pan.

"You're going to meet Seth and see Kat," she said. "That much I've figured out. I don't see how you think this will work. You know it's only a matter of time before you're caught. When that happens, you'll be putting your daughter in danger—"

"I don't need you pointing out the pitfalls of my situation."

"*Our* situation. You decided to implicate me in a crime. *You* have no choice but to learn to be a team player."

"Team player?" He swung around to face her. "You're not clear on what's going on here. We're in completely different situations. I'm *going after* something. You're *fighting against* something. A team has a common goal. We aren't a team, Alyssa.

"You have to know that no matter what happens now, your so-called salvage process isn't going to be as simple as holding a press conference and declaring your innocence. This is going to be complicated. There will be repercussions, no matter what. Your brother will tell you that. We're talking about the State of California here. We're talking about the prison system. A secret society of guards who've made a pact that what happens in prison stays in prison. This is not a he-said, she-said deal. They have teams of attorneys that will blow your brother away. They have union attorneys that will jump onboard. You're fighting a system of people who watch each other's backs, a system you won't—can't—break into unless you know someone on the inside."

He turned back to the sink, reliving the gnawing frustration he'd experienced in the search for answers to that life-altering fire—the one he was sure, more sure with every passing day, had put him in this situation. No one could stonewall like the government. And, not for the first time, Teague wondered if Desiree would still be alive if he hadn't gone to her for help in getting his answers.

He chucked the soapy sponge in the sink. Bubbles puffed into the air, splattered over the counter, and his shirt. With his hands gripping the sink's edge, he turned his head and met that direct, intelligent, determined gaze of hers. "I'm trying to enlighten you on how the criminal *justice* system works. How the *government* works. Believe what you want, Lys. Just get your shoes on. We're going out."

He reached over the counter, pulled a khaki-colored baseball cap off a hook and frisbeed it to her across the kitchen. "And throw this on, too. Cover up that camera-ready face."

Lys. His use of her nickname softened another of Alyssa's many barriers, despite his occasional bark. Growing up with four brothers and a snippy mother had taught her to attach little significance to minor verbal blowouts.

She cast a glance at Teague's face to gauge his mood now. His brow was tight, mouth thin, fingers flexing over the steering wheel. Tense, as always. That wouldn't change anytime soon.

They'd been driving twenty minutes, and as they descended in elevation on their way into town, patches of ground showed through the thinning snow layer.

She focused on the strip mall coming up on their right. "What are we doing here?"

"Cruising." His jaw twitched beneath tanned skin. The creases at the corners of his eyes peeked out from beneath the sunglasses he'd pilfered from the cabin. He could have easily been a model with those rugged good looks. Alyssa could see him as a firefighter, decked out in yellow turnouts, hauling hose, issuing orders, driving into the face of the flames. For as little as she knew of him, somehow she believed that profession suited him to perfection.

"You don't strike me as a random cruising kind of guy," Alyssa said. "Why are we here?"

"What kind of guy do I strike you as after our whole fifty-six hours together?"

"Like a guy who has secrets."

"That's not news, now is it?"

He turned into the parking lot, his attention scanning each row as he drove. An Albertson's supermarket crowned the center of the outlet. Other stores included an optometrist's office, a donut store, a barber shop, a one-stop photo place and a pharmacy. On the streetside, a Taco Bell, a Wendy's and an AM-PM mini-mart rounded out the center.

A fast food banner set off a craving for comfort food. "Can we go to Wendy's?"

He looked at her, one brow quizzically dipped below the edge of his sunglasses. "You just ate."

"I want a frostie."

"Ice cream at this hour of the morning?"

"I haven't eaten in two days. I'm making up for lost time."

"You're insatiable." He sighed, and shook his head. "In a minute."

Alyssa watched people bundled for the weather walk to and from their vehicles. "What kind of car are you looking for?"

"How do you know I'm looking for a car?"

"I'm smart, remember? Four eyes are better than two. What kind?"

He hesitated. "A white 2004 Volvo S70."

As they passed through another row, Alyssa asked, "What are you going to do if you find them?"

He shrugged.

Unease pinched her stomach. "I don't want to be part of a kidnapping here, Teague. I've got enough trouble to straighten out as it is."

He didn't respond. His jaw twitched.

She twisted toward him. "You need to start thinking clearly and stop running on your emotions. You need to start thinking about Kat and stop thinking about yourself."

He flicked a look at her, then away.

"What do you think it will do to Kat if you steal her away from the parents she's known for three years? How do you think she'll react to seeing you out of jail, to you taking her from the security of her life?"

"She's *my* daughter. She belongs with me."

"And what are you going to do once you have her? Does she deserve a life of running? Is that the way you want to raise her?"

"We won't always be running. We're going to settle . . . somewhere. She'll be with me. I'll be with her. That's all that matters."

"To you, maybe. But I imagine a lot of other things matter to her. Like her favorite stuffed bear and her favorite blanket and her favorite pair of sparkly slippers. Like her morning routine and her friends at school and her teacher—"

"*Stop.*" He shot her an angry look, but Alyssa saw such desperation in his eyes it made her ache. "She's all I have. She's all I want. There is no reason to live if I can't be with her."

The thought of a little girl living without a father who loved her as dearly as Teague obviously loved Kat was like a knife in Alyssa's chest. She didn't know who or where she'd be without her own father. And honestly, she didn't know where her father would be without her, either.

"I'm not disagreeing," she said. "But we're talking about a five-year-old here. You can't just rip her from her life and whisk her off with no plans."

"I have plans."

"And *somewhere* would be the crux of your plans?"

A sound scraped from his throat. "I just want to see her, for God's sake. I want to set my eyes on her, know where she is—exactly. I need to know her *physical* location. I can't explain it."

He didn't need to. Alyssa understood that, because she wanted to see the little girl, too. She wanted to see the child that had driven such a strong man to these extremes. Kat seemed ethereal in Alyssa's mind, like a magical nymph that had cast a spell over him.

"There's one." Teague whipped the Jeep in a U-turn so fast, Alyssa had to grip the door handle to steady herself.

Her heart was hammering when he stopped behind the Volvo and put the Jeep in park. He climbed out and cupped his hands around his face to peer through the window. His shoulders slumped. He pulled back and returned to the Jeep.

"No booster seat," he said.

"Are you sure they have one?"

"Seth would never let Kat ride in a regular seatbelt."

"Why not?"

"Six years old and sixty pounds—that's the law. Kat isn't six yet, and she's not anywhere near sixty pounds. We've both seen way too much tragedy in our job to take that risk." He shook his head. "He'd put her in a bullet-proof bubble if he could."

"Jesus, Teague, do you *hear* yourself? What is taking Kat going to do to Seth? Don't you care?"

"Of course, I care." He pounded the steering wheel with his palm, making Alyssa jump. "There is no win-win here. It is what it is. Sometimes life throws shit your way. You can't always control it or avoid it or even fight your way out of it. You just have to find a way to deal with it. I did. Seth will, too."

"We've had this discussion before," she said. "It revolved

around the phrase 'shit happens' and you know what I think of that theory."

He rubbed a hand over his face. In front of Long's Drugs, Teague pulled to a stop and left the engine running as he rounded the front of the Jeep and headed for a newspaper kiosk. He dug in the front pocket of his jeans for change and slid it into the slot.

He returned to the car and tossed the paper in Alyssa's lap, his gaze focused into the parking lot. "There's another one."

The Jeep shot forward, pinning Alyssa to the seat. He swung around the next aisle and pulled up behind another white Volvo, just as an elderly man climbed into the front seat. Teague crept past, swearing under his breath.

Irritated, Alyssa laid her head against the seat. "There aren't any more here and your driving is making me sick. Can I get something to settle my stomach now?"

Teague grumbled an undecipherable response, but he headed down the row, turned into the drive-thru lane and stopped behind a black Ford F250. "Where did all these people come from? It's not even lunch time."

"There's *one* car ahead of us."

"And one behind us and one at the pick-up window. It's only ten—" He gestured to the dash. "Eleven-forty-five? Where did the morning go?"

"We slept late."

The moment the words were out of her mouth, the atmosphere inside the car shifted. Intimacy thickened the air between them.

"Yeah. I guess we did." The softness of his voice sent shivers sliding over her shoulders. She shook them away and scanned the menu board as Teague pulled up.

"I'll have a number three with a large Coke," she called to the speaker.

Teague looked at her with stark disbelief. "You just inhaled a table full of food at breakfast."

"If you hadn't gone all NASCAR on me, I could have settled for a frostie." She raised her voice again, directing her words to the speaker. "Oh, and a large frostie." She sat back and settled a look on Teague. "If you want something, get it because I'm not sharing."

"There is no way you're going to eat all that."

She shrugged. "You had your chance."

Teague pulled forward and waited behind the rumbling truck. Alyssa focused on the paper in her lap with a mix of resentment and fury. "Oh, look, we're not headline news anymore. We're just a little footnote directing people to the back page."

"Hallelujah."

"But our pictures are still here." She lifted the paper to show him their thumbnails in the bottom right-hand corner next to the caption, "Murderer and Accomplice Still at Large."

"Fucking fantastic."

"Puh-leeze." She drew out the word in irritation with his continued swearing. He ignored her. She turned to page ten. " 'Police continue to search for Teague Creek, thirty-four, convicted three years ago of . . .' " She flicked a glance at Teague. "I'll just skip that part."

"Appreciated."

" 'Creek is suspected to be accompanied by the woman who allegedly aided him in his escape.' " An angry sound scraped her throat. "It's all the same character-bashing crap."

Teague shifted in his seat, gestured toward the front of the line and let his hand drop against the window ledge. "What happened to the concept of *fast* food?"

" 'It is unclear, but suspected,' " she read on, " 'that Foster had arranged for the team's . . .' " No way. She was not reading these words. " '. . . getaway car'? Getaway car? Now they're saying I'm responsible for . . . Jesus, I'm so pissed I can't breathe."

Teague ran a hand over his face and rested his forehead on his fingers.

" 'Sources inside the hospital tell the *Tribune* that—' "

Alyssa skimmed ahead, barely able to believe the bull in front of her eyes. " 'Foster and Creek met and developed a relationship over the several visits Creek made to the facility'? You have got to be kidding me."

She crumpled the paper in her lap and looked at Teague, but she didn't see him, not really. Her mind had filled with visions of Dyne leaking this crap to reporters. Of that good old boys' club sucking it up.

"It's just sensationalism." Teague's smooth voice cut into her nightmare. "You're today's news, tomorrow's memory. No one will remember this shit a week from now."

"Oh, yes, they will. Maybe not the public at large, but everyone who counts will remember—the people I have to work with at St. Jude's will remember. Everyone in the medical community will remember. And my family will always remember."

"Everyone who counts?" Teague asked. "How in the hell do those dicks at the hospital count? That's your own twisted perception, Lys. The reality is that the only people who count are those who believe in you no matter what. The ones who stand beside you when hell crawls through, nipping at your heels because they know who you *really* are. Anyone who would spread lies, discount your integrity . . . they don't count for shit."

Alyssa's gaze focused on Teague's profile. His words, filled with certainty and finality and truth, sank in and gave her a whole new perspective. The tension in her chest loosened.

"You're right." All it took was a fresh outlook and Alyssa felt in control again. After experiencing the rigors of her fellowship, she could work anywhere. She could do research anywhere. The fact that leaving St. Jude's would make her mother happy didn't even phase Alyssa, because her mother's opinion didn't matter either.

She looked out the passenger window, her mind drifting toward new priorities, new horizons, new ideas of what really mattered in life. A woman caught Alyssa's eye. Or rather, a little girl with a woman. They exited a shop together, the girl cuddled in the woman's arms.

Maybe Alyssa noticed them because they seemed mismatched—the petite, thirty-something woman with a contemporary blond bob, the little girl with long, dark waves. Or maybe because that's who they were looking for—a woman and a child. Whatever the reason, something about them held Alyssa's attention.

"Teague?"

"What?"

"Look." Alyssa pointed to the twosome, who had stopped at a blue Volvo. It was brand new, the paper dealer plates still in place.

A sound drifted from Teague. Something painful, guttural. Alyssa looked back at him. He'd taken off his sunglasses and was peering past her at the woman and child, his eyes sharp and hot.

"Kat." His one murmur, filled with such longing, such love, touched Alyssa like someone reaching into her chest and stroking her heart.

"Are you sure?" She refocused on the pair. The woman was bent inside the backseat and the little girl stood beside the car.

"Of course, I'm sure." He threw the driver's door open.

Fourteen

Teague pushed himself from the driver's seat.

Alyssa reached across the console and hooked her fingers in the front pocket of his jeans. "What the hell are you doing?"

Without letting go, she looked over her shoulder toward Kat and the woman who had to be Tara. The little girl stopped playing with her doll and looked up, honing right in on Teague as if they had some psychic connection.

"Kat," Teague called to her.

"Don't do this here, Teague," Alyssa warned. "This isn't the place."

Kat started toward Teague, wandering away from the other car as if she were in a trance. Excitement broke out on her face, a smile as bright as a shining star.

A cop cruised along the drive between the Jeep and the Volvo, cutting off the view of Kat. With a curse, Teague ducked back into the car and closed the door, peering past Alyssa in search of his daughter.

"Dammit, Teague, you idiot." Alyssa looked out her window toward Kat. "She's in a parking lot, for God's sake."

"I didn't plan it like that. I just saw her . . . I just . . . I want to run over there and pick her up."

The cruiser passed, revealing a perplexed Kat. She craned her neck toward the Jeep, a worried frown creasing her face.

She said something, but Alyssa couldn't hear her from this distance. Then she said it again and Alyssa read her lips—*Daddy*. She resumed walking in their direction, then started running.

Teague was up and out of the car again before Alyssa could grab him. She pushed open the passenger door and stood just as Kat tripped. The little girl fell forward, hands outstretched. Her forehead collided with the bumper of a parked truck. Alyssa shot her hand out and caught Teague's arm as he pushed into a run.

"You can't." She curled her fingers into the sleeve of his shirt, holding him back. "The cop. You can't."

He pulled against her grip. "She's hurt."

"I'll go. Get back in the Jeep." Alyssa didn't wait for his agreement. She turned and jogged to the other side of the parking lot, where Tara bundled Kat into her arms.

"Oh, baby," Tara crooned, her voice tight with distress. "You know better than to wander in a parking lot. Your poor little head."

"Is she okay?" Alyssa stopped a few feet away.

Tears tracked down Kat's cheeks as she focused on Alyssa.

Tara's head snapped up. She stepped back and glanced around the parking lot. "Where did you come from?"

Kat whimpered and looked at the palms of her hands, where asphalt scrapes marred her skin. "Mama, it hurts. . . ."

"I was just . . . I'm a doc—"

"I know what you are." Tara cut Alyssa off in a low voice that sounded more like a growl.

"I came to—"

"And I know why you came. Your partner just left and I'm not going to tell you anything different than I told him." Tara drew Kat close. "Why can't you all just leave us alone? I did everything you told me. I've kept my mouth shut. Kept my part of the bargain. You can't come back now, years later and ask for more. I won't let you blackmail us for the rest of our lives."

Alyssa stood there stymied. Her gut told her there was important information in that monologue somewhere, but without more background, she had no idea how to decipher the significance.

Tara turned away, buckled Kat into a booster seat, then locked and shut the door.

Alyssa took a steadying breath. "Look—"

"No, you look." Tara faced Alyssa with rock-hard resolve. "I tried to reason with Vasser. I should have known you people wouldn't let up. The answer is no. I will not get involved again, and no one is taking Kat from me. Ever. Do you understand? *Ever.* So just back the hell off."

As Tara climbed into the Volvo's driver's seat and searched her purse for the keys, Alyssa inspected Kat's forehead through the window. The bump was mild, Kat's response normal. The little girl did indeed have dark eyes, supposedly her mother's, but they were shaped like Teague's. And she had Teague's mouth, too. He'd been more than just a proud father when he'd said she was beautiful. He'd been right.

Tara started the car and backed out of the parking spot, the Volvo's tires squealing as she exited the lot. Alyssa watched the vehicle disappear with a myriad of unsettling currents racing under her skin and even more questions firing off in her brain.

Vasser? You people? Involved? Take Kat? Mysterious men lurking? Something ugly was definitely going on here. Something beyond a wrongly convicted man. Something Teague was damn well going to start explaining.

She twisted toward Wendy's. The Jeep no longer sat in the drive-through. She scanned the parking lot. No cop. No Tara. No Teague. As she spun in a slow circle, she realized she was alone.

"That damn—"

Her thoughts broke off as her gaze landed on a man near Albertson's. He was tall, muscular, and dressed in casual clothing with a military style—drab cargo pants, boots and waist-length navy jacket. His head was shaved and he wore mirrored sunglasses over his eyes. He pushed away from a brick pillar and stepped off the curb, his attention on the asphalt as he spoke on the phone and walked toward the lot. The position gave Alyssa a clear view of the right side of his face, the large, triangular-shaped scar there and his partly missing, partly mangled right ear.

She sucked in a breath, as uncertainty rushed through her brain. Had Teague spotted him and run? Or had they seen Teague and hijacked him?

She made one more sweep of the lot. Still no sight of Teague or the Jeep. One thing was for sure, Alyssa wasn't going to stand around in the freezing weather and wonder. She was done taking orders and following rules. With no one telling her what to do, she was damn well going to start doing things her own way.

"Yeah, Joce, I'm a little cranky," Jason Vasser said into the phone. "Forgive me. It's like three fucking below out here, and I haven't slept more than two hours chasing this asshole all over the damn state."

He stuffed his free hand into his jacket pocket and fished for his keys, wishing he'd worn something to cover his freshly shaved head. If he'd known Creek was coming to the Arctic, he'd have waited to get the cut.

"Well, where the hell is he?" Jocelyn's voice rose in pitch with each day Creek remained free. "We're talking one man here. You've taken down armies, Jason."

They were a hell of a lot easier to subdue, too. Jason would take an army over Creek any day of the week.

"I can tell you he's not going for the girl. I've scoured this town. He hasn't been seen anywhere. I scared Tara Masters within a breath of a coronary. I've dumped her phone records, followed her, threatened her, bribed her. If he had contacted her, she'd have broken by now."

"Maybe he's not up there. Maybe that sighting was—"

"He's here. I saw the pet store surveillance tape. It was him."

"If he's not there for the girl, then why the hell is he there?"

Jason rubbed his throbbing forehead between his fingers. "Hell, if I know. Maybe he's taking the scenic route to the Canadian border. The F.B.I. is staging at Ransom's house. I'm going to horn in over there, see what they've got."

He lifted the key from his pocket and pointed it toward his car door. A hand came out of nowhere and covered the lock. Jason twisted. Put up his hand in a defensive gesture. And looked into the light hazel eyes of Alyssa Foster.

"I'll call you back." He snapped the phone closed and stuffed the device into his pocket. "Where did you come from?" He clasped her wrist and did a quick pat of her pockets while scanning the parking lot. "Where's Creek?"

She looked at him with what Jason could only describe as liquid venom. "I will only say this one time. Listen closely." Her voice came out low, raspy and far more menacing than she appeared capable of delivering. "Let go of my hand—right now—or I will scream *rape* so loud I will filet your eardrums."

It took Jason a second to process her words. The tone, the directness, the content, they didn't fit the sweet face, the petite build. . . .

"Right. *Now*," she said in a feral growl from between clenched teeth.

Reflexively, Jason released her. An unsettling current rippled beneath his skin, partly embarrassment that this woman had unnerved him, partly anger that he'd succumbed to her order.

"Who are you?" she demanded. "And how are you related to this situation with Creek?"

"Let's talk in the car." He reached for her again. "I'm freezing out here."

"Then talk fast." She twisted out of his grasp. "I'm not getting into that car with you."

She crossed her arms, cocked her hip and raised her brows, daring him to try again. Bitch wasn't afraid of a goddamned thing. All he had to do was blink at Tara to have her shivering. And he wasn't quite sure how to play this woman. She wasn't at all what he'd expected.

"I know about Teague's past," she said. "About his wife, his girlfriend, his daughter. What I want to know is where you fit in."

"If he told you that much, why didn't he tell you the rest?" He took another sweep of the lot. "Where is the bastard anyway? Couldn't face me himself? He sent a woman to do a man's job?" His eyes fastened on her face again as a new realization settled in. "And why aren't you worried I'll arrest you?"

She held up her hand, tapped her index finger. "One, I haven't done anything wrong. Two, since Creek dumped me here, I've got to find a way back to reality one way or another. Three, it will give me another reason to file a lawsuit against you and yours. Beyond that, all that matters is why *you're* following *him*."

Dumped her? Jason's mind chugged. Purpose emerged. The jitter in his chest settled as he reached for his back pocket.

Alyssa's fists clenched. She took two quick steps back.

"Just getting my wallet." Jason held his free hand up. "Look, Dr. Foster—Alyssa—my name is Jason Vasser. I'm with the Department of Defense. The reason Mr. Creek doesn't like seeing me is because he's done a lot of illegal things, and he knows I mean to put him back in prison."

"How does a murder involve the Department of Defense?"

Jason was all for strong women, but this chick was getting on his nerves. "Creek never did listen very well. Didn't listen when he was told to stop asking questions. Didn't listen when he was told not to involve outsiders in his quest. He just didn't listen. You strike me as far more intelligent."

Jason pulled out a card, and pushed his wallet back into his pocket and turned on the compassion.

"I've done extensive research on your background, and I know you've worked hard to get where you are. I'd hate to see all those years go to waste when you could be out there in the community helping people."

He offered her the card. "I have a lot of pull in a lot of places, Alyssa. If you help us out here, help us get Creek back where he belongs, I can make all those ugly stories floating through the media disappear."

The fight in her shoulders eased. Her gaze dropped to the card as she tapped the paper against the fingers of her opposite hand. "Those guards are telling convincing stories."

"Not a problem." Jason didn't like the sense of being tested, but he grinned. "It's a specialty of mine."

"They have a whole web of correction officers backing them up."

"Sounds like you've been talking to your brother."

Her head came up again and a sincere surprise lit her eyes. "You know Mitch?"

Damn. He just couldn't read her. If it were anyone else, he would swear she was baiting him, but she just didn't look the part and her history suggested she was a straight shooter.

"Doesn't everyone who's anyone?" he said.

"I suppose so. He's on his way to pick me up."

That news definitely put a kink in Jason's hopes of drawing her over to his side. He had to make a decision—try to net her and pull her in or arrest her. He couldn't see any immediate benefit in the latter.

"Mitch has quite a reputation," he said. "He does great work, Alyssa, but honestly, this situation is well out of your brother's league. I guarantee he can't do half of what I can do for you." He tapped the card, pointed at her and smiled as he pulled his keys from his pocket. "Think about it. You know how to contact me. But don't wait too long. If I find Creek first . . ." He shrugged. "Would be a shame to see a bright future like yours wasted." He paused for effect and met her eyes directly. "Or cut tragically short."

Alyssa shivered as Vasser's car exited the lot and turned onto Highway Eighty-nine. He'd just told her who he was, who he worked for and what he was doing. He'd oh-so cleverly alluded to the fact that he and / or his department had been involved in Teague's imprisonment and Desiree's murder. Then had balls enough to stand there and threaten Alyssa's reputation, her career and her life if she didn't act fast and spill Teague's location. And they knew all about her. Even about her brother. At this moment, her lie about Mitch coming to get her didn't sound like a half-bad idea.

"Department of freaking Defense?" she muttered. "Good thing you always love a challenge, Mitch."

She closed her fingers around the card and refocused on the parking lot. A heavy sigh filtered past her lips creating a thick plume of smoke in the cold air.

Holding her jacket closed across her chest, Alyssa wandered through the parking lot, searching for the Jeep, but after five minutes of failure, her emotions started to play nasty tricks on her mind. She still couldn't believe Teague had actually left her stranded. She was alone.

Finally free.

Or was she? This situation just kept getting more and more complicated. And after that conversation with Vasser, her immediate circumstances had gone from tangled mess to hopeless knot. She felt so lost. So confused. Maybe she'd developed Stockholm's syndrome over the last few days, because she found herself wandering toward Wendy's, hoping for a sign of the Jeep. She was cold and tired. Her side hurt. Her head hurt. And she wanted more of the TLC Teague had offered her last night. Not to mention a good shot at his ribs for holding back this information, when all she *should* want was an instant connection to Mitch's cell and a direct flight to San Francisco International.

"I'm sick," she muttered as she crossed into the Wendy's parking lot. "I'm a sick, twisted idiot." Why else would she want to go back to Teague? Why else would she put up with the abusive atmosphere of St. Jude's? "My mother is right. There is something wrong with me."

Alyssa rounded the corner of the fast-food restaurant and scanned the rear alley. The Jeep sat alongside the building in the shadow of a Dumpster. Excitement buzzed in her chest, followed by an immediate lick of fear, when she realized the engine was off. Something wasn't right.

"Oh, God." Alyssa pushed into a jog. "No. No, no, no."

Alyssa was still ten feet away when she saw the silhouette of Teague's figure in the driver's seat. Her feet stopped moving, as if they had their own controls. She pushed each foot forward with deliberate effort and angled to look through the passenger's window, peering into the driver's seat.

Teague wasn't moving. His head lay against the window, tilted at an odd angle. One limp hand covered his face.

A jolt of adrenaline-laden terror pushed her arm forward. She fumbled with the handle. Jerked the passenger's door open. Lunged across to touch his face.

"Teague!"

He jumped and grabbed her arm, his eyes sharp with surprise and fear beneath a sheen of wetness.

Alyssa closed her eyes and dropped her head as relief coursed through her chest loosening all the coiled muscles. She released all her breath in a heavy whoosh, then panted quick and shallow to get a normal rhythm back.

"Oh, my God. You scared the crap out of me." She rubbed a palm over her forehead and pressed her suddenly stinging eyes. She would not cry in relief. She would not. To force herself to obey, she opened her eyes and glared at Teague.

He released her hand and turned away, swiping at tears he

obviously didn't want her to see. "Why aren't you halfway to San Francisco by now?"

"Because I'm as demented as you are infuriating. What in the heck are you doing? How could you just leave me there? With *him*?"

"You're the one who walked right up to him," Teague shot back. "I couldn't very well waltz over and interrupt."

"He's been gone fifteen minutes. What happened to staying close?"

His mouth compressed at the same time as his eyes darted away. "This would be a good time for you to head home. Take care of business like you've been wanting to."

"*Excuse me*? After everything . . . after *this* . . ." she sputtered. "I'm not even going to acknowledge that asinine comment with a response. *You jerk*." She slapped the business card against his chest. "Tell me how the Department of Defense got involved in this, Teague. And who is this Vasser guy?"

He looked down at the card, taking it from her at the same time. "He gave you his damn *business card*? Man, this guy is un-freaking-believable. *You* are un-freaking-believable, approaching him like that. What were you thinking?"

"I was thinking that you abandoned me. I was thinking that I'm up to my dang eyeballs in this and that my future is at stake. I was thinking that there's a lot you're not telling me, and I want answers, Teague. And after Tara assumed I was *one of them*"—she used her fingers to put air-quotes around the words—"and treated me like the plague, insisting she, and I quote, 'wasn't going to get involved again,' I thought it best to just go to the source of all this mayhem when he walked right in front of me."

The blue of Teague's eyes darkened to stormy gray. "And what did you learn from the source?"

"That he's as cunning as a snake, as manipulative as my competition at St. Jude's, and as heartless as Taz. That he already knows every detail about my past and in the five minutes we talked, he tried to flip me against you and all but confessed to framing you and killing Desiree."

His eyes lowered to the card, his long, dark gold lashes sweeping down to cover the emotion within. "So colossally screwed up," he murmured. "Kat's okay, right? Just bumped her head?"

Kat's bump? He was worried about Kat's bump?

Alyssa's blood boiled. A scream ramped up in her throat, but before it escaped, Teague lifted his hand to his eyes and swiped at them again. A fine tremor rocked his fingers, his arm, his shoulders.

All her frustration evaporated. Her heart broke open. She reached across the Jeep and squeezed his forearm. "Kat's fine. A bump and a few scrapes. She's fine."

He heaved a breath and nodded. Then in one swift move, he leaned across the Jeep and pulled Alyssa into his arms. She stiffened in surprise as he pressed his face to her neck, then whispered, "Thank you. Thank you for checking on her."

Teague stuffed the wicked anger of raw injustice deep inside and let a sweeping sense of gratitude wash over him. Still, nagging guilt encroached. Alyssa was the last person on earth who should have done anything for him. Yet not only had she risked her safety, she'd come back.

"Why?" he said against her neck, still holding her, smelling her, feeling her. "Why didn't you leave?"

"I evidently have some sort of masochistic streak."

He huffed a laugh, more relief than humor. Then the warmth of Alyssa's hands smoothed over his head, down his neck and rested on his shoulders. He'd never felt anything so good in his life.

Teague lifted his head and looked into her eyes. He didn't know who moved first, only felt her mouth against his. And it was so right. So perfect.

Her lips were soft and warm as she kissed him. Tentative.

Gentle. Then again. And again. Her arms tightened around his shoulders. He slid one arm around her waist and cupped her face with the other hand. He wanted to devour her, drive in and take her all at once, but forced himself to hold back. And gained a huge payoff when Alyssa was the one to demand more.

She sucked his lower lip between hers and pulled his mouth open, then kissed him fully. Her tongue slipped in and touched his. Heat streamed through his chest and expanded in his groin, and Teague moaned with the feel of it.

Alyssa twisted toward him, sliding one arm around his neck and locking on. She took the kiss deeper and, oh, the feeling of being wanted—for who he was in the moment, even at his worst—made Teague lose all sense of place and time and circumstance.

When Alyssa finally pulled away, they were both breathing hard, tangled in an impossible position in the cramped Jeep. Teague's head was swimming, his cock straining against his jeans and pounding to the beat of his heart. Before he had fully cleared his head, Alyssa took his face in both hands. One thumb slid over his cheekbone, the other over his lips, all while those smoky eyes scanned his face with a mixture of tenderness and need. He kissed her thumb as it passed.

"Wow," she breathed. "Could this get any more complicated?"

Stupid, stupid, stupid. A little voice warned. *Don't do this. No matter how badly you want her. Don't do this.*

Teague closed his eyes, his heart heavy with resignation, and pulled back. He curled his fingers around hers and released her grasp on his face, set her hands back in her lap. "I imagine it could, but I don't want to think about how."

He turned away and stared out the windshield, forcing his mind back to his purpose.

"Where were they coming from?" He cleared the desire from his throat. "Tara and Kat? Which store?"

"Um. The photo shop, I think."

Teague turned the engine over. "Let's see what they were doing there."

In front of the photo shop, he slammed the Jeep into park, pushed the driver's door open and rounded the front of the vehicle, trying to get that damned kiss and the fantasies it created out of his head.

Before Teague could reach the passenger's door, Alyssa was out, her gaze direct and focused. "Are you sorry you kissed me?"

His chest grew heavy with emotion—so much emotion. Past, present, future. All knotted and matted. He lifted one hand to her cheek, ran his thumb over the soft, blushed skin. He wanted to kiss her again. Push her against the Jeep and feast on her. Take her back to the cabin, carry her into the house, lay her down on the sofa in front of the fire and undress her and touch her and taste her.

"At a different time, a different place . . . God, I wish I'd met you years ago." He shook his head, dropped his hand. "But I didn't. And I've already screwed up your life enough, don't you think?"

He didn't wait for a response, just closed his hand around hers and headed into the store.

Alyssa remained unusually quiet. He'd expected her to argue or pick a fight or at least tell him he was wrong and render her own opinion. But she didn't, which made him feel even worse. Maybe she agreed. Maybe she had her own second thoughts about their kiss, given what was at stake.

At the rear of the shop, three Asian women sat in front of large, complex machines processing photos. They didn't look up from their work. A man appeared from behind a curtain leading to a back room and scurried up to the front counter. "Can I help you?"

"Yeah, hi." Teague searched for a relaxed demeanor. "My sister sent me to pick up her pictures. She was in earlier with my niece. Last name is Masters."

The man turned and chattered at one of the women in Vietnamese. The two shot conversation back and forth like arrows before the woman dug in a pile of white envelopes and handed one to the man. Without asking for ID or questioning Teague further, the man rang up the sale, made change and offered Teague the envelope.

He dragged Alyssa out of the store and shook the envelope's contents into his hand. Several two-by-two head shots of both Tara and Kat filled his palm. Teague frowned and checked the envelope again, but found it empty.

"Passport photos." Alyssa's voice drew Teague's attention to an advertisement painted on the shop window for one-hour passport photos.

Teague's stomach tightened up. "What did Tara say to you? Tell me everything."

Alyssa's eyes went distant as she recalled the conversation. "Ah . . . she didn't let me get much of a word in edgewise. I told you she jumped on me about being 'one of them.' She said she'd already talked to Vasser, called him by name. Said she'd die before anyone took Kat from her. She talked about already having done what they'd wanted, mentioned blackmail . . ."

Dots started connecting in Teague's brain, and he didn't like the picture they were creating. At all. "Let's go. Vasser will have the cops here any second."

FIFTEEN

Teague dialed Seth's number as he drove the route back toward the cabin, splitting his attention between the road, the rearview mirror and Alyssa, who sat far too silently in the passenger's seat.

After the first ring, Seth picked up, breathless and expectant. "Tara?"

"No, it's me, Teague. What's going on?"

"Did you contact her, you dumbass? I told you I'd set something up and call you."

Teague's mind hit an invisible wall and broke into several different pieces. "No, I didn't contact her. Why would I call her? Why would you ask that? What's wrong?"

"She got a call this morning and after that she was acting totally freaked out. When she'd been gone too long and stopped answering her phone, I got a weird feeling and looked through the house. Her stuff is missing. Kat's favorite toys and books are gone. I can't find the suitcases we keep in the garage. She's gone, Teague. She's gone and she took Kat. Why would she do that if you hadn't spooked her?"

An ice storm of reality rolled through Teague in prickly, painful waves. Kat was out there somewhere and even the man who'd been a father to her for years didn't have any idea of how to find her. "Thanks for the vote of confidence. But if she ran, it wasn't because of me."

"I called the police."

"Wh—what?" An unexpected stab of betrayal stole Teague's breath.

"Not on you, idiot. On Tara. For Kat."

That didn't help the sting much. "What did they say?"

"That if her legal guardian has her and there is no evidence that Kat is in any danger, then they can't call her missing yet. They told me to stay home and wait for Tara to phone or come back. To call if anything changes."

Teague nodded to himself. At least if Tara changed her mind, he'd have a link to the information through Seth. "That's good advice. I'm already out here, looking. Believe me, buddy, if anyone is going to find her, it's me."

Seth grumbled something unintelligible.

"Couple quick questions that might help me," Teague said. "Had you planned on taking a trip anytime soon?"

"What? No."

"Any big purchases recently? Say, a new car?"

"No. Why? How is this important?"

"Call me if Tara calls you, Seth, and I'll call you if I find them first. Deal?"

More grumbling. A few creative curses. "Find her, goddammit."

Seth hung up on him. Teague disconnected, set his elbow on the window ledge and rested his head in his hand.

He's fallen back in time—to the days before he'd gone to prison, when he'd been digging into the source of the warehouse fire and the contents of the building that had burned too hot and too fast. Contents that had exploded and blown their team to hell. An explosion that had taken Quaid's life.

This situation with Tara's behavior was eerily reminiscent of the way reporters Teague had spoken to had been fired and disappeared or suddenly relocated to parts unknown. Followed by documents taken from his home, evidence stolen from Desiree's office files and death threats on Desiree's doorstep.

"What's this whole custody thing about?" Alyssa's voice brought Teague back to his ugly reality.

He glanced at her. She was resting her head against the window and looking at him from barely open eyes.

"What about it?"

"Why are Luke and Seth and Tara fighting over Kat? Luke is family, Seth and Tara aren't. You all used to be friends. What happened?"

"Luke hates me. Blames me for Suzanna's death."

"Your wife? You said it was suicide."

"It was. She overdosed on depression meds." He pushed through the words without attaching emotion or memory. He couldn't relive the guilt and loss all over again. "It started with hormones from the pregnancy, normal stuff, but got progressively worse. Luke doesn't think I did enough to help her. He's been fighting for custody of Kat ever since Suzanna died. Thinks I was a lousy husband and an unfit father."

"Why did you choose Seth and Tara?"

"Seth's been one of my best friends since I was a kid. He and Tara have been trying to have a baby for years, but can't. They're Kat's godparents and they adore her. Seemed like the best choice."

"Why weren't you shocked when I told you Vasser all but confessed to framing you for Desiree's death?"

Teague shrugged. "I knew someone did. I mean, I knew I sure as hell didn't kill her. But I couldn't find a trail, a motive. Never found any evidence. Besides, it doesn't matter anymore. What's done is done. I had to let it go or it would have eaten me alive."

He pulled into the drive at the cabin just as a light snow dotted the windshield. They fell into a tense silence. No new tire tracks lay in the driveway. No changes to the house.

"Vasser said he was going to Luke's," Alyssa said. "He said the F.B.I. was staging there."

Teague's gaze swiveled toward her. He must have had a what-the-fuck look on his face because she answered his unasked question with, "He was talking on the phone when I approached him. I caught his side of the conversation."

"Why didn't he arrest you?"

"He must think I'm more valuable to them free."

He wanted to ask her why she didn't just turn him in, but his instincts told him that might start World War III. His instincts also told him that what he was about to say was going to come damn close.

He turned toward her and laid one arm over the steering wheel. "Look. This has gotten . . . well, completely out of control would be a gross understatement. I took you when I shouldn't have. I kept you when I should have let you go." Teague ran a hand over his prickly hair. "I want you to call your brother and arrange to have him meet you in Colfax at the gas station where we stopped after the pet store. I'll drop you there a half hour ahead. This is just beyond dangerous. Vasser knows who you are. If he thinks you have information, if he thinks you're holding back . . ."

"Um, hello." She straightened in her seat. "Beyond dangerous? Have I not had a gun at my head? Were we not attacked by gang members? Do I not have stitches in my side? Did I not just have my career and my life threatened by a member of the government whose salary is paid for by my own taxes?"

"I know you're pissed off. You have every right, but you don't understand the magnitude—"

"Pissed off? Now *that* is a gross understatement." But she didn't sound as furious as he'd expected. Mad, yeah, but also hurt and disillusioned as she shoved the door open. Frozen air whooshed in, stinging Teague's lungs on his next breath.

"News flash, Creek." She glanced over her shoulder just before she got out of the car, her eyes veiled, the way she used to look at him days ago, before they'd meant anything to each other. "I'm making my own decisions now."

* * *

"And just what would those decisions be, genius?" Alyssa muttered to herself as she lay in the middle of the bed she'd slept in the night before—or part of the night before—at the cabin. The other part of the night, she'd lain skin to skin with Teague.

The memory sent a delicious shiver along the length of her body and made her groan in a combination of want and anger.

"Jerk." She flung her forearm over her eyes. "Didn't leave me many freaking options."

She could stay here with a man she wanted, but shouldn't want. For a million reasons. Or she could go home to allegations that would cause a troublesome immediate future at best, very well change the course of her life at worst. And if Vasser wanted to get nasty, he could wipe out her career with the same ease he'd stolen Teague's freedom.

Mitch had more pull, more power than Vasser gave him credit for, but there was merit to the power structure Vasser had eluded to. An attorney could only get so far fighting the all-powerful government.

The mere idea that someone had that type of supremacy infuriated her. The fact it was her government, agents the people had placed in a position of power, twisted her with an injustice that gnawed deep in her belly. And maybe for the first time, Alyssa had a sense of the blinding passion that drove her brother to do what he did for a living.

Mitch was her safety net. Her go-to guy. He would be the one to give her answers, to guide her through the mess that had become her life. She could trust him with her reputation, her career, her life. And she would. When the time was right. When she had more information.

Alyssa pushed up on her elbows and stared at the wall. She knew about Desiree's death. Teague had told her a little about the warehouse fire. She could work with that, take the information and tap deeper sources as she had during college or while performing research, but she had no resource—no library, no Internet. Just Teague, and he liked talking about his past about as much as Alyssa liked working with Dyne. She could call Mitch, but she wasn't willing to deal with his overprotectiveness yet. She'd rather try to get Teague to tell her more on his own first.

Alyssa turned into the hallway, her gaze drifting to a door that was cracked open, leading to a room she hadn't noticed before. She peered around the doorjamb and scanned the space—an office, with an eight-foot map of the United States covering one wall and encyclopedias and reference books lining another. That was enough to have Alyssa's mouth dropping open. Then she saw the giant flat screen computer monitor on the desk, its blue glare shining on Teague's quickly lengthening crop of deep gold hair as he ran his fingers through it over and over again, his head tilted down, elbows planted on the desk blotter. To his left sat an all-in-one fax-scanner-printer.

"What in the heck . . . ?" Alyssa muttered.

Teague's head came up. "I thought you were going to get some rest."

"And I thought this was a hunting and fishing cabin."

"It is."

She shot him a don't-even-start look.

"Doesn't mean it has to be archaic," he added.

"Whose cabin did you say this was?"

"I didn't."

"So, whose is it?"

Teague let out a long breath and sat back in the black leather chair. "It belongs to the father of a friend. A man who's been like a surrogate father to me. He's a history professor at U.C. Davis."

"What happened to your father?"

Teague shrugged, his gaze locked on the spinning hourglass on the screen, indicating that the system was still booting up. "Never knew him. Ditched me when I was little."

"And who is the friend?"

"His name is . . . was Quaid."

Something connected in Alyssa's brain. "The firefighter who died at the warehouse?"

Teague nodded.

"Friend to Seth and Luke, too?"

Teague's jaw pulsed. His eyes darted to hers, then back to the desk, where he picked up a pen and slid it through his fingers. And nodded.

She tipped her head to the side. "And you don't think the cops are going to figure out where you are?"

Teague rubbed at his eyes. "I know they'll find me here, *eventually*." He dropped his hand to the desktop and glared at her. "That's why the sooner I get this research done, the better."

"What are you researching?"

"Not what, who—Tara. Trying to figure out where she'd go."

"Mexico?" she offered. "Europe?"

"Canada, more likely. She grew up in Banff. Her mother and stepfather lived in British Columbia for a while. Her brother moved to Anchorage to work in the fisheries for several years. The stepfather died about seven or eight years ago and her mother and brother moved to Oregon."

"How do you know so much about them?"

"I asked. I wanted to know the person raising my daughter."

"Canada seems like an obvious place to go if she's trying to hide."

"The thing you learn quickly about Vasser and his group," he said, his voice flat and serious, "is that there is no limit to their reach. They can find you anywhere. They can get to you anywhere. So if Tara was trying to feel safe, it would make sense to go somewhere she knows people, where she would have a community that might rally around her." He shrugged and met Alyssa's eyes. "She's not exactly your typical criminal mastermind. She's just a woman afraid of losing her only child."

As good as any other theory, Alyssa guessed. She had a few theories of her own to check out.

"Does there happen to be another computer in this place?" she asked.

He eyed her for a moment too long, and in that instant she knew there was indeed another computer source. "Why?"

"Because I'd like to do some research, too. Vasser threatened my career, not to mention my life. I'd like to get a jump start on some background information for Mitch."

Teague wiped both hands down his face, leaned over to pull open a bottom desk drawer and lifted out a laptop.

Alyssa's heart picked up speed as she stepped forward and took a blank notepad and pen from the desktop. "Does it have an Internet connection?"

"Wireless. But don't—"

"Puh-leeeez give me some credit." She took it from him over the desk. "I'm here by choice, remember?"

"Yeah," he muttered. "And I'm still questioning your sanity."

"Join the club."

Alyssa retreated to the privacy of the bedroom. She would have preferred the ambiance of the living room with the big, soft sofa, high ceilings and the crackling fire, but she didn't want Teague seeing all her topics of research. Yes, Vasser was on her list, but so were Teague and Luke and Seth and Quaid and Desiree and the murder and the warehouse fire and anything else that popped up along the way that connected the previous topics. She also planned on looking into these abilities Teague had and what chemical change in the body could cause them.

She sank into the soft bed, propped herself up on the slatted wooden headboard with a mound of pillows and tried to squeeze months of research into a few hours.

* * *

By the time the computer battery waned and the screen went black, Alyssa couldn't squish another word onto the notebook and she was seeing double. She rubbed her eyes and looked at the clock on the nightstand, only slightly shocked to see that over three hours had passed as fast as three minutes.

She'd always been absorbed by research. And she had found some interesting tangents regarding DNA mutagens that could cause the powers Teague had experienced the last several years. She'd also uncovered loads of photos of Vasser with Senator Schaffer and Jocelyn Dargan, the Director of D.A.R.P.A., both of whom were well-known advocates of experimental scientific studies for the advancement of military warfare. Amped and ready to dig back in, she stretched her back. All she needed was a power cord . . . and maybe a cup of coffee.

Standing, she tuned in to the silence. No Teague tapping on the keyboard. No distant, muttered curses. She started toward the office and poked her head around the jamb. Computer and lights were still on, but no Teague. She turned toward the living room where the hallway opened into the main space, and paused when she saw paper and folders. Everywhere. Piles on the coffee table. On the sofa. Lining the floor. And Teague, asleep on the sofa, with what looked like photographs lying facedown against his chest.

On a quick indrawn breath of excitement, Alyssa realized what lay spread out before her. Information. Research. Answers. All at her fingertips.

She darted a look at Teague where he lay sleeping and tiptoed around the piles as she made her way closer. Then she stopped and simply admired him. He wore nothing but those gray gym shorts again. Bare chest, bare arms, bare belly, bare legs, bare feet. She could stare at all that muscle definition forever. And that face—the masculine jaw. The straight nose.

The full lips. And the golden eyelashes brushing his cheeks. There should really be a law against men getting the great lashes.

In sleep, his intensity simmered down a notch to merely serious. When her brothers slept, Alyssa always saw the youth come out in their eased faces. But whatever little boy had once lived in Teague was gone. This man was definitely one-hundred-percent warrior, one hundred percent of the time. And, she had to admit, she admired that about him. She also knew the toll that role took on a person. She lived it.

Alyssa took in the piles again. Two empty boxes sat by the coffee table, two full boxes with the lids askew by the arm of the opposite sofa. Colorful photographs drew Alyssa in that direction.

Excitement sparked like firecrackers. The same burning inquisitiveness that drove Alyssa to uncover the source of a patient's illness nagged at her now.

With another glance at a still-sleeping Teague, she crouched and lifted the edge of the top box. Inside lay more photographs, along with files and notebooks. She fished out a handful of pictures and eased to a seat on the edge of the sofa, studying the image of someone dressed in full firefighter gear. The heavy, yellow turnouts were covered in soot, the man's face so black the only immediate part visible was a gleaming, white grin.

She looked closer, searched the shadows and found Teague's face. His smile was so clear, so crisp, so pure. She hadn't believed him capable of such joy, and her stomach tightened with a mix of sadness for what he'd lost and hope for the possibility that grin held.

The next photo was of Teague centered in a group of five other firefighters in some type of training setting with a crumpled vehicle in the background and monstrous-looking tools scattered around the asphalt at their feet. Each of them—three men, two women and Teague—wore heavy turnout pants held up by thick red suspenders and navy T-shirts with Nevada County Fire stretching across their chests. Every one sported a grin that spoke of serious fun, loyal camaraderie and common purpose.

Envy stirred deep inside Alyssa. She was not a jealous person. Competitive, yes. Driven, sure. Ambitious, absolutely. Envious? Never. But, as she turned through picture after picture of Teague in his element, at the height of a meaningful career he loved with people he adored, Alyssa definitely felt a little on the green side—both jealous of a camaraderie she'd never experienced and sick over what he'd lost.

With her curiosity electrified, Alyssa crouched beside the boxes and peeked in again. A pastel floral cover stood out against the cream file folders.

She drew out the notebook and looked at the front cover. Dates from six years ago were scrawled on the front in a woman's cursive handwriting. Alyssa opened the book to a random page about one third of the way in, chose a passage and read.

> *It's nice to have Teague home, but I'm worried. He's not the same man who left the house that day before the warehouse fire. He's distracted and preoccupied. He says he's just worried about me, but I know something's going on. He's researching doctors for me again.*
>
> *He also found a woman to watch Kat on the days he works. We both know I can't take care of her. From one moment to the next I can't recall if I've fed her or changed her. It scares me. I'm afraid to be alone with my own baby.*

Sympathy bloomed in Alyssa's chest. She turned to a halfway point in the book and skimmed another passage.

I've felt like death all day. I've cried from the moment I woke up. I feel as if I'm dying from the inside out. What scares me the most is that as I have more and more days like today and the hopeless, deep, dark, torturous feelings last longer and longer. I feel as if I don't have anything left to fight with.

The fire crackled. Alyssa started, her gaze darting to Teague. But he remained still, eyes closed, chest rising and falling in a peaceful rhythm. His words filtered back through her mind: *She's dead. And before you ask, no, I didn't kill her. She committed suicide. . . .*

The quick beat of Alyssa's heart created a painful stab beneath her ribs, but she needed to know how the dominoes had fallen, how Teague had ended up in this position, and how her own life had been ultimately and irreversibly changed because of it.

She opened the diary past the halfway point and picked another passage.

Ambilify, Zoloft, Prozac, Paxil, Citalopram, Celexa, Ativan, Xanax, Lorazepam, Ambien, Lexapro . . . I've tried them all. I still can't get rid of the headaches. I can't stop crying. I can't sleep. I can't eat. I can't FEEL. I'm dead inside.

"Jesus." Alyssa breathed the word. Those were heavy drugs for severe depression—bi-polar, manic depression.

She overdosed on depression meds.

She sure as hell had. Alyssa's mind tripped over the course of events. Fire, Teague's strange powers, Suzanna's suicide, Desiree's murder, Teague's imprisonment. A downhill spiral destroying a previously perfect life—all starting with that fire.

She turned to the last page of the diary. This passage was

different from the rest. Suzanna's writing was smooth and clear, the words centered and double-spaced, more like a letter than a journal entry.

> *Teague, I love you dearly. I'm so very sorry for everything I've put you through. You have been the best husband I could have ever dreamed of, the best father Kat could ever want or need. I hope you'll both be able to forgive me someday.*

The torment throbbing in Alyssa's chest had to be nothing compared to the pain Suzanna had gone through or the trauma and loss Teague had suffered.

Exhaustion layered over Alyssa like a heavy blanket. A person could only take so much physical and emotional turmoil. And as she closed the diary with Teague's promises that he'd die before he went back to prison floating through her head, she couldn't help wondering how much stress was too much. At what point did a person break and do the unthinkable?

She couldn't let that happen. Not here, not now, not for her or for Teague or for Kat. She had the determination, the intelligence, the resources to make a difference. And, she had to admit, she often shared her brother's passion for slaying dragons. Especially the ones out to burn those she cared about.

Alyssa set the photos aside and picked up the top file on the coffee table. A soft jingle brought her attention to the car keys. She darted a look at Teague, but he was still asleep.

Settling into the soft cushions, she scanned the documents inside—court transcripts. After skimming four pages of dry court proceedings, Alyssa rolled her eyes and set that file aside, muttering, "No wonder I decided against law."

She snuck a glance at Teague before perusing the other piles for something interesting. He remained completely still, his chest rising and falling easily. The pile farthest away, at the edge of the coffee table, caught her eye. She made out the partial word: *Autop*. Alyssa scooped up the autopsy report and rifled through the other papers in the pile. Radiology reports, toxicology results, crime scene notes.

Jackpot.

SIXTEEN

Teague peered through cracked eyelids toward Alyssa, who was perched on the edge of the couch. He had to clench his fingers to keep from ripping those files out of her hands. Of all the things for her to latch on to, the autopsy report and crime scene details were two of the worst. If she'd picked up the file with the actual autopsy photos, he wouldn't have been able to hold still. As it was, he had to continue to remind himself that if she was horrified enough by what happened to Desiree and he was able to convince her she was in the same danger, he might actually get her to leave. Which would be best for both of them.

His stomach churned as she flipped each page. He'd scoured that damned information so many times, he knew exactly what she was reading. And with every word, she seemed to get deeper into the details. Brow furrowed, lips compressed, she flipped pages back and forth, scooted to the edge of the sofa, then laid the reports side by side on the coffee table.

After another twenty minutes of total focus, she finally sighed, propped her elbow on one thigh and dropped her forehead into her hand. "Jesus Christ."

Her tone of disgust tore at Teague. He'd wanted that reaction, but hated witnessing it.

She planted one finger on a line of type and followed it to

the end of the paragraph. A low moan escaped her throat, and it cut through him like a razor blade.

Teague swung his feet to the floor and sat up. "Seen enough?"

Alyssa startled but didn't respond, just stared at him with a complex mix of emotions he couldn't read.

"What is wrong with you?" he asked. "Why would you torment yourself with all this stuff?"

Her beautiful eyes sparked with something hot, something intelligent. She grabbed for the knot of keys on the table and, in one quick, fluid move, chucked it at him.

Teague barely lifted his hand in time. He caught them an inch from the cheekbone she'd already cracked once days earlier.

"That's it." She pushed to her feet. "I knew something wasn't right."

"What the hell was that for?" Teague dropped the keys on the table and rubbed at the sting in his palm.

"Confirmation."

"Of what?"

"That you're right-handed," she said as if the answer should be self-explanatory. "You held the scissors to my throat with your *right* hand. You stitched my side with your *right* hand. You caught those keys with your *right* hand. I thought you were right-handed, but I was just making sure because whoever killed Desire was *left-handed*. It's not evidence of who else killed her, but evidence that *you* didn't."

His mind stopped turning. He darted a look at the papers she'd been reading. "I've read those reports over and over and over. I know for a fact the medical examiner didn't say whether the killer was right or left-handed."

The look in her eyes shifted from distracted consideration to frustration. "M.E.'s don't draw conclusions like that. Not on paper. They state the facts, offer opinions on those facts relating to the manner of death, not *who* might have caused that death. Detectives and attorneys take those facts and twist them to fit their respective cases. But I don't know how anyone could come up with anything other than a left-handed killer given the realities in that report. It's all in the details—the area of her body damaged by blunt force trauma, the angle of the stab wounds—"

"This may all be clear to you, Alyssa, but you're a doctor, for Christ's sake."

She snatched the report up from the sofa and started reading. " 'Blunt force trauma . . . right skull fracture, broken right humerus, cracked right ribs.' "

"She also had a broken left hand and bruising on her left hip, shoulder, knee—"

"If someone hit you in the head with a bat or a pipe, wouldn't you have less severe injuries on the opposite side of your body from falling in that direction?"

Neurons long dormant fired off in a chain reaction of little explosions. "Oh, my God."

"What do you mean 'oh, my God'? Any halfway decent attorney—" She stopped mid-sentence. "You *had* a halfway decent attorney . . . right?"

Shame made Teague break eye contact. "I had a public defender. Evidently, he was about ten-percent decent. All he managed to do was save me from the death penalty."

"Why did you trust something so crucial to a court-appointed attorney?" she asked in breathless shock. "You had a good job, you could have afforded—"

"No, I couldn't." He forced his voice down. "I spent every last damn dime I had on an attorney for the custody battle against Luke. When this hit me, I had nothing left."

They stood there, staring at each other in the midst of thick silence. Teague's stomach roiled with memories of terror and agony. He wiped at the sweat on his forehead. "What about the stab wounds? Those were everywh—" A rush of nausea took him off guard. "Those were everywhere on her body. A crime of passion, they said. Personal, they said. Someone who knew her."

"What? You're the only person who knew her? She'd never had another boyfriend? She'd never had a fight with someone? For Christ's sake, Teague, she was an assistant district attorney. Half the prison population probably wanted her dead."

He didn't believe her. Couldn't believe there was evidence that he hadn't committed the crime staring him in the face while he'd been trying to aid in his own defense. Evidence that his attorney had missed and the prosecution had skimmed over at best, repressed at worst.

"Humor me," he said. "How could you possibly tell if all those stab wounds were inflicted by someone left-handed? I read the report. They crisscrossed, overlapped. There were some places that had so many they dug a hole in her tissue—"

He wiped a hand down his face and rested it over his mouth to quell the urge to puke. He couldn't do this. Couldn't go back through all these gruesome details.

Alyssa snapped the papers back into place in front of her, one finger following the text as she read. " 'Penetrating stab wound of the skull passing through the skin and into the brain tissue diagonally *upper left* to *lower right*.' And here." She flipped to a new page. " 'Four slanted stab wounds passing through the sternum in a roughly diagonal fashion with a penetration angle of *left* to *right*.' "

She lifted her hands and let them fall to her sides in a that-should-tell-you-everything type of gesture.

Teague shrugged, lifted his right hand and made a cutting motion across Alyssa's torso using his right hand for demonstration. "Yeah. Upper left to lower right."

"No. That's *your* left, not the victim's left. From the wounds we know Desiree was facing her attacker, so this," she shook the report, "is talking about *her* left side." Alyssa took Teague's left hand by the wrist and lifted it across her body to her left shoulder, then made a cutting motion across her body toward her right hip, saying, "*Her* upper left to *her* lower right. That is not a normal right-handed movement."

The physical demonstration instantly registered with Teague. He tried to twist the information to fit a right-handed attacker, but couldn't. Based on the angle of the wounds, the depth of penetration, there was no way someone could have made them with their right hand.

"Good God." Teague pulled out of Alyssa's grasp and smacked his hands against his head, raking his fingers down the sides of his face. "How could I have missed something so obvious?"

"Teague," she said, her voice easing into a compassionate tone. "Even top physicians can operate on the wrong organ or amputate the wrong limb. You were stressed, you were terrified and you expected your attorney to do his damn job." She paused and got that rock-solid serious look on her face. "Which begs the question . . . where did your attorney *really* come from? The DOD could have slipped anyone into the lineup that day to become your public defender."

Teague's stomach pitched. He covered his face and rubbed his eyes. "I feel sick."

He turned to the fire, opened the grate and added several logs to the flames. He stayed crouched there and watched them catch.

His mind needed a few minutes to rest. If he focused on everything he'd lost, he'd definitely snap. He needed to think about all he still had. He was free. He would find Kat. He would follow through with his plan and live a quiet life with her under the radar. And, Alyssa . . . No, he couldn't think about losing Alyssa. She wasn't his to lose.

"Okay." Her voice finally brought Teague's gaze around. She paced the room, her focus blurred in the middle distance as her mind twirled in thought. "Okay, here's what we'll do. I'll call Mitch, explain everything. He can refile your appeal. This is more than enough information to get you a new trial. In fact,

I wouldn't be surprised if Mitch got all charges dismissed. You and I will go through these files together. We'll highlight all the discrepancies. Mitch can get copies through the court. He can track down your previous attorney and look into the circumstances of how he was assigned to your case."

As Alyssa rambled, Teague grabbed her hand and tugged her to a seat beside him on the sofa. "No."

She leaned forward in earnest. "He's good. I wasn't lying when I said he's the best criminal defense attorney in the state. He knows everyone—attorneys, judges, politicians, cops, detectives, private investigators. Once I explain this to him, he'll jump on it—"

"Alyssa . . ." He waited for her to focus. The hope he saw in her eyes both healed and broke his heart. "What's done is done. The life I had is gone. No matter what happens, nothing will ever be what it was. It's over."

"Once you're exonerated, you can rebuild. You're an amazing man. You're intelligent, educated, skilled. What you've been through has made you a deeper, richer, more compassionate person. You can have an even better life. You can have your career back. You can have Kat back." She ran her hands up his forearms and held on. "Teague, please, trust me on this."

She pleaded with so much sincerity and conviction, he ached. She believed in him. After everything he'd done to her, and with so little evidence, she was ready to fight for him. His firefighting team had been steadfast and loyal throughout the process. They had visited Teague in prison, initially battling for his innocence. But as the weeks turned into months, the months into years, he'd urged them to move on. And eventually, they had. And while each of his team members—other than Luke—had continued to believe in his innocence, in him, this felt different. This felt deeper. So much deeper.

He wished he could hold on to her confidence, to her faith. To her. Aside from being a father to Kat, there was nothing he'd like better than to imagine Alyssa in his future. Unfortunately, he knew the horror of the legal system firsthand and just how it could be manipulated. And he sure as hell wouldn't let her ruin her own life. He'd done enough damage already.

He lifted one hand to her face, cupped her jaw and ran his thumb over the skin of her cheek. "At this moment, there is no one I trust more." He dropped his hand and leaned back. "But I told you before, I'm not going back to prison."

"You won't have to. With the evidence, you could get out on bail—"

"You aren't listening. I have no money, no home, no collateral. No family money, no rich friends. I don't have any means for bail—"

"I can pull from credit. Mitch can get your bail reduced—"

He squeezed her hands hard, then dropped them and stood. "No, Alyssa. I'm not going through it again."

She stood and faced off with him. "You should want to clear your name, if not for you, then for Kat."

"Should? According to who? You? You didn't sit through a yearlong trial. You didn't lose custody of your daughter. You didn't spend three years in San Quentin."

"So a rough life is your excuse for taking Kat away from everything and everyone she knows? For putting her life at risk when you have the means to prove your innocence and provide her with a good life here in America?"

A big part of him knew she was right. An even bigger part did want to prove his innocence. To be a living example for Kat. To show whoever had created this nightmare they hadn't beaten him. But he knew the hell of a trial, the horror of prison. He knew all about manipulation, cover-ups and stonewalling. And he wouldn't risk Kat's safety by living within reach of whoever had killed Desiree.

"A life with me in another country is better than no life with me at all. You don't have to like my plan. You don't have to agree with me. Hell, there's the door. You don't even have to stay."

"Oh, that's mature."

"Don't you get it? This isn't just about the murder charge anymore. I've committed new crimes—crimes I'm actually guilty of." He put out his hand and ticked off fingers. "Escape, kidnapping, assault, grand theft auto. For Christ's sake, Lys, I *killed* Taz."

"That was self-defense."

"Says who? You? The woman who aided and abetted my escape?"

She got that you-little-shit look on her face, crossed her arms and leaned back.

He put his hands up in surrender. "Look, I'm done fighting with you. I'm doing what I think is best for Kat and me, and you're not going to change my mind. Now, I need to try to get a couple hours of sleep so I can think straight."

Alyssa watched him walk away. He passed the bedroom she'd been sleeping in earlier and turned into the last door at the end of the hall.

"Why did God make men so damn stupid? So stubborn? So . . . ? *Grrrrrr.*"

She stared at the doorway he'd disappeared into. She wanted to follow him, hammer him with common sense until he got past his fear. But he was so obstinate, and she had to admit, he had solid justification for his beliefs and actions.

Alyssa let out a frustrated breath and paced. She didn't presume to know what Kat really needed. But she did believe she had to be the one looking at the big picture, because his vision was limited by love, obligation and fear.

With fresh dedication to a new mission, Alyssa started her work. She scoured the files, arranged information in piles of priority. The deeper she looked, the more injustice she found and the angrier she grew. When she and Mitch were finished, the attorney Teague had gotten stuck with would be sitting in front of the bar. His negligence warranted prison time, although if this had been orchestrated by a larger entity, Alyssa guessed the guy would either be dead or on permanent vacation before he was ever called to account for his actions.

She took the most important documents into the office, taped Vasser's business card on the top page and wrote below: *Creek is right-handed.* Alyssa knew that was all she needed to say. Mitch would thrive on a case like this, especially because it involved her. And when Mitch sank his teeth into something, he didn't let go until it was dead.

With the fax machine piled high, Alyssa dialed her brother's home office number and pressed "send."

While the papers rolled through the machine, Alyssa went back into the living room. She looked at the stacks she'd created, heaved a breath and dropped to the sofa. Paper crinkled, and she pulled photos from under her butt. She looked at the pictures, the ones that had been lying on Teague's chest when she'd first come into the room.

The images blurred in front of her tired eyes. She fought to bring them into focus and found photos of Teague and Kat as a dark-haired toddler. The girl's smile illuminated her from the inside out and radiated around her like a golden aura. Teague was smiling, too, his face pressed against her cheek in a big, fat kiss. Kat was laughing, eyes shining, every little tooth showing.

The next photo hit Alyssa oddly—an image of four adults and Kat around a restaurant table. Kat was in the middle with a couple on each side of her. Teague and a woman on the right, Tara and a man on the left. Alyssa guessed the unknowns had to be Desiree with Teague and Seth with Tara. Alyssa looked closer, trying to identify the source of her discomfort. Something about the women.

Desiree, a pretty strawberry blonde, had her arm around Kat, squeezing the little girl to her side. Tara wasn't looking into the camera, and she wasn't smiling. She was staring at Desiree and Kat with total absorption.

The look on her face was one Alyssa had learned to recognize over the years—envy. Not the I-wish-I-had-that kind of wistful yearning, but a that-won't-be-yours-much-longer anger. Alyssa had seen it when she'd made the highest grades in her courses, when she'd graduated top of her class, and every time she outshone Dyne at the hospital.

The fax machine beeped, signaling successful transmission. Her attention shifted and a weight Alyssa hadn't realized she was under, lifted.

She set the pictures down and looked around the living room. Nothing more to do now but wait. She'd talk to Teague again in the morning. Try a different approach to get him to see her point of view. Right now, she needed the same thing Teague needed. A few hours of rest.

She paused at her room, her gaze on the next door. She wanted to peek in, check on him. See him. Her body stirred at the thought. *Another place, another time . . .* How many times did she need to be rejected to get the message?

Instead of following her desire, she turned into her room and pulled a man's T-shirt from the dresser. In the bathroom, she changed and brushed her teeth. When she looked at herself in the mirror, her reflection surprised her. Instead of the emaciated, exhausted shell she expected, Alyssa found color in her cheeks and light in her eyes. Thanks to Teague's healing touches, the marks on her face and neck had completely vanished.

Getting back to normal, she supposed. Only, what was normal? Surely not what had been her norm a few days ago. And while that didn't make her feel particularly comfortable, it didn't feel wrong either. For the first time in her life, not knowing what would come next felt right.

She opened the medicine cabinet to replace the toothbrush. Her gaze landed on a clear Ziploc bag, the one Teague had pulled from his package of clothing in the GTO. Sample-size toiletries filled the plastic—toothpaste, soap, mouthwash . . . condoms? Her brows lifted. She picked up the bag and turned it, checked the packaging. Yep, condoms.

For the longest time she just stared at them. Her mind veered toward Teague. Snapshots of his body filled her head. The sight of him undressing to get into the shower. That night in the motel when he'd dropped his towel and she'd seen him in all his naked glory. The feel of his hard bare body stretched out next to her, keeping her warm the night before. Then their kiss earlier that day invaded her thoughts. And, finally, his words: *God, I wish I'd met you years ago.*

She pulled a handful of condoms from the bag and pushed them around in her palm. Turned them all so the packaging was face up and in the same direction the way bank tellers arranged dollar bills. Stacked them between her fingers. Counted.

Eight. She snorted. She'd never used more than one in a night and couldn't say that any of those interludes had been particularly memorable. But even the thought of using one with Teague tightened her body with anticipation.

With the condoms sandwiched between her fingers, Alyssa wandered out of the bathroom. She walked past her own bedroom, paused at Teague's door and watched him sleep. If he was asleep. She didn't truly know if the man ever slept. In the light spilling out of the bathroom, she could see him lying on his back, a blanket covering his legs. His chest was bare, his arms clasped behind his head. Eyes closed.

Indecision zinged around her chest like a firefly trapped in a jar. She pulled in a slow breath, then blew it out.

"Wrong room, Lys." His voice came out low and languid and lusty, giving her firefly a shot of adrenaline. But his eyes stayed closed, his body still.

"I . . . don't think so." She grabbed another ounce of confidence and walked toward the bed.

Seventeen

Each step closer to Teague intensified Alyssa's nerves and her excitement.

"I don't want to talk anymore, Alyssa."

He didn't move even a millimeter, but his lids cracked, and he tracked her with his eyes. The heat there, the longing, gave her the final flash of confidence she needed to make her move.

"Neither do I." She dropped the condoms on his chest. Watched as they scattered over muscle. "I had something else in mind."

Teague's gaze darted to the little packages and held. Slowly, his eyes lifted to meet hers again. His hands slid out from behind his head. She anticipated him reaching for her, pulling her down on top of him. But instead, he wrapped his fingers around the vertical slats in the headboard.

"I'm not the guy for you, Lys."

"I am sick of you telling me no." She lifted a knee and rested it on the bed beside him. His gaze dropped and lingered on the bare legs extending beneath the hem of her oversized T-shirt. "A woman can only hold her patience for so long and you've been testing mine from the moment I set eyes on you."

His chest moved with quick breaths. His fingers wrung the

wood of the headboard, making his arm muscles flex and roll. His eyes sparkled from beneath partially closed lids.

Alyssa pulled one arm through the sleeve of her shirt, grabbed the hem with the other hand and tugged the shirt over her head. Slowly. When she dropped it on the floor and looked at him again, his eyes were fully open and on fire.

"Fuck. Alyssa . . ."

"That's exactly what I was thinking." She grinned, hooked her thumbs in the edges of her panties and scooted them over her hips, letting them drop to the floor. "You're finally getting with it? I'm all for slow, but maybe not at first, if you know what I mean."

She reached for the blanket and pulled it off his legs. He still wore boxer briefs, and his erection already strained against the cotton.

"Mmm." She licked her lips, her mouth suddenly dry. "That's what I want."

With a hand planted on either side of his chest, she climbed onto the bed and straddled his hips. Teague's gaze roamed over her like a hungry touch, but it wasn't nearly enough. She wanted his hands on her. His mouth on her.

"Alyssa." He said her name in a pained growl. "Dammit. It's been three years."

She flipped her hair to the side and leaned in to kiss his lips. He didn't kiss her back. "Good. Then we're even."

"Not even close." His eyes lifted and burned into hers. "I can't . . . I won't be able to stop once I start. I don't know . . . I don't want to hurt you."

She slid her palms up his sides, over his chest and down his belly. He shivered, making her smile. "You've had these abilities a long time, Teague. Did you hurt Suzanna?"

"No."

"Did you hurt Desiree?"

"No, but . . ."

She leaned in and kissed his chest. "But what?"

"I've never wanted anyone as much as I want you."

Her insides melted into warm, golden liquid. "As I said"—she lifted her mouth to his chin and nipped it—"we're even."

"You don't get it. It's not just the heat. You make me so damned insane. This won't be easy or sweet or . . ."

A surge of lust hit her low in the gut. "Then you'll just have to make it up to me, won't you?"

She sat back on his thighs and pulled on the waistband of his briefs. Dragged the fabric past his hipbones, exposing the first inch of curly, dark golden hair and more of the smooth reddish mark low on the right side of his pelvis.

"Birthmark?" she asked.

Teague hesitated. "Scar."

She traced one finger around the edge. Not a normal scar. Too smooth. Too even. "Looks a little like a phoenix. Appropriate, don't you think?"

"I . . ." His breath came fast, his pupils dilated. "Can only think about one thing right now. And that isn't the damned scar."

She scooted back, stripped him of his boxers and smiled. "I knew I wouldn't be disappointed."

Her tongue wet her lips, teeth raked over her bottom lip as she assessed his abundant size and just how she was going to feast on every delectable inch.

"Don't even think about it." By the time the rasp of his voice drew her eyes up, she was nearly drooling. "I'll never last."

"But—"

"But nothing. No."

With a pout in place, she decided to make him pay in some other way. She slid her palm over the length of his shaft, her fingers closing around its thickness, her dissatisfaction forgotten. He was hard and smooth. Hot and silky. Huge and throbbing. Teague groaned, and arched into her touch. His eyes squeezed tight, fingers white on the headboard.

A sense of power and strength flooded her with pleasure. Her throat squeezed with the anticipation of taking him. Of sliding that thick length between her legs. Of filling herself with his hardness, his fire, his passion.

She pushed the fabric down his legs, kicked it off his feet with her own. With her free hand, she picked up a condom and pushed the rest off his chest. She ripped the foil and tossed the wrapper to the floor. Positioned the smooth latex over the tip of his penis. The touch made him flinch, then tremble.

Enjoying the moment of control, Alyssa rolled the condom down, slowly, stroking him luxuriantly as she did. The heat and intensity in his eyes eased another layer of Alyssa's nerves and amped her blood pressure.

She lowered her body to his and rubbed the ache between her legs against his swell. Her hands explored, hips to chest. He was warm and supple and hard—in all the right places.

She tilted her chin, kissed his throat and whispered, "Touch me."

His arms came around her almost before she finished speaking. One hand slid up her back and around her neck to guide her face to his. And then he kissed her. Openmouthed, hot and hungry. His lips were searching and relentless. The whiskers on his jaw, cheeks and chin scraped her skin, abrading her lips. She thrived on the desperation. On the pent-up need. Even the fact that he'd want anyone to this degree didn't dim the thrill. Because, for the moment, he was hers. All hers.

His other arm locked tight around her back as he rolled with her. Up onto their sides, over onto her back. All while still kissing her.

Alyssa lost herself in the passion. He made her feel fragile, feminine and so intensely desired. Restraint sent fine tremors through his shoulders, down his arms. His thigh slid between hers, then his hips. One hand caressed her shoulder to hip, then slipped between her legs.

A jolt of heat shot through Alyssa, teasing her with a preview of what was to come. She broke the kiss on a gasp. Teague's mouth skimmed her cheek, her neck, her shoulder. His palm stroked her, his fingers teased. Then they were inside her, moving, filling her with a deep, languid heat. She'd never felt anything so erotic. Her nails dug into his shoulder. Her hips rose to his hand.

"God, you're wet," Teague murmured against her shoulder. "And so hot."

Hell, yeah, she was, and it mystified her. Sex had always been a lukewarm experience, ending with an is-that-it?

Now, as his cock pressed against her opening, she lifted to meet him, more than eager. And, without hesitation, he accepted the invitation. He positioned himself and pressed into her. Steadily. Insistently. Deeply.

Alyssa's throat constricted with the new pressure and the rush of excitement it brought. Her hands ran down his back to his hips. His ass flexed beneath her hands as he rocked into her. Stretched her. Filled her. Completely. He supported the bulk of his weight on his forearms, continued to kiss her everywhere his mouth could reach. Endlessly.

As the sensation of his body, his hands, his mouth, layered upon each other, Alyssa's thoughts dissipated. Her mind filled with a hazy, iridescent cloud. Her body with luscious currents and undercurrents.

Teague's climax built fast and strong. She knew the moment his restraint broke and his body took over. His thrusts were hard and deep. His fingers dug into her skin, her muscle. His teeth closed at the base of her neck. To her surprise, her body responded in kind. Thriving on the intensity. The edginess. The ruthless need.

She was almost there, could nearly taste the powerful release, when Teague let go. Hands on her ass, he held her tight and drove deep. His hips undulated with the spasms, rubbing just the right spot, just when Alyssa needed it, and within seconds, her intense, scorching climax followed.

Pleasure flooded her body on a hot wave. Second thoughts evaporated in ecstasy. And that long-empty space floating beneath her ribs filled with joy.

The distant ring of a phone intruded on Teague's blissful sleep. The first real sleep he'd had in three years.

He came awake slowly, reluctantly. The phone clicked over to a long, high-pitched, steady buzz. Just as his eyes opened, the buzz ceased, leaving him disoriented and wondering if he'd been dreaming. It had to be close to midnight.

The front of his body was aligned with the back of a woman's. A warm, slim, soft woman. His arms were wrapped around her, holding her close. Their legs entwined. The fingers of one hand threaded through thick, silky hair, the fingers of the other, clasped with hers.

Alyssa.

Teague smiled and closed his eyes on a sigh. She was definitely a dream.

With his face snuggled into the sweet-smelling strands, he rocked his hips forward, rubbed against the softness of her sexy ass, seeking relief for yet another hard-on. Alyssa didn't stir. No surprise, considering she'd kept him busy for hours. He brushed the hair away from her face and pulled her earlobe between his teeth. If he could rouse her, they could stay busy for a few more.

Ring.

Teague froze.

Ring.

He propped himself up on his elbow.

Ring.

What the hell was that? Not the cell phone. Not the house phone.

Buuuuuuuuuuuuuzzzzzzzzz.

Teague sat up and swung his legs off the opposite side of the bed. "What the fuck?"

Click. Silence.

"Don't swear," Alyssa murmured.

His fingers released the clenched blanket. Probably a wrong number. The longer he stayed at the cabin, the more tense he felt about being here.

"Come back to bed." Alyssa rolled toward him and held out her hand, eyes still closed.

"That'd be a great offer if you were actually awake."

"I'm 'wake," she slurred, and dropped her hand when he didn't take it.

"I'll make you a deal." He leaned over and kissed her forehead. "If you're still awake when I get back, you can have your way with me."

Her mouth curved in a lazy smile. "Deal."

She fell instantly back to sleep. Teague grinned and reached out to brush her hair back.

Ring.

His heart jumped. His fingers froze. No way in hell was this a wrong number. He pushed to his feet, pulled on shorts and went to the bedroom door.

Ring.

He checked the hall before stepping out. Paused at the entrance to the living room, where the smoldering fire lit the room with a low glow.

Ring.

He crossed to the kitchen counter and snapped up his gun. Then he stopped and stared at the phone.

Buuuuuuuuuuuuuzzzzzzzzz.

Teague spun toward the sound. The office. The fax machine in the office. Not the kitchen phone.

He turned into the room, half expecting to find cops waiting for him. Of course, it was empty. The computer had gone into hibernation and the space was dark. He flipped on the overhead light and headed for the fax machine, where papers lay in the tray facedown as if they'd been sent.

The hair on his neck prickled. He lifted the stack on the tray and turned them over. *Creek is right-handed,* was the first thing he saw. A handwritten note. It could only be Alyssa's hand. And the note was on the autopsy report title page. With Vasser's business card.

A dark sensation dripped into his gut. He set the gun down and turned the pages. Autopsy report, crime scene reports, trial transcripts.

His hand was already shaking when the phone rang again. *Ring.*

And now he knew why it was ringing. By faxing this information, she'd also given out the phone number. Which meant their location was now traceable.

Ring.

He closed his eyes, clenched his teeth, picked up the receiver. And waited.

"Alyssa?"

The hope in the man's voice made Teague cringe. "No."

"Creek." The voice transitioned from hope to barely restrained fury.

Teague didn't respond.

"How do I know you?" the man asked. "And what do you want?"

Teague's mind skidded to a halt, reversed directions. Stalled.

"I recognize your name," the man said. "You tried to get me to take your case at some point, didn't you?"

Mitch. It had to be Alyssa's brother. Teague dropped his head back, both furious she'd involved him after Teague had clearly told her not to and touched she believed in him so deeply she would enlist her family in his fight. Clearly, Mitch didn't find it touching at all.

Teague pulled in a breath to steady his temper. "No."

"You did," Mitch said. "I'm sure of it. You're a desperate man to go to such lengths to get my attention."

"And you're fucking full of yourself. I don't want or need your help. I never have."

"Then why target my sister?"

"You've got it wrong."

"I'm not going to argue with you. I don't care how the hell your twisted mind conjured up this idiotic scheme. I only care about Alyssa."

That made two of them, but he doubted Mitch would find his concern valid.

"You'll be happy to know that I've gone over the papers Alyssa sent me," Mitch continued, his tone now flat and businesslike. "And I've been looking into some of my own resources. It does appear as if your attorney fucked you over. In fact, you might enjoy knowing, Hal Brueger died shortly after you were convicted. Cause of death is listed as undetermined. When I talked to the M.E. who performed the autopsy, he said he couldn't conclusively determine whether it had been suicide or murder."

"Why would I enjoy knowing that?"

"Because it supports the conspiracy theory you tossed around early on in your defense."

Okay, this guy had to be as good as Alyssa claimed if he'd dug up that sliver of information. "Yeah, and, look how well that worked out for me."

"In fact, it will help you now. New evidence is grounds for a new trial."

An acrid chemical scent brought Teague's attention to the plastic receiver melting beneath the heat of his fingers. He switched hands and worked to tamp his temper. "I don't want a new trial."

"How about an appeal, then? Brueger was also being investigated for disbarment when he was found dead. Misrepresentation or lack of quality representation is all you need."

Teague closed his eyes and rubbed his head. "That's not what it said on my appeal denial."

"I looked into that, too. It was signed by a judge who retired immediately after and left for parts unknown."

"None of this means anything to me now."

"It should," Mitch said. "Because I'm calling to offer you a deal."

Teague's eyes came open, his vision blurred over the desktop. "Didn't you hear me? I'm not looking for any fucking deal. I don't *need* any fucking deal. I don't *want* any fucking deal. In fact, you don't have a goddamned thing I *do* want." *Except the most beautiful sister on earth.* "So you've wasted your time."

"There's something big going on here, Creek. Big and deep and ugly. I happen to prefer these types of cases. The bigger, the deeper, the uglier, the better. And because this particularly nasty case involves my sister, I'm offering you representation. I will take on your case at no expense. All you have to do is let Alyssa go, safe and sound."

Let Alyssa go. The words twisted inside him like a knife. He knew he had to let Alyssa go, but not in the same way Mitch meant. He also knew, after tonight, he'd never be ready to let her go.

"I'll take it under advisement."

"Creek," Mitch said as Teague started to remove the phone from his ear. "Couple more things. One, for what it's worth, I don't think you're guilty of Desiree's murder. And I'll prove it. But, if you're involved in any way, shape or form with this mess, I'll prove that, too."

"Reassuring." Teague switched the phone to the opposite hand again, grimacing at the metal and wires now showing through holes in the plastic casing.

"And two," Mitch said, "there is an ex-San Francisco homicide detective and two ex-members of the San Francisco S.W.A.T. team sitting outside the cabin at Fallen Leaf Lake.

You have until eight a.m. to release Alyssa. If you don't, they will arrest you, using deadly force as necessary."

An icy trickle slid down Teague's back. He automatically scanned the living room windows, still covered by the shutters.

"Just so we're clear," Mitch said. "If that happens, all offers are rescinded. Of course, that is if you're not already dead."

EIGHTEEN

The cool sheets on the mattress next to her pulled Alyssa fully awake. She opened her eyes and scanned the bed. Then the room. And found both empty.

Her heart picked up speed as she propped herself on her elbows. That's when she heard it—the sound of running water. The shower.

"Jesus," she breathed and fell back against the pillow, her arm over her eyes. She hated the way fear crept into her heart whenever she didn't know his exact location. Worrying was not her thing. She didn't do it well. She didn't like the way it felt. She'd never wanted to be that caught up in someone. But, here she was.

Restless for the sight of him, for the feel of him, she tossed back the covers and stood. A groan escaped her throat as she took her first few steps toward the bathroom. He had worked her over in the most delicious, erotic ways and Alyssa smiled at the memories.

The bathroom door stood ajar. She pressed the flat of her hand to the wood and stepped in, closing it quickly to keep the warm, humid air in the small room. Teague's silhouette stood beneath the spray, head bent, one hand pressed against the tile.

Already naked, Alyssa pushed the curtain aside just enough to slip in behind him. She closed the distance and wrapped her arms around his torso from behind. Before she could lay her cheek to his back, Teague whipped around. One arm slashed across her throat, the other shoved her against the shower wall. The force of the thrust snapped her head on the tile. Pain exploded beneath her skull. She cried out.

When she opened her eyes, she found Teague staring at her with an expression she could only describe as menacing. His eyes were dark and flat and glazed, filled with violence.

"Teague." She gripped his forearm, and tried to pry it off her throat. "Stop."

His eyes cleared, but he didn't release the pressure. Water sizzled as it hit his skin, evaporated and filled the shower like a steam bath. Heat seared through her neck where his arm nearly cut off her air supply.

"Teague," she tried again, "you're hurting me."

The hostility in his eyes shifted to fear, then to a sick regret as he fully focused. "Oh, my God." Teague instantly released her, hands up, palms out. "Oh, my God. Lys. I'm sorry." In the next instant, he swept her up in his arms. "I'm so sorry."

She didn't immediately return the embrace, still stunned and confused.

"I—I—" he stuttered. "Oh, my God." He pressed his face to her neck and let out a sound somewhere between a sob and a growl. "I didn't think. I just reacted. I thought—I thought—" He shook his head and buried his face deeper. "Fuck."

His turmoil churned her own gut. She wrapped her arms around his shoulders, ran her hands over the smooth course of his new hair growth. "Okay. It's okay. I'm okay."

"It's not okay." He let her go as quickly as he'd pull her close and turned away. He slammed both fists against the shower tile, knuckles first. "It's *not* okay. Nothing about this is okay."

Alyssa jumped at the outburst, then cringed. She reached past him, grabbed his wrists and pulled him around to face her again. "Stop. You're going to break your fingers." He hung his head, closed his eyes, shoulders slumped with what looked like a lifetime of guilt.

"What did you think?" Alyssa asked, running her lips over his bleeding knuckles.

He shook his head. The water dripped off his perfectly straight nose. "I didn't think. It's just, in prison, the showers . . . It's the place where you're most vulnerable. It's where . . . Guys, you know . . ." His expression compressed in pained memory. "Goddamn, I wish I could get that shit out of my mind."

She stepped closer to him, and again wrapped her arms around his waist. Hardening herself, preparing herself for the answer to her next question. "Did that happen to you?"

"No! God, no. But, I couldn't take a fucking shower without seeing it. Hearing it." That disgusted, pained sound came from his throat again. "Goddamned sick sonsofbitches."

Relief swamped her stomach and pushed tears to her eyes. She wrapped her hands around his wrists and gently pulled them away from his face. "Look at me, Teague."

His eyes opened and focused, filled with pain. But it was the edge of hopelessness that worried her the most. "Let's make new memories. We'll wipe out the bad memories with good ones."

She wrapped her arms around his neck, pressed her body fully against his and pushed up on her toes to kiss his mouth. Their lips slid together effortlessly. Teague sighed, tightened his arms around her and took the kiss deeper. His tongue circled hers and Alyssa tasted that same desperation she'd sensed in the Jeep. The same need he'd shown her in bed.

She kissed her way down his chest, low on his belly. Just when she was about to take him into her mouth, he pushed back.

"No. Don't."

Alyssa looked up to find his face twisted with torment, a mixture of dreams he wanted to realize and nightmares he wanted to banish.

"I'm sorry, Lys." He pulled her to her feet. "I can't do this."

He tore the curtain aside, got out and slid it closed again. He grabbed his gym shorts on his way out the door. Alyssa stood beneath the steaming water confused. She wanted to help him so badly, but her impatience had once again gotten the best of her. She'd pushed him too hard, too soon.

She took several minutes to tip herself back into emotional balance, get her thoughts straightened out, and push the hurt away. When she came out of the bathroom, she peered down the hall and saw the bright glow of the fire.

A pinch of fear tore at her stomach. If he found out she'd faxed Mitch that information . . . It wasn't that she didn't want him to know, just that she didn't want him to know now, in this frame of mind.

She traded her towel for the oversized T-shirt and wandered down the hall. At the living room entrance she paused and watched Teague for a moment where he sat on the sofa. He was looking through something on his lap. With her bottom lip between her teeth and her mind conjuring excuses and arguments for passing the information to Mitch, she walked up behind him. When she peered over his shoulder, a breath of relief exited her chest. He was looking at photos.

She touched his shoulder to let him know she was there. No more surprising him, that was for sure. He tensed. When she was sure he wasn't going to go haywire, she slid both arms around his shoulders, crossed them over his chest and kissed his neck from behind. "I'm sorry I startled you."

"I'm sorry I'm so fu— Screwed up."

She rested her chin on his shoulder and looked at the photos in his hands. The top one was a close-up of Kat, wearing a flowered bikini, soaked head to toe, with blurred sprinklers in the background.

"She's got your eyes," Alyssa said.

Teague chuckled, the sound filled with absurdity. "They're brown."

"They're your shape. She's got your mouth, too." Alyssa kissed his cheek. "She's beautiful, and she's lucky she has a father who loves her so much."

"Doesn't seem so lucky to me," Teague grumbled in disagreement. "I just keep hurting the people I love."

Alyssa's heart stuttered. Had he just told her—albeit in a roundabout, convoluted way—that he loved her? She shook the possibility away and reached over his shoulder to pull out the group picture she'd looked at earlier.

"Tell me about this photo," she said.

"What about it? That's Desiree, Seth. You already know Kat and Tara."

"Desiree looks pretty chummy with Kat there. Were they close?"

"Oh, no. In fact, that was the first time I'd introduced her to Kat." He shrugged. "Desiree wasn't all that comfortable around kids, but Kat's such a dream. She's so easygoing, fun, social."

"When did you ask Seth and Tara to be Kat's guardians? Was it during the trial?"

"No." Teague set the pictures on his lap and laid his head back against the sofa. One hand came up and caressed Alyssa's arm. "After Suzanna died. In case something happened to me."

"Which was how long before Desiree died?"

"Two years." He looked up at her. "Why?"

She shook her head. "Just playing with numbers. Did you date anyone before Desiree?"

"No. Kat was just a baby, and I was trying to work these crazy shifts. Besides, Suzanna's suicide really dragged me under. I couldn't even think about anyone else. The guilt was horrendous. If it wasn't for Kat . . ." He shook his head. "It was a rough couple years."

Alyssa pulled another photo of Kat as a toddler from the bottom of the pile and set it on top. "Looks like you did a damn good job, Daddy."

Teague let out a heavy sigh. He set the photos down on the coffee table, took hold of both of Alyssa's hands and looped her around the sofa. With a gentle tug, he pulled her into his lap. Both hands came up to frame her face. He looked directly into her eyes as if he was trying to communicate something. Alyssa saw sadness and regret and affection. She also recognized smoldering passion.

She turned her head and kissed his palm. He lifted her face to bring her mouth to his. The kiss was slow, tender, meaningful. Something uncomfortable niggled in her chest. He couldn't be closer, yet she felt as if he were pulling away.

Alyssa intensified the kiss, demanding more, giving more. Teague groaned into her mouth, shifted with her until they lay on their sides. His bottom arm curved beneath her neck, his hand on the back of her head, fingers tangled in her hair, as he seemed to prefer them. His other hand settled on her thigh, slid under the hem of the T-shirt and caressed her butt. Squeezed and pulled her into his erection buffered by the cotton shorts.

"Mmm," she murmured against his mouth. "I want you more every time. I can't get enough."

His hand swept up her back, around her side, and cupped her breast. "I love the way you look." He kissed her long and deep and slow, his hand caressing, teasing. "I love the way you kiss." His thigh slid higher, pressing between her legs. She arched into the pressure, rubbing against him. "I love the way you touch me."

She smiled, trailed kisses over his jaw and down his neck. With a nudge, she pushed his shorts over his hips and wiggled them off his legs with her feet.

Teague pulled her earlobe between his teeth and nipped gently. "I love your passion." He continued kissing his way down her neck. "I love your commitment. Your determination. Your courage." His mouth moved over her shoulder. "I love your intelligence. Your compassion."

He shifted her onto her back, worked his hips between her

thighs. With every word, every kiss, every touch, Alyssa's heart picked up its pace.

He slid lower and kissed his way to her right breast. "I especially love your forgiveness. And your faith. There's so much to love." He took her nipple between his teeth, then entirely into his mouth.

"Teague," was all she could manage to drum up from her flooded brain.

He kissed his way back up her body. His hands slid beneath her butt and lifted. He entered her slowly, deeply.

"Teague . . ." Tears clogged her throat. She was so confused. She felt as if he were telling her he loved her in one breath, yet saying goodbye in another.

"Shhh." He kissed her. "Don't say anything, Lys. Just *feel*."

Alyssa woke with a subtle sense of panic that had become familiar. Teague wasn't lying beside her in bed, where they'd migrated after making love on the sofa. The house was silent, but it was the drop in temperature that worried Alyssa most. It meant Teague hadn't stoked the fire. And if he wasn't in bed with her and he hadn't tended the fire . . .

She dragged the blanket around her shoulders and rose, ignoring the aches and pains—both good and bad—tugging all over her body. Something jingled and hit the floor with a thud. Alyssa looked down. A roll of money and two sets of keys had landed by her bare feet.

"What the . . . ?"

Fury and fear rose in tandem. She hurried through the house, casting a quick look in each room to assure herself Teague wasn't holed up in some corner doing research.

When she reached the living room, her fears were confirmed. The fire wasn't just smoldering. It was out. Which meant Teague had been gone for hours.

With betrayal and hurt seething through her heart, Alyssa returned to the bedroom and pulled on the clothes she'd already worn two days in a row. She couldn't think. She had to move. Had to *do* something. Like find that jerk and ream the crap out of him. Then figure out why.

"What the hell kind of man does that?" she growled as she tightened the belt on her jeans. "Teague, you ass."

She pulled on her sweater, dug her feet into her clogs and scooped up the money and keys from the floor.

An explosion of sound came from the living room—the *crack* of wood, a loud *boom*. Alyssa jumped. The contents in her hands hit the floor.

"Freeze, police!" The words echoed from several different voices. "Hands up! Police!" Then a domino chorus of: "Clear. Clear. Clear."

A man turned into the bedroom and swept some type of rifle in Alyssa's direction. He wore all-black, military-style gear, helmet to boots. "Freeze."

Uh, yeah. Already there. Her entire body was stiff with terror. Alyssa couldn't have moved if she'd wanted to.

"Foster!" the man yelled. "In here."

A wave of confusion made Alyssa dizzy. Then Mitch stepped into the room. Mitch. Her brother. Also decked out in a black jumpsuit. Also carrying a weapon. Teague—gone. Mitch—here. What the hell was going on?

"Jesus Christ, Alyssa." In two steps, Mitch reached her, swept her up into his arms in a fierce hug. The equipment at his waist jammed into her side. Pain twisted through her belly. She cried out.

Mitch immediately put her down. "You're hurt?" He started pulling at her clothes. Before she could stop him, he'd lifted her shirt. "That fucking sonofabitch." He dropped the fabric. "Where is he? I'm gonna kill him."

Overwhelmed with physical and emotional pain, all she could do was press a hand to her side and shake her head.

"Find him." Mitch directed the other man with a sweep of his hand.

"Search the perimeter." The other man's authoritative

voice came muffled from the hallway, followed by the creak of leather, the clink of metal and the rustle of canvas as their boots clomped down the front steps.

Mitch put an arm around Alyssa's shoulders and turned her toward the bed. "Come over here. Sit down."

He dropped to a crouch in front of her, lifted her head with one hand on her jaw, swept the hair away from her cheek. Looking into his familiar face was so reassuring, yet not. The only hint of their Japanese ancestry was evident in his high cheekbones and too-long, jet-black hair. His eyes, the same color as hers, sparked bright green with intensity. In the safety of his presence, she broke.

"Mitch." She sobbed his name and fell forward, into his arms.

"Okay, Lys." He held her gently this time. "It's okay. It's all going to be okay."

It's not okay. Nothing about this is okay. Teague's words filled her head. Words she wanted to scream at her brother now.

"Where else are you hurt?" Mitch's gaze traveled over her, his hands sweeping down her limbs. "What else did he do to you?"

"He didn't do this. He didn't hurt me."

Her brother pulled away. His skeptical eyes met hers. "He's gone. Don't protect him, Lys."

"*He* protected *me*. If it hadn't been for him, I'd be dead." She gestured to her abdomen. "This is Taz's fault. He provoked a fight with a gang and Teague couldn't get me out of the way fast enough. He's the one who stitched me up. He's a—"

"Paramedic. *Was* a paramedic. I know all about him. And he shouldn't have had you there in the first place."

Mitch's frustrated gaze traveled over the room, paused on the rumpled sheets, dropped to the floor and held. His jaw went hard. His eyes went dark. Alyssa followed his gaze to a torn condom wrapper. Mortification pierced her belly and her eyes fell closed.

"Did he . . . ?" Mitch's hands closed over her arms. "Did he rape you, Lys? Fuck. We need to get you to a hospital."

"Stop." Alyssa resisted her brother's attempt to pull her to her feet and grabbed his forearms, squeezing until he met her eyes. The sickness there made her own stomach clench. "He did *not* rape me."

It took Mitch a long moment to absorb the meaning behind her statement. When he did, his eyes narrowed as he dropped his arms and leaned back. "You *slept* with him? What in the fuck . . . ? Jesus Christ, Alyssa, how . . . ? What . . . ? Why would you put yourself at risk like that?" He squeezed his eyes closed, pushed to his feet and smacked his forehead with his hand. "This is so not like you. He manipulated you when you were at your weakest—"

Alyssa stood, furious with every man in the universe. "Don't you dare insult my mental stability. I knew what I was doing. *I* made the choice. *I* went after *him*. If you knew the real man, you'd know *why*."

For a long moment, Mitch didn't speak, didn't move. He finally took a deep breath and met her gaze. The disillusionment in his eyes hit her hard, like one of those head butts he used to deliver as a kid when he was losing one of their many wrestling matches.

"Where is he, Alyssa?"

"I don't know." She crossed her arms against the pain in her torso, this pain originating from her heart, not her wound. "He walked out on me while I was sleeping."

His eyes said *I told you so*, but his lips didn't move. Finally, he let out a frustrated sigh and closed his arms around her again, kissing her forehead. "You have no idea how worried I've been."

"I'm sorry."

"It's not your fault. It's Creek's." He pulled back. "When

did he leave? And how the fuck did he get out of here? We've been watching this place all night."

"Watching? What do you mean, watching?"

"I thought telling him we were here would make him cave, but it only gave him information to escape. Again."

"You told him . . . ? When, how . . . ?"

"On the phone last night. I called the fax line until he finally picked up."

A chill started at the middle of Alyssa's chest and spread outward. "What time?"

"He finally answered around midnight."

The origin of her chill turned hard and icy. He *had* been pulling away. Saying goodbye. She'd been right. She'd *felt* it.

He'd made love to her, gone to the verge of telling her he loved her, then held back, knowing he would never have to live up to the declaration.

She lifted her eyes to meet her brother's. "What did you say to him?"

"That I knew where he was and that I would represent him if he'd let you go. I gave him until eight a.m."

"That you'd . . . ? Why?"

"I knew I recognized his name. He petitioned my office to take his case a little over a year ago. I didn't take it because I was already swamped. Looks like he found a way to get my attention."

All of the air whooshed from her lungs as if she'd been punched. Her mind bounced through the past few days. What had happened to make her believe his claim that he'd kidnapped the wrong woman? Were there signs, in retrospect, that he'd in fact targeted her?

Listen, Creek, I heard about your appeal, but you're not out of options, man. You can petition for another one.

Girl, you are the only thing I really need.

How does Luke live with you?

She's a bargaining chip, nothing more.

You give me Kat; I give you Hannah. Simple. Easy.

Back and forth. Back and forth. Alyssa grabbed her head to keep it from exploding. She didn't know what was real anymore, what was fiction, what were out-and-out lies. Now, with her head pounding, she couldn't remember if she'd ever actually heard Luke's voice. Had no idea if Luke was even real.

Then she thought of Suzanna's diary. Yes, Luke was indeed real. And only Luke could tell Alyssa if Hannah had been his girlfriend. Only Luke could tell her if Teague had actually made that phone call to him or if it had all been a fabrication.

She gathered herself and looked at her brother. "What now?"

"Now"—he pushed to his feet, settled his hands at his hips—"we work damage control. I've already put wheels in motion. My paralegal is organizing and filing papers for a suit against the hospital—"

"No." A few days ago, maybe, but now, everything was different. "I don't want a lawsuit."

"It's not going to be a real lawsuit. They'll settle the minute they see the charges. I've got suits against Dyne for defamation of character, the hospital for negligence, the Department of Corrections—"

"No, Mitch. I know you're trying to help, but—" She shook her head, and rubbed at her eyes. Her head pounded in time with her heart, and both hurt like hell for completely different reasons. "Just, no."

Mitch's arms closed around her shoulders again. Alyssa turned her face into the coarse material against his chest.

"You'll not only get your fellowship back, but you'll get the job you wanted—"

"I don't know if I want it anymore. I just want this to be over. I want my name cleared. I don't want people saying the things they're saying about me. I don't want people thinking I'm a criminal."

Which made her think of Teague and how he must have suffered.

"Okay. Fine," Mitch said. "I'll keep the lawsuit going against CDC, get the investigators to tear apart the guards' stories. When Creek is caught, he'll back up your story and we'll have them."

Alyssa closed her eyes and rubbed her forehead. "It's way bigger than that, Mitch. If we don't find Teague first, he may not live to tell any story." She dropped her hand and looked at her brother. "That business card I sent you, Vasser? He's—"

"Bad news. I know. Real bad news."

"He's been following Teague. All but confessed to killing Desiree and framing Teague. Tried to blackmail me into turning on him."

"I had a bad feeling about this from the beginning." Irritated resignation slid over Mitch's handsome face as he stood and held out a hand to help Alyssa to her feet. "I'll get my guys on Creek's trail while I drop you at Mom and Dad's—"

"No. I'm going with you." Teague wouldn't get to take the coward's way out. If he didn't want her, he would damn well tell her to her face.

Mitch heaved a breath. "How did I know you were going to say that?"

"And I know where to start," she said. "Right here in town. I want you to help me find someone."

With a cigarette propped in the corner of his lips, Jason pushed the cheap motel chair back on two legs and balanced there as he dug his pocket knife into the branch he'd found outside his door. He hadn't carved wood since he'd been a boy in Cub Scouts, but he sure as hell needed more than a smoke to relax him. At this point, he'd try anything.

"It was a calculated risk, Jocelyn," he said around the cancer stick. "She was no good to us sitting in a cell."

"Well, she sure as shit isn't any good to us now, is she? And her brother? Her *brother*? Do you realize what a problem that man is going to be?"

The knife in Jason's hand slid through the bark and a wood chip came off in an unsophisticated chunk, flying through the air and hitting the wall with a *clunk*. A smile curled Jason's mouth. He knew exactly what a problem Mitch Foster would be. The man was a perfect legacy. An appropriate parting gift. The ultimate payback for Schaffer forcing Jason to take on this shit case in his last weeks on duty.

"You think I spend all my time thinking of ways to make problems for you, Joce?" he said. "Come on. You're hot, babe, but, really—I don't have that kind of time."

"This isn't funny, Jason." God, he hated it when she got all intensely stressed and bitchy. "And just how did Foster find them before you did? How do you expect me to explain that to the senator?"

"Tell *the senator* Foster has nearly unlimited resources. If *the senator* would like to stop bitching about my expense reports—"

"Jason"—Jocelyn bit out his name, then hesitated and cleared her throat. "Along those lines, I'm calling to inform you that I've been authorized to provide you with additional resources. Dillon Burton will be joining you until Creek is . . . no longer a threat."

The knife in Jason's hand dug into the pale flesh of the tree limb and his hand paused. For a long moment, he couldn't form words. He'd worked alone for . . . as long as he could remember.

He yanked the knife from the wood and chucked the branch at the wall, pushing to his feet at the same time. "*What?*"

"You heard me." Her voice shook. Most people wouldn't have noticed, but Jason did because he'd heard it before. He'd heard it during extreme moments, like when he'd made her climax the fourth time in a row after she'd begged him to stop. "He'll be at your hotel room tomorrow morning, six sharp. Get this under control, Jason. For your own good."

Nineteen

Alyssa drove Mitch's BMW along Route Eighty-nine, listening to her brother relay the information to his investigators over a conference call via his cell phone. The deep blue waters of Lake Tahoe, the majestic pines, needles still sparkling with a fresh dusting of snow tried to steal her attention. But, the scenery couldn't compete with the thoughts and memories of Teague floating around in her head.

Mitch disconnected his call, looked down at the file in his lap and started talking to Alyssa. "Looks like Luke Ransom drifted after high school. Spent his summers fighting fires and his winters on ski patrol while getting his associate's degree at a local junior college. The firebug stuck and he went to California Polytechnic State University, San Luis Obispo, to get his bachelor's in Fire Protection Engineering. Graduated in the top ten percent of his class."

He flipped to another page. "Spent most of his firefighting career in the Nevada-Placer County of our fine state, while getting his master's via a correspondence program with University of New Haven. Signed on with the Bureau of Alcohol, Tobacco and Firearms a year ago."

Alyssa rubbed at the ache in her head. "So he was a firefighter when his sister committed suicide."

"Fire captain," Mitch murmured, looking directly at her. "And it was his *twin* sister."

"His twin?"

"Yep." Mitch returned his attention to the file. "I have to admit, if you'd committed suicide because I thought your husband had neglected you, and I had a niece out there somewhere being cared for by that person, I'd sure as hell fight to get custody of her, too."

Mitch's words created warmth that mingled with hurt and confusion. This situation was so complex, so wrought with emotion and turmoil. She'd been working up a lecture for Luke, filled with guilt-provoking facts. But after seeing it from Mitch's perspective, she found herself rethinking her whole approach.

As they neared the outskirts of Truckee, Mitch gave her directions through the business area, and into the narrow side streets making up one of the many residential communities, toward Luke's home, where they had learned the agencies involved in both the manhunt for Teague and the search for Kat had created their joint command center.

"Make a left turn," Mitch said. "It's up on the right. Drive past and double back to find a place to park."

Alyssa glanced in her rearview mirror for the S.W.A.T. guys who'd been following from Fallen Leaf Lake. "What about them?"

Mitch didn't bother looking up. "Those guys need no instruction."

Something that had been nagging at Alyssa for the last hour came to the surface again. "How are you paying those guys, Mitch? Teague doesn't have any money, and you know I've got student loans I'll take to my grave."

"Not to worry. I called in a few favors."

She'd known he would dodge the question. "Mitch—"

"Alyssa." He looked at her with that stern expression that conveyed the end of the discussion. "Believe me, I've done more for those guys than they could ever repay. Now, you and I can argue about this another time if you insist. But, right now"—he gestured up the street—"we have other problems to take care of."

Alyssa followed the direction of his hand toward an area of the street cluttered with knots of vehicles. F.B.I., A.T.F., and sheriff rigs lined the road. Alyssa's chest tightened, but not in excitement as it had just a few days ago at the prospect of seeing the police. Now she felt like a criminal. Now she feared getting caught and arrested. Now she had a whole new appreciation for what Teague had gone through. Was still going through.

"Looks like we've found the ant hill." Mitch pushed his sunglasses to the top of his head as Alyssa maneuvered through the tight space. "Better vantage point from the top of the street. Go a couple more blocks, make a U-turn and park." He pointed through the windshield toward a home whose front yard was a conglomeration of rock. "Behind those honkin' boulders. And don't scratch my car."

"Shut up. I've always been the better driver."

"Do I need to remind you how I beat you at the driver's test?"

"By *one* point," she said.

"Or how I've never been in an accident."

"That wasn't my fault. The other guy hit *me*."

"Or that I've never gotten a ticket."

Alyssa set the brake, turned off the engine and looked at her brother. He was smiling at her from the passenger's seat with that got-you smirk. And, God, it felt good.

"That," Alyssa said, enjoying the familiar banter, "was a *parking* ticket."

"Facts are facts. So let's find a few more that can help us here." With a flick of his wrist, he opened a new folder. "I think you were right about waiting until Ransom broke from the group before we approach him. If we called him out, he'd bring muscle, even if we told him not to. Stupid cops never listen. They're like insecure two-year-olds—can't go anywhere alone."

Movement down an adjoining street caught Alyssa's eye. The black sedan the S.W.A.T. guys had been driving pulled alongside the road in view of Mitch's BMW and parked.

"Isn't he more of a fireman than a cop?" Alyssa asked, turning her attention to a few men milling outside the white craftsman-style building that was Luke's home.

"He's a fire cop. A cop is a cop is a cop, as far as I'm concerned."

As the group of officials mingled and shifted location, another figure came into view.

"There he is," Alyssa said, pointing at Vasser, dressed almost exactly as he had been the day before at the shopping center. "Just like he said he'd be."

Mitch's attention veered from a computer-generated list in his hands to the crowd. "I thought he worked alone."

"What? Yes, he does. I mean, he did. I mean . . ." Confused, Alyssa frowned at her brother. "How do you know this stuff? I never told you that, but yeah, every time we've seen him, he's been alone."

Mitch tapped his temple with one finger, a sign he used to indicate what he humbly referred to as his stellar brain. "He's got a friend with him today."

Alyssa's gaze scanned the group again and paused on another man in plain clothes, no emblem on his Navy Windbreaker. Tall, hefty, mid-thirties, dark complexion. "Do you know him?"

Mitch aimed his iPhone at the man through the windshield, manipulating the photo until he had an amazingly clear close-up of the guy. "What, you think I know every spy in the business?"

"Yes." She tapped his temple.

A big, boyish grin transformed Mitch's face into the one Alyssa knew and loved with all her heart. He looked at her with those sparking green eyes. "That's the sweetest thing you've said to me in years."

She lifted her chin to the image on his phone as he clicked a still. "That's some camera."

"They say it's not the equipment, it's all in how you use it. But we know that's bullshit. I'll send this off and have this guy's whereabouts since birth in a couple hours."

"When this is all over, you and I need to sit down and have a heart-to-heart about who you're working with nowadays."

He slid her a look. "Uh-huh. That'll happen."

"Like that." She pointed to the papers in the folder he'd been looking at. "Ransom's bank account records? How could you possibly have obtained those legally?"

The Cheshire cat grin was back. "That's what investigators are for. Important stuff here. Tells me he's a caffeine addict and he'll be needing a hit soon."

Alyssa closed her eyes and laid her head on the seat. "This is so messed up. I really don't want you—"

His hand landed on her shoulder, and squeezed. "Alyssa. Stop. I've been doing this a long time. I can sure as hell take care of myself." He released her shoulder. "Well, look who's decided to show his beautiful face."

Alyssa opened her eyes, and focused on the house. A man came out onto the porch, dropping into conversation with a group of others. She'd seen a few older pictures of Luke from Teague's memorabilia, but nothing recent. Because of the porch overhang and the distance, all she could distinguish about the man who'd come outside was that he was taller than average, about Teague's height, wore a navy blazer and had blond hair.

"How do you know it's him?" she asked, waiting for the group to shift so she could get a better look at his face.

Mitch flipped another page in the folder and lifted it for Alyssa to see. "Here's his most recent photo. Can't be too many guys who look like that around."

Alyssa turned her attention to the picture, an eight-by-ten headshot of Luke that appeared to be some type of work-related photo. He wore a navy uniform with the badges on his chest shining bright gold, both of which accentuated his light, wheat-colored hair and deep blue eyes.

"Wow." Alyssa hadn't meant to say it out loud, but honestly, this guy was beyond handsome. "I think I may have seen a couple guys like that in one of your *GQ* magazines."

"Don't start harping on my choice of reading material, Miss I-only-have-time-for-medical-journals-boooooooooooring." Mitch jerked the photo back. "I think he looks a lot like that lifeguard at Mission Beach you pined over for months in high school."

"Oh, my God. I can't believe you'd bring that up."

"Definitely your type." Mitch shoved the photo back into the folder and turned more pages.

"If you weren't my brother, I'd think you were jealous."

"Fire up the engine, Lys. He's headed out to score."

Alyssa turned the key, and her heart accelerated in time with the engine. Luke climbed into the black SUV sitting in his driveway and backed out. Alyssa pulled in behind him, her fingers wringing the steering wheel, butterflies banging against her ribs.

"You're too close," Mitch complained. "Drop back, Lys."

"These streets are so convoluted, I'll lose him."

"I think I've done this a few more times than you have. If you spook him, he'll call in reinforcements and you won't get the chance to talk to him alone. An idea I'm still not thrilled about."

With a frustrated growl, Alyssa slowed, but not enough to placate Mitch. They followed Ransom's Explorer to the main road, and Alyssa turned out right behind him.

Mitch rubbed a hand over his eyes. "Don't quit your day job. You'd never make it in surveillance."

"Shut up."

"You've got time, Lys. He always goes to Peet's, which is in the shopping center two miles—"

The SUV took a sharp right and coasted into a parking lot where three small stores sat in a row: Molly's, a restaurant; Rush, a snowboarding-slash-rafting company; and Wild Cherry's, a coffee house.

Alyssa followed and cruised past Luke, who was parking in front of the coffee house, and continued to the end of the row, pulling in near Molly's. The S.W.A.T. guys magically appeared beside them, stopping two spaces away on the far side.

" 'You've got time,' " she mimicked in a high-pitched voice. "Peet's is two miles—ooooh, look at that."

"Shut up." Mitch frowned at the papers in his lap, his fingers skimming the list of Luke's recent purchases. "He's never come here. At least not in the last three months."

Alyssa watched Luke uncurl himself from the Explorer and wander toward the shop. He looked tired. No. He looked exhausted. He moved slowly, shoulders dragging, head bowed as he checked his phone.

"He doesn't want to go to the regular place," Alyssa mused. "Everyone knows him there. Too many questions. He can't face the fact that he doesn't have answers."

Mitch looked at her from the corner of his eye. "You're a psychic now?"

"I see the same behavior in the doctor's lounge. I know what people do when they don't want to face hard questions."

"They evade." Mitch closed the folder. "Like you're doing with Mom and Dad."

"I called Dad this morning. He's fine."

"You know what I mean."

Luke pulled the dark sunglasses from his face and held Wild Cherry's glass door for an older couple on their way out. They exchanged greetings; then Luke disappeared into the building.

"It's been fun getting needled by you, Mitch. Just like old

times. Sorry I have to cut it short." She reached into the backseat and pulled out her own manila file folder, then reached for the door handle.

Mitch caught her arm. "Lys . . ."

She turned back to Mitch and covered his hand with her own, squeezing his fingers. "I'm a smart girl. I've done my homework. I know what I'm doing. I'll try not to make so much of a mess that you can't clean up after me."

"Alyssa—"

She shut the door on his warning. Mitch covered his face with both hands and rubbed hard before glaring at her through the windshield. For his benefit, she smiled and blew him a kiss, then tugged down the white ball cap Mitch had given her and ran a hand over the ponytail threaded through the hole in back. With those captive butterflies in her stomach, she pulled the front door to Wild Cherry's open and stepped inside.

The welcoming scent of fresh, rich coffee made her salivate. She hadn't had a latte or mocha or frappachino or even a simple decent cup of coffee in days.

A quick survey of the shop was all she needed to release some of the pent-up anxiety. One word described the setting: cozy. Upholstered lounge chairs lined the periphery, while wooden bistro-sized tables and ladder-back chairs occupied the center area. One wall of windows looked out onto the street, another toward the parking lot. Alyssa glanced through them now to locate Mitch.

He and his S.W.A.T. playmates hovered around the hood of Mitch's BMW, where they studied a map they had spread over the shiny, black surface.

Alyssa pulled off her sunglasses and tucked one arm into the collar of her long-sleeved thermal shirt—another of Mitch's hand-me-downs.

Alyssa's gaze fell on Luke's back where he stood in line behind a college-aged man with a laptop hooked under his arm. She took a deep, calming breath and stepped into line behind him. The navy blazer stretched across wide shoulders, and his hair brushed the collar, the color a rich, deep wheat underneath, lighter on top. The gently curving mass was a little on the longish side, bordering on unruly. Alyssa thought of the photos she'd seen of Teague as a firefighter, his golden hair similar in length and style, darker in color.

Luke's voice rumbled into Alyssa's thoughts as he ordered a cappuccino, and the reality of the situation tingled through her chest. She pressed the apprehension away. She could do this. She'd faced far more daunting men than Luke, although, in those cases, she'd had far less to lose.

Luke pulled out a card from his wallet and handed it to the girl behind the counter. As he replaced it in the worn leather fold, Luke wandered to the end of the counter and leafed through a newspaper.

"What can I get for you?" The cashier's voice brought Alyssa's attention around.

"A tall, non-fat vanilla latte, double pump, extra hot, please." She held out a five-dollar bill, one from the wad of cash Teague had left on the bed—the jerk—and offered it to the girl.

"Your name?" she asked.

Alyssa stared at the girl. Her name? Should she use a false name? Her real name? What repercussions would either have? Unable to juggle the consequences of the decision here and now, she straightened her shoulders, took a deep breath and said, "Alyssa."

In her peripheral vision, she saw Luke's head come up. His whole body went still, fingers paused on the corners of the newspaper.

No pulling out now.

Alyssa stepped out of line and turned directly toward Luke. She met his dark blue eyes and held out her hand. "Alyssa Foster."

Luke's eyes widened with shock and disbelief. And he was even better looking in person. Definitely Malibu lifeguard material. He and Hannah would have been an absolutely stunning couple. Move over Brad and Angelina.

His gaze flicked between her face and her extended hand, which hung there feeling heavy and awkward. For a long moment, she was sure he wouldn't take it, but then his hand snaked out. Only he didn't accept her greeting; he grabbed her wrist.

"What is it with the wrist? Is that a guy thing?" she asked, twisting it in his grasp. "That is so damned irritating I can't even tell you."

In one step, he was an inch away, his other hand sliding handcuffs from somewhere beneath his blazer.

A current of fear zinged through her chest. She didn't pull out of his hold, but caught the wrist of his free hand with hers, evening the score.

"I suggest you hear what I have to say before you arrest me," she said.

"Give me one good reason."

"Because as soon as those cuffs close, so does my mouth. That won't help you find Kat."

His lips compressed. Eyes darted around the shop, surveying. She didn't resist when he pulled her toward a corner table, then pushed on her shoulder until she sat in a chair. He perched himself on the edge of a seat opposite her, positioning himself between her and the front door.

"But there are so many other good reasons," she said. "Why stop at just one? Let's consider the reasons related to Teague." As she talked, she pulled a handful of photos from her pocket. "He was your best friend for over *twenty* years."

She snapped a photo onto the table: one of Luke and Teague as kids, bare chested and muddy, both holding up fish almost as big as they were, grins splitting their faces. Luke's gaze fell to the photo and held. Alyssa knew a captive audience when she had one.

She set another photo down—Teague's wedding picture with Luke standing at his side as his best man. "He dedicated five years of his life to your sister." She added the photo she'd first seen at the cabin, one of Teague kissing Kat's cheek and glee written all over Kat's face. "He is the father of the niece you've sacrificed so much for."

And then the *coup de grace*, an image she'd discovered buried at the bottom of the box stuffed with photos of Teague's life. This one had been taken at the scene of a fire. Teague was in full gear, kneeling on the pavement in front of a burning building. His respirator dangled from the strap on his helmet as he cradled an unconscious Luke in his lap.

The anguish on Teague's face still made Alyssa's heart pound in her throat. She stabbed the picture with her finger and tried to meet Luke's shadowed, pained eyes, but he wouldn't look at her. "And how many times has he risked his own life to save yours over the years, Luke. I'd guess a few. Maybe even a few *dozen*. He deserves at least an ounce of your loyalty."

"Luke." The woman behind the counter announced his order. A moment later, another young girl said, "Alyssa."

The interruption seemed to snap Luke out of a trance. Without meeting Alyssa's eyes, he scooped the pictures off the table and stuffed them into a blazer pocket. "Don't move."

He turned toward the counter, picked up both coffees and returned. With a click, he set her drink on the table in front of her. "An ounce is all he gets. Talk. And start with how you know Teague."

She had to admit, he was intimidating, and Alyssa didn't intimidate easily.

Alyssa took a sip of coffee to soothe her nerves. The brew hit her tongue, scalding hot.

Luke ignored his own drink and pounded the table with his knuckles. "*How* do you know Teague?"

"For a smart man, that is a really stupid question."

"Papers say you're an accomplice, not a hostage. And I don't see any sign of Teague holding a gun to your head. So if you don't start talking, I'll take you down to county jail right now."

"Guess Teague was right. He said everyone would believe those guards."

"It's not much of a stretch to believe a law enforcement officer over a murderer." He nearly sneered at her. "Not for *most* people, anyway."

Alyssa's temper shot to full boil. "I never saw Teague before the day he wrapped a chain around my neck and dragged me out of the hospital. Instead of Hannah—or so he claimed. Which is one of the reasons I came to talk to you. Are you, or were you, truly seeing Hannah Svelt?"

"I don't see how that—"

It was Alyssa's turn to hit the table. Her open-palmed slap resonated through the small space, drawing attention. She turned away from the curious eyes. "Were you or not?"

He hesitated. "Yes, but that doesn't have anything to do with—"

"And you broke up when?"

"A couple weeks ago."

A rush of relief clogged her throat and stung her eyes. In her heart she'd known Mitch had been wrong. Teague hadn't targeted Alyssa to get to Mitch.

"Look," Luke said, "I don't care what Teague does as long as he stays away from Kat. He can go hide on the opposite side of the world as far as I'm concerned. Right now, I need to find my daughter."

"*Teague's* daughter."

"Not anymore. He gave up his life with Kat when he neglected his wife's pleas for help. When he killed Desiree. I've got court papers that say Kat is mine."

"She's not a dog, for God's sake. Nobody owns her."

He leaned forward, his face hardening with anger and impatience. "What are you, his personal activist? Why isn't that coward here talking to me himself?"

His gaze darted toward the window, as if he might find

Teague lingering outside, and his attention paused on the S.W.A.T. guys. His back straightened, body went on alert. "What's going on here?"

Alyssa followed Luke's gaze. Two of the S.W.A.T. guys stood at the passenger's door, smoking and talking. Mitch and the third ex-cop stood in front of Mitch's BMW. The cop was on his cell phone. Mitch had his arms crossed over his chest, his butt resting against the hood, one ankle over the other. And his unwavering stare was directed at her and Luke through the window of the coffee house.

"That's my brother, Mitch Foster," she said. "Maybe you've heard of him. He's a—"

"Shark," Luke said. "Trolling the waters of the Pacific Coast, freeing criminals up and down the state of California. Yeah, I've heard of him."

"Innocent men convicted of crimes they didn't commit. Not criminals."

"My ass. He's just another scumbag bleeding heart. And he can't be much of an attorney if he's letting his client come in here and talk to me alone."

So much for the benefit of the doubt. Luke obviously had deeply rooted issues Alyssa couldn't smooth over here or now. "I told you, he's my brother, not my attorney. I don't need representation. I haven't done anything wrong."

"Harboring a fugitive is wrong, Ms. Foster. Felony-level wrong."

"I'm not harboring anyone. Teague disappeared sometime last night while I was sleeping. My brother and his . . . associates . . . found me this morning."

One side of his mouth lifted in a sneer of doubt. "Coming to see me with an attorney and muscle in tow is hardly convincing me of your lack of involvement."

"I didn't say I was uninvolved. Thanks to Teague and the accusations of those guards, to the gossip and buzz surrounding the escape, I'm involved up to my goddamned hair follicles now. My reputation has been trashed, my future—

one I've worked toward over half my life—put at risk. Hell, yeah, I'm involved. And to be honest, there aren't any positive outcomes in this situation for me. I'm trying to salvage what I can."

Luke's lids lowered halfway and the skin beneath his left eye twitched. He huffed out a cynical laugh. "You're trying to manipulate me. Don't think I don't see it."

A burn sliced beneath Alyssa's breastbone. That was it. The last straw. Her patience had snapped. "You want to talk manipulation, Luke? Let's talk Department of Defense. Let's talk a warehouse fire some five years ago that changed six lives and ended another. Let's talk blackmail, murder, suppressing evidence, wrongful conviction. Does the name Jason Vasser mean anything to you?"

Luke leaned back. Way back. His head tilted sideways, eyes narrowed. He'd put up every shield available to block what Alyssa was throwing. But it didn't matter. As Mitch loved to argue—facts were facts.

"Yeah, that guy who's at your house, hovering, devouring all the information you're digging up? He's using you. He's been following Teague since the warehouse fire. When I confronted him yesterday, he threatened my reputation, my career and my life if I didn't tell him where Teague was. He insinuated that bad things happen to people who ask questions and said that Teague just didn't listen when he was told to stop asking. That Teague didn't listen when he elicited the help of others—namely Desiree Tapia."

Luke shook his head, waved flattened hands across the table. "Make up all the shit you want, girl, it's not going to change the fact that Teague Creek is a convicted murderer who escaped prison. He will eventually be caught, will go back and will spend his life behind bars. This is bullshit. This is all smoke and mirrors."

Alyssa crossed her arms and let out a long breath. She hadn't expected this level of pent-up anger and resentment. Hadn't bargained for such concrete convictions. And for the first time since she'd concocted this crazy notion, doubt crept in. But she wouldn't let that stop her. It sure as hell never had before, and then she hadn't been fighting for things that mattered half as much.

She pulled out her best card and played it in a much harsher fashion than she'd planned. "You're even more bull-headed and stubborn than your sister said."

"My sister?" Luke's brow wrinkled in anger. "You know nothing about my sister."

"But I do. I know a lot about your sister. More than you do, evidently." Alyssa set the journal on the table and pushed it toward Luke. "Have you seen this before?"

His gaze darted down, but he didn't touch it. "No, why?"

"Because it's Suzanna's diary."

The skin below Luke's eye trembled as he looked up at her again. "Where did you get it?"

"From a box of Teague's things." She waved at the diary. "Open it. Look. You should recognize your own sister's handwriting. Your own *twin's* handwriting. Mitch and I are twins, too." She waited until his gaze lifted to hers. "We could nearly read each other's thoughts for the better part of our lives. Still can on some level. You'll never convince me that you and Suzanna didn't have that connection. Not after what I read in that diary. Your sister talks about begging Teague not to tell you her problems, their problems, but then goes on to say she was sure you already knew without being told."

He looked at the notebook again with pain washing his features. Still, he didn't touch it. "She's been gone five years. None of this matters now."

Alyssa had an intense desire to wrap her fingers around Luke's neck and choke some sense, some patience, some compassion, some human kindness into him. "I'm beginning to see where you and Teague ran into trouble." She pushed the diary toward him until it met his fingers. "I marked a few passages I think will speak to you. Or at least I thought they would before I met you. Now I can only *hope* they do."

He pushed the diary back by the edge as if he couldn't stand to touch it. His expression was one of dread masked by lack of interest. "This isn't important now."

"It's *crucial* now. It's the root cause of everything that has happened in the past five years. One thing led to another, which led to another and another. And it all started with a warehouse fire."

Luke's eye twitched again. The blue of his irises hardened into murky steel. His gaze darted down and away in uncharacteristic apprehension, sparking a random thought in Alyssa's mind.

"You were there," she said. "You were at that fire six years ago, weren't you?"

"Yeah. I was there." His gaze came back sharp, but pained. "I went through everything he did and I didn't go off neglecting or killing people. That's no excuse."

Alyssa studied him, looking for signs of increased body temperature, considering how angry he was, but nothing struck her. He wasn't sweating, didn't take off his jacket. His fingers weren't burning the wood table or melting the Styrofoam coffee cup. Had Teague been the only one affected? Did Luke even know about Teague's abilities?

"He's not using it as one." She tapped the diary. "Are you going to look at it, Luke? Or are you afraid of what it might say? Then again, maybe you already know. Did you finally discover over the past few years what your sister knew early on? That the warehouse fire affected you all differently and to varying degrees? That she believed whatever Teague had been exposed to worsened her depression until it ate her soul clean away? That it was the chemical in that warehouse, the warehouse fire and ultimately the government that killed her, Luke? Not Teague?"

TWENTY

Teague took one final glance down the rural Oregon road, the only sight dozens of black-and-white cows grazing the neighbor's fields and another farmhouse half a mile in the distance.

Buddy Rawlings, Tara's half-brother, wouldn't be home from work for another hour, and before Teague talked to him, he wanted to pilfer the house and Rawlings's files for information. That way he'd know what questions to ask as well as what answers to expect. And if Buddy was lying to him, or holding out on him, Teague would know.

But he had to find a way into the house first, because evidently, even in rural Oregon, people locked their doors and windows. At least Buddy Rawlings did.

He pulled open the barn door at the rear of the property. The hinges moaned and wood edges scraped the ground. Late afternoon sun speared the dark interior, illuminating the dust colonies floating like sea nymphs in the deep blue. The musty scent of earth mixed with the smells of tobacco, oil and gasoline. A 1960's truck filled the right side of the garage, and Teague instantly knew where Buddy Rawlings spent every spare moment of his time.

How a man could keep a machine as pristine as that with a workbench stretching across the left side of the barn cluttered with wall-to-wall shit, Teague would never understand, but neither did he have to. He only had to find something to jimmie a lock.

In the far corner of the musty space, fertilizer and weed killer sat on the hard-packed dirt next to a shovel, rake and hoe. Nearby, a five-gallon can of white paint and an antique five-gallon can of gasoline sat next to an ancient lawnmower. The workbench lay scattered with empty Camel cigarette packages, spent cigarette butts and tools—wrenches, screwdrivers, a hammer, a putty knife, painting supplies.

Teague picked up the largest screwdriver and tested the weight. "This has potential."

He prowled up the back steps of the house and peered through the glass on the top half of the rear door. It led to a tiny kitchen, beyond which Teague could see an equally tiny living room. He knew from casing the place, the files he wanted were probably in the closet-sized bedroom just off the kitchen.

With the flat of the screwdriver wedged between the lock and the doorjamb, he had the door open in seconds without enough damage for Buddy to notice until well after Teague was gone. He'd already disconnected the telephone landline in the event that Buddy decided to call the cops right after Teague left. And if the guy had a cell phone, Teague had parked the truck he'd stolen from a home in Fallen Leaf Lake well out of sight so at least Buddy couldn't tell the cops what he was driving.

He left the door barely ajar and went directly to the office. Without wasting a second of time, he dove straight into the files, searching for anything related to Tara, their parents, or their family. He scoured tax records and real estate holdings while keeping one eye on the clock.

A car engine sounded outside the window, startling Teague from his research. Gravel crunched under tires in front of the house.

"No, dammit," he muttered and shut the file cabinet door. "It's too early."

Staying low, he crept to the window and peered over the edge. An olive-green Jeep Laredo stopped in the drive. Rawlings flung the driver's door open.

Teague ducked below the window ledge and squeezed his eyes shut. "Shit, shit, *shit*."

He scuttled back to the file cabinet, sent his fingers flying through the folders, plucking out anything remotely helpful. He pulled up his shirt, stuffed them into the waistband of his jeans and secured them by tucking in his T-shirt.

Footsteps sounded on the porch and Teague realized too late that he couldn't escape through the back door now. The bedroom lay directly off the open living area with a direct line of sight into the kitchen and his planned escape route.

The front door slammed shut. He'd have to settle for Plan B.

With his heart beating double-time, Teague coiled by the window like a snake, pressed his palms to the sash and pushed. He held his breath, only nothing happened. The window didn't move a millimeter.

Dammit.

Teague inspected the sill. Painted shut.

Fuck me.

Would anything ever go right?

His thoughts shot to the screwdriver he'd used to jimmie the lock. With slow, careful movements, he scored the paint along the sash, over and over, cutting through years, possibly centuries of paint layers as Rawlings rummaged in the kitchen.

By the time chips started to fly, sweat ran down the sides of Teague's face. He set the screwdriver down, pressed his palms to the sash, bent his knees, put his shoulders into it and pushed.

The window gave. Slid. An inch. Another. Then stuck.

Teague wiped his brow with the back of his hand and rubbed the sweat off on his shirt, then picked up the screwdriver again.

Movement outside caught his eye. A car passing the house. He stepped back, pressed up against the wall and peered out.

No, not passing. Stopping. Right out front. A navy-blue sedan with government plates.

Fucking government plates.

The gun at the base of his spine took on weight. His breathing picked up pace and his eyes honed in on the passenger door, closest to him. A dark-haired, dark skinned man appeared. Not Vasser.

Teague's heart tripped. What the . . . ?

Then the driver emerged and Teague's moment of hope popped. Vasser passed the other man on his path to the house without a glance and continued toward Rawlings's front door with single-minded purpose.

Alyssa had told him Vasser was convinced Teague wasn't after Kat. And yet, if Vasser believed that, why was he here? Rawlings had no tie to Teague but Kat.

Even though he knew it was coming, the pound on the door made Teague jump. He edged toward the bedroom door, listening.

"Look, I can't be leaving work early at your beck and call," Rawlings said. "I already told you guys—"

The sharp smack of flesh and a visceral grunt sounded almost simultaneously. "You lied to me," Vasser said, his voice tight. "You said you hadn't talked to Tara."

The front door slammed. Creek took one step to the opposite side of the door where he could peer through the crack. Rawlings, nearly three hundred pounds, was bent over holding his face, Vasser circling him like a rabid animal. The unknown man stood silently at the front door, watching.

"I . . ." Rawlings stammered, "I . . . didn't talk to her about Creek. I just—"

Vasser backhanded the side of Rawlings's head. The big man hit the floor with a solid thud. "You wired her money, which means you *talked* to her, you motherfucker. You also told me you hadn't seen Creek. Was that another lie? Another *partial* truth?"

Vasser, for all his psychopathic twists, was an even-keel

personality. Teague could never remember seeing him riled. Not like this.

"No," Rawlings said. "No. I haven't seen or talked to Creek. Ever."

"He's never come looking for his kid?"

"No. Never. I swear."

Vasser looked at the guy standing by the door. "I think he's lying, Burton. What do you think?"

Burton didn't answer, which didn't seem to surprise Vasser, who only looked back down at Rawlings.

Rawlings straightened, hands held out. "Tara loves that kid. Just wants to take her somewhere safe. I gave her money so she could do it, that's all."

"Where'd she go?"

Rawlings rubbed blood off the side of his mouth. "Vancouver."

"As in fuckin' Canada?" Vasser asked in disbelief. "Why?"

"Because my dad, he has a house up there."

"Yeah?" Vasser straightened, assessing Rawlings with suspicion. "What's the address?"

"Uh, Jesus, I don't know the address. Somewhere around Queen Elizabeth Park."

Vasser looked at Burton. "What do you think of all this, *partner*?"

To Teague's knowledge, Vasser had never worked with a partner. The distaste in the word came through loud and clear. Something was seriously wrong.

Burton's dark face remained expressionless as he moved forward. Nearly as tall as Rawlings at six feet, Burton looked in the other man's eyes as if to search for truth or lie. Long, slow, silent seconds ticked by.

"I think we're done here." Burton's voice was so soft and low, Teague almost didn't hear the words. Without warning, Burton lifted his weapon, shoved the muzzle against Rawlings's forehead and pulled the trigger.

The muffled pop made Teague jump. Rawlings jerked back

the same instant the rear of his skull exploded. He stumbled two giant steps, eyes wide and blank before he fell like a logged tree.

Teague's stomach clenched. Buckled. Shriveled.

Vasser's arms flew out to his sides. At some point, Vasser had drawn his weapon, because it was in his hand, but Teague hadn't seen him do it. "What the fuck is wrong with you? Why'd you do that?"

"Why?" Burton asked. "Did we need him for something?"

"No, but did you ever stop to think about how we're going to explain how this guy got an agent's bullet in his brain, you dumbfuck?"

"Freeze!" The authoritative, familiar voice sent another zing down Teague's spine, and not in a good way. "Federal Agent."

Vasser and Burton swung toward the front door, weapons raised and aimed at the newcomer.

"Funny," Vasser said. "Me, too. Up for a game of chicken, Agent Ransom?"

Teague shifted to get a better view. Sure enough, Luke stood there, backed up by a man Teague didn't recognize. The other guy was tall, with black hair, wearing a crisp suit. But there was something familiar about him. The eyes, the chin, the bone structure . . . in a masculine sort of way, this guy looked a lot like . . . Alyssa.

Shit. Her brother Mitch.

Shock and dread congealed in Teague's belly. He moved to the window, peered toward the street, scanned for another car, and spotted a black BMW parked inconspicuously half a block away and, yes, Alyssa, skulking behind a tree.

"Fucking A . . ." he whispered and scuttled back over to peer toward the foursome in the living room, his mind spinning for options like a cyclone.

"What the *fuck* is going on here?" Luke growled in the other room. "Put your weapons *down.*"

"Sorry to say," Vasser said, "that's not going to happen,

Agent. But this doesn't involve you. At least not right now. Unless you'd like to end up like this"—he tipped his head toward the carnage on the floor at his feet—"I'd suggest you walk out of here and let us handle Creek. Think about it. There's a lot of incentive. Once we find him, he will never show up on your radar again."

Teague's heart beat too fast. His head went light. The Luke that Teague used to know would never back down. His former friend's values, ethics, ego, training, would have made it impossible for him to turn away in this moment. But now, after all that had happened between them, with all Luke had to lose, Teague didn't know what to expect.

He eased the weapon from the back of his jeans and crouched by the door leading to the living area and open to the kitchen. The space was so small, one wrong move and they could easily end up in wall-to-wall blood.

Movement out the room's side window caught Teague's attention. His gaze jerked left, where he peered through the glass and found Alyssa creeping up the rear walk, past the barn and toward the back door.

After that one shot, Alyssa couldn't stand the silence. Luke had told her to stay put like she was a freaking dog. Mitch had left her to play cop without a second look, just as he had their entire childhood, running off with his friends and leaving her behind.

Now, movement inside the house passed through the single-sheet glass like shadows on the surface of a lake. She crouched as she neared the back door and the upper window panel. Standing to the side, she eased in until her eyes just cleared the edge of the glass.

Luke and Mitch stood opposite Vasser and the other man she'd seen at Luke's house earlier in the day. All had their weapons drawn in a room the size of a large bathroom. Alyssa's throat tightened as she scanned their faces. No one looked ready to back down.

Then her gaze caught something else. Something lower. On the floor. Legs. That led to a body. That led to a head. No . . . yes . . . She squinted, trying to make sense of the . . . *Oh, God.* A partial head. And blood. And something sprayed across the room . . . something that looked like . . . tissue.

Her breathing stuttered. Her mind numbed out.

"Lys . . . Alyssa . . . *Alyssa.*"

The hushed sound of her name floated at the edges of her brain, somewhere far away. Her head wavered, legs weakened.

"Alyssa *fucking* Foster." The furious hiss penetrated her foggy head. "Get the *fuck* out of here. Right this *fucking* minute."

The swearing pierced the remaining haze and when her mind came around, she looked to her right. Teague met her gaze through the window and mouthed: *Get out. Now.*

Then he opened the door separating him from the four men and entered the living room. He swept up behind Vasser in one stealthy move and pressed the weapon in his hand to the other man's cranium.

"No." Alyssa's voice came out as nothing more than a ragged whisper. "No, no, no."

"Here I am, Vasser," Teague said. "Silver platter. This is between you and me. Let them go."

Every method of coping she'd ever learned failed. Nothing met this level of extremity, not even medical life and death. These were two of the men she loved most looking death in the face well before their time. This was her watching those two men test fate partially because of decisions she'd made. No, this had definitely not been in any crisis-planning curriculum or life lesson she'd ever learned.

Alyssa backed down the walk, her mind stumbling for traction. What could she do? Calling the cops was out. She didn't have a weapon. If she walked in there, she risked causing havoc. But dammit, she couldn't just stand outside and wait. There had to be something she could do.

Her gaze swept the old ranch house falling apart at the seams. Unlike the gas station where she'd first stopped with Teague, this place had plenty of loose siding and broken pipes lying around, only those were no weapons against four guns.

"Oh, my God. Oh, my God. Oh, my God." With panic crawling up her throat, Alyssa sprinted toward the barn, its door partly open. She was already panting when she stepped into the rancid space, filled with nothing but junk, save a stunningly restored old truck.

"Come on, Lys, *think*." Her heart pounded hard against her ribs, hands poised to grab the first thing that made sense. Only, nothing made sense. After all, what the hell did she know about breaking up a gun fight? Give her a ruptured aorta, a severed spine, a failed heart—no problem. But, this? She couldn't even begin to fathom how many things could go wrong in this situation.

She eyed a shovel in the corner—throw it through the window? What if it startled one of them so badly his weapon discharged and she inadvertently started a gun war? Make noise in the barn? What if they simply ignored it?

Alyssa pressed both hands to her forehead and wandered around the darkened space, her gaze searching for something, anything that would pop an idea into place. And dammit, she was desperate.

A crowbar, hammer, lighter, screwdriver, wrench, paint supplies, bag of weed killer, can of gasoline.

Click.

Her mind stopped on the gasoline, though she didn't immediately know why. She bent over and tested the weight. Her arms and ribs flexed with effort. It was full. Thirty awkward pounds full.

"Holy crap."

The car with government plates so blatantly parked right up next to the house as if it belonged there appeared in Alyssa's mind. A sinister plan snapped together so perfectly, so clearly. Wrong—legally. Yet right—on so many other levels. And there was a vindictive element that tempted Alyssa in a way she'd never experienced before. She wanted to see the people that had torn Teague's life apart pay, and she was going to use her act of revenge to get Teague and Mitch and Luke out of there safely. It was the kind of distraction they couldn't ignore. The kind they would have to act on. And it was all Alyssa could think of in the moment. Which was *all* she had. A moment.

She swept a lighter off the workbench and flicked the metal wheel with shaking fingers. It sparked. She tried again, and when she got a flame, Alyssa stuffed the Bic in her pocket and bent to grip the handles on either side of the gas can.

She dragged the awkward metal canister close to her body and waddled out of the barn. Then she stumbled down the side of the house. The injury over her ribs pulled as if her healed scar was ripping apart. After two feet, she was sweating. After ten, she was panting. After twenty, she was moaning. Fifty, and she turned the corner of the house.

Overgrown weeds caught her ankle. She tripped and stepped on a piece of downed siding. The wood splintered, shot up and dug into her forearm. A muffled cry lifted from Alyssa's throat. She dropped the can, then instantly tried to grab and right it. Inside, liquid sloshed. Gas fumes burst from the canister and burned Alyssa's nasal passages, searing her throat.

The metal handles cut into her palms as she rehoisted the can. She staggered the last fifteen feet and set it down by the sedan's driver's door.

"I can't believe I'm doing this," she muttered as she swung the door wide and looked over her shoulder. Through the living room window, the men remained shadowed watercolors behind the glass.

She hadn't heard any more shots, which she considered a good sign. If anyone could talk his way out of a situation, it was Mitch. But for some reason, she didn't expect him to talk his way out of this one, only hoped he could bullshit these guys long enough for her to light up this damn car and get them out of the house.

Crouching, she unscrewed the two-inch-diameter pour hole in the lid, lifted the edge of the can to the driver's seat, grabbed the bottom and tipped it up until gasoline spilled out. The potent liquid sloshed over the seat and spilled onto the floorboards. Alyssa kept tilting the can until it was empty, then shoved it into the passenger's seat.

With a fumbling hand, she drew the lighter out of her pocket, struck the wheel and brought the flame to the driver's seat before she had time for her conscience to kick in.

The flames whooshed from her hand like a blowtorch. Heat scorched her face. She sucked in a breath of supercharged air and shrank from the flames. One arm came up to shield her face as her feet scuttled backwards on dirt and gravel. Fire traveled through the car like a windstorm. Within seconds, the vehicle looked like a crazed Halloween pumpkin, fire swirling, eating away the guts.

Alyssa gained her feet and ran back the way she'd come, heart beating hard, but somehow lighter, strangely liberated.

A loud *pop* sounded behind her, like a gunshot. The shatter of glass rained on gravel. When she reached the barn, Alyssa turned toward the car. Flames licked at the metal frame where the windshield had been. Shards of glass glittered along the hood like diamonds. A line of fire flowed from the open driver's door and across the ground to the corner of the house where it devoured the old siding board by board like a starving creature. In front of her eyes, the fire jumped from the side boards to the roof and streamed across the tinder-dry shingles as if they were painted in oil.

Fear burned through Alyssa's chest just as fast. "Oh, *shit*. No!"

She whirled toward the back of the house and ran up the walk. A window on the opposite side of the house shattered. Charcoal smoke coiled into the dusky sky. By the time she reached the kitchen's rear door, the interior undulated with shades of neon orange. Black silhouettes lunged against the backdrop. Alyssa cupped her hand around her eyes to peer through the glass, but the smoke obscured her view.

"Mitch!" She yelled as loud as her searing throat allowed. "Teague!"

The back door flung inward. Alyssa jumped back and screamed. Smoke poured out, choking her. Luke appeared, stepping into the middle of the doorway, face bloody, suit jacket burned away in sections. As if the fire knew he was planning escape, flames raced overhead, split at the center of the doorway and traveled around and down the frame.

"Get the hell out of here!" he yelled at Alyssa.

Without waiting to see if she listened, he opened both hands, reached up and planted them, palms down, on the doorframe, directly over the flames.

Alyssa sucked in a breath of horror. "Luke, no!"

The fire sizzled beneath his hands just before smoke plumed out. He continued to run his palms down the frame, smothering the flames with his bare skin.

Alyssa grabbed one of his hands and turned it over, but all she found was one perfect, intact palm. "Oh, my God."

Luke grabbed her arms and pushed her back. "I said get out of here."

Then he turned and disappeared into the smoke and flames.

The first hint of sirens perked up Alyssa's ears. She turned toward the sound with a new fear filling her heart. Firefighters were coming. Cops wouldn't be far behind.

"Teague!" she called into the house. "Mitch! Luke!"

Grunts sounded in the murky din, amongst the angry roar of fire, the pop and crack of old wood. Something flew past the door where Alyssa stood, and she jumped. It hit a wall, bounced off, darted across the floor and stopped at her feet. A gun.

She reached for it. Teague appeared, skidding across the

floor. He grabbed the weapon and looked up at her. "Get out of here, goddammit! Don't you ever listen?"

Vasser walked out of the mist, gun pointed down at Teague's chest, blood dripping from his forehead. "Didn't I ask you that once, you stupid sonofabitch?"

Teague tilted his chin to his chest, lifted his foot and kicked at Vasser. The other man dodged, but not completely and went down with a scream. Teague disappeared once again into the swampy darkness.

"No, Teague! Cops are coming." Alyssa peered through the smoke and stepped farther into the house with the hem of her shirt pulled up over her mouth. "Luke!" Smoke invaded her eyes like thousands of tiny needles. Tears poured down her cheeks as she pushed farther into the gloom. "Mitch!"

Scuffling sounds came from somewhere to her left. She started in that direction, but Teague caught her arm from behind. "You're not going in there."

She yanked her arm from his grip and turned on him. "Stop pulling at me and help me get them out."

Someone rammed into her and she pitched sideways, her breath locked in her chest. Teague caught her as the other person hit the floor. Mitch. Alyssa registered the blood covering his face in the second before Burton pointed a gun at Mitch's chest.

"No!" Alyssa heard her voice, but didn't register the sensation of speaking.

Everything beyond that whirled into a successive blur of motion. Teague struck out. The gun flew from Burton's hand. A scavenge, then a struggle for the weapon. A shot.

Alyssa screamed—a rip in her throat and a stab in her heart.

Burton collapsed on top of Mitch.

"Mitch!" She kept screaming his name, coughing, wheezing, screaming. She couldn't breathe, couldn't think. Couldn't live without him. "Mitch!"

"Goddamned fucking fat bastard." Mitch hefted Burton off him using his whole body.

A shaking whoosh of air left Alyssa's chest. She swallowed back the urge to throw up in relief. "Oh, my God."

Mitch slowly got to his feet, rested his elbows on his knees and met Alyssa's eyes. "I'm fine, Lys."

"*Fine?*" she wheezed. If this was what an anxiety attack felt like, she was going to be far more liberal handing out Xanax prescriptions in the future. "I almost watch you get *killed* and that's all you have to say to me? I'm *fine?*"

When Teague reached for Alyssa, Mitch pushed off his knees and intervened, taking her arm while giving Teague a death stare. "Where's the other one? Vasser?"

The sirens grew ear piercing and stopped in front of the house. Luke passed through the group and stepped out the back door. "Incapacitated. Let's go. Unless you'd like to explain that kill to the cops right this minute."

TWENTY-ONE

Teague's chest ached, but it wasn't from the solid military-style elbow shots Burton had hammered to his sternum or the smoke burning his lungs. His pain came from looking at Alyssa and knowing he'd never touch her again.

Damn, she looked good. Great. Amazing. Had she looked that gorgeous when he'd left her? Just that morning?

Had he really walked out on her lying naked, tangled in a sheet, still warm and damp with their sweat from hours and hours and heavenly hours of lovemaking? Had he? Really?

Luke passed, purposely knocking Teague's shoulder hard. "Come on, Houdini. Think up something to get us out of here."

Teague wiped the smoke burn from his eyes with his forearm and turned toward the barn, but stopped short. Did Luke just say *out of here*? Why were they all walking away from him? Why wasn't anyone holding a gun on him? Cuffing him?

No sense in questioning it, at least not for the moment. The answers and the pain that went with them would come soon enough.

"How in the hell did you get here so fast?" Teague knew how they'd found him—Alyssa. But how had they caught up with him? "I had a five-hour lead on you."

Mitch scowled at Teague from beneath a mess of black hair falling over his forehead. "They're called planes, Creek."

While Luke cased the scene for cops and Mitch and Alyssa bickered, Teague pried open the second door to the barn and inspected the wires beneath the dash of the ancient Ford. He prepped the truck by stripping and twisting wires, then unlatched and opened the gate hidden behind the barn by overzealous morning glories. It led to a barely noticeable gravel back road he'd found earlier in the day during his inspection of the property.

When he returned to the truck, he took a deep breath, focused and directed his energy until the engine turned over. The well-kept vehicle started like a brand new Corvette and purred like a damn Ferrari.

He didn't have to beckon the others away from the inferno; they automatically climbed into the cab of the truck. But Teague didn't miss the suspicion on Mitch's face as he slid into the bench seat alongside Luke.

"Why am I the only one who doesn't find the fact that he can hot-wire a car surprising?" he asked.

"Long story," Alyssa muttered, sitting on Mitch's knee, holding the dash to balance herself as Teague turned onto the rutted back road.

"Well, everything about this is a long fucking story, isn't it?"

"Mitch," she scolded.

"Excuse me for swearing, Lys. You've only uncovered some festering conspiracy that my gut tells me is way beyond anything I've ever seen and, oh, by the way, I just killed a guy." His voice rose until it vibrated through the truck cab. "Sorry if I'm a little upset."

She heaved a sigh. Teague rolled his shoulders and purposely loosened his grip on the steering wheel. How in the hell had this gone so wrong? All he'd ever wanted was a simple, quiet life with his daughter.

"What in the hell are you all doing here?" he spat at them collectively. "I tried to cut you out of it."

"You're trying to take Kat," Luke yelled back from the center seat next to Teague. "How the hell does that cut me out, asshole?"

"She's *my* daughter, that's how. She belongs with me."

"And you belong in prison," he shot back. "Explain how that would work, brainiac."

"If you really think I belong in prison, why haven't you arrested me? What in the hell are you doing with them?" He jerked his hand at Mitch and Alyssa. "Why don't you have your A.T.F. buddies with you? Where's the fucking F.B.I.? Would someone tell me what the hell is going on here?"

Alyssa put up her free hand in a stop gesture. "Could you wait to scream until we're out of an enclosed space so you don't rupture my eardrums, please?"

The farther they drove from the light of the fire, the harder it became to follow the road. Teague finally turned on the headlights.

Mitch dropped his head back and rubbed a hand over his forehead. "My God. I shot a federal agent with my own damn gun. Motherfuckingsonofabitch."

"Mitch, that's enough," Alyssa complained. "I know this is bad, but come on."

"Creek, stop the car." Mitch sat up, and reached for the door handle. "I need some air before I puke on everyone in this truck."

It was a good thing Teague was driving slow, because Mitch didn't wait for him to make a full stop. He pushed the door open and took Alyssa with him when he dropped to the ground. She squealed as she fell on her butt in the grassy gravel.

"Mitch, you jerk." Alyssa's voice carried in the silent night, the sirens and fire only distant background noises now.

By the time Teague put the truck into park and jogged

around the front, Alyssa was standing, brushing gravel off her jeans, her scowl fully visible in the headlights' side beams shining down the path.

Luke leaned against the bed of the truck, arms crossed, eyes keen as he followed everyone with that watchful gaze. Mitch paced, head down, hands threading and rethreading through his collar-length, black hair.

"You're not getting how serious this is for me, Lys." His voice rose to a shrill tone, eyes wide with panic. "They'll match the slug they pull from Burton to a shooting I was involved in last month."

"A shooting last—" Alyssa started.

"It doesn't matter"—Mitch cut her off. "What matters is, when they do that, they'll know my gun killed Burton. They'll know *I* killed Burton."

Teague opened his mouth to speak, but Mitch started waving his hands again, muttering. "You know how long I've worked for what I've built? As long as you've worked for your M.D. Those goddamned government freaks are going to try to take me out right along with you and Creek and anyone else they damn well feel like eliminating."

"Hello." Teague waited for Mitch to take a breath. Alyssa looked over at him with a hollow, helpless look in her eyes. Mitch, on the other hand, turned on Teague with clear contempt. "About that gun . . ." Teague lifted his shirt to reveal a weapon in the waistband of his jeans. "This is the gun that killed Burton."

Mitch pulled his gun from a holster on his hip. "No, this is mine."

"Yes, that is yours," Teague said. "But this is the one that killed Burton. You grabbed it by mistake."

Mitch walked in front of the headlights, pulled the magazine of his weapon open and checked it in the light, squinting.

"What the hell?" Mitch said.

"It's full, right?" Teague said. "I kept track of all the weapons. All the shots. In the end, I made sure the right ones ended up where they belonged."

Mitch looked up from the weapon, his suspicion as clear as the darkening evening sky. "How could you possibly have kept track?"

Teague shrugged. "You learn to do that in prison. Lose track of one fork at breakfast, end up dead in the shower at lunch. A sharp mind and quick hands keep you alive inside."

"You couldn't see your hand in front of your face in there with all that smoke."

"He was a fireman for over a decade," Luke said. "You learn to see through smoke."

Anger stirred in Teague. He wanted to tell Luke to shut the fuck up. His defense came about five years too damn late.

"Why would you *do* that?" Mitch asked, his brows drawn together in disbelief.

"This is my fight, not yours." His voice rose and Teague let it. For once it felt good to yell at someone. "I hightailed it out of that cabin to keep as many people out of this mess as possible. I let her go, just like you wanted, and look where it got me."

He pulled the murder weapon from his waistband with the hem of his shirt, walked over to Mitch, and shoved it at him. "But, fine, whatever. If you don't want to believe me, it's your hide. I was just trying to help."

Mitch pulled his sleeve over his hand and took the gun. But his eyes screamed *what the fuck?*

"By the way," Teague added. "Just for fun, I put Vasser's prints on it while he was unconscious. I'm sick like that. The prison effect."

Teague was about to turn away, but his gaze passed over Alyssa, and he stopped. How could he not? Even sooty and sweaty and cut and bleeding she was heart melting. And every time he looked at her, all he could think about was how she tasted, how her body fit against his, how it felt to be inside her. Heaven. Absolute heaven on earth. Now, he'd have to spend the rest of his life without her, which would be sheer hell.

He channeled the pain into frustration. This huge, ugly mess was no place for her. These people would never leave him alone. If she continued to follow him, if he continued to allow a relationship, she'd never be safe.

"A fire?" he mocked. "A car fire? What were you thinking, *genius*? If I'd wanted to start a fire, I could have done it myself."

Her eyes narrowed, and her mouth curved into a sneer. "You can't even catch a paper bag on fire. For your information, I've done more research on your powers and what you have isn't pyrokinesis, it's thermokinesis. So you may be able to change your body temperature—note, I said change, not control, because God knows you're not in control of much—but, babe, you aren't starting any fires."

Smart-ass little . . . He leaned into her and lowered his voice. "That's not what you said last—"

"Whoa, whoa, whoa." Mitch put a hand on Teague's chest and pushed him back. "Powers? Pyrokinesis? What the hell are we talking about here?" He put himself squarely between Teague and Alyssa, his hands on her shoulders. "Who are you and what have you done with my diehard scientist sister?" He released her and turned on Teague. "An even better question is why do these guys have a hard-on to see you dead? What is this about?"

Silence gapped in the stark absence of their bickering and quiet night sounds filled the void in contrast, the loudest and most cliché, the sharp chirp of crickets.

"Another long story," Alyssa finally offered. "One we haven't fully figured out."

"Think I'm ready for a drink," Luke said. "Or ten. Foster, why don't you use that fancy phone of yours to track down the seediest bar you can find?"

"I don't have time for that." Teague started for the driver's side. "You can do all the detective work you want, but I don't give a shit about Vasser anymore. I'm getting the hell out of here."

As soon as Teague slid behind the wheel, the familiar *shhhh* of a Glock slide sounded beside him. In his peripheral vision, Teague registered the weapon pointed at his chest and the man behind it.

"You're not going anywhere without us," Luke said. "You've pulled us all into this, Teague. Our lives, our careers—we're all exposed. You made your choices. Now you're going to live with them, just like we have to."

Anger, frustration and uncertainty zapped like an electric current in the air of the cab as they all piled back into the truck. Teague took the back roads until he pulled up behind Mitch's black BMW and cut the lights, letting the truck idle as Alyssa pushed the passenger door open and climbed out.

While Mitch finished up a phone call, Teague watched flames and water battle over Rawlings's rooftop, creating billows of charcoal smoke that rose and then disappeared into the night. A painful twist of emotions ached in his chest, too many to define and identify before Mitch disconnected and scribbled an address on the back of his business card.

"You two ditch this eyesore and take that piece of shit Creek stole and meet us here," Mitch said. "We can clean up, regroup and do some research—"

"Look," Teague started, "I don't mean to be unappreciative, but—"

"I'm obviously not making myself clear." Mitch slapped the card onto the dash and slid off the seat, turning to settle one of those Foster family this-is-the-way-it-is stares on him. "That was not a request."

He slammed the door, took Alyssa's arm and strode to the passenger's side of the BMW, opening the door for her.

"Even though he's a shark," Luke said, moving along the

bench seat toward the passenger's door, "I think I kind of like him."

"I think I kind of hate him." Teague turned on the next street, driving toward the Toyota 4Runner he'd stolen and parked.

"I know. That's a big part of why I like him."

Teague slid a look at Luke. "Don't point that fucking gun at me again."

"Then don't think of doing stupid fucking things, like running."

Teague pulled in behind the 4Runner, reached under the dash and yanked at the wires of the Ford, cutting the engine. This was going to be one long-ass night.

Luke got out of the truck and crossed to the driver's side. "I'm driving."

"Sure you want to risk getting caught driving a stolen vehicle?"

"I'll just tell them you took me hostage."

"Funny. Then get your ass under the dash and see if you can still hot-wire a car, *Agent*."

Luke swung the driver's door open. "Still a premium asshole."

Teague rounded the truck, dropped into the passenger's seat and waited. He'd already done all the groundwork, Luke only had to twist a few wires. Without Teague's sparking ability, it took Luke longer to get the engine turned over, but he managed.

He settled himself behind the wheel and let the truck idle. A little too long. Teague knew what was coming. It was inevitable. The anticipated knock-down, drag-out fight for Kat. His shoulders tensed in anticipation of the pending confrontation.

Luke had the clear advantage. All he had to do was deliver Teague to the closest police car at the fire scene, claim he'd started the whole thing and killed the men inside. Luke could send him straight back to prison, never to be heard from again. Simple plan. Effective solution to Teague ever taking Kat back.

"Why didn't you tell me about Suzanna?" Luke turned in the seat, partially facing Teague. "Why didn't you tell me about the depression, about the problems she was having?"

Teague's brain stopped spinning, leaving him woozy from the sudden tilt. This was not the confrontation he'd been expecting. "What . . . ?"

"Alyssa showed me her journal." Pain and anger seethed through Luke's words. "*Why*? Why didn't she tell me? Why didn't you tell me? Why didn't *someone* tell me my sister was suicidal?"

Alyssa. The journals. It all made sense now. A sweet, sick, convoluted kind of sense.

And while his past with Suzanna was the last thing Teague wanted to talk about at this moment, the pain in Luke's voice touched something deep inside him.

"Nobody knew she was suicidal," he said. "Not even me. She was depressed. She couldn't think straight enough to walk to the mailbox. She sure as hell wasn't in the right frame of mind to go around explaining her bizarre feelings.

"She and I were separated so long after the fire because of that damn quarantine that by the time we figured out how bad it was . . . she asked me not to tell you. She was ashamed of how she'd changed. She felt like a failure—as a wife, as a mother, as a sister. We tried every doctor, every specialist, every medication. But nothing worked. Neither of us had an answer or a solution and without one, she didn't want to face you."

Luke turned to look out the driver's window, one hand over his forehead. A lone streetlight created vague light and shadow over his face, but Teague couldn't miss the signs of anguish there. He'd seen it in his own expression too many times to count.

"And Desiree?" Luke asked in a hoarse voice.

"You blamed me for Suzanna's death. You tried to take my

daughter from me because you thought I was an unfit father." An old, deep wound split open. Pain seeped out. So much pain, it threatened to drown him. "Of all the people in the world, I shouldn't have had to tell you I didn't kill her. You should have known."

Teague clamped his mouth shut. There were so many other accusations he wanted to make. So many other blames he wanted to lay at Luke's feet. But that was all moot now.

Let's make new memories. Alyssa's voice drifted through Teague's head. *We'll wipe out the bad memories with good ones.* That's what Teague wanted. More than anything else. He wanted to let go of all the pain, the resentment, the anger and just move forward.

Luke remained silent another long moment. There was no point in either of them apologizing now. They'd both already suffered so much, the words would only magnify the chasm created by events that couldn't be changed.

"Alyssa and Mitch are into this up to their fucking eyeballs now, Teague. And look at what happened to Desiree. Jesus, if you'd just taken Hannah, none of this would have happened. You'd probably have dumped her over the side of the Bay Bridge just to get rid of her."

"There's a vote of confidence in your choice of women. But then, everyone but you knows how royally you fucked up when you let go of Keira." Teague huffed a laugh of disappointment. "When I got that first push back from Alyssa, saw that first spark of personality, I thought, shit, maybe he's pulled his head out of his ass and started dating real women again. But no. I should have known Alyssa was far too much woman for you. Just like Keira."

"I didn't *let* Keira go." Anger and pain vibrated in his voice. "She walked away."

"You *pushed* her away."

Guilt slid through Luke's eyes before he broke contact, which gave Teague the opening he needed to hammer the idiot like he'd wanted to ever since he'd heard of their breakup.

"Ever heard of a fucking phone?" Teague taunted Luke with his own words. "A goddamned letter? Ever think of discussing something before you go and cut your own throat? You could have talked to someone about it before you ruined the best thing you had going in your life."

Luke jammed the SUV into drive and doubled back on the street, avoiding the emergency vehicles spread out for the fire. "You're a fucking asshole."

Jason felt a cough crawling up his chest and lifted a hand. "Hold up, Doc."

The kid suturing his scalp at the emergency room in Klamath Falls, Oregon, who couldn't have been older than twelve, pulled the needle from his head and waited while Jason convulsed, hacking up a fur ball of black lung. At least that's what it felt like.

"If you hadn't smoked for twenty-five years," the tiny tot of a doctor said, "your smoke inhalation wouldn't have affected you as severely."

"I've been telling him to quit forever." The female voice brought both men's gazes to the door where Jocelyn stood. She wore skintight black yoga pants and a purple spaghetti-strap top that dipped in the front to show off her cleavage and left those toned, evenly tanned arms bare.

Inside, hope floated to the top of Jason's murky emotions. "Did someone tell you I was dying? What the hell are you doing here?"

She flicked another glance at the doctor, then settled her clear, blue eyes on him with a not-now message. "We need to talk when you're done."

Hope turned to lead and bottomed out in his stomach. She hadn't come because she'd feared she'd almost lost him when she'd heard the firemen had dragged him out of the burning structure unconscious just seconds before the roof had caved in. No, this was a how-could-you-have-fucked-up-so-badly call.

The doctor tied off the last of Jason's eighty-seven stitches over various parts of his body and excused himself with promises of a nurse coming in to bandage.

"Sorry to have pulled you away from your all-important workout, Joce." Jason pushed himself off the gurney, tugged his singed T-shirt over his head and stuffed his arms in as pain bounced around his body. "Give me the abbreviated version of the lecture, which I'm sure starts with, '*The senator . . .*' and maybe you can make it back in time for six a.m. aerobics."

"All right then." Her chin dipped. "To say the senator is . . . upset . . . with your lack of results on this case would be an extreme understatement."

"I'd like to see his fat ass out here on the line. I'm guessing the prick didn't use the words 'lack of results.' "

"Uh, no. No, he didn't. The point is that he wants you to put an end to this. It's obvious Creek is going for the girl after all. If he gets her, Creek might disappear, but we'll never know for how long. He'll always be a liability. And Tara Masters will also become a problem."

"I'm going to get Creek," Jason said. "He's learned a few good tricks inside prison, for God's sake. I just need a couple more days."

Jocelyn didn't respond. She didn't have to. They both knew the senator wanted this problem solved yesterday. There was no "a couple more days."

"What's the senator's brilliant plan?" he asked.

"To get to Tara and the girl before Creek does, use them to lure Creek to us. And once we have him, eliminate all three."

Jason picked up his jacket. "Well, see, Joce, there's a little twist *the senator* doesn't know about yet."

She rolled her eyes and crossed her arms. "What now?"

"If he's looking to eliminate everyone who's in the know

about Creek and that trial and Tara's involvement, he's going to have to up the numbers, because now Ransom and the Foster twins have joined the fun." He leaned into her, enjoying the shock in those wide beautiful blue eyes as he whispered, "I told you *the senator* should have either faced the American public with the truth or gotten rid of the evidence. But he wanted to play mad scientist. He wanted to go for the big, secret payout." He whisked a piece of her soft blond hair off her temple and let his finger trail over her smooth cheek. "We all make sucky decisions we have to face eventually, don't we, baby?"

Twenty-two

Teague crossed from the massive bathroom where he'd just showered to one of the two bedrooms in the guest wing of the house—correction, mansion—Mitch had secured for them for the night in Klamath Falls, Oregon. Mitch had already designated sleeping arrangements for the rooms, each furnished with two queen-sized beds, dressers, desks, lounge chairs and huge flat-panel televisions. Teague with Luke, Mitch with Alyssa. No surprise. But there was just something about a guy who could make one phone call from a random city and arrange lodging, clothing and food on the fly like this that you couldn't trust. Mitch Foster was sure as hell no ordinary defense attorney.

Teague paused at the banister over the stairs leading to the living room, where the four of them had set up shop with all their evidence. The fact that they were all sacrificing their time, their resources, their reputations to clear him . . . it still made him shake his head in disbelief.

Alyssa had brought documents from Teague's boxes at the cabin, Mitch had collected accordion folders filled with research, Teague had thrown the papers he'd pulled from Rawlings's house into the pot and the four of them had pored over the information until Teague thought his eyes would bleed. Mitch, Alyssa and Luke were still huddled around the room, flipping through papers and God-only-knew what else.

Mitch's voice drifted up from below. "Where did you get these pictures of Vasser with Jocelyn Dargan? And Dargan with Senator Schaffer?"

"Internet," Alyssa answered.

"Where on the Internet?"

"*Washington Post* image archives."

"You hacked my account?" Mitch's voice rose. "Someone gave me that access as a favor, Lys. Do you know how confidential those files are?"

"I wasn't hurting anything," Alyssa tossed back in a huff. "I just downloaded a few pictures. And you gave me your user name and password yourself. That doesn't qualify as hacking."

"Like, two years ago when you were trying to dig up dirt on that psycho internist stalking you."

"Mmm, yeah," Alyssa said. "Maybe that's where my skewed sense of 'highly confidential' came in. Besides, if you're really worried about people using the passwords you *gave* them, you should change them more often."

Mitch grumbled something under his breath that made Luke laugh.

"How did you connect the three of them anyway?" Mitch asked.

"Internet," she said.

"Alyssa."

"It's called Google, Mitch. I think you've been letting your paralegals do a little too much of your research."

Teague leaned his elbows on the rail and raked his fingers through his now inch-long hair. These two had far too much brain power. They were obviously dangerous enough on their own, but put them together and—

"Well." Mitch's voice cut through Teague's thoughts. "I think we've got enough. At least for now."

"Enough to what?" Luke asked, irritation boiling in his voice. "We still don't know what was in that warehouse, or what the seven of us were exposed to, or what killed Quaid. We sure as hell don't know where Kat is."

"Enough to keep Teague out of prison," Mitch answered. "Enough to get these assholes off our backs so we can search for Tara and Kat without guns in our faces and freak car fires lighting up houses."

Alyssa dropped her stack of papers with a *thwack*. "When are you going to stop harping on me about that? How many times do I need to say I'm sorry? It didn't go the way I planned."

"Whatever," Mitch mumbled. "You just stick to gouging people with needles and shooting dye in their veins and shit, okay? Look at my hair. It's freaking singed. It's going to take me an hour to convince that damn two-hundred-dollar-an-hour hairdresser—wait, excuse me, *stylist*—of mine not to whack it all off."

"Good." A note of superiority edged Alyssa's voice. "I've been telling you it's too damned long for months."

"Hello?" Luke interrupted. "Back to my daughter, please."

"*Teague's* daughter."

Alyssa's bite stopped the conversation dead. Emotion welled up inside Teague, pressing his lungs against his ribs. She was still fighting for him. Fighting for Kat. Fighting for them to be together. Even after everything she'd been through because of him.

"Right," Luke conceded with a mixture of anger and anguish in his rough voice. "Teague's daughter."

Teague hung his head. He hadn't expected to feel guilt toward Luke. There had always been too much betrayal standing in the way, but it was only natural for Luke to feel as if Kat were his own child after all this time. Being here not only put Luke's career and life at risk, but it put his custody of Kat at risk as well.

"And on that note," Mitch said. "I'm going to get a couple hours of sleep before we head north."

North? Teague straightened, his mind clearing. When had they decided to move?

"Lys." Mitch's voice sounded in the hallway, directly beneath the walkway where Teague stood. "Come here a minute."

Teague stepped back from the railing, out of their line of sight.

"Alyssa, I haven't had a chance to talk to you about—"

"Mitch, don't. I'm tired."

"I've seen the way you've been looking at Creek all night."

"Like I'm dying for a game of pin the tail on the donkey with a handful of spinal needles and Teague as the ass?"

Teague winced and dropped his head back against the wall.

"I'm not going to lecture you. I just want you to know what I know. I've worked with guys like Creek a long time. No man I've ever met came out of prison the same way he went in—innocent or not. These guys are tormented. They drift. They have problems with depression. They have nightmares. You know post-traumatic stress disorder is real. Guys like Creek have learned violence as a way of life in prison and use it when they get out. They can't get a good job, and they can't hold a job once they get one. They need years of counseling." Mitch paused and let out a long, frustrated breath. "I just—"

"I hear you, Mitch." Her voice softened. "And I love you for worrying about me. Get some sleep."

They said good night and Alyssa returned to the living room. Mitch started up the stairs and Teague considered ducking into the bedroom, but why? Everything Mitch had said was true. And Teague found he was tired of running. Tired of hiding.

When Mitch reached the top stair and caught sight of Teague standing in the shadows, he stopped in midstep.

"Why are we going north?" Teague asked without moving.

Unease passed over Mitch's features, followed by resolve. He crossed to the banister, planted his elbow on the painted wood and looked down at where he'd just been standing with Alyssa. "Because according to the papers you pulled from Rawlings's office, his father, Tara's stepdad, owned two properties under a defunct corporation. One in Coos Bay, here in Oregon, and one in Victoria, British Columbia."

Vancouver. British Columbia. Somewhere near Queen Elizabeth Park. Vancouver, not Victoria.

"Victoria?" Teague asked, thinking back to what Rawlings had said in that house.

"Yeah. Canada. I figure we may have a headstart on Vasser. He may not know about the corporation ties. They can be a little tricky to unravel. We'll split up tomorrow and cover both locations. I'm betting Tara took Kat to either Coos Bay or Victoria."

"Alyssa and I should go to Coos Bay."

Mitch's expression turned defensive with a firm mouth.

"It only makes sense," Teague said before Mitch could argue. "Neither of us can cross the border into Canada. You and Luke can get special privileges. Get on the next plane and get back almost before Alyssa and I can drive to Coos Bay from here."

Mitch's eyes, so much like Alyssa's, sparkled with thought.

"If Tara and Kat aren't there," Teague pushed, "you can just come straight to Coos Bay from the airport."

"I guess," Mitch conceded, but his jaw rolled as if that thought was anything but "okay."

"Say whatever is eating at you, Foster."

Mitch turned to fully face him. "I meant every word I said to Alyssa. You may have been a good man in your past life, but *past* is the key word here and we both know it. Regardless of how the system screwed you over, you're not the same man you were before. Bottom line, Creek—today, right now, even five years from now—you don't have a thing to offer my sister. Any connection to you, even after you're exonerated, will hurt her career. Which is all she lives for."

Teague crossed his arms over his chest, counterpressure to the pain. "Didn't sound to me like that was going to be a problem."

Mitch cast a look toward the living room, then shook his head and started for his own room. "Where that girl is concerned, there's always a problem."

Teague waited for Mitch's door to close before he headed down the stairs, all the while telling himself it would just be smarter to do exactly what Mitch wanted. Which was stay away from Alyssa and not prolong the inevitable. But he couldn't. With Alyssa in the same house, he was on auto pilot, drawn to her regardless of his conscience.

"Mutagens are found in chemical compounds or ionizing radiation." As Alyssa spoke to Luke about the science behind their abilities, Alyssa's voice was filled with an excitement Teague couldn't ever remember hearing before. "Chemical compounds could be anything. They're just two chemical elements stuck together. Ionizing radiation comes from radioactive materials, and based on the burns you've described, the quarantine they put you under, this whole conspiracy they've developed and the lengths they will obviously go to keep the incident classified, that's where I'd put my money."

He wandered into the dim living room. Only one light was on, casting a warm glow over the sofa, where files and papers were strewn across the floor, on the cushions, teetering on the arm.

Luke spotted Teague first, long before he came out of the shadows. Alyssa either caught sight of movement with her peripheral vision or she was following Luke's line of sight, because she cast a glance his way as he came into the room. The excitement lingering in her eyes from her previous topic died. She turned her attention to the papers on her lap, straightened them and set them aside.

"There he is," Luke said. "Lys was just telling me how it is that you're so screwed up."

"*We're* screwed up, Mr. Fireproof."

Luke shrugged and pushed up from the sofa. "Yeah, but you're way more screwed up than me. You definitely got a higher dose of that radioactive shit." He narrowed his eyes. "Come to think of it, I'm sure I've seen you glow now and then."

Teague lifted his brows. "You think? Did you tell Alyssa how your powers used to change when Keira—"

"Don't go there."

Luke's warning stare should have brought Teague a sense of accomplishment, but it didn't. It only made him miss Keira, and all his other former team members, and his old life.

Teague crossed his arms over his chest, wandered to the floor-to-ceiling windows and looked out on the expanse of Upper Klamath Lake. The calm waters glittered in the moonlight.

Alyssa remained silent after Luke said good night, his footsteps echoing up the stairs. They were finally alone for the first time since he'd abandoned her. Yet she didn't say anything, which, he discovered, was worse than if she'd screamed at the top of her lungs.

"Who are Mitch's clients?" he asked.

She didn't immediately answer. "I've never asked specifically. His work, like mine, is very confidential. Why?"

He lifted his arms to the cathedral ceiling, and turned to face her. "This." He gestured to the T-shirt and gym shorts he'd been given upon arrival. "These." He waved a hand at the light blue halter she wore with straps as thin as yarn, the bodice so fitted he could see every curve of her breasts, and the loose-fitting silky pajama bottoms of the same color. "Those. On a moment's notice."

Fire sparked in her eyes. "You don't trust him?"

"I'm asking a question no one seems able or willing to answer."

"After all he's done for you?"

"I never asked for help."

She stood and pointed at him. "That's because you don't know how to *ask* for help, and you don't know how to *accept* help. You don't know help when it's staring you in the face. How in the hell are you going to help Kat?"

Her question hit him square in the chest. He hissed out a breath and rubbed his face with both hands, trying to quell his anger. She wasn't his target. He was angry with himself. He was angry with all the mistakes he'd made, all the people he'd hurt along the way. He was angry that his own stupid choices kept him from reaching for her now.

"Why are you here, Alyssa? You should be as far away from this as you can get."

"I'm as caught up in this as you are."

He shook his head. "With a brother who could obviously take care of you, with resources you could use while the mess is getting straightened out, you could be doing this research from anywhere in the country with Mitch's contacts. Where you'd be safer, comfortable. Why are you *here*?"

She planted her hands on her hips, pressed her lips into a thin line and kept those eyes on him. "You walked out on me. I fully understand that what we had may have been a fling for you. A biological need. I knew that going in. But the least you could have done was face me when you left. After everything, I deserved that much."

Regret, guilt, loss grew in a burning pressure at the center of Teague's chest. "We both know how that would have gone, Alyssa. Look at where we are now. There is no easy goodbye for us."

The anger in her eyes flattened into resignation, but the pain he'd sensed before remained. She walked toward him, stopping only a foot away. Her sweet scent swirled in his head, bringing memories of her taste, her touch, that were forever burned into his mind. Everything inside him screamed to act. Take what he wanted. What he needed. What he loved.

Ease her pain. Fix this mess. Make it right. Only it wasn't that simple.

"There is," she whispered. "Just tell me you don't want me. To my face. Right now."

The look in her eye told Teague she would accept nothing but an answer. There would be no excuses, no rationalization, no middle ground.

He drew a shaky breath through a tight throat. "I . . . don't . . ."

"You are so full of *crap*." She nailed him with a glare as hot as the flames snapping in the fireplace. "You know what you are? You're a coward. Plain and simple. I should have seen it before. Oh, yeah"—she made a sweeping gesture over him from head to foot—"you've got the macho exterior, the bark, the occasional bite, but underneath it all, when it comes to the strength that really matters . . . nothing, *nada*." She leaned forward. "Go ahead and lie to yourself if you want, if it makes you feel safe. But we both know better, Teague. We both know you are full of *shit*."

She dropped her arms and turned away.

He should have let her go. That would have been the end of it. But he was pissed—because she was right. Too damned right.

He barely had to touch her to have her whipping back around, ready for a fight. Her hair swung around and over her shoulder. Her eyes sparked with fire. Her hands balled into fists at her sides.

"You're right, dammit. Is that what you want to hear?" He sucked in air and forcibly lowered his voice. "You're right, okay?" He darted a glance at the stairwell for signs of the others, but the hallway remained dark and silent. "My God, you are a pain in the ass. Do you always have to push? Can't you let anything go?"

She crossed her arms, cocked her hip and pressed her lips in a firm, frustrated line.

"This is so screwed up." There was too much to say and it

was all too little, too late. "I didn't want . . . I'd already made such a mess. . . . I left because—" He dropped his head, rubbed his face with both hands. He was so screwed. So utterly, royally screwed. "Dammit, Alyssa, I can't tell you I don't want you, because I want you more than I want to breathe."

"Well, you sure have a piss-poor way of showing it," she muttered, the fight gone from her voice.

Teague huffed a humorless laugh and squared his eyes with hers.

"I know why you left," she said, dropping her tight stance. "I just had to hear it from you. That's why I'm here."

He closed the distance between them, squeezed her shoulders and slid his hands down her arms. "I know it's not enough, but I'm sorry." He looked down at their hands, entwined. "I'm so sorry, for so many things."

"So make it up to me."

"Huh?" He looked up at her, confused.

She opened her hand and threaded their fingers. The slide of her strong, lean fingers along his sent sparks up his arm. "Make it up to me." She took one step closer, but didn't press up against him. "I know you know how. And as I recall, you're pretty damn good at it."

The invitation was on the table, but she wasn't going to make the move. She was giving him the opportunity to back out. He could still walk away. He *should* still walk away. But those beautiful eyes were searching his with a film of pain he wanted to erase. Everything in him said yes—mind, body and soul.

"Alyssa." The last syllable of her name floated in his throat as he leaned in to kiss her.

She returned his kiss with an immediate hunger that shocked him—a mixture of passion and anger and frustration and need that shot sparks through his body. He answered her demand, increased pressure, swept his tongue past her lips and rolled it against hers. She murmured into his mouth, part whimper, part moan. Her hands slid up his chest and locked around his neck. Her body pressed against his in all the perfect places, and his mind evaporated in the sweet heat.

He lifted her, and she immediately wrapped her legs around his waist, putting direct pressure against his erection. Alyssa added fuel to the fire by running her hands under his shirt, over his chest and belly. On a groan, he turned and pressed her against the wall, driving his hips into the softness between her legs. He held her head with both hands, slanting it so he could kiss her one way, then the other. No matter what he did, he couldn't get enough. He needed more, needed to fully and completely reconnect with her.

A sound caught Teague's ear. The *click* of a door, followed by running water. Reality chilled over his shoulders. *You don't have anything to offer her.* He gripped Alyssa's waist and set her feet on the floor.

"What . . . ?" Her eyes opened, glazed with passion.

"I think that was a wakeup call, baby." His excuse didn't relieve the choking regret. "Too many people here. Your brother's right upstairs."

With a spark in her eye, she flattened her palms against his belly, turned until they'd switched positions and pushed him back against the wall. "I don't care who's where." She slid her hands under his shirt again, scraped her nails across his lower abs. Heat gushed into his groin. "But this is your call."

His call. Oh, man . . .

"Jesus, Lys." He looked around the open room. No private corners, no enclosed spaces. "This isn't the best place." His hand lifted to brush the hair out of her eyes. "Not that I'm complaining, because Lord knows I'm not, but you're not exactly quiet, baby."

She rested her chin on his chest, eyes heavily masked by low lids and thick lashes. "Ever think that might be your fault?"

A grin started in his chest and traveled to his mouth. "God, I hope so."

"I have a place." She took his hand and led him to a door a short distance away made out of the same paneling as the wall.

"What's this?"

"Wine closet." She took his hands and walked backwards into the darkness. "Found it earlier."

Teague squinted around the space. Sparse light drifting in from the living room, illuminating rows and rows of wine bottles stacked neatly in racks along three walls, leaving a walkway five-feet wide and one solid, flat wall.

You don't have anything to offer her.

"Lys . . ." He searched for the strength to turn her down, but his body pulsed with need and his soul ached for the connection only she could give him.

"Teague." She pulled him into the closet and shut the door. The intoxicating aroma of sweet wine and pungent spices filled his nose, wafting through his head.

"Wow." Her surprised whisper made a smile creep over his face. "I didn't expect it to be so dark. I can't see a thing."

"You don't need to." Excitement pulsed through his blood. He *might* not have anything to offer her in the future, but he had plenty to offer her in the moment. "I know your body. I know what you like."

He slid his hands down Alyssa's body until he felt the hem of her halter and swept it off over her head. Her deep-throated murmur rippled through his body, urging him to satiate the white-hot burn radiating from his groin. But his heart begged for slow and deep, longing to mend the bond he'd damaged by abandoning her the night before.

With nothing but blackness surrounding them, he swept his hands over her shoulders, down her sides and across her belly, avoiding her wound. She was so warm, so soft. He pushed her against the one free wall and trailed his hands up to cradle her breasts. The supple masses teased his hands with their swaying weight. He rubbed his thumb over the nipples and kissed his way along her neck, over her collarbone and finally replaced one thumb with his mouth, exciting the flesh with slow, hard, suckling strokes of his lips and tongue.

Alyssa's initial high-pitched cry drifted into a sighing moan. When her back arched off the wall, she pushed her breast into his mouth. He added pressure, and bit gently at her nipple.

"Teague," she groaned as if she couldn't stand another minute, her hands clawing at him. She had a way of making him feel like a superior lover, which only made him want to work harder to both prove her right and maybe even outshine her wildest fantasies.

Her hands slid from the back of his head, scratching her nails over his scalp and all the way down his back to his ass. She gripped him hard, pulled his hips to hers and rubbed against him with a groan of barely restrained patience. "I want you inside me."

She pushed at his shorts and boxers, and the fabric slid past his hips and dropped on the floor. Then her hands skimmed his belly as she reached for her own pajama bottoms.

Teague grabbed her wrists and pinned them against the wall at her sides. "That's my job."

"Then hurry up."

"You're getting a little bossy, Lys." Teague bit his way down her neck. "I like it."

He bent his knees enough to get his hips between her legs and with heavy pressure rubbed his way to her soft center, wedging himself there. She shivered with need. One he could fill, right here, right now. Being wanted, needed, to this degree, by this woman, was so incredibly erotic, Teague could hardly hold back. But he wasn't ready for this to end. Wasn't sure he'd ever be ready. She was a heady mix of sex and sweetness he wanted to possess.

He lifted both hands above her head, clasped both wrists in one hand and held them against the wall. With his other hand, he explored. When he caressed her face, she turned her head and took two of his fingers into her mouth and sucked. He ran his wet fingers over her lips, down her neck. Circled her nipple over and over before moving on. Scraped his fingers down her belly, as she'd done to him, and smiled when she trembled.

When his hand dipped below the low waistband of her pants, Alyssa lifted her hips to him. A sexy offering he couldn't resist. As slowly as he could, he let his hand drift lower. Hers strained against his hold, even as her fingers wrapped around his. He toyed with the thin strip of curls between her legs, let her hips rock and sway beneath his hand until she whimpered.

"Teague, please."

"God, that sounds good." He kissed her, gently. Sucked her lower lip between his, then her upper. "Say it again. Just one more time."

"Teague," she put more deliberation behind the word and lifted her hips higher. "Please."

He pressed his hand downward, pushing between her legs. Simple sensations passed through his foggy mind: hot, soft, wet, sweet, good. And those simple concepts kept replaying over and over in his head, music to the amazing sound of Alyssa's pleasure.

Rocking his hand deeper into the soft flesh between her legs, Teague searched. With the tips of his fingers, he stroked the wet crease. Pressed his finger into her.

"Yes." Her whisper sounded high-pitched, a little frantic, like she was about to lose it. Too soon. But it couldn't happen too soon for Teague.

He pressed deep and hard, massaging her clitoris with his thumb.

"Wait," she breathed. "Teague. Wait."

"No waiting, baby. You wanted it. You got it. Now give it back to me."

As Alyssa approached the peak, Teague released his grip on her wrists and used his hand to cover her mouth, muffling her cries of release. He kept pressure between her legs until the thrust of her hips eased.

He pulled his hand from the throbbing heat. With a nudge of fabric, her clothes fell to her feet. She swayed, and gripped his waist with both hands.

"Don't wimp out on me now, Lys. The best is yet to come." He smiled. "No pun intended, but it works, don't you think?"

She let out a breathy laugh. "I can't think."

"That's okay, you don't have to." He lifted. "Put your legs around me."

The feel of her hands braced on his shoulders, fingers biting into his skin, only made his cock throb harder.

Teague pushed in a few inches and pulled back. "Jesus, you're so wet."

"Mmm." She lifted her hips to take him in again, deeper. "For you."

He gritted his teeth, letting her lead at a comfortable pace. The result was excruciating pleasure. The complete darkness focused his attention on every detail of sensation. A quarter of the way in. Out. Halfway. Out. Three quarters. Out. And finally—finally—she took him completely.

He paused there, pressed balls-deep. She tilted her hips, driving him just that much deeper and rubbing herself against him. Her body rocked with each quick breath.

"Damn, girl." He wiped the droplet of sweat trickling down his temple on her shoulder. "I can't keep up with you."

"Try harder." With only a tip of her pelvis, Alyssa drew back, dragging him out of her warm wetness, then drove him back in.

He shuddered, the pleasure shockwave rippling though his torso. "I'm not gonna last like that."

"Good," she said and did it again, then groaned. "Neither am I."

He imagined every thrust even more vividly than if the lights were blazing. He saw every inch of her, heard every breath, felt every movement, tasted every sultry bit of skin and curve of lips.

"Teague." One simple word and he knew she was on the edge, wanting to know if he was there with her.

"I'm here, baby. Let go."

Even if he'd wanted to hold back at that point, he couldn't have. Her orgasm pumped the climax right out of him, siphoning every ounce of energy from his body. He pressed his face against her neck to muffle the guttural sounds bubbling up from his throat.

It took what seemed like forever to come off the sexual high. He couldn't seem to catch his breath. Didn't want to let her down, even though his legs were shaking with the effort of maintaining their position. He wanted to stay inside her until he got hard again. Then repeat the whole amazing event. Wanted to make love to her in a bed, where he could linger and explore, then lie with her curled warm and comfortable in his arms until morning.

Alyssa groaned, but this time it wasn't in pleasure.

"What's wrong?"

"Cramp. In my back."

"Okay." His hands drifted up from her butt and gripped her waist. With what felt like all the strength he had left, he lifted her enough to pull out, then set her on her feet.

Skimming his hands down her legs, he found her pajama bottoms and her top and helped her back into them, then tugged on his own shorts.

He cupped her face in his hands, swept back the hair from her face and kissed her. "Let's sleep on the couch. I'll wake you up before your brother—"

A creak sounded overhead. Then another.

"Someone's up," he whispered.

Teague felt along the wall for the doorknob, turned it slowly and nudged Alyssa into the living room, then closed the door, leaving it open only a crack to see out.

"Alyssa, why are you up?" Mitch didn't come into Teague's field of view, but the irritation in his voice came through loud and clear.

"Looking over the files," she said without a hint of hesitation in her voice. He'd have to remember what a polished liar she was for future reference.

"Where are Ransom and Creek?"

"They went to bed."

Teague couldn't help feeling foolish, hiding in a closet like a kid. He wanted to wrap his fingers around Mitch's neck and tell him to mind his own damn business.

"What's in there?" Mitch asked.

"Wine closet." Alyssa lifted her hand toward Teague's hiding place. "I was thinking about opening a bottle."

"You don't need a bottle of wine; you need some sleep." Mitch walked up to Alyssa and slid a hand around her upper arm, tugging her toward the stairs. "We need to be up and out in a couple of hours."

She pulled out of his grasp and started toward the couch and her papers. "I'll be right up. Just let me put these away."

"Leave it, Alyssa. Come on. It's three in the morning."

Alyssa cast a covert glance at the closet. Her shoulders drooped in concession. "Okay, okay."

Teague's heart sank. He closed his eyes and laid his forehead against the doorjamb. Above him, stairs creaked as Alyssa and Mitch headed back to their room.

Goddammit. That wasn't what he'd wanted. The fear that he would lose her when this was all over hung heavy in his chest. Hot sex was all well and good, but he wanted more. He wanted to make himself irreplaceable to her. And the amount of time in which he had to do that was quickly ticking away.

TWENTY-THREE

Distressing dreams brought Alyssa awake in the passenger's seat of the Escalade Mitch had rented for Teague and her to drive to Coos Bay that morning. She blinked against the hard sunlight slanting through the windshield and repositioned herself, glancing over at Teague.

When he had insisted on a lower-profile vehicle, Mitch had said that's exactly what the cops would be looking for and ordered the most expensive car on the lot. Teague still wore the same tight mask he'd worn all morning. The stubborn set of his mouth indicated he was no more ready to talk about whatever was bothering him than he'd been hours earlier when Mitch and Luke had left to catch their plane to Victoria and Teague and Alyssa had started out on this road trip.

Too many things about this situation reminded her of their first tense days together—his expressions, his demeanor, his unwillingness to talk. Something was eating at him. Something she instinctively knew would ultimately drive them apart unless she faced it head-on.

She watched his profile for long seconds, working up the nerve to slice the artery on this subject.

"About last night," she finally started with the equivalent of a shaking surgical hand, "I should have . . . I mean, I should have told Mitch to mind his own business. It's just that, I mean, I know it wouldn't matter in the end, because he's a professional and he'd never let his personal feelings interfere with a case, but in the back of my mind, I also know he's your best hope of getting out of this as unscathed as possible and, well, I just . . . I mean—"

"Lys," Teague cut in, his voice soft. "You're rambling."

She clamped her mouth shut. Took a breath through her nose. Blew it out through her mouth. "I should have stood up to him and stayed with you. I'm sorry I didn't."

A smile curled one side of his sexy mouth and the fear hiding in the shadows of Alyssa's heart eased. "You did the right thing. Your relationship with Mitch is more important than my ego." He reached out, took her hand and brought it to his mouth for a gentle kiss. "Although, I did miss you."

"If that's not what's bothering you, then what is it?"

The mask returned, and a chill spread over Alyssa's shoulders. She didn't like the way he could turn on and off.

"You're keeping something from me," she said. "What is it?"

His fingers released hers, then wrapped and rewrapped the steering wheel.

"You may as well tell me now. I'll find out eventually, and then I'll be really pissed."

"We're almost there," he said.

"Teague." She put her hand on his head and let it slide down the soft layer of golden hair to rest on the warm skin of his neck. "You have to trust people. Especially those closest to you. Especially me."

He tilted his head away and sighed in frustration. "You're going to be pissed either way. It's a no win. There's no point."

She laughed, but didn't feel any humor. "Well, now you have to tell me. I'll never let up after that comment."

He hesitated. "Kat isn't in Victoria. That's why I wanted Luke and Mitch to go there."

"How do you know?"

"Because when I was in Rawlings's house, he told Vasser

that Tara took Kat to *Vancouver*, where his dad owned a house."

"You probably just heard him wrong. He probably said Victoria."

"No." Teague shook his head. "He said it was somewhere around Queen Elizabeth Park. That's in Vancouver."

"Maybe he was mistaken."

"He sent money to Tara to help her. That's why Vasser came back. He found out Rawlings had lied to him. Rawlings said Tara loved Kat. He stood up for Tara, told Vasser to leave them alone. My gut tells me he was leading Vasser purposely off track."

Alyssa picked up the cell phone Mitch had given her from the center console. "We need to tell Mitch and Luke. Vasser might be—"

He covered her hands. "It will take days for Vasser to get the correct addresses for the father's real estate holdings. Vasser will be running around like a chicken, nowhere near Luke or Mitch, while I get to Kat here."

Her hands dropped to her lap, eyes narrowed as her mind honed in on his underlying meaning. "You arm-wrestled Mitch into letting me come with you because . . ." She huffed a dry laugh and looked out the windshield as Teague turned onto a residential street. "Because you thought I'd be a pushover. Because you thought that once you found Kat, you'd simply take her and run and I wouldn't stop you like they would."

He pulled his hand from hers and didn't respond.

"I . . ." she started, confused. "You sonofabitch." She couldn't work up the anger to put behind the curse.

After coming so very close to losing him and Mitch in that fire and feeling so completely out of control, so ready to do such crazy, haphazard things to save them, could she really blame him for making every insane effort to save his daughter and restore their life together the best way he knew how?

"Guessed I pissed you off good," Teague said, studying

her from his peripheral vision with suspicion as if he expected her to explode any second. "You swore."

"More like a reaction. Your bad habits rubbing off on me." She shook her head. "I really don't know how to feel about that right now."

Hurt, angry . . . yet compassionate about what he'd been through. She'd have to contemplate it all later, because they were coming up on the address of Tara's father's home.

"There it is." Anticipation pushed her confusion aside as she pointed to a house down the street on the right. "The one with a jungle for a front yard."

Teague slowed, but continued past the house.

Alyssa's gaze scanned a detached garage positioned at the back of the house. Old-fashioned, partially open, double vertical doors exposed a blue Volvo inside.

"Oh, my God, you're right. She's here." She clamped onto Teague's forearm, excitement bursting in her chest. "The car. It's there. It's in the garage."

"Calm down." He wiped a fresh burst of sweat from his forehead. "Let's make sure."

As Teague swung a U-turn and cruised back by the house, Alyssa worked at keeping her emotions under control. The yard was overgrown, the windows covered by interior blinds. When they passed the east side of the structure, Alyssa craned her neck to look back toward the rear of the small property. Sure enough, there it sat: a blue Volvo, the temporary dealer plates still in place.

"Did you—?"

"Yeah," he breathed, wiping his forehead again. "I saw it."

Half a block down, Teague made another U-turn and pulled over. He turned in his seat and studied the house. Alyssa could see the heat building inside him: Sweat broke out over his face and neck, darkening the T-shirt over his chest.

"Teague. Teague." She reached for his forearm. Heat pierced her fingers. "Ow!" She jerked her hand away. "You're burning again. Focus, Teague. This is not the time to lose control."

"I'm trying."

His intense gaze returned to the house. Alyssa dialed her brother's cell. "Hey, we found her."

"Wait for us," Mitch said. "We just landed. We're on the tarmac. Did you see them?"

Teague opened the console and pulled out the weapon and cuffs hidden there. She put a restraining hand on his arm, ignoring the burn through her skin, and shook her head at him.

"No," she said into the phone. "But the car is in the garage."

"Try to get a visual to confirm," Mitch said, "but don't spook them. We'll be there as fast as we can. Luke will call authorities when we're closer, when we're sure we already have control of the scene."

She disconnected from Mitch and looked down at the gun and cuffs. "If whatever you're thinking involves those, think again."

Anguish tightened his features and darkened his eyes. "You can't really expect me to wait for them. There is no way in hell I'm going to sit here when my baby is right inside that house."

He reached for the door handle. Alyssa tightened her grip on his arm and pulled him back. "Wait, Teague. Wait. Just think about this for a minute. Remember what happened the last time you let your emotions drive you? Kat could have been seriously hurt in that parking lot. She's lucky she only got a bump on the head." She pulled her hand back, shook it, then blew on her fingers. "You're so out of control."

Teague ground his teeth. He wiped a hand over the sweat on his forehead and looked out the windshield toward the house again. "I'm running on adrenaline here, Lys. I don't expect you to understand, but I have to get to her."

"You have to get to her *safely*. In this condition you could do her more harm than Tara. You're burning my hand within seconds. What are you going to do to Kat's tender skin?"

"I won't touch her skin. I'll wrap her in a blanket or a jacket or my damn shirt if I have to."

"Look at me. Listen to me." She fisted her hand in the chest of his T-shirt and gave it a hard shake. When his eyes finally met hers, she leveled her voice. "Let me just go look. As soon as I see them, I'll come back and we'll decide what to do next. Okay?"

"I should be the one to go look."

"They'll both recognize you instantly. If Kat sees you, she'll go ballistic. If Tara knows you're here, she could use Kat as a hostage. Neither of them will remember me from a two-minute exchange days ago." She paused, put her free hand on his jaw and kept his face turned toward her. "You need to trust me."

He swallowed. "Just a look. Three minutes."

"Five." She leaned in and kissed him solidly on the mouth, sealing the deal.

Alyssa climbed from the car and set a brisk pace for the house with new hopes for the future. He'd put his trust in her when he'd wanted to act on his own. A huge first step. All she had to do was see both Tara and Kat and she could return to reason with Teague.

As she neared the house, her gaze swept over the empty neighborhood. A mild wind whipped leaves in mini whirlpools, then chased them down the street. A light gray sky promised rain. No one paced their lawns with a mower. No one played basketball in their driveway. No one hauled groceries from their car.

Alyssa cut through the neighbor's side yard and skimmed along the hedge between for cover. From there she could see the entire back side of the house, which was one flat wall with a few small windows, their blinds raised a couple of inches.

Alyssa hurried from the security of the hedge and flattened herself against the wall. Sound drifted from a window just to her left. Music?

She inched closer. No, not music. Singing. Someone was singing. It was a quiet, soothing tune, but the voice was tense and shaky. Alyssa eased forward and glimpsed inside. She saw nothing but a blank wall and a doorway leading to another room.

Maybe she was hearing things.

She changed her position and peered through the window at a different angle. Huddled in a corner, Tara lay on the floor in what looked like a makeshift sleeping area, cradling something swaddled in blankets. Excitement hitched in her chest and made it hard to breathe. Alyssa pulled back. Kat. She had to be holding Kat.

Hoping for a better view, Alyssa ducked beneath the window and darted to the other side. She held her breath, pushed onto her toes and peered past the window ledge. Yes, Kat was there, lying on the floor, tangled in blankets, asleep. But Tara was gone.

A crunch sounded behind her. Alyssa started to turn. Pain exploded in her head and radiated beneath her skull. Glass crashed somewhere in the distance. Blurred darkness swamped her, while intense flashes of light stabbed at her eyes. Her legs lost strength, and she sank toward the ground.

Someone grabbed her from behind and dragged her. Nothing was working. She couldn't maneuver her brain, her limbs, her vocal cords. Her skull was about to rip open like a weak seam.

Something jabbed her spine. Her head hit the ground again. She clenched her eyes and fought the unconsciousness clawing at her.

"Come on, Katrina." The voice drifted to Alyssa from a distant tunnel. An eerie singsong quality tainted the sweet tone. "Time to go. Come to mommy."

The thought of Kat gave Alyssa the will to open her eyes. She stared at a ceiling, blinking away the darkness. As she tried to push herself up, her head spun. She whimpered, grabbed her temples with both hands and fell back to the ground.

"I told you people to leave us alone." Tara's voice stabbed into Alyssa's brain. "I *told* you."

Alyssa winced, slid her hands lower to cover her ears. A cold shiver crawled down her spine and spread like fingers into her gut. She pushed her eyes open. Tara looked down with an unconscious Kat swaddled in her arms. And the look in Tara's eyes—Alyssa had seen it before, the same semi-absent, malevolent glimmer she'd seen in patients very high on either street drugs or meds or just plain crazy.

How much stress was too much? At what point did a person break and do the unthinkable?

She squeezed her eyes shut and managed to roll onto her side, then paused there to catch her breath. "I'm not . . ." Every word was like a mini-bomb exploding in her brain. "I'm not one of them. But they're coming. They're . . . looking for you. What did you do to her? Is she unconscious?"

Tara pulled Kat closer to her chest and cast a frightened look toward the front door as if someone would come bursting through any second. Alyssa wished she'd stuck with Teague's three minutes instead of pushing for five.

"No, she's sleeping," Tara said, as if incensed at the insinuation she could have hurt Kat. "A little Benadryl always helps her sleep. She's been so upset. All she wants is to go home. She doesn't understand that we can't go home anymore."

"But you can, Tara. You can take her home. I'm here with Teague." Alyssa pushed all the way over to her stomach and pressed her palms against the carpet, getting her knees under her. "He'll keep you both safe from Vasser. He loves her so much. Don't take her from him. She's all he has."

"She's all *I* have." Tara's voice came out harsh and bitter.

"She's all I'll *ever* have. He was going to marry that girl. He was going to take Kat away. I tried to talk to her. Tried to reason. But she didn't understand. She wouldn't listen. It was just an accident. She tripped. Fell and hit her head on a table. An accident. But they said I'd go to prison. Said I'd never see Kat again."

"Vasser says anything he has to say to get people to do what he wants." Alyssa's head throbbed. Her stomach swirled. "You won't go to prison. You're right, it was an accident. Teague knows you love Kat. He would never take her away from you."

"I'm not taking that chance." Tara leaned down and kissed Kat's forehead, the sugar voice returning. "No one's going to take my Katrina, are they, baby?"

She started for the door. Alyssa pushed off her hands and knees and took one desperate lunge. "Tara, wait!"

Alyssa's hand locked around Tara's ankle and the other woman stumbled, hit the door frame and cried out. She stumbled, dropped to the floor and immediately scuttled out of sight.

"What the hell is taking so long?"

Teague pried his gaze from the house and looked at the dashboard clock. She'd been out there four minutes, yet it felt like she'd been gone an hour. But that probably had more to do with the way his thoughts kept drifting back to the decisions he'd have to make once Alyssa returned to the car.

The fact was, they had different priorities. No matter how he twisted things, he came back to the same bottom line—he couldn't see how he could keep Kat and Alyssa and his freedom. He'd have to sacrifice something.

He lifted his gaze from the dash to scan the street again. Movement near the house caught his eye. His heart lifted for a split second, until he realized it wasn't Alyssa coming back to him. It was someone else, moving toward the house. A man. Disappearing alongside.

Fear zipped up Teague's spine and spiked the hair on his neck. "Sonofabitch."

Every muscle contracted. Flexed. Pumped into action. He shoved the car door open. Hit the ground running. How had he found them so fast? How would Teague keep him away from Alyssa, Kat and Tara? Questions, tactics, worst-case scenarios raced for the trophy like thoroughbreds at the Kentucky Derby.

Following Alyssa's path toward the rear of the house, Teague held the gun tight to his thigh. The small detached garage sat twenty feet away from the rear corner, one door askew on broken hinges, alongside a rusted propane tank overgrown with thick vines. The remainder of the yard was bordered by unkempt hedges and patchy grass.

With his shoulder pressed against the stucco wall, his heart beating hard and fast, Teague peered around the corner and down the length of the house.

Something hit the side of his head. Pain exploded. His brains scrambled, vision blackened. Before he could right himself, another blow hit his left kidney. He went down. Hit the grassy dirt on his knees. Fell to his side. A foot stomped on the wrist of his gun hand.

"Hello, there, Creek." Vasser's voice ricocheted through Teague's head. "Let's go inside and join the others."

The others meant Kat was here. Alyssa and Kat were inside. Everything he wanted, everything he loved was in that house. Within reach. This one man was standing in his way.

A familiar desperation welled up from a primitive place inside Teague. A desperation that instilled men with superior strength, unimaginable stamina, terrifying brutality. One that drove men to fight to the death. A place he'd discovered in prison.

The sensation grew inside him until it overwhelmed him. Dominated him.

And it raged.

He dropped the gun and grabbed Vasser's leg. Using the

limb as leverage, Teague coiled his stomach muscles, pulled both legs back and kicked out, slamming Vasser in the sternum. The other man's air wheezed out of his lungs. He stumbled backwards, arms flailing. His spine hit the side of the house, and his gun discharged.

The bullet pinged a decorative metal sun hanging on the side of the garage. The huge hunk of metal fell, hit the top of the propane tank and bounced off with another loud *clank* as it landed. An instant later, a high-pitched, angry *hissssss* signaled the break of the gas line and a thirty-foot high-pressure stream of volatile propane shot from the two-hundred gallon tank.

A fireman's worst nightmare.

Teague popped to his feet and maneuvered for his next attack. If Vasser took another shot, he would be instant toast. And most likely Teague would be, too.

He charged Vasser again, driving his head into the other man's chest. Teague grabbed Vasser's gun hand and slammed it against the house. The crack of bone sounded in Teague's ear, followed by Vasser's howl and the *plunk* of the gun on dirt.

The propane fumes invaded Teague's nose, his throat, his lungs. His head felt as if it would spin off his neck. He straightened away from Vasser, searching the ground for the weapon while the vertigo seemed to whirl him three-hundred-and-sixty miles an hour.

His stomach pitched, rode up his throat. The gun swirled in his vision. He kicked out, caught the handle and knocked it across the yard. But not far enough from the concentration of fumes.

Vasser pushed off the house and stumbled after it.

"Don't!" Teague yelled. "You're going to blow us up."

Vasser dove for the gun, picked it up, and squeezed off another shot.

The weapon's spark ignited the surrounding vapors in a ground-shaking explosion. Flames grabbed Vasser and feasted.

Teague could do nothing but watch as Vasser flailed and

screamed, fire eating at his clothes, his skin, his muscle, his bone. He stumbled, turned, and swatted. The propane followed, a relentless, ravenous predator until the man's charred remains hit the back of the house and slumped to the ground. One feast over, the fire lost interest in devouring Vasser and started in on wood.

The vile scent of seared human flesh reached down Teague's throat and gripped his stomach. He pressed his hands to his knees, gagged, and dry heaved.

His gaze landed on the gun lying on the ground. He swooped down, grabbed it. Pushed it into his jeans and forced his feet toward the house.

Alyssa couldn't see anything but black. She couldn't hear anything but an incessant drone. And she couldn't breathe.

Orange flames snaked along the junction of wall and ceiling.

Tara. Fight. Fire. Kat. Oh, God, Kat.

She rolled to her hands and knees, wheezed smoke into her lungs, and slid her hands over the floor, searching blindly.

The ringing in her ears dimmed, immediately replaced by the roar of fire. Glass burst nearby, spraying Alyssa with razor-sharp debris. Light speared the room, illuminating the solid gray clouds of smoke spilling out the new opening. A trickle of flames devoured the oxygen, then exploded across the ceiling.

She pried her gaze away from the undulating, consuming, orange river and peered past the tears pouring from her eyes. "Kat!"

As soon as the word was out of her mouth, Alyssa's lungs seized and she convulsed in a coughing fit. She continued to run her hands over the carpet in one direction. She found a wall. Doubled back to the opposite wall.

She kept moving. Touched something soft. Relief mixed with adrenaline and fear. Her hands worked fast, pulling at fabric, palpating limbs, bodies, until she distinguished Kat's body from Tara's. Her fingers immediately pressed against the little girl's neck and found a pulse, regular and strong.

By the time she hefted the unconscious girl into her arms, panic had taken root. Using the wall for support, Alyssa pushed up and turned toward the door, only to find a curtain of fire. She wrapped the blanket tightly around Kat and drew one end over her own head like a tent, then dropped to her knees. With one hand on the floor, one arm around Kat, she crawled beneath the flames and into a hallway. Her side burned from injury and exertion. Lungs ached from searching for every molecule of oxygen. Head throbbed from Tara's attack.

She pushed herself toward the next doorway. Assessed the distance to an exit and found a huge hole in the front of the house where the roof had caved in. A hundred yards of burning building stood between her and safety.

"Alyssa!" Teague's voice drifted to her above the howl of flames and crack of wood. "Over here. This way."

She peered from under the blanket. Across a trench of whipping, snapping flames, Teague stood waving frantically. He was covered in soot, his clothes torn.

"Run," he yelled. "Bundle and run. I'll catch you."

Christ. He couldn't be serious.

You need to trust me.

Crap. She hated it when her own words came back to haunt her.

Overhead a loud crack signaled a beam giving way.

TWENTY-FOUR

Before Teague could reach her, before she cleared the danger zone, the beam gave. A massive sheet of flaming drywall fell, crushing Alyssa and Kat right in front of his eyes.

"No!" Teague didn't think, only reacted. He dove into the burning mass, chucking fiery boards and debris until he cleared a space. If he burned, he didn't feel it. He felt nothing but the utter torment of losing Alyssa and Kat.

Water showered him, the first realization that firefighters were on scene. He'd blocked everything else out. He worked, throwing tiles, kicking debris, heaving wall sections.

When he peeled back a piece of smoldering sheetrock and saw the familiar blanket, a sob rumbled up his throat.

Please be alive.

You have to be alive.

You both have to be alive.

His stomach felt like a feather in a storm, twirling, spinning.

Teague reached down to grab whatever part of Alyssa he could reach. The flooring cracked, swallowing Teague's foot. He fell back, struggling to regain traction. By then, Alyssa was moving. *Yes*. She was alive. Teague reached for her.

"I'm here." He grabbed her upper arm and dragged her partially from the rubble.

"Take her." Alyssa pushed the soot-covered, swaddled bundle toward him. "She's okay. Take her."

Teague lifted Kat from Alyssa and held her to him with one arm, grabbing Alyssa's with the other. Smoke swirled around them. Flames snapped and snarled.

Another set of hands delved into the pit and grabbed Alyssa's other arm. Teague jerked his head around to find a familiar sight: a firefighter staring at him through the Plexiglas facing of a breathing apparatus.

"Get the kid out." The firefighter's voice came as a muffled yell from behind the mask. "This place is gonna go."

Which told Teague he had seconds before the entire structure collapsed. Teague lifted Kat from his chest and thrust her at the firefighter. "You take her. I've got this one."

The man plucked Kat from Teague and retreated. Teague leaned down, grasped Alyssa's arms with both hands and lifted her from the pit. He turned toward the exit as he tugged one arm up and around his shoulders and dragged Alyssa across the debris and out onto the grass.

In the street, he spotted the firefighter, still holding Kat, blankets unwrapped to display his baby unconscious, while a paramedic pressed a stethoscope to her chest.

"She's alive." Alyssa's assurance instantly calmed him. "She's not hurt. I think she's just drugged."

"Are you sure?" he asked, only wanting one answer.

Alyssa coughed, then nodded, wiping the black film from her eyes. "Her pulse is strong."

Thank you.

More sirens pierced the fire's turbulence. Teague surveyed the vehicles on the scene: fire trucks, battalion chief, emergency medical. There was only one group who hadn't shown up yet: cops.

"You should go." Alyssa's voice refocused him. "Get out of here before they come."

No. He wasn't leaving without Kat. He wasn't leaving without Alyssa. He wasn't willing to make the sacrifice he'd known all along he'd have to make.

He led Alyssa to the ambulance just as the paramedic

looked up at them and removed the stethoscope from Kat's chest. Another EMT crawled out of the rig with an oxygen mask. "This will help."

That might help, but Teague knew what Kat really needed, something only he could provide. He drew close, wiped his hands on his jeans and laid his palm over the top of Kat's head like a cap. Eyes closed, head bowed, he focused.

He pooled his fear and anxiety, blended it with all the love he had for his daughter and Alyssa and directed all the emotion into his touch. In his mind's eye, a soothing, healing heat glowed in the center of Kat's chest. Slowly, he added strength to his visualization, growing the energy until it filled Kat's body.

"She's coming around." The paramedic's voice brought Teague's eyes open.

Kat had gone from sooty pale and limp to sooty pink and squirmy. She hadn't opened her eyes, but was pushing at the mask over her nose and mouth.

The firefighter still holding Kat turned toward them and, as if instinctively laying the child in her mother's arms, offered Kat to Alyssa. "You got her?"

Alyssa nodded and took possession of Kat. The sight shifted something inside Teague. They looked so right together. So natural. Alyssa had risked her life for Kat. For him.

"Tara." The name popped out of his mouth almost sooner than it entered his mind. He swung toward the house. "Tara's still inside."

He thought of Seth, of how dedicated he'd been to Kat, what a solid friend he'd been to Teague, and started toward the burning house.

"You're not going back in there."

A hand fell on his shoulder. Teague turned to find himself facing a cop. His stomach dropped.

A black Lincoln Towncar pulled up in a cloud of dust, drawing his gaze past the cop. A petite, blond woman emerged from the back, four large men clustering around her, all headed directly for Teague.

Dargan. He recognized her from the photographs.

Her eyes, a light, icy blue, chilled him from yards away. The freeze started at his shoulders and slid down. Spine, chest, belly, limbs. He could have been standing naked in a snowdrift.

And as if he could visualize his future, Teague saw himself getting into that Lincoln and never getting out alive. A shiver rocked his upper body.

He moved close to Alyssa and Kat, put his arm around Alyssa's waist from behind and tilted his chin so his mouth was right next to her ear. He wanted to tell her he was sorry. Wanted to tell her he loved her. But there was no point. They had no future.

"Arrest him." Dargan's curt voice cut through the chaos. "That's Teague Creek. Arrest him, now."

The cop standing near him went into immediate action, drawing his weapon and pointing it at Teague. "Sir, step away from the woman and child."

"Teague?" Alyssa's voice wavered.

"Take care of Ka . . ." His voice broke on Kat's name. Tears pushed at the backs of his eyes. "Make sure she gets to Luke. Call Mitch the second this is over. You'll be okay. They won't take you or Kat with so many people watching."

"I said, arrest him!" Dargan barked.

Half a dozen dark blue uniforms closed in around them. Half a dozen weapons pointed at him. And Alyssa. And his daughter.

"Do it *now*, Creek," the officer behind him said, clearly pushed by the little blond bitch.

Teague did what he swore he'd never do when he'd walked out of prison. He released Alyssa, lifted his hands above his head and stepped back, putting as much room as possible between them before the cops took him down.

He didn't pay attention to the who, what or where of the takedown, but gave himself over to it. Resisting would only cause pain and injury. There was already enough of that to go around.

One cop yanked the weapon from his jeans. Another shouted orders. It didn't matter that Teague followed them to the letter, he still got the royal treatment. A shove to his back, a knee to his spine, a wrench of his arm, his face scraped in the dirt. Yeah. This was familiar. Pain. Shame. Control. So familiar, part of him believed it was what he deserved. That prison was where he belonged.

He kept his eyes fixed on the ground as the cuffs closed around his wrists. Kept his mind averted from all he was losing, where he was headed.

Another vehicle thundered close and came to a quick stop. The burn of rubber met Teague's nose. The screech of a heavy metal door scraped his ears, followed by the clomp of boots and the clack of weapons.

"Stand down, Director Dargan." An authoritative male voice joined the rush of fire hoses, sirens and shouts of working firefighters. "Senior Special Agent Marshall, A.T.F. We've been authorized to take control of this scene and this prisoner."

Teague tried to lift his head. Someone from above him slapped a hand against his skull and slammed his face back into the gravel. Rock ground against his teeth.

"The hell you have," Dargan yelled. "I want to see paperwork. Official, signed paperwork."

"I have a copy of that documentation right here for you, Director Dargan."

Teague recognized Mitch's voice immediately, although it sounded far more congenial than he'd ever heard it before.

"Help me get him up." Luke's voice joined the mix.

Two strong sets of hands grabbed Teague's arms and lifted him from the ground. When Teague gained his feet and looked up, he found a dozen A.T.F agents in full S.W.A.T. gear had joined Dargan, her security detail and the cops. Luke took the cuff keys offered by one of the cops and unlocked Teague's hands.

"Need medical attention?" Luke muttered as he pulled the metal off Teague's hands. "Aside from psychiatric, I mean."

"Shut the fuck up," Teague shot back, but couldn't keep the half grin off his face. He spit gravel and blood out of his mouth.

He scanned the crowd for Alyssa and found her, swaying with Kat, stroking her hair where the child's head lay on her shoulder. Relief eased Teague's shoulders.

"She looks good with Kat," Luke said with a casual air as he pocketed the cuffs. "Try not to screw that one up."

"You have no room to talk."

"Okay, Director"—Mitch held out a sheaf of papers toward Dargan—"it's a little complicated, so I'll go slow. First, I have a Change of Custody form signed by Judge—"

"How could he *change* custody when he wasn't *in* custody at the time the judge signed that form?" she asked.

"Now, now, let's not get hung up on details. Second"—Mitch licked his finger and flipped the page—"I have filed an expedited exoneration hearing based on new evidence." He paused and gave her an award-winning grin. "No worries, I've taken the liberty of forwarding a copy of all that paperwork to your office."

Teague leaned toward Luke, lifted his chin toward Mitch and kept his voice low when he asked, "What's with him?"

Luke shook his head in an expression of uncertainty, then guessed. "Vindication. Retribution."

"Big words for you, Ransom."

Luke shot him a shut-the-fuck-up side-glance.

"Three"—Mitch flipped the page again and pointed to a line midway down—"you'll see it says here, that one Mr. Teague Creek, that's him"—he pointed at Teague—"has been released into the custody of one Mr. Lucas Ransom, that's him"—he pointed at Luke—"pending hearing date."

Teague couldn't keep the shock from his expression when he looked at Luke again. "How in the hell . . . ?"

"Let me give you a bit of advice: Don't ever travel with

that man." Luke crossed his arms over his chest, frowning at Mitch where he stood with Dargan. "Getting through security was a nightmare. He carried his laptop and portable printer on the plane. He spent the entire flight either on the damn phone or on the Internet, and took up both tray tables with all his shit. 'Put these together.' 'Staple that.' You'd think I was his goddamned secretary.

"But I have to admit—and if you tell him I said this, I'll kick your ass—that man works magic. Sheer magic. You may have kidnapped the wrong woman from that hospital, but you hit a gold mine when you grabbed Mitch Foster's sister."

Yards away, where Mitch tortured Dargan, the woman's face grew red and lined with anger. "And how do you plan on keeping him out of jail for the crimes he's committed since his prison break?" she asked.

"Ohhh, right. Did I forget to mention that?" Mitch flipped back through the pages. "On this exoneration page, there's a section here . . . I'll read it for you, 'blah, blah . . . *to include all crimes stemming from the escape attempt for which Creek was wrongfully imprisoned.*' " Mitch straightened all the paperwork in his hand, secured the paperclip and offered them to Dargan with a charming smile. "I think that covers it."

At the last second, he pulled them back. "Oh, I almost forgot. My card." He took a business card and a pen from his pocket, slid the card beneath the clip, then scribbled on the card. "And I don't usually do this, but for you"—he tossed her a wink—"I'll put my cell on here, too. Just in case."

She kept her arms crossed, rejecting the packet when he offered it again. "This is bullshit. Complete and utter bullshit."

"Oh, no, no, no. I promise you, if I were slinging bullshit, Director, you'd know," Mitch said, remaining maddeningly congenial. "In fact, I'll let you use my phone to call each and every judge—at home if necessary—to confirm their signatures."

The spark of uncertainty in Dargan's eyes started the thaw

of Teague's numbness. Hope trickled in, and even though he tried to keep the flow regulated, his retaining walls crumbled quickly.

At a short distance, Alyssa continued to monitor the conversation, eyes sharp, hopeful. Kat woke up, rubbed her dirty face and squirmed in Alyssa's arms.

Dargan snapped the papers from Mitch's hands. "I will investigate each and every word on these documents, Mr. Foster. If one thing is out of place, just one, I will have your ass in front of the bar." She turned and pointed at Luke, who looked at her from several yards away. "And I'll have your badge, Agent."

A news van rolled up in the background and a cameraman jumped out, dragging gear in his wake.

A pretty, dark-haired female reporter shoved a microphone in Dargan's face. "Deputy Director Dargan, can you speak to the allegations of misconduct by D.A.R.P.A. regarding taxpayer funds in recent military scientific research projects, specifically—"

"No comment." Dargan swiveled and set a brisk pace for her Lincoln, flanked by her wall of security.

"Oh, and Director," Mitch called, "I went ahead and cc'd Senator Schaffer on all that paperwork. Good for everyone to be on the same page, don't you think?"

Alyssa passed Dargan on her way toward Teague. He couldn't keep his eyes off the sight of Kat in her arms, his daughter's eyes fighting to focus. Nerves squeezed his chest, as he wondered how she'd react to seeing him unexpectedly and outside prison walls. There was always the chance that she really wouldn't want to be with him.

"Uncle Luke?" Kat asked.

Teague's heart stopped.

"Yeah, baby, right here." Luke walked over and took Kat gently from Alyssa's arms. She immediately curled into him and buried her face in his shoulder.

A violent rip of pain tore across Teague's chest.

Alyssa came to him, stood close, and threaded their fingers. It helped. But . . . Shit.

Luke hesitated. He took a moment with Kat, ran a hand over her hair, closed his eyes, pressed an extended kiss to her head.

Pressure built behind Teague's forehead, eyes and nose. His throat thickened. If she rejected him . . . Teague couldn't do it. He could face a man with a gun. Face running into a burning building. Face going back to prison. He couldn't face his five-year-old rejecting him.

Luke walked up beside Teague. "Princess, look who's here."

"I want to go home," she cried against his shoulder.

"Luke," Teague said, his voice raspy, thick. "Don't."

Luke ignored him. "Come on, baby. One quick look. You'll be happy. I promise."

She lifted her head, her dark curls a tangled mess over her bleary eyes and soot-streaked cheeks. Luke pushed them aside as Kat assessed him.

He held his breath.

Tightened his fingers around Alyssa's.

"Daddy?" Her head tilted. She reached out a hand to touch his chest, as if testing to see whether he was real. "I saw you, but you disappeared. Like a dream."

His breath leaked out from between tight lips. He lifted his free hand, wrapped his fingers around hers and brought them to his mouth. Kissed them. Pressed them to his cheek. When she didn't pull back, the rest of his tension ebbed. Tears burned his eyes.

"I'm real," was all he could find to say.

"You're not in jail?"

"Not anymore."

"Forever?"

Teague opened his mouth, but nothing came out.

"Forever, kid." Mitch walked up from the sidelines. "Your dad is out of jail forever."

Kat smiled, leaned toward Teague and reached out to him with both arms. "Uncle Seth told me you'd come home someday."

Alyssa squeezed his hand, then released him to allow Teague to pull Kat into his arms. When he did, his entire world telescoped into view and focused. Like the heart of a labyrinth. Right here. Right now. With the woman and child he loved.

"He did?" Teague asked.

"Your file *did* come through my office," Mitch said. "Seth submitted it."

Teague's eyes fell closed. Gratitude pushed the last remnant of fear aside. He dropped his face to Kat's feather-soft hair despite the residual fire debris.

"It was a secret," Kat said, resting her cheek against his shoulder, her lids growing heavy.

Tara. Teague swung toward the house, where most of the flames had been conquered, but charcoal smoke still flooded the sky. "Did they—?"

"In the ambulance." Alyssa's soft voice floated over his shoulder. "Critical, but alive."

"Are you going to live with us now, Daddy?"

Teague returned his gaze to that cherub face he'd dreamed of every night in prison and picked up one of Kat's dark curls, twirling it around his finger over and over. "I, uh, I—"

"Yeah." Luke grimaced, raked a hand through his own hair and pushed out a breath. "He is." Then he muttered, "Whose freaking idea was that?"

"Forever?"

"No." Luke gave Teague a hell-no look. "Just for a while."

Kat's dark eyes landed on Luke with a clearly disapproving, disconcerted expression.

Luke held up his hands, palms out. "Don't worry. None of us is going anywhere. We'll all be here whenever you want us. Me, Uncle Seth, your dad . . ."

"Sucker . . ." Teague teased, a half-grin lifting his mouth

despite a sudden wave of exhaustion settling in. "She's got you wrapped."

"What about Mommy Tara?"

Teague's grin dropped. Everyone went silent.

"She's not feeling well right now," Alyssa said, saving them from answering. "But when she's better, I'm sure you can see her."

Kat's dark eyes slipped to Alyssa. "Who are you?"

"I'm Alyssa."

"Are you going to live with us, too?"

Alyssa smiled, tilted her head, and opened her mouth to respond.

But Mitch spoke first. "I heard rumors that Gregory Dyne has resigned from St. Luke's. The scuttlebutt is that as soon as an accusation of defamation of character hit the airwaves, he hit the pavement. Seems St. Jude's is trying to locate you to offer you a permanent position."

Alyssa's mouth froze in that open position as she stared at her brother. Teague couldn't read her expression past the shock. But how could he possibly compete with that offer? Despite the fact that he'd always suspected he'd have to give her up eventually, he hadn't anticipated the immediate and complete shredding sense of loss that hit him now.

"But"—Luke slid his hands into the front pockets of his jeans and glared at Mitch while speaking to Alyssa—"if you decide you'd rather not go back to an overpopulated, polluted, crime ridden hellhole of a city and prefer to live in the pristine Sierra Nevadas instead"—he turned his gaze on Alyssa—"I happen to know the head of H.R. at Tahoe Basin Community Medical Center. I'm sure they would jump at the chance to have a physician with your qualifications on staff."

"Ransom," Mitch said, "mind your own damn business."

"This is more my damn business than it is yours now, Foster. I don't see him sleeping on your couch."

The news reporter sidled up to the group, but she only had

eyes and one hell of a flirtatious smile for Mitch. "Excuse me, Mitch. Do you have a minute?"

"Beautiful job, Brittany." He turned on the charm like a light. "I believe I owe you dinner."

As Mitch wandered off with Brittany, Luke looked toward the A.T.F. van. "I'm going to check in."

Teague watched Luke go, twirling Kat's hair in an attempt to calm the nerves in his stomach. Finally alone with Alyssa, all the emotion bottomed out. He turned and nearly fell into her, wrapping his free arm around her shoulders and pulling her to him, sandwiching a now snoozing Kat between them.

"My God, you scared me to death." He closed his eyes and absorbed the all-consuming relief. "I thought I was going to lose you."

She closed her arms around his waist and fisted the shirt at his back. "Now you know how I felt when I saw you in that house with Vasser and all those guns. Only you weren't near as nice to me as I'm being to you now."

"I know. I was a shit." He turned his head in and kissed her neck.

"There you go with your famous understatements," she murmured against his shoulder. "Just so you know, I won't be accepting the extenuating-circumstances excuse ever again."

Teague looked down at her. With the fear washed out of her eyes and the stress drained from her face, she looked tired. He longed to drag all the anxiety of the last several days from her body, wished he could ease the worry of the next few weeks from her mind. But he couldn't.

He could only give her what he had. And based on the fact that he was now free and the shadow government was off his back, that was a hell of a lot more than he'd had to offer several days ago.

He took a breath, brushed stray black hair off her forehead with his fingers. "What if I were so over-the-top insane about you that I lost my head and did crazy things? Would that be an acceptable extenuating circumstance?"

The shadow of fatigue drifted out of her eyes, replaced by a spark of surprise and a grin of interest. "Depends on the offense. What kinds of crazy things?"

"Like . . ." Oh, shit, here he went. The biggest risk of his life. "Like if I asked you to stay in Truckee with me and Kat, even though I know the job in San Francisco is better. And promised we'd go anywhere with you once we got things straightened out back home. And told you I love you more than is rational for time or circumstance and that the thought of losing you scares me as much as the thought of losing Kat again."

"W-wow." Her eyes grew wider with each confession, their irises glittering with unshed tears. "Those are pretty crazy."

He tried to smile, but his stomach was wound in knots waiting for her response. "That's me. Impulsive. Reckless." He paused, searching for another word to finish off the trio. "Foolish," tumbled out.

Alyssa laughed. The sound bubbled out of her chest like a fountain of champagne. She squeezed close and swept her palm across his cheek, her skin warm and smooth. "Those are just a few of the things I love most about you. And if you *hadn't* asked me to stay, that house"—she tipped her head toward the charred remains behind them—"wouldn't have been the only thing on fire around here."

This time, Teague's smile spread across his face and stuck. And when Alyssa pushed to her toes and pressed her lips to his, he knew it was way too late to think about starting fires. Or smothering fires.

"Baby," he murmured, a breath away from her mouth, "where you're concerned, I'll always be on fire."